Beneath the Sky

Carol Prescott

Published by Carol Prescott, 2024.

BENEATH THE SKY

First edition. October 6, 2024.

ISBN: 979-8227909725

Written by Carol Prescott.

Chapter 1: A Taste of Freedom

As the night deepened, the yard transformed into a twinkling wonderland, each light flickering like fireflies caught in a gentle breeze. The air was thick with the sweet scent of blooming jasmine, wrapping us in its embrace, while the music floated through the space, weaving its way into our laughter. Guests mingled, their faces illuminated by the soft glow of string lights, creating a tapestry of joy and connection that felt almost surreal.

I stood at the edge of our gathering, a glass of sparkling lemonade in hand, the tartness dancing on my tongue like the excitement in the air. Noah was lost in conversation with a local artist whose vibrant paintings lined the makeshift gallery we had crafted from old sheets hung between trees. Each piece told a story, much like the moments we had shared over the last few weeks, and I felt a swell of pride at what we had accomplished together. This wasn't just a showcase; it was a testament to the resilience we had cultivated, both individually and as a team.

As I sipped my drink, a sense of awe washed over me. I was witnessing a community coming alive—people who, only a short while ago, had been strangers in passing. Now they exchanged smiles and stories, connecting over art and the shared desire to create something beautiful. It was a vibrant tapestry of human experience, each thread essential to the whole.

"Noah, look at this!" I called out, beckoning him to join me. I pointed at a piece depicting a sunset over a mountain, the colors bleeding into one another, resembling the very sky that had watched over us during countless evenings. "Doesn't it remind you of those moments we've spent together?"

His eyes lit up as he approached, the warmth of his presence grounding me. "It's like the artist captured the essence of every sunset we've shared," he said, a hint of admiration in his voice. "I love how art can encapsulate emotions and memories, turning them into something tangible." His fingers brushed against mine, a fleeting contact that sent a thrill coursing through me.

In that moment, the world around us faded into a gentle hum, the clinking of glasses and distant laughter dissolving into a backdrop of soft melody. "Do you think they understand how much power they have?" I mused, my gaze drifting back to the painting. "Each brushstroke, every color choice—what if they knew their work could bring people together?"

"They probably do," Noah replied thoughtfully, his expression serious yet tender. "Artists are like magicians. They create something from nothing, weaving stories that touch hearts. Just like you with your words." His compliment sent a flush to my cheeks, and I smiled, feeling a warmth radiate from within.

As the night wore on, the showcase grew in life and vibrancy. The laughter swelled, echoing through the air, becoming a part of the evening itself. A local band took the makeshift stage, their melodies rising like a wave, inviting everyone to join in the revelry. The music pulsed through my veins, and before I knew it, I was dancing, the world spinning with joy and freedom.

Noah joined me, his movements fluid and carefree, and together we swayed beneath the starlit sky, our bodies entwined in a rhythm that felt both natural and exhilarating. I could see the happiness mirrored in his eyes, and it filled me with an overwhelming sense of gratitude. This was the life I had always dreamed of—full of laughter, love, and a deep sense of belonging.

Suddenly, the music shifted to a slow ballad, and Noah pulled me closer, his arms wrapping around me protectively. I rested my head against his chest, listening to the steady beat of his heart, which seemed to sync with the rhythm of the song. We swayed gently, our surroundings fading into the background as if the universe had conspired to grant us this singular moment, untouched by the chaos of life outside.

"I can't believe we did this," I whispered, feeling the weight of everything we had accomplished together. "It's everything I've ever wanted."

"It's only the beginning," Noah replied softly, tilting my chin up so our eyes met. "Whatever we do next, we'll face it together." His voice was laced with a certainty that calmed the tempest of excitement within me.

As the last notes of the song faded into the night, I caught sight of the sky, a canvas splashed with starlight, each twinkle a reminder of the countless dreams waiting to be chased. The laughter continued to weave through the air, a melody of connections forged, friendships rekindled, and stories shared under the gaze of a million stars.

In that moment, surrounded by people who believed in us, I felt a profound realization wash over me. Life was not just about the milestones we achieved but also about the relationships we nurtured along the way. Each person in attendance was a thread in the fabric of my journey, a reminder that love and creativity could flourish even in the darkest of times.

As the night drew to a close, guests began to trickle away, their hearts lighter, their spirits lifted by the energy we had cultivated. Noah and I stood side by side, watching as the last remnants of our magical evening began to fade into the night.

"I can't help but wonder what tomorrow holds," I said, a blend of excitement and apprehension swirling within me.

"Whatever it is, we'll face it head-on," Noah assured me, his voice steady and reassuring. "Together, we can tackle anything."

His words hung in the air, echoing with the promise of new beginnings. We began to clean up the remnants of the evening—the empty glasses, the crumpled napkins, and the lights that had sparkled like stars. With each task, the world around us grew quieter, a gentle reminder that even the most vibrant moments must eventually give way to stillness.

As the last light was dimmed and the final piece of trash was tossed away, I turned to Noah, my heart swelling with gratitude. "Thank you for believing in us, for this incredible night. You make everything better."

He smiled, his eyes reflecting the remnants of our shared joy. "And you make me believe in the impossible."

The stars above shimmered like a promise, and I knew that whatever lay ahead, we would navigate it together, hearts intertwined and spirits unbroken. The journey was just beginning, and as we stepped into the dawn of a new day, I felt ready to embrace every moment, every dream, and every challenge that life would throw our way. Together, we would chase the stars, crafting a love story that would forever echo in the chambers of our hearts.

The door swung open, and the rich aroma of slow-cooked meats and freshly baked bread enveloped me like a warm embrace. It was the kind of place where the hum of conversation mingled with the clinking of cutlery, creating a symphony of life that seemed to promise comfort. I stepped inside, my heart fluttering in a way that had become unfamiliar over the years. Each table was adorned with rustic wooden placemats and cheerful flower vases, contributing to the homey atmosphere that beckoned patrons to linger. I let out a soft sigh, attempting to shake off the unease that had settled in the pit of my stomach.

As I scanned the room, my eyes fell upon a table in the corner, occupied by a solitary figure. A woman sat with her back to me, her hair cascading like dark waves over her shoulders, and I couldn't help but wonder if it was Amelia. Memories flooded in—a childhood spent giggling over shared secrets, the warmth of sisterhood now a distant echo. Yet, the years had carved deep lines between us, both in the physical distance that separated our lives and the emotional chasm created by silence. I took a deep breath, steeling myself for the reunion that felt more like an impending storm than a homecoming.

I made my way to the bar, ordering a glass of deep red wine to calm my racing heart. The bartender, a cheerful man with a welcoming smile, poured me a generous serving. "First time here?" he asked, his voice smooth and engaging. I nodded, taking a sip of the wine, the rich flavor dancing on my palate. "You'll love the duck confit," he added. "It's a house specialty. Just like grandma used to make, if your grandma were a master chef." His infectious enthusiasm sparked a flicker of excitement within me, momentarily distracting me from my impending confrontation.

Sipping my wine, I stole another glance at the woman in the corner. She was now leaning forward, engrossed in her phone, completely oblivious to the world around her. There was something about her posture, an unmistakable tension in the way she held herself that resonated with me. It mirrored my own uncertainty, and for a moment, I almost felt a kinship with this stranger, this potential sister. I set my glass down, mind swirling with thoughts, and felt an urge to take the plunge.

I approached her table, heart hammering in my chest, and cleared my throat softly. As she turned to face me, recognition washed over her features, quickly replaced by confusion and perhaps a hint of resentment. "What are you doing here?" she asked, her voice steady yet laced with the sharpness of years gone by.

"Amelia," I began, surprised at how the mere sound of her name brought forth a flood of emotions I had buried deep. "I... I thought it was time we talked."

For a heartbeat, she stared at me as if gauging whether to indulge my intrusion or send me away with a wave of her hand. Her expression softened, just a fraction, and the walls between us seemed to waver like the flickering candlelight on the table. "Talk? After all this time? You think a lunch at some bistro can fix everything?"

I opened my mouth to respond but found the words caught in my throat. What could I possibly say that would convey the whirlwind of regret, longing, and love I felt? "I miss you, Amelia. I've missed you for years." It was an honest admission, raw and unfiltered, and as it left my lips, it felt like a revelation, a step into uncharted territory.

The silence stretched between us, heavy with the weight of unspoken words. I could see her grappling with emotions that had long been buried. Finally, she sighed, her shoulders relaxing just a little. "You missed my life, you missed my wedding, you missed everything," she shot back, the hurt in her voice palpable. "You've been too busy chasing food reviews to notice."

Her words stung, yet they were an undeniable truth. The sacrifices I had made for my career loomed large, eclipsing the personal connections I had once cherished. "I know," I said softly, feeling a deep shame wash over me. "And I can't change the past, but I want to try and be a part of your life again."

With a huff, she glanced away, focusing on the bustling restaurant instead of the sister sitting before her. "You don't just get to walk back in, you know. Life doesn't work that way."

"Then let me take you to lunch," I proposed. "Not as a critic, but as your sister. I want to know you again, to understand who you've become. Let's start over, one meal at a time."

She hesitated, her eyes darting between my hopeful gaze and the chaos of the restaurant. The idea of connection dangled before us like a tantalizing dish, yet she seemed reluctant to take the first bite. Eventually, her defenses softened slightly. "Okay," she relented, a hint of surprise coloring her tone. "But this doesn't mean we're best friends again. It'll take more than a few meals to get there."

Relief surged within me, as if I had just been granted a second chance at a long-lost recipe, one I hoped to savor slowly. We spent the next hour talking, the initial awkwardness gradually giving way to laughter, stories shared over plates of fragrant dishes. Each bite of food seemed to break down the barriers we had erected, allowing us to glimpse the sisters we once were.

The world outside the bistro pulsed with life, but within those four walls, time seemed to bend, giving us space to explore the contours of our relationship anew. As we finished our meal, the sunlight spilled in through the window, illuminating the table where a shared history began to unfold. My heart, once heavy with regret, now felt buoyant, lifted by the promise of renewal. Amelia smiled, a genuine spark igniting in her eyes, and for the first time in years, I felt a glimmer of hope that perhaps we could weave the threads of our lives back together, one meal at a time.

As our conversation unfolded, the initial hesitance began to dissolve like sugar in warm tea. Amelia's laughter, once an elusive memory, echoed through the restaurant, bringing with it a lightness I had forgotten existed. Each story shared was a small offering, a crumb leading us back to each other. She spoke of her life, detailing the ordinary magic of her days—an afternoon spent at a local farmer's market, the joy of learning how to bake sourdough, and the newfound passion for painting that had transformed her once-empty weekends into vibrant canvases filled with color.

With every word, I felt myself leaning closer, hungry not just for the details but for the intimacy of sisterhood we had allowed to slip away. I shared snippets of my life, too, tales of culinary escapades that had led me to hidden gems across the country. I recounted the thrill of discovering a secret speakeasy in New Orleans and the regretful flavors of an overcooked soufflé in a pretentious Parisian café. Yet, beneath the thrill of my experiences lay a current of loneliness, a void that my relentless pursuit of gastronomic excellence could not fill.

"Why did you really come back?" Amelia's question hung between us like a delicate thread, one that might snap if tugged too hard. I considered my answer, feeling the weight of vulnerability pressing down. "I realized that food—though it brings joy—is not as fulfilling without people to share it with. I've spent years savoring flavors, but I miss the taste of companionship. I miss you."

Her gaze softened, and I could see the flicker of understanding glimmering in her eyes. It was a spark that lit a small fire in the depths of my heart, one I dared to nurture. As we finished our meal, I noticed the way the sunlight bathed her face in a golden hue, highlighting the freckles dusting her cheeks—remnants of our childhood days spent chasing after butterflies in the fields behind our house. The sight tugged at something deep within me, a longing for the simplicity of our past.

The warmth of that moment gave way to a shared silence, a mutual acknowledgment that while we had years to bridge, we could start with this lunch. It was a fragile beginning, but the promise of more lingered in the air like the lingering scent of garlic and rosemary. As we rose to leave, the restaurant buzzed with life, the din of laughter and clinking glasses serving as a reminder of the connections we often took for granted.

As we stepped out into the bustling street, the world felt vibrantly alive around us. The sun was shining brightly, casting long shadows on the pavement as people meandered about, lost in their own narratives. I took a deep breath, inhaling the mingled scents of fresh pastries from a nearby bakery and the earthy aromas of the street vendors selling roasted corn. "What's next for you?" I asked Amelia, eager to delve deeper into her world.

She glanced at me, a spark of mischief in her eyes. "I've been wanting to check out that new wine bar down the street. They say it has a selection that would make a sommelier swoon." Her laughter was infectious, and I couldn't help but join in. "Or," she continued, a playful glint igniting her gaze, "we could get creative and host a little cooking session at my place. I've been wanting to try making homemade pasta, and trust me, it's a spectacle."

The idea filled me with warmth, a rush of excitement coursing through my veins. "I'm in! But you have to promise not to judge my technique."

"Only if you promise not to critique my choice of wine."

With that playful exchange, we headed towards her apartment, a charming two-bedroom tucked within a historic brownstone, its exterior covered in climbing ivy. As we approached, I marveled at the inviting atmosphere of her neighborhood. Colorful murals adorned the walls of nearby buildings, each telling a story of the vibrant community that thrived here. It was a far cry from the impersonal high-rises of my own world, where life seemed to blend into an unremarkable blur.

Inside, the apartment was filled with sunlight, illuminating her eclectic decor—a mix of thrifted finds and artwork from local artists. Each piece held a story, a testament to her personality. The faint sound of jazz wafted through the air, setting a relaxed tone as we settled into the cozy kitchen, the heart of her home.

As Amelia rolled out the dough, we fell into an easy rhythm, laughter punctuating our efforts as flour dusted the countertops like freshly fallen snow. She instructed me on how to knead the dough properly, her enthusiasm infectious as she demonstrated the technique with graceful movements. I tried my best to replicate her actions, but inevitably ended up with dough stuck to my hands, and we both erupted into laughter.

"Not bad for a critic who spends more time tasting than cooking," she teased, handing me a glass of wine to accompany my culinary efforts. The laughter and clinking of glasses filled the room, slowly weaving a tapestry of memories that began to eclipse the years of silence. We shared stories—about friendships lost and found, heartaches endured, and the dreams we had nurtured in our separate lives. Each story was a thread, stitching together the patchwork of our relationship.

As the evening unfolded, I found myself savoring not just the delicious homemade pasta but the undeniable magic of rekindled connection. It was intoxicating, like the finest wine—a heady mix of joy and relief, accompanied by the bittersweet taste of all that we had lost. With every bite, I felt the walls between us continue to crumble, revealing the heart of our bond, vibrant and pulsing beneath the surface.

"Do you remember those summer nights when we'd sneak out to the backyard and pretend we were chefs in a fancy restaurant?" I asked, the nostalgia washing over me like a gentle tide.

Amelia's eyes sparkled with recognition. "And we'd serve our parents the most ridiculous concoctions, insisting they were gourmet. I think Mom was convinced we'd put her out of business."

We both laughed, the sound resonating in the room like a melody.

As the sun dipped below the horizon, painting the sky in hues of pink and orange, I realized that in this simple act of cooking together, we were crafting something much deeper than a meal; we were redefining our relationship, one shared experience at a time. Each layer of pasta we rolled out was akin to peeling back the layers of our lives, exposing the raw, unfiltered truth of our experiences.

Finally, as we set the table, the warmth of connection enveloped us, and I couldn't help but marvel at the beauty of this moment. The food was just a backdrop to the genuine connection we were forging. In the chaos of our lives, we had carved out a sacred space where laughter reigned, memories were forged, and the taste of freedom lingered in the air, rich and fulfilling. This was just the beginning, a new chapter waiting to be written, and I was ready to savor every moment.

Chapter 2: The Uninvited Guest

The cozy bistro, a hidden gem tucked away in the heart of a bustling city, was a refuge from the chaotic world outside. Its rustic wooden beams and walls adorned with vintage culinary posters invited patrons into an intimate atmosphere, a space where time seemed to slow, allowing for whispered conversations and shared laughter. The soft glow of Edison bulbs cast a warm light across the room, illuminating the lively chatter of diners and the rhythmic clinking of cutlery. My senses were enveloped by the enticing aromas that danced through the air, a fragrant symphony of roasted garlic and rosemary teasing my anticipation as I sank into the plush upholstery of the corner table.

As I carefully opened the menu, the elegant script of the daily specials caught my eye, each dish promising an exploration of flavors that ignited my culinary curiosity. My stomach rumbled softly in response, and my mind raced through the possibilities. Just as I began to mentally select my meal, the sound of footsteps approached, the familiar cadence both unexpected and thrilling. "Is this seat taken?" The voice, smooth like silk, sent an involuntary shiver down my spine. I looked up, and there he was—Jackson. His presence seemed to shift the air around us, a familiar energy sparking in the space between us.

Jackson, the sous-chef with an infectious smile and a talent for making the mundane feel extraordinary, stood before me, slightly breathless, as if he too was surprised by this serendipitous encounter. His tousled hair caught the light, revealing soft waves that framed his chiseled face. I could see the flecks of green in his eyes, an iridescent reminder of the verdant hills where I imagined he found solace after long shifts in the kitchen. The casual way he leaned against the table, one hand tucked casually into his jeans pocket, exuded a relaxed confidence that I found immediately disarming.

For a moment, I was transported back to the kitchen of the bustling restaurant where we first met, the air thick with the sizzling of pans and the vibrant energy of chefs in their element. I remembered the way he moved, deftly chopping vegetables with precision, his passion evident in every slice. It had been a whirlwind of tastes and aromas, a culinary ballet that left me both awed and enchanted. Now, sitting across from him in this serene setting, the memories flooded back, almost overwhelming in their intensity.

"No, not at all," I managed to reply, my voice steadier than I felt. I gestured to the seat across from me, and he slid into it with an easy grace. We exchanged pleasantries, the kind that felt like warm hugs, easing the tension that had been building in my chest. It was as if no time had passed since our last encounter, yet the undercurrents of our previous interactions hummed beneath the surface, creating a tension that was both thrilling and terrifying.

As we settled into conversation, the initial awkwardness dissipated, replaced by a genuine warmth that enveloped us. We reminisced about the chaotic energy of the kitchen and shared stories about our culinary escapades. He told me about his latest dish, a sumptuous risotto infused with saffron and topped with fresh herbs—a creation that was not only a feast for the palate but also a visual delight. I could see the passion igniting in his eyes as he spoke, a flame that flickered brighter with every detail he shared.

The laughter that erupted between us felt familiar yet thrilling, like a dance I had long forgotten but remembered perfectly once the music started. I could see the sparkle in his eyes, a glimmer that suggested he was equally enchanted by our unexpected reunion. As we delved deeper into conversation, the restaurant around us faded into a soft blur, the chatter of other diners becoming a gentle hum in the background. My focus remained entirely on him, on the way his hands animatedly illustrated his stories, and the way his laughter felt like a melody that danced in the air.

Just as I began to relax, the mood shifted slightly. A shadow flickered across his face, and I noticed a hint of hesitation in his demeanor. It was a subtle change, a mere crack in the charming facade that made me wonder what lay beneath the surface. Had I misread the spark between us? Was this moment a mere echo of the past, a fleeting illusion? I couldn't help but lean closer, my curiosity piqued as I attempted to decipher the thoughts that momentarily clouded his expression.

"Are you still with that restaurant?" I asked, trying to gently probe into the depths of his current life, hoping to uncover the story behind that flicker of uncertainty. The question hung in the air, heavy with the weight of unspoken words and untold stories. He hesitated, a slight furrow forming between his brows as he searched for the right words.

"I left, actually," he finally confessed, the admission accompanied by a rueful smile. "It was time for a change. I've been exploring new opportunities, but..." He trailed off, a shadow of uncertainty lingering in his eyes, the flicker of ambition dimmed by a hint of vulnerability. I could sense the shift in the energy between us, a tender moment of shared struggle that connected us more deeply than I anticipated.

Before I could respond, the waiter appeared with our drinks, a timely distraction that broke the tension and allowed us to momentarily retreat from the weight of the conversation. The clink of glasses against the wooden table echoed like a promise, a fleeting reminder that even amidst uncertainty, moments of joy could still be found. Jackson raised his glass to mine, and as our eyes met, I felt the warmth of connection enveloping us once more, igniting a flicker of hope in the air between us.

The conversation flowed easily again, the laughter returning to fill the spaces between our words. With each passing moment, I realized that this unexpected reunion was more than just a chance encounter. It was a doorway to rediscovering not only him but also the parts of myself that had remained dormant in the whirlwind of life. I found myself leaning in, captivated by the way he effortlessly navigated through stories of his culinary adventures, and how his passion for food seemed to intertwine with a passion for life itself. Each shared laugh and meaningful glance drew us closer, the allure of the evening wrapping around us like the inviting aroma that had first lured me inside.

The conversation drifted like the steam rising from our glasses, each word wrapping around us in a comforting embrace. Jackson animatedly recounted tales from his time in the kitchen, illustrating the intensity and camaraderie of the bustling environment where the clattering pans sang a raucous tune. He painted a vivid picture of late-night shifts spent experimenting with flavors, where laughter echoed off the tiled walls and culinary disasters were transformed into inside jokes. I leaned in closer, enthralled by the way his enthusiasm lit up his face, the lines of worry momentarily forgotten as he embraced the joy of his craft.

"Do you remember that time you nearly set the fire alarm off with that flambé?" he asked, laughter dancing in his eyes. I couldn't help but chuckle, recalling the chaos that had ensued as I stumbled through my review, attempting to contain a small kitchen disaster that had erupted into a hilarious spectacle. The memory of his teasing grin made my heart flutter. "Your face was priceless!" he continued, his laughter infectious. "I thought we'd have to call the fire department!"

I playfully swatted at him, a feigned look of indignation plastered on my face. "Hey, I was just trying to bring some excitement to the evening! Besides, isn't that what you chefs live for—turning the mundane into something memorable?"

He grinned, a spark of mischief lighting his expression. "I suppose you have a point. We thrive on chaos; it's our secret ingredient."

As our laughter filled the cozy nook of the bistro, I could feel the walls between us crumbling, revealing a vulnerability I hadn't anticipated. There was something electric about this moment, an unspoken acknowledgment that perhaps we were both searching for more than just culinary companionship. I found myself wanting to know the man beyond the chef—a kindred spirit hidden beneath layers of laughter and culinary bravado.

"So, what's your next big adventure?" I asked, genuinely curious, leaning back slightly to give him room to express himself. The question lingered between us, and I could see him weighing his options, the gleam of ambition and uncertainty flashing in his eyes.

He took a sip of his drink, the thoughtful silence stretching out comfortably. "I'm considering starting my own pop-up," he finally confessed, his tone earnest. "Something different, more personal. I want to create a dining experience that tells a story, that connects people through food."

His dream resonated with me, igniting a flicker of inspiration that danced in the pit of my stomach. "That sounds incredible! You have such a gift for storytelling through your dishes. I can only imagine how magical it would be to experience that firsthand."

A shy smile tugged at the corners of his mouth, and I noticed a blush creeping across his cheeks, a rare moment of vulnerability that endeared him to me even more. "Thanks. I just want to bring something special to the table, you know? Food has this unique ability to bridge gaps between people, to create connections we often forget exist in our daily lives."

Our conversation flowed seamlessly, weaving through dreams, fears, and the little quirks that made us who we were. He shared his experiences with different cuisines, detailing the spices that ignited his imagination and the textures that inspired him. Each story was laced with a tenderness that suggested a deeper longing—a desire not just to create dishes, but to create experiences that lingered in the hearts of those who tasted them.

I found myself captivated, feeling an unexpected kinship with his aspirations. It was as if he were reaching out to me through the veil of his culinary world, inviting me to see life through his eyes. In that moment, I wanted nothing more than to cheer him on, to be the wind beneath his wings as he soared toward his dreams. "I would love to help in any way I can," I offered, my words tumbling out before I could think twice. "Maybe I could write about your pop-up when it happens? I mean, a great story deserves to be told, and you have the heart to make it truly special."

His eyes sparkled with a mix of gratitude and surprise. "Really? That would mean a lot. I can only imagine how much of a boost it would be to have someone like you sharing the experience with the world."

The sincerity in his voice sent a warm flush through me, and I couldn't help but smile. It felt good, this connection we were forging—a delicate thread woven through laughter, ambition, and the shared language of food. Just then, our meals arrived, the beautiful presentation eliciting gasps of delight from both of us. The waiter placed a plate in front of me, artfully arranged with vibrant vegetables nestled beside a perfectly seared piece of fish, its skin golden and crisp. Jackson's dish looked equally enticing, a fragrant risotto glistening with fresh herbs and garnished with a delicate touch of saffron.

"This looks almost too good to eat," I remarked, letting my gaze linger on the colors and textures before me.

"Almost," Jackson agreed, lifting his fork with a teasing smirk. "But not quite. Prepare to have your taste buds blown away."

As we dug into our meals, the flavors danced on my palate, each bite an explosion of carefully crafted taste. Jackson watched me with eager anticipation, his eyes lighting up as I savored the dish. "What do you think?" he asked, leaning forward, his enthusiasm palpable.

I closed my eyes, allowing the flavors to wash over me like a gentle tide. "It's exquisite! The seasoning is on point, and the fish melts in my mouth. I could eat this every day!"

His laughter rang out, bright and unrestrained, and in that moment, I realized how easy it was to forget the world outside—how the clamor of life faded into the background, leaving only the delicious food, the lively banter, and the warmth of connection. We continued to share bites and laughter, feeding off each other's energy as the evening progressed, losing track of time as the outside world became a distant memory.

Yet, amid the laughter and the shared joy of culinary exploration, a gentle current of unease began to creep in. A nagging thought nestled itself in the back of my mind, whispering doubts I had tried to suppress. Did this spark between us mean something more? Or was it merely a momentary flicker, destined to be snuffed out by the demands of reality? I glanced at Jackson, engrossed in sharing his culinary dreams, and I felt an inexplicable urge to leap into the unknown, to embrace whatever this was between us, regardless of the consequences.

It was a choice, one that lingered tantalizingly in the air, like the sweet scent of rosemary that wrapped itself around us, binding us in this delightful dance of flavors and feelings. As our plates emptied, I felt an overwhelming urge to bridge that final gap, to take a leap into the unknown and see where this connection would take us. Would it be the start of something beautiful, or merely a bittersweet memory tucked away like a cherished recipe? Only time would reveal the answer.

Jackson leaned forward, the candlelight flickering in his eyes, casting a warm glow that added to the intimate ambiance of the bistro. Our conversation flowed like a well-practiced dance, each exchange a step toward something deeper. As we savored our meals, the flavors igniting our senses, I became acutely aware of the world outside our little bubble. The murmur of other diners was a distant hum, punctuated only by the occasional clink of glasses or burst of laughter.

"What if we took this outside?" Jackson suggested, glancing toward the patio where twinkling fairy lights dangled from above, illuminating a space that beckoned like a scene from a romantic film. His voice was low and inviting, and I felt an unexpected thrill at the thought of escaping the enclosed warmth of the restaurant for the starry night. The invitation felt less like a suggestion and more like an irresistible lure, calling me into the open air where the night sky could cradle our budding connection.

"Absolutely," I replied, unable to suppress the smile tugging at my lips. The thought of sharing a moment under the stars ignited a rush of excitement within me. We gathered our things, the lingering taste of exquisite food dancing on my palate, and made our way to the patio. The gentle night breeze wrapped around us like a soft shawl, the sounds of the city fading into a comforting backdrop.

Once outside, the atmosphere transformed. The patio was alive with its own energy, filled with laughter and the clinking of glasses, yet somehow it felt more serene than the bustling interior. Jackson led us to a small table adorned with a flickering candle, the soft glow casting delicate shadows that danced across our faces. I could see the stars twinkling overhead, each one a silent witness to our burgeoning connection.

"So, tell me more about this pop-up idea of yours," I prompted, eager to delve into the world he dreamed of creating. His eyes lit up, the passion within him spilling over as he spoke.

"I want it to feel like a secret gathering, a place where people can come together to celebrate food and the stories that accompany it," he explained, his hands animatedly illustrating his thoughts. "Imagine an intimate setting, a communal table where strangers become friends over shared dishes. Each meal would have a theme, perhaps inspired by a different culture or season, weaving together flavors and experiences into something memorable."

I could see it in my mind's eye—long tables adorned with rustic centerpieces, laughter filling the air, the clatter of cutlery blending with lively conversation. It was a vision infused with warmth and connection, a stark contrast to the isolation that often marked the modern dining experience. "That sounds enchanting," I said, genuinely moved by his vision. "It's like you want to create a tapestry of human connection through food."

"Exactly!" he exclaimed, his enthusiasm palpable. "Food has this incredible ability to break down barriers. I want people to feel something—joy, nostalgia, connection. It's about more than just nourishment; it's an experience."

As he spoke, I could see the wheels turning in his mind, the way he envisioned each detail—the decor, the menu, the ambience—all coming together to create a perfect evening. His passion was contagious, and I found myself daydreaming of attending this pop-up, savoring the carefully crafted dishes while sharing stories with strangers who might soon become friends.

"I would love to be a part of that," I admitted, my heart racing at the thought of being involved in something so meaningful. "I can help you with the promotion, document the stories behind each dish, perhaps even gather a few friends for your first event."

Jackson's eyes sparkled with appreciation. "You'd really do that? It would make all the difference. I want to showcase the connection between food and people, and having you there to share it would be incredible."

The night wore on, and we exchanged ideas, bouncing thoughts off one another like sparks flying from a flame. It felt as if we were two kindred spirits unraveling a shared dream, and with each suggestion and insight, the bond between us tightened. In those moments, I could hardly believe that just hours before, I had entered the bistro alone, yearning for a night of solitude. Now, the air was thick with possibilities, electric with the kind of chemistry that made my heart race.

With laughter bubbling up between us, I teased him about his culinary prowess. "I hope you're not just all talk, Jackson. If I'm going to write about this pop-up, I expect food that makes my taste buds sing!"

"Challenge accepted," he replied, his grin widening, a playful glint in his eye. "I'll make sure the dishes are unforgettable. Just wait until you taste my signature dessert—it's a revelation."

A challenge lay in the air, playful yet tangible, and I found myself craving that dessert more than ever. "Now you've piqued my interest. What's the secret?"

He leaned closer, his voice dropping conspiratorially. "Ah, that's for another time. But I will say this: it involves chocolate, a hint of spice, and a story that ties it all together." The way he spoke, his words weaving a tantalizing narrative around something as simple as dessert, only fueled my curiosity further.

Our laughter intertwined with the soft strains of music drifting from the restaurant, each note a gentle reminder of the world continuing around us. As the night deepened, the conversation meandered, touching on everything from childhood dreams to our current struggles. I found myself revealing more than I had intended, sharing snippets of my life, the fears that sometimes gnawed at me in quiet moments. With Jackson, vulnerability felt safe, a welcomed release rather than a burden.

"So, what's your biggest dream?" he asked, genuine curiosity shining in his eyes.

I paused, the question hanging in the air like a shimmering thread. "To create something that resonates with others," I replied, feeling the weight of my own ambition settle over me like a comforting blanket. "I want to write stories that matter, that connect people to experiences they've either lived or long to live. There's so much beauty in the mundane, and I want to capture that."

A moment of understanding passed between us, a silent acknowledgment of the desires that intertwined our lives. "You're already doing that," he said softly, his tone sincere. "Every time you share a review, you're connecting people to the heart of a place, a dish, a story. Your words have power."

I felt warmth spread through my chest, a sense of validation that had been elusive in my career. "Thank you, Jackson. That means a lot coming from you."

With the evening stretching on, the world around us continued to fade, and it was as if we were suspended in our little oasis. Just when I thought the moment couldn't get any more perfect, the patio lights flickered, casting a soft glow across Jackson's face, illuminating his features in a way that made my heart flutter. He was more than just a charming sous-chef; he was a passionate dreamer who somehow had woven his way into my thoughts, igniting a flame I hadn't realized was flickering within me.

But as the night wore on and laughter turned into quieter reflections, I couldn't shake the feeling of impending change. With each shared secret and playful tease, the walls I had so carefully built around my heart began to crumble. It was exhilarating and terrifying, a whirlwind of emotions that left me breathless.

As we finished our drinks, a comfortable silence settled between us, and I felt the weight of what lay ahead. Would this spark lead to something more? Or was it a moment meant to remain suspended in time, a beautiful memory to treasure as life continued its relentless march forward?

"Shall we go back inside?" Jackson finally suggested, breaking the spell. I nodded, not ready to let this moment slip away but aware that reality awaited us inside the bistro, with its familiar aromas and vibrant energy.

As we rose from the table, our fingers brushed against one another, a fleeting touch that sent shivers down my spine. In that instant, I knew something significant was unfolding, a new chapter waiting to be written. Whatever came next—friendship, collaboration, or something more—was a journey I was eager to embark upon, hand in hand with the charming sous-chef who had unexpectedly stepped into my life and ignited a spark I had thought long extinguished.

Chapter 3: The Flavor of Regret

The clinking of silverware and the soft murmur of conversation enveloped us in a warm embrace as I sat across from Jackson, my heart a dissonant blend of anticipation and unease. We were nestled in a small, rustic restaurant tucked away in a bustling corner of New Orleans, a hidden gem that beckoned with the promise of flavor and familiarity. The rich aroma of spices danced through the air, mingling with the faint notes of jazz that floated from the nearby street musicians, their soulful melodies painting the evening with vibrancy.

Jackson was in his element, animatedly sharing stories about his culinary escapades as a chef. His hands moved expressively, punctuating his words with an enthusiasm that was infectious. "You won't believe the first time I attempted to make gumbo," he said, a twinkle in his eye. "I used every spice I could find, convinced I was crafting a masterpiece. Let's just say, my kitchen smelled like a hurricane of chaos and flavor." Laughter spilled from him like the smooth bourbon in the glass beside him, and I found myself hanging on every word, captivated by the way he embraced life and all its messy intricacies.

Each dish that arrived at our table told a story of its own. The fried green tomatoes were golden and crisp, their tartness balanced perfectly by a drizzle of tangy remoulade that danced on my tongue. I savored each bite, yet the flavors seemed to whisper secrets of simpler times, drawing me away from the dazzling present into a haunting reflection of what I had sacrificed for my career. My reviews had become more of a rigorous evaluation than a celebration of culinary art; I had become a relentless critic instead of an enthusiastic appreciator.

As Jackson enthusiastically described his latest experiment—a fusion of traditional Cajun spices with Asian influences—I couldn't help but feel a twinge of envy. Here he was, a man so vividly alive in his passion, creating joy with each plate he served. I could almost envision him in a bustling kitchen, his brow furrowed in concentration yet illuminated by the fiery spirit of creativity. How long had it been since I had felt that spark? My own culinary experiences had dwindled to mere footnotes in my quest for perfection, a relentless pursuit of critique that had dulled the palate of my soul.

"Why do you do it?" I asked, the question escaping my lips before I could think to filter it. "Why put yourself through the chaos of the kitchen?"

He paused, the warmth of his gaze steadying me, as if he could read the turmoil beneath my casual inquiry. "Because, for me, it's not just about the food," he replied, his voice soft yet firm. "It's about the connection, the stories behind each dish, the laughter shared over a meal. Cooking is a way to express love, a way to build bridges." His words resonated with an intensity that enveloped me, igniting a flicker of longing deep within.

The evening deepened around us, and as the decadent dessert arrived—a chocolate lava cake oozing with molten richness—I felt the weight of my own discontent settle heavily in my chest. The cake was a masterpiece, rich and indulgent, yet I couldn't shake the bittersweet aftertaste of regret that lingered like a stubborn specter. I cut into it, watching as the warm chocolate flowed out, pooling onto the plate. It felt symbolic, the way it spilled forth, an eruption of sweetness mixed with the complexity of emotions that I had kept tightly contained.

"I used to love cooking," I confessed, my voice barely above a whisper. "But somewhere along the way, I let the pressure of my reviews consume me. I forgot what it meant to enjoy food, to savor it." I could see the understanding flicker in his eyes, a silent acknowledgment that made me feel strangely vulnerable yet oddly liberated. "Now, it's all about the next critique, the next headline. I feel like I'm losing something essential."

Jackson leaned forward, his expression earnest, the soft light from the chandelier above catching the thoughtful curve of his mouth. "Maybe it's time to find that joy again," he suggested, his tone gentle yet firm. "Food is meant to bring people together, not tear them apart. It's about the experience, the laughter, the stories. You've gotten so wrapped up in the details that you've forgotten the bigger picture."

His words struck a chord within me, resonating in the hollow space I hadn't realized existed. I felt the tension in my shoulders ease slightly, a crack forming in the facade of perfection I had so carefully constructed. Perhaps it was time to rediscover the joy I had lost in the pursuit of excellence, to embrace the messy, chaotic beauty of life beyond the review.

As I took a bite of the lava cake, the chocolate enveloping my senses, I couldn't help but envision a different path. One where food wasn't just a means to an end but a vessel for connection, a canvas for stories waiting to be painted with laughter and love. The flavor of regret lingered, yes, but perhaps it could also be the catalyst for something new, a reminder that life was not meant to be lived in rigid lines but rather in the delightful, swirling colors of spontaneity.

Jackson's laughter pulled me back from my reverie, and for the first time in a long while, I felt a smile bloom on my face. The warmth of the evening wrapped around us like a comforting blanket, and in that moment, I realized that the journey to reclaiming my love for food and life might be the most delicious adventure of all.

The warmth of the evening settled like a gentle sigh around us, wrapping us in a cocoon of flickering candlelight and the tantalizing scent of rich spices. I could hear the soft jazz notes weaving through the air, an enchanting backdrop to the unfolding conversation. Jackson's enthusiasm for food was infectious, the way he animatedly spoke of his culinary adventures had a rhythm that drew me in, urging me to relax and let go of my tightly wound apprehensions. Each story was an invitation to a world I had nearly forgotten—a world where food was a celebration rather than a critique.

"Last week," he said, his eyes sparkling with mischief, "I decided to try my hand at a traditional jambalaya. You know, the kind that makes you forget your troubles and want to dance on the tables?" He leaned closer, lowering his voice conspiratorially. "Let's just say my first attempt involved more smoke alarms than I'd like to admit." I laughed, the sound spilling from me like champagne, light and effervescent, and it felt good. It felt freeing, as if his stories were coaxing out the joy I had buried beneath layers of professional ambition.

With every bite of the rich dishes he described, my senses awakened, each flavor bursting forth with a vividness that reminded me of the pleasures I had let slip away. I could almost taste the smokiness he spoke of, could almost feel the rhythm of the kitchen as he recounted the hurried dance between the sautéing vegetables and simmering sauces. The images he painted were as vibrant as the colorful murals that adorned the streets outside, splashes of life and spontaneity that seemed to call out to me.

"I miss that," I admitted, my voice softer now, tinted with a wistfulness that surprised me. "I used to find joy in the kitchen, in experimenting with flavors, but it feels like a lifetime ago." The admission hung in the air between us, delicate and fragile, as if revealing a hidden scar. Jackson's gaze bore into mine, unwavering, and for a moment, the busy restaurant faded away, leaving just the two of us in a cocoon of understanding.

"Why not rekindle that flame?" he urged, his tone gentle yet filled with conviction. "What if you tried cooking again, just for the sheer love of it? No reviews, no critiques. Just you and the ingredients." The idea hung between us, tantalizing and risky. I could feel the stirrings of something long dormant within me—a flicker of excitement that was both exhilarating and terrifying.

I took a sip of my wine, the velvety liquid sliding down my throat, and considered his words. "I'm not sure if I remember how," I confessed, my brow furrowing. "What if I've lost my touch? What if I can't capture the magic anymore?" The self-doubt crept in like an unwelcome guest, uninvited but very much present. Jackson chuckled softly, his laughter warm and enveloping.

"Cooking isn't about perfection; it's about connection. It's about flavor and feeling. It's messy and chaotic, just like life. You'll find your way back if you let yourself."

His faith in me was an unexpected balm, and I could feel the tension in my shoulders easing as I considered the prospect of reclaiming a piece of myself I had nearly forgotten. Perhaps Jackson was right; perhaps it was time to rediscover the kitchen—not as a battleground of expectations but as a sanctuary of creativity and joy.

"Let's do it together," Jackson suggested, his eyes lighting up with enthusiasm. "Next week, we'll make dinner. You can teach me your favorite recipe, and I'll introduce you to some of my secret techniques." His invitation felt like a lifeline, a chance to reconnect with the art of cooking and with a sense of joy I had let slip through my fingers.

"Are you sure you're ready to handle my cooking? It could get messy," I teased, the playful banter lightening the mood, and for the first time in ages, I felt the corners of my mouth lift into a genuine smile.

"Messy is my middle name," he quipped, raising his glass in a mock toast. "Bring it on!"

As we clinked our glasses together, a spark of camaraderie flickered between us, a burgeoning connection forged over shared plates and laughter. I felt buoyed by the prospect of our culinary adventure, the promise of stepping outside my meticulously crafted boundaries to embrace the spontaneity Jackson so effortlessly embodied.

The evening unfolded like a beautiful tapestry, each moment rich with layers of flavor and warmth. The restaurant around us thrummed with life—families celebrating milestones, couples stealing kisses across the table, friends raising glasses to toast to each other's dreams. It was a symphony of connection, each note resonating with a reminder of what I had been missing.

"I love this city," Jackson said, his gaze sweeping across the bustling room, the vibrant energy reflected in his eyes. "There's a magic here that seeps into everything—into the food, the music, the people. It's alive, and I can't imagine being anywhere else."

His passion was palpable, igniting a spark of longing within me. I had always adored New Orleans—the chaos of the streets, the allure of the cuisine—but in my quest for perfection, I had become a spectator in my own life. I was so busy dissecting the flavors for my reviews that I had forgotten to simply taste, to revel in the experience.

"Let's not just taste; let's savor," I replied, my voice gaining strength. "Let's embrace the chaos and the flavors, the laughter and the messiness." I felt a sense of determination bloom within me, a promise to reclaim the joy I had allowed to slip away.

"Exactly," Jackson beamed, his enthusiasm infectious. "We'll dive into it all—each layer, each flavor, and each experience. Together."

As the night wore on, the candles flickered low, their warm glow casting soft shadows around us, and I knew that this evening would linger in my memory, not as a moment of regret, but as a turning point. A chance to rediscover not just the flavors of food but the essence of life itself. The table before us, filled with remnants of our shared meal, stood as a testament to the magic of connection—an invitation to embrace the beautiful mess that life had to offer. I took a deep breath, feeling alive in a way I hadn't in years, ready to step boldly into the flavors of my own life once more.

The evening slipped into a delicate hush, a sweet interlude where the bustling sounds of the restaurant became a gentle murmur, allowing the intimacy of our conversation to fill the air. I watched as Jackson animatedly described his upcoming plans for a new menu, his hands weaving through the air as if conducting an orchestra of flavors. Each dish he envisioned seemed to burst with life—a vibrant ratatouille that spoke of sun-soaked fields, a velvety crème brûlée that promised a satisfying crack of caramelized sugar. I found myself captivated not just by his words but by the sheer joy that radiated from him, a stark contrast to the cloud of obligation that had hovered over my own culinary experiences.

"I want to bring people together," he said, his voice low and earnest. "Food has this incredible power to connect us, to forge relationships. It's not just sustenance; it's a shared experience, a story waiting to be told." His passion washed over me like the warm breeze that flowed through the open windows, mingling with the scent of jasmine from the nearby trees, wrapping us in a fragrant embrace.

As I sipped my wine, its rich notes swirling on my palate, I felt a wave of longing for that kind of connection, for the simplicity of sharing a meal without the weight of judgment or analysis. My life had become a series of reviews, dissecting flavors and textures as though they were pieces of art rather than experiences meant to be savored. I realized, in that moment, that I had been so focused on documenting every nuance of my meals that I had neglected to fully immerse myself in them.

"Let's do something crazy," Jackson suggested, a mischievous grin dancing on his lips. "Let's host a dinner party! Just us and a few friends. We'll cook together, make a mess, and share stories over a table overflowing with food. No critics, just laughter and good company." The idea was exhilarating, igniting a spark of adventure within me.

"I'm in," I replied, my heart racing at the thought of rolling up my sleeves in the kitchen once more, creating something from scratch with no strings attached. "But I warn you, my cooking might be a little rusty."

"Rusty or not, it'll be fun," he reassured me, his confidence enveloping me like a warm hug. "Let's plan it for next weekend. We'll hit the local markets, pick out fresh ingredients, and just let the magic happen."

The very thought of wandering through vibrant stalls overflowing with fresh produce, fragrant herbs, and artisanal cheeses brought a swell of nostalgia. I could picture it vividly—crisp greens gleaming under the sunlight, the earthy aroma of fresh basil filling the air, and the riot of colors that could only be found at a farmer's market. The anticipation of it all felt intoxicating, an elixir of spontaneity that I had been craving.

The evening continued to unfold, each moment layered with richness as we shared anecdotes, laughter spilling from us like the wine we enjoyed. Jackson's stories were infused with warmth, and with every laugh, I felt the burdens of my career begin to lift, replaced by a growing sense of connection. He spoke of his childhood, of watching his grandmother prepare gumbo on lazy Sunday afternoons, the kitchen filled with laughter and the warmth of family—a stark contrast to the sterile, lonely atmosphere of my own culinary experiences.

"You know," I said, my heart swelling with a sudden rush of vulnerability, "I used to find that kind of joy in cooking. I remember helping my mom in the kitchen, tasting sauces, and getting flour everywhere. It was a beautiful mess, and I loved every moment."

"Then let's bring that back," Jackson encouraged, leaning forward, his enthusiasm infectious. "Let's make a mess together. Let's be like kids again, unafraid to explore and experiment."

With each story shared, I could feel the walls I had built around myself begin to crumble. The dining room around us seemed to fade into the background, and in that small bubble of warmth, I was reminded of the very essence of food—the joy of creation, the delight of discovery. It was a simple yet profound truth that I had overlooked, buried beneath layers of expectations and the relentless pursuit of perfection.

As we lingered over dessert, savoring the last bites of the chocolate lava cake, I felt a renewed sense of purpose bubbling to the surface. The flavor of regret was still there, a bittersweet reminder of what I had lost, but it no longer felt overwhelming. Instead, it became a catalyst, propelling me forward into the realm of possibility.

"I can't wait for this dinner party," I said, a smile stretching across my face. "It feels like the beginning of something wonderful."

Jackson beamed back at me, his eyes bright with anticipation. "It will be! We'll create something beautiful—together."

The next week unfolded like a delightful culinary adventure. We spent our days planning, gathering recipes, and crafting a menu that celebrated the vibrant flavors of New Orleans. The farmer's market was a treasure trove of inspiration, each stall bursting with fresh produce, artisan bread, and fragrant herbs. As we strolled through the colorful booths, I felt a thrill of excitement coursing through me, a joy I had long forgotten. Jackson and I filled our baskets with ripe tomatoes, glossy eggplants, and fragrant bunches of basil, the air rich with the scent of summer.

"Let's not forget dessert!" Jackson exclaimed, his eyes twinkling with mischief. We made a beeline for a small vendor selling homemade pastries. A few minutes later, we emerged with an array of sweet treats, including delicate macarons that promised to melt in our mouths and a rich, buttery tart that would round off our meal beautifully.

The day of the dinner party arrived, the sun dipping low in the sky, casting a warm golden light across Jackson's cozy apartment. The kitchen buzzed with energy as we prepped side by side, laughter bubbling over as we chopped vegetables and seasoned our meats. Flour dusted the countertops like a fine layer of snow, and the air was thick with the rich aromas of sautéing garlic and onions. I felt an exhilarating freedom in the chaos, an invitation to embrace the messiness of the moment.

"Here, try this," Jackson said, handing me a spoonful of his simmering gumbo. I closed my eyes as the flavors danced across my palate, the warmth of spices igniting a nostalgic memory of family gatherings.

"Wow, that's incredible," I gasped, grinning ear to ear. "You really captured the essence of it!"

"Thanks! But I need you to give me your honest opinion on the seasoning," he replied, handing me another spoonful, his playful confidence infectious.

As the evening wore on, friends began to filter in, each one greeted with warmth and laughter. The dining table, set with mismatched plates and flickering candles, overflowed with the bounty we had created. With every clink of glasses and bite of food, I felt the burdens of my career lift further away, replaced by the joy of shared experiences and the thrill of creativity.

The laughter flowed freely as we indulged in our culinary creations, stories blending with flavors, creating a rich tapestry of connection. I watched as Jackson navigated the kitchen with an effortless grace, embodying the very spirit of what cooking was meant to be—a joyful exploration, a dance of flavors and emotions. And in that moment, as I savored the fruits of our labor, I realized that the regrets of the past had transformed into the promise of a vibrant future.

It was a celebration of everything I had missed—the laughter, the mess, the connections forged over food. I was reminded that life was not just about the destination but the journey itself, a delicious adventure filled with unexpected flavors and heartfelt moments. As the night stretched on, the candles flickered low, and I knew I was finally home, right where I was meant to be.

Chapter 4: Crumbs of Comfort

The aroma of freshly baked bread wafted through the air, wrapping around me like a warm embrace as I stepped into the quaint little kitchen of the culinary studio. Sunlight streamed through the large windows, casting a golden glow that danced over polished wooden countertops and the vibrant assortment of ingredients laid out before me. Jackson stood at the front, a master of ceremonies in his element, gesturing enthusiastically as he described the day's menu. His charisma was infectious, a spark that ignited something deep within me—a flicker of excitement I hadn't felt in ages.

I found a spot at the far end of the long, rustic table, my fingers instinctively tracing the grain of the wood, each knot and groove telling its own story. Around me, an eclectic mix of people buzzed with anticipation. A couple in their late thirties whispered conspiratorially, their laughter punctuating the air like bubbles popping in a fizzy drink. A young woman with a fiery mane of curls was already engrossed in a lively conversation with an older gentleman who wore glasses perched precariously on the bridge of his nose. My heart swelled slightly; this felt like a gathering of kindred spirits, each of us seeking solace in the simple pleasure of food.

Jackson's voice broke through my reverie, snapping me back to the moment. "Today, we're making a classic—homemade pasta! Who here has never made pasta from scratch?" His playful challenge echoed around the room, and hands shot up, accompanied by a chorus of giggles. I smiled, recalling my own culinary misadventures, the countless times I had stood in my tiny kitchen, flour dust swirling around me like a soft snow, as I tried (and often failed) to recreate my grandmother's recipes. That kitchen, with its mismatched utensils and faded paint, was my sanctuary, yet it had become a place of frustration and sadness without Amelia.

As the class began, I focused on the rhythm of the moment—the sound of hands kneading dough, the symphony of laughter mingling with Jackson's instructions. My fingers moved instinctively, working the flour and eggs together, the dough slowly transforming under my touch, warm and pliable. There was something liberating about it, the way the world outside faded into a blur as I lost myself in the tactile nature of cooking. Memories of my sister flooded back, her laughter echoing in the corners of my mind like a haunting melody. She was always the adventurous one, the fearless explorer of flavors, while I had been the cautious one, afraid to step outside my culinary comfort zone.

But today felt different. I looked around, watching people pair up, forming connections over shared tasks. I could hear snippets of conversation, a blend of stories and laughter, as the smell of garlic and basil began to permeate the room. It made my heart ache for the kind of bond I once shared with Amelia—those late-night chats filled with dreams and secrets, the comfort of knowing I had a partner in crime.

"Okay, everyone! It's time to roll out that dough!" Jackson's exuberant call snapped me back to the present, and I grabbed a rolling pin, my heart racing with a blend of anticipation and anxiety. The sound of the dough stretching beneath the pin was oddly soothing, like the gentle thrum of a heartbeat.

With every stroke, I felt a piece of my worry melting away, giving way to a sense of freedom I hadn't realized I was missing. I glanced up, meeting Jackson's eyes for a fleeting moment. There was a warmth there, an understanding that perhaps today wasn't just about cooking. Maybe it was about reconnecting with parts of myself I had neglected in the wake of Amelia's absence.

Once the dough was rolled thin enough, I cut it into delicate sheets, the edges fraying slightly as I worked, reminiscent of lace. "Perfect!" Jackson called out, moving between the stations, offering encouragement and gentle guidance. I couldn't help but laugh when he pointed out my imperfect edges, a delightful tease that pulled me further into the moment. It reminded me of those little jabs Amelia used to make about my ineptitude in the kitchen.

"Let's see those sheets of pasta!" Jackson announced, and I carefully draped mine over the back of a chair, a small triumph blossoming in my chest. As I stepped back to admire my handiwork, I realized that I had stepped outside my comfort zone, and that exhilarating rush was intoxicating.

Before I knew it, we were mixing a sauce, the bright scent of tomatoes and fresh basil filling the air, and I was laughing with my new companions. The camaraderie felt foreign yet welcome, and I was grateful for it. A young man across the table, with a wry smile and twinkling eyes, had been sharing terrible puns about pasta that made my heart lift in a way I hadn't expected. I felt lighter, unburdened by the weight of sadness that had draped over my shoulders like a heavy cloak.

"Who knew cooking could be this much fun?" I remarked, wiping flour from my cheek, catching a glimpse of the young man's grin. He leaned closer, eyes sparkling with mischief. "Just wait until we taste it! It might just change your life."

We both laughed, the sound ringing out like a bell in the quiet space. And in that moment, as we stirred sauce and rolled out pasta, I could almost hear Amelia's voice cheering me on from somewhere distant. Perhaps I was ready to embrace joy again, to create new memories in this bustling kitchen and to honor the love I once shared with my sister by rediscovering my passion for cooking.

As the class continued, I found solace not only in the food but in the connections being forged. My heart, once heavy, now danced to a lighter tune, twirling alongside the notes of laughter and the sizzle of olive oil in a pan. Each ingredient was a reminder that life, much like cooking, is a delicate balance of flavors—sweet, salty, bitter, and sometimes a little sour. Yet it is the blend of all those elements that creates something truly beautiful.

The sun hung low in the sky, casting a warm, golden hue that seemed to paint the world in a more forgiving light. I stood at my kitchen counter, the faint aroma of spices lingering in the air from lunch. Yet, despite the cheerful ambiance, the heaviness in my chest remained stubbornly present. The memories of Amelia weighed on me like a well-worn backpack, its straps digging in with every thought. I placed my phone down, the screen dimming into darkness, mirroring the shadows that seemed to creep into my heart.

Jackson's invitation sat there like an unturned page, promising an escape, a new story waiting to unfold. Cooking was his love language, each class an opportunity to share not just recipes but snippets of his vibrant spirit. I could almost hear the laughter echoing in my mind from past classes, the kitchen a cacophony of sizzling pans and playful banter. Yet, the idea of stepping away from my carefully structured life felt like balancing on the edge of a tightrope. Would I fall into the abyss of chaos, or could I find the thrill of freedom I so desperately craved?

After a moment's hesitation, I found my fingers dancing across the screen, typing a simple reply: "Count me in!" With that, a flutter of excitement coursed through me, dispelling some of the melancholy that had taken up residence in my thoughts. Perhaps this was the nudge I needed to stir things up, to infuse my routine with a sprinkle of spontaneity.

The days leading up to the class felt like a countdown to a long-awaited event, the anticipation buoying me through mundane tasks. I found myself daydreaming about the ingredients we might use, the smells wafting through the air, and the camaraderie that always emerged in the kitchen. Each day, I carved out a little space in my heart for the possibility of rekindling my joy. As the weekend approached, my excitement morphed into a palpable energy, igniting a spark of hope.

On the day of the class, the world outside my window was alive with color. I dressed with care, choosing a vibrant apron that felt like an armor against the heaviness that had lingered for too long. I navigated the streets with a newfound lightness, the car radio filled with upbeat melodies that accompanied my eager thoughts. Each note seemed to push the shadows further away, as if music could rewrite the narrative of my heart.

Upon arrival, the familiar hum of conversation enveloped me, the kitchen bustling with familiar faces and a few new ones. Jackson stood at the center, his presence a warm beacon in the crowd. His enthusiasm radiated, drawing people in like moths to a flame. He spotted me, his grin widening as he waved, an invitation to join the merry chaos.

As we began chopping, stirring, and sautéing, I lost myself in the rhythm of the kitchen. The knife danced across the cutting board, the vegetables yielding to my touch, while laughter bubbled up like the simmering sauces on the stove. Each interaction felt like a thread weaving itself into a tapestry of connection, a fabric I had longed to mend. The world outside faded away; there was only the sizzling of ingredients and the warmth of camaraderie.

During a brief break, Jackson pulled me aside, his eyes sparkling with mischief. "You know," he began, leaning closer, "you've been missed. Your energy brings a certain magic to these classes." The compliment landed softly in my chest, stirring something deep within. The emptiness I had felt in Amelia's absence seemed to fill with the promise of friendship, of a bond that could flourish despite the tumult in my personal life.

As we transitioned from one dish to the next, I began to notice how the act of cooking was not just about creating a meal; it was an act of expression, a form of art. Each ingredient had its story, just

like each participant in the class. With every chop, every sprinkle of
seasoning, I felt a layer of my own guarded heart peel away, revealing
a tenderness I hadn't realized was still alive within me.

By the end of the class, we gathered around the table, plates
adorned with colorful creations that looked almost too beautiful to
eat. As laughter filled the air, the warmth of shared stories enveloped
me. I found myself seated next to a woman named Claire, who
shared her own struggles with relationships and family. Her
vulnerability echoed my own, and as we swapped anecdotes, I felt
the walls I had built around myself begin to crumble, brick by brick.

Later, as I cleaned up, Jackson approached again, holding a plate
of leftovers, a glint of excitement in his eyes. "Want to join me for a
taste test? I've got a new recipe I've been dying to try." The invitation
was irresistible. It felt as if he was extending a hand, not just to
share food but to build something deeper—a connection beyond the
confines of our cooking class.

We moved to his kitchen, the space alive with the smell of herbs
and spices. As he cooked, we talked effortlessly, the conversation
flowing like the wine we sipped. He shared stories of his culinary
adventures, of mishaps that turned into masterpieces, and gradually,
my laughter mingled with his. In that moment, I realized how often
I had confined my joy to the shadows, allowing fear and regret to
dictate my interactions.

The evening wound down with the setting sun casting a warm
glow through the window, illuminating our faces as we shared our
hopes and dreams. It was in that small, unassuming kitchen that I
began to understand the importance of nurturing connections, of
allowing oneself to be vulnerable in the presence of another. As we
savored the last bites of our impromptu feast, I couldn't help but
think that perhaps this was the beginning of something beautiful,
a rekindling of joy and the promise of friendship, one crumb of
comfort at a time.

The sun dipped below the horizon, casting a soft glow that transformed the ordinary into something magical. I found myself sitting at Jackson's kitchen island, the countertop a symphony of colors as the evening light played over the vibrant vegetables and fragrant herbs. The air buzzed with the residue of laughter and shared stories, a melody of connection that I had almost forgotten existed. It was a world apart from the isolation I had come to know in my routine.

Jackson moved fluidly, his hands deftly chopping herbs while humming a tune that seemed to merge with the sizzle of garlic in a pan. Each movement was a dance, and I felt like a spectator, mesmerized by the ease with which he navigated his culinary kingdom. "Cooking is an act of love," he said, glancing over his shoulder with a grin. "You pour your heart into it, and it reflects back." I found myself pondering those words, reflecting on how I had poured so much of myself into avoiding pain rather than embracing joy.

As he prepared a dish I had never seen before—an intriguing fusion of Italian and Thai flavors—Jackson shared stories of his culinary adventures, each tale laced with humor and insight. He recounted the time he accidentally mistook chili flakes for oregano, resulting in a dish that nearly scorched the eyebrows off his dinner guests. It was in these moments of vulnerability that I felt a connection blossoming, one that felt richer than the bonds forged in superficial exchanges. I was reminded that every person carries their own tapestry of experiences, woven with threads of joy, sorrow, and laughter.

With the meal almost complete, Jackson set a plate before me, the presentation both beautiful and inviting. "Here's to taking risks," he toasted, raising a glass of chilled white wine. I followed suit, clinking my glass against his, feeling the vibrations of the moment resonate through me. I took my first bite, and the explosion of flavors sent a rush of warmth through my veins. Each mouthful was a revelation, a reminder of the joy that came from sharing not just food, but also moments of genuine connection. It was the first time in ages that I felt truly alive, my heart echoing with the thrill of rediscovery.

As we savored the meal, the conversation flowed effortlessly, touching on dreams, fears, and the unyielding passage of time. Jackson spoke about his aspirations to open a restaurant, his eyes sparkling with passion. I shared snippets of my life, allowing him glimpses into my world—my work, my heartache over Amelia, and the burdens I had carried for so long. It was cathartic, a release that felt like shedding a heavy coat after a long winter.

As the night wore on, our laughter mingled with the soft glow of the kitchen lights, creating an intimate atmosphere that felt cocoon-like. Jackson leaned against the counter, wiping his hands on a towel, his gaze steady and warm. "You know, sometimes it's the connections we make that heal us the most," he said, his tone turning earnest. "It's easy to retreat into ourselves, to build walls. But real magic happens when we allow others in." His words hung in the air, a truth that resonated deeply within me.

In that moment, I felt a shift within—a flicker of hope igniting where darkness had settled. Perhaps I didn't have to carry the weight of Amelia's absence alone. The possibility of forging new bonds, of allowing friendships to flourish, seemed within reach. It was as if a door I had long shut was now ajar, letting in a rush of fresh air and the promise of new beginnings.

After dinner, Jackson suggested we clean up together. The act of washing dishes while still basking in the afterglow of a shared meal felt oddly intimate. We worked in comfortable silence, the only sounds being the gentle clinking of plates and the soft swish of water. As I scrubbed a particularly stubborn pot, I felt Jackson's gaze on me, a curious warmth that made my heart flutter. "What do you want?" he asked, the simplicity of the question layered with meaning.

I paused, water dripping from my hands, and pondered. "I want to feel whole again," I admitted, my voice barely above a whisper. "I've been lost in my own grief, clinging to the past." Jackson nodded, his expression one of understanding. "Then let's carve out a space for that wholeness," he suggested, wiping his hands on a dishcloth. "Let's create a tradition—weekly cooking nights, a way to connect, to share, and to heal."

The thought of establishing such a ritual ignited a spark of excitement within me. It felt like a lifeline, a way to anchor myself to something positive amidst the chaos of my emotions. I imagined the laughter, the culinary experiments, the camaraderie that would blossom over pots of bubbling sauces and freshly baked bread. "I'd like that," I replied, my heart swelling with a mixture of hope and apprehension.

As we finished cleaning, the remnants of the meal transformed into memories that would linger long after the plates were washed. Jackson began to clear away the dishes, but before he could turn away, I reached out, touching his arm lightly. "Thank you," I said, the sincerity of my gratitude spilling forth. "For tonight, for reminding me of the beauty in connection."

His smile widened, illuminating the space around us. "No thanks needed. Just promise to bring your appetite next week." As I stepped out of his kitchen and into the cool night air, I felt a warmth that had been absent for far too long. The stars twinkled above, casting their glow like a blanket of comfort, and I knew this was just the beginning.

Days turned into weeks, each cooking night a delightful adventure filled with laughter and camaraderie. Jackson and I created a rhythm, exploring new cuisines and experimenting with daring flavors. The kitchen became a sanctuary, a place where I could set aside the weight of my worries and immerse myself in the joys of culinary creation. With every dish we crafted, I found healing—each chop of the knife, each stir of the pot, felt like a small step toward reclaiming the joy I had lost.

With Jackson by my side, I learned not just about cooking, but about life itself—about the delicate balance of flavors, the patience required to create something beautiful, and the importance of savoring each moment. I began to understand that the path to healing wasn't linear; it was a winding road dotted with unexpected turns and delicious detours.

One evening, as we prepared a particularly ambitious paella, I looked over at Jackson, his brow furrowed in concentration. "Do you think it's possible to fall in love with someone while still holding onto the pieces of your past?" I asked, the question hanging between us like the fragrant steam rising from the pan.

He paused, thoughtful. "I believe we can love deeply, even amidst the remnants of what we've lost," he replied, his voice steady. "It's all about allowing ourselves to be vulnerable, to trust that love can coexist with grief." His words resonated within me, a balm to the tender places in my heart still raw from Amelia's absence.

In that moment, I realized that I was not just rediscovering my love for cooking, but also the capacity for connection and love. It was a slow, gentle unfurling—a blossoming that felt like homecoming. The memories of my sister, once a source of pain, began to coexist with the new joys I was cultivating. I felt her spirit with me, urging me to embrace life fully, to savor each crumb of comfort that came my way.

As I stood there, stirring the vibrant mixture in the pan, I felt a sense of belonging. I was no longer merely moving through life, but actively participating in it, crafting a narrative filled with flavors, laughter, and connection. The cooking nights had evolved into something more than just culinary adventures; they had become a lifeline, a bridge to a new chapter where healing and love could thrive, nourished by the rich experiences we created together.

In Jackson's kitchen, I had not only found comfort but also a reminder that life, in all its complexity, was meant to be celebrated. And as I stirred the paella, I did so with a heart open to new possibilities, ready to embrace whatever came next, one delicious bite at a time.

Chapter 5: Chopping Away Barriers

Sunlight poured through the expansive windows of the community kitchen, illuminating the space with a warm glow that seemed to dance with the vibrant colors of fresh produce strewn across the countertops. The air was alive with a medley of scents—basil mingling with garlic, the earthy sweetness of ripe tomatoes merging with the sharp tang of lemon zest. Each breath I took felt like a plunge into a sensory whirlpool, pulling me deeper into this world where chaos met creativity.

Participants darted around, each wrapped up in their own culinary quests, but I was hyper-aware of every detail—the sound of knives skillfully chopping, the soft bubbling of sauce simmering on the stove, and the laughter erupting from a group attempting to roll fresh pasta. It was a beautiful cacophony, a soundtrack of collaboration and camaraderie, and it tugged at something deep within me. I had long resigned myself to a quieter existence, cocooned in the safety of my solitude. But here, in this bustling kitchen, I felt the stirrings of a forgotten joy.

Jackson stood at the front, his tall frame commanding attention without the need for raised voices. He wore a fitted apron that accentuated his lean physique, and his hair, a tousled mess of curls, framed a face that was equal parts charming and inviting. There was a spark in his hazel eyes that seemed to ignite a fire in everyone around him, as if he possessed a magical ability to turn mundane ingredients into something extraordinary. I watched him as he moved, fluidly transitioning from one task to another, sharing tips and encouragement with a smile that could brighten the gloomiest day.

As he demonstrated how to julienne carrots, my gaze lingered on his hands, deftly slicing through the vibrant orange flesh with a precision that made it look effortless. It was in these small, intimate moments that I began to feel my own barriers start to chip away, like ice melting under a radiant sun. I had spent so long shielding my heart from the world, building walls so high that even I felt trapped inside. Yet, with each laugh and every shared recipe, I felt those walls begin to tremble, the cracks allowing flickers of light to seep through.

"Who's ready to get their hands dirty?" Jackson called out, his voice a melodic blend of enthusiasm and playfulness. I couldn't help but grin at the challenge, feeling an impulse to dive into the fray rather than hover at the edges, a wallflower cloaked in hesitation. I joined a group of eager cooks, each of us wielding our own knives with the ferocity of warriors preparing for battle. We chopped, diced, and stirred, the rhythm of our movements creating an unspoken bond among us, and I found myself laughing at our shared clumsiness.

As I struggled to keep up, a particularly unruly onion slipped from my grip, rolling across the floor with a defiance that made the entire room chuckle. Jackson, ever the gentleman, knelt down to retrieve it, his laughter infectious. "Don't worry; onions are resilient. Just like us," he quipped, shooting me a wink that made my heart skip a beat. I could feel the heat rising in my cheeks, a combination of embarrassment and exhilaration, and I couldn't shake the feeling that there was something deeper brewing between us, simmering just beneath the surface.

The recipes unfolded like stories, each ingredient contributing to the narrative of our meal. We crafted a hearty ratatouille, layering flavors and textures like brushstrokes on a canvas. I became entranced by the process, losing track of time as we navigated the colorful array of vegetables. Chopping, stirring, seasoning—each action felt like a step toward something transformative. I discovered not just a newfound passion for cooking but also a reawakening of the part of me that had long been dormant, buried under layers of fear and uncertainty.

The room vibrated with shared laughter as we recounted culinary disasters and successes. The atmosphere was charged with a sense of community, an unspoken agreement that we were all in this together, forging connections over simmering pots and shared struggles. I felt a sense of belonging creeping in, like a warm blanket wrapping around my shoulders on a chilly evening. It was a feeling I hadn't dared to invite into my life for a long time, but in this moment, it enveloped me, softening the edges of my guarded heart.

As we gathered around the table to share the fruits of our labor, the colorful array of dishes glistened under the overhead lights, each one a testament to our collective effort. My heart raced as Jackson moved closer, pulling out a chair beside me. The subtle scent of his cologne mingled with the aromas wafting from the table, creating an intoxicating blend that made my head swim. We exchanged a look, a fleeting moment that felt charged with electricity, and I found myself holding my breath, waiting for him to speak.

"Not bad for a group of amateurs, huh?" he said, his smile widening as he took in the feast before us. I could only nod, overwhelmed by the warmth spreading through me, as if the meal had ignited something long buried within my spirit. In that moment, with laughter and food surrounding us, I felt a flicker of hope ignite within—a glimmer that maybe, just maybe, I could allow myself to embrace this connection, to explore the possibilities beyond the confines of my well-guarded heart.

And just like that, as the dishes were passed around and the stories flowed, I realized that I was ready to chop away the barriers that had held me back for too long.

As Jackson chopped vegetables with a precision that made me question my own culinary skills, I leaned against the counter, absorbing the scents wafting through the air. The aroma of garlic sizzling in olive oil mingled with the sweet undertones of ripe tomatoes, creating a symphony of flavors that danced around us. He moved with a casual elegance, his hands deftly turning the mundane act of cooking into an art form. Each slice of the knife seemed to echo my thoughts—sharp, decisive, and sometimes hesitant.

"Are you hungry, or are you just here to watch me impress my friends?" he teased, glancing over his shoulder with a grin that made my heart flutter.

"Definitely a bit of both," I replied, my voice light, though my heart felt heavier. As I watched him, I couldn't help but wonder if he sensed the weight I carried, the hidden burden that felt increasingly like an anchor weighing me down. But as we shared banter and laughter, it seemed easier to ignore the shadows lurking in the corners of my mind.

With each passing day, Jackson became a beacon of warmth in my life. Our conversations began to unravel the tightly wound threads of my insecurities. He shared his own fears, exposing a vulnerability that matched my own, and in those moments, I felt the barriers I had built around my heart begin to crumble. We spoke of dreams—his aspirations of becoming a chef, the thrill of creating dishes that brought people together, and the quiet yet profound joy of sharing a meal. My dreams felt less defined, like wisps of smoke that disappeared before I could grasp them fully.

The kitchen was alive with the chatter of friends, but as I stood there, I felt like a ghost—visible yet disconnected. The family portrait caught my eye again, a stark reminder of the past that had shaped my present. The smiling faces seemed to reach out to me, urging me to reclaim what I had lost. Memories of laughter filled my mind: the way my sister's eyes sparkled with mischief, her laughter like music that enveloped me in a cocoon of safety. I longed to recreate that bond, to bridge the chasm of silence that had formed between us.

In that moment, I realized that the cooking lesson Jackson was imparting wasn't just about food; it was about connection. I watched as he explained the importance of seasoning, of layering flavors to create depth. It struck me as a metaphor for life itself—every experience, every moment, seasoning the soul, contributing to the richness of our stories. Yet here I was, paralyzed by fear, afraid to add my own spices to the mix, terrified of the unpredictable nature of reconnection.

As the evening unfolded, laughter filled the air like a comforting blanket. Friends gathered around the table, plates piled high with Jackson's culinary creations. I sat among them, sharing stories and exchanging glances, but a part of me remained distant. The shadows of regret loomed over my heart like a heavy cloud, the weight of unspoken words pressing against my chest.

"Hey, what's on your mind?" Jackson asked, his eyes piercing through the laughter like sunlight breaking through clouds.

"I've just been thinking about family," I admitted, my voice barely above a whisper, hesitant to break the spell of the evening.

His expression shifted, curiosity piqued. "Family can be complicated, can't it? Mine is a mixed bag of personalities, but somehow we make it work."

I nodded, feeling the truth of his words resonate within me. "I used to have that too—someone I felt close to, someone I could share everything with."

"Are you still in touch?" he inquired gently, his tone a blend of interest and empathy.

"No," I replied, the word tasting bitter on my tongue. "I... I haven't spoken to her in a while. It's complicated."

"Complicated usually means it matters," he said, a knowing smile tugging at the corners of his lips. "Maybe it's time to add a little seasoning to that relationship."

As the evening wore on, I found solace in Jackson's words. He had an uncanny ability to see beyond the surface, to peel back the layers of my hesitations like he did with the tomatoes in the kitchen.

The laughter of his friends, mingled with the delightful sounds of clinking glasses and shared stories, felt like an invitation to embrace the chaos of life.

In the glow of candlelight, I could almost feel the warmth of my sister's presence, as if she were seated at the table, laughing alongside us. The nostalgia washed over me, bringing with it a longing that felt tangible. I realized that perhaps I had been too focused on the fear of rejection, too preoccupied with the shadows of the past, to see that the future could hold something beautiful.

Jackson's laughter brought me back to the moment, his easygoing demeanor reminding me that connection was worth the risk. "So, are you going to let fear hold you back, or are you going to reach out and see what happens?"

His question lingered in the air, an unspoken challenge that stirred something deep within me. Perhaps it was time to step beyond the walls I had built, to embrace the uncertainty and reach for what I had lost.

As the night deepened, I found myself swept up in the magic of the moment. The worries that had weighed heavily on my heart began to dissipate, replaced by a flicker of hope. Jackson's kitchen had transformed into a sanctuary, a place where laughter and warmth intertwined like the ingredients of a well-seasoned dish. And as I watched him move gracefully through the space, I felt a renewed sense of purpose blooming within me—a desire to reconnect with my sister and savor the flavors of our shared history.

In that fleeting moment, surrounded by friends and the comforting chaos of the evening, I resolved to reach out. No longer would I let fear dictate my actions; I would embrace the unknown and allow the past to blend seamlessly with the present. I would find my voice again, and perhaps, just perhaps, rekindle the bond that had once brought me so much joy.

As Jackson expertly stirred a vibrant sauce, the rich aroma of basil and roasted garlic filled the kitchen, wrapping around us like a comforting embrace. The flickering candlelight illuminated the walls, casting playful shadows that danced along with the laughter of his friends, who were gathered around the dining table, their chatter punctuated by the clinking of glasses. It felt like a scene from a movie, one that captured the essence of connection—a moment suspended in time where joy was the common language.

"Alright, chef, what's next?" I asked, leaning in closer, my curiosity piqued by his deft movements.

"Now for the pièce de résistance," he replied, a mischievous glint in his eye. "The secret ingredient: a splash of red wine."

With a flourish, he poured a generous amount into the bubbling pot, the liquid swirling like a vibrant promise of warmth and richness. It was mesmerizing to watch, and I couldn't help but feel that Jackson, in many ways, embodied the very essence of this dish—complex, layered, and wholly captivating. Just as he blended flavors to create something remarkable, he was piecing together the fragments of my heart, pulling them from the shadows where they had lingered far too long.

The lively atmosphere of the evening wrapped around us, yet within me simmered a quiet conflict. Every laugh shared, every story told, only amplified the longing I felt to bridge the gap between my past and my present. I stole another glance at the family portrait, the smiling faces frozen in time—a perfect encapsulation of what once was and what could still be. My sister's face shone with a brightness I longed to see again, yet the weight of silence stretched between us like a vast chasm, threatening to swallow the possibility of reconnection.

As the meal came together, Jackson's friends joined in, setting the table with an assortment of dishes that transformed his cozy kitchen into a festive banquet. The warmth of friendship enveloped us all, filling the space with an infectious energy that made the worries of the world feel far away. I found myself swept up in the spirit of the evening, participating in lighthearted debates over which wine paired best with the meal, my laughter mingling seamlessly with theirs.

"Here's to good food and even better company!" someone raised their glass, and the sentiment echoed around the table, bringing a smile to my face. I toasted along, the familiar tingle of hope rekindling within me. Perhaps life could be more than the weight of my past. Perhaps it could be flavored with new beginnings.

As the evening wore on, my heart danced with joy, but the specter of Amelia's absence never fully dissipated. I could see her face in the laughter of Jackson's friends, hear echoes of her voice in the clinking of silverware. The juxtaposition of my longing for her presence against the reality of my situation tugged at me, urging me to reach out, to break the silence that had woven itself into the fabric of our relationship.

"Tell us about the best meal you've ever had," one of the guests prompted, and I felt the gaze of the table shift toward me. A perfect opportunity to bring Amelia into the conversation—a chance to share a piece of her with this newfound community.

"Actually, it was with my sister," I began, feeling the words spill from my lips like a cherished secret. "We used to have these elaborate Sunday dinners, just the two of us. She'd try new recipes while I acted as her taste tester."

Laughter erupted as I recounted the time Amelia's ambitious lasagna had turned into a bubbling disaster, the cheese spilling over like an overzealous performer on stage. It was a memory tinged with warmth, each detail pulling me closer to the love we once shared. As I spoke, I felt the barriers within me start to crumble, the connection to my sister reigniting like a flame that had only smoldered in the ashes of time.

"Sounds like you two had a blast," Jackson chimed in, his eyes sparkling with appreciation. "Cooking is so much more than just a meal; it's about the stories we share, the connections we make."

"Yes," I agreed, a sense of clarity washing over me. "And that's exactly what I've been missing. I've let fear keep me from reaching out to her, from rekindling what we had. It feels daunting."

Jackson leaned closer, his expression serious yet gentle. "Reaching out is the first step. You never know—she might be waiting for you to take that leap. Life's too short to let fear dictate your connections."

His words hung in the air like the lingering aroma of the meal, striking a chord deep within me. I knew he was right. What if Amelia was also feeling the weight of our silence? What if she longed for reconnection just as fiercely as I did?

With the taste of the meal still fresh on my palate and the warmth of the evening enveloping me, I made a decision. Tomorrow, I would reach out to her. I would not let the fear of rejection keep me shackled to the past any longer.

As the night drew to a close and friends began to filter out, their laughter echoing in the hallway, I lingered, savoring the last remnants of joy that filled the space. Jackson busied himself with the dishes, his movements fluid and graceful. The kitchen, now dimly lit, felt intimate and inviting, a cocoon of warmth that shielded us from the outside world.

"Thank you for tonight," I said softly, stepping closer to where he stood. "You've created something truly special here—not just the meal, but the connections."

He turned, a smile breaking across his face, illuminating his features. "It's all about the moments we create. We should do this more often."

The unspoken invitation lingered in the air, and my heart fluttered with anticipation. Jackson was becoming an anchor in my life, a source of light in the murky waters of my emotions.

"Definitely," I replied, my voice steady with newfound resolve. "Let's plan for a Sunday dinner soon."

As I left his home, the night air was crisp and invigorating, invigorating me with possibilities. I felt a spark of determination igniting within me, a flame fueled by the joy of the evening and the promise of reaching out to Amelia. The streets felt alive, every shadow shifting like a breath of encouragement whispering in my ear.

Perhaps the flavors of the past could blend with the future, creating something uniquely beautiful. Tomorrow would be a new beginning—an opportunity to connect and reclaim the bond that had always been there, waiting for the right moment to flourish once more. With each step, I felt lighter, ready to embrace the challenges ahead, to stir the pot of my life and see what delightful concoction might emerge.

Chapter 7: Ingredients of Healing

The moment I stepped through the door, the warmth of my little apartment wrapped around me like a familiar embrace, the rich scent of vanilla wafting from a candle I'd lit earlier filling the air with a sweet promise of comfort. I kicked off my shoes, the soft thud echoing in the quietness, a gentle reminder of the day's chaos left outside. The world felt vast and unyielding beyond my walls, but here, nestled within this modest space adorned with mismatched furniture and half-finished paintings, I found my sanctuary.

The kitchen was the heart of my home, a vibrant mosaic of culinary experiments. Pots and pans hung like trophies, testament to countless evenings spent whipping up dishes inspired by flavors that danced through my mind. The gleaming countertops bore evidence of my adventures: a splotch of tomato sauce, the remnants of a failed soufflé, and the joyous smudge of chocolate that had escaped during a moment of sheer delight. It was here, amid the chaos of my culinary trials, that I had discovered the power of creation. Yet tonight, the usual excitement felt muted beneath a layer of uncertainty.

I sank onto a stool, letting the cool surface soothe my restless thoughts. My phone sat nearby, a silent sentinel that held the weight of my heart. My fingers twitched, hovering above the screen as I recalled the message I had sent to Amelia—a fragile offering of hope wrapped in words I had carefully chosen. Memories of laughter and shared dreams floated to the surface, mingling with the pang of past grievances. She had been my confidante, my partner in crime, until the shadows of misunderstanding had pulled us apart like a curtain drawn too tightly.

Jackson's voice echoed in my mind, urging me to embrace vulnerability, to peel back the layers I had so carefully constructed. I wondered if he could sense the tremors of fear coursing through me. His support was a steady flame, illuminating paths I had long since abandoned. With him, I felt the thrill of adventure, the intoxicating rush of rediscovering myself, yet the thought of reaching out to Amelia felt like standing at the edge of a precipice, the depths below shrouded in uncertainty.

With a determined exhale, I flicked on the kettle, the rhythmic bubbling soothing my nerves. I rummaged through my cabinets for my favorite tea—a fragrant blend of chamomile and lavender that seemed to whisper promises of serenity. As the water danced and boiled, I reflected on the fragility of friendship. Each bond is a delicate tapestry woven from shared experiences, laughter, and trust, but when frayed, it takes courage to stitch it back together.

The kettle sang, a soft chime that pulled me back to the present. I poured the steaming water over the loose leaves, the floral aroma rising to envelop me in its calming embrace. With a sip, the warmth spread through my chest, igniting a flicker of resolve. I had spent too long running from my past, burying my feelings under layers of flour and sugar, and it was time to confront what I had avoided.

As I settled into a corner of the couch, my thoughts drifted to Jackson. His laughter was a symphony, buoyant and rich, always echoing in my mind like a beloved song. He had a way of drawing out my truest self, coaxing me from the shadows into the light. It was strange to feel this swell of affection, a burgeoning connection I hadn't anticipated, yet it filled me with a warmth that overshadowed the loneliness I had once worn like a cloak.

The door creaked open, and my cat, Marigold, sauntered in, her tail held high like a flag of independence. She hopped onto my lap, purring as she settled in, her presence grounding me. I absentmindedly stroked her soft fur, a rhythmic motion that echoed my swirling thoughts. In this moment, I felt the delicate balance of joy and fear—joy at the possibility of reconciling with Amelia and fear of rejection.

The minutes slipped away, each tick of the clock amplifying my unease. I glanced at my phone, the screen still blank, waiting. What was taking her so long? The anticipation felt like a tightrope walk, each second stretching into eternity. I had poured my heart into that message, but perhaps it wasn't enough. Maybe my words felt empty, lacking the substance that once defined our friendship.

As the night deepened, I switched on a soft lamp, casting a warm glow over the room, enveloping me in a cocoon of light. Outside, the city pulsed with life—honking horns, laughter spilling from nearby cafés, the distant sound of music weaving through the air. Yet here, within my sanctuary, the world felt like a distant dream, blurred and muted.

The silence was deafening, wrapping around me like a fog, each breath echoing in the stillness. I couldn't shake the feeling of inadequacy that gnawed at my insides. The taste of fear lingered on my tongue, sharp and metallic, but amid the chaos of emotions, a small flicker of hope persisted. I had taken the first step; now all that remained was to wait, to allow the universe to unfold its plans in its own time.

Marigold shifted, nudging my hand as if sensing my turmoil. I smiled down at her, grateful for her unwavering presence. In her emerald eyes, I saw the reflection of a friendship that had stood the test of time—a bond unbroken by misunderstandings or silence. If only I could channel that same strength in reaching out to Amelia. With each passing moment, I reminded myself that vulnerability could pave the way for healing, for rekindling a friendship that had once been my anchor in life's tempestuous seas.

The city outside whispered its secrets, and I closed my eyes, envisioning a reunion, a moment when we would sit across from each other, laughter spilling like sunlight through the cracks of our shared past. A soft sigh escaped my lips, mingling with the steam that rose from my cup, and I found myself wishing, hoping, praying for a miracle wrapped in the simplest of gestures: a response from a friend who had once been my everything.

The night wore on, my thoughts swirling like the steam rising from my now-cold cup of tea. Marigold had drifted off, a small bundle of warmth nestled against my leg, her gentle purring the only sound in the room. In the stillness, I felt the weight of the silence, a soft but persistent reminder of the fears I had laid bare with my message to Amelia. I imagined her reading my words, the familiar rise and fall of her laughter mingling with the echoes of our shared memories. What would she think of my attempt to bridge the gap?

As dawn approached, a sliver of light broke through my curtains, painting the room in hues of gold and peach. I threw off my blanket and headed to the kitchen, where the light felt alive, illuminating the little details—the chipped ceramic tiles, the pots hanging like glistening ornaments. I set to work, determined to immerse myself in the familiar dance of chopping, stirring, and creating. Cooking had always been my refuge, a place where I could pour my heart into ingredients, transforming mundane elements into something beautiful.

This morning, I opted for blueberry pancakes, a dish that held the kind of nostalgia that warmed the soul. The plump berries burst against the batter, releasing their sweet juices, filling the air with the tantalizing scent of summer. I hummed softly, allowing the rhythm of the spatula against the skillet to soothe my nerves. With each flip, I imagined flipping through the pages of my past, seeking out the cherished moments with Amelia that I longed to reclaim.

As the pancakes sizzled, I grabbed my phone and glanced at the screen. Nothing. Just a blank canvas, a silent testament to my vulnerability. I tried to dismiss the gnawing anxiety, but it tugged at me like a persistent child demanding attention. Perhaps she was busy. Perhaps she hadn't seen it yet. I forced myself to focus on the batter, pouring it with the precision of an artist creating a masterpiece.

When I finally plated the pancakes, I drizzled maple syrup like a finishing touch on a canvas, the golden liquid pooling in delightful little puddles. I sat at the table, the warm sunlight spilling in, illuminating the feast before me. As I took my first bite, the burst of sweet and tangy flavors enveloped me, a reminder that joy could still exist amid uncertainty. The warmth settled in my belly, a comforting presence that nudged me to relax.

But in the back of my mind, the thought lingered. I needed to reach out again, to break the ice if it remained frozen. So, I decided to make a plan, a casual invitation perhaps. Something light, like a warm breeze inviting the sun into a chilly day. I could suggest meeting for coffee, to talk about the good old days, to share a laugh, and perhaps a few tears.

After breakfast, I shuffled to the living room and sank into the couch, my mind racing with ideas. I imagined our reunion, her laughter lighting up the room like sunshine breaking through clouds. Would she be hesitant? Would there be a moment when silence enveloped us, filled only by the weight of unspoken words? I hoped we could fill those spaces with the sound of our old camaraderie, a testament to our shared history.

The hours dragged, each tick of the clock an echo of my impatience. I busied myself with chores—dusting the shelves that held my collection of cookbooks and knick-knacks, all the while imagining Amelia leafing through those books, her brow furrowed in concentration, her laughter bubbling over as I fumbled through a recipe.

I paused, my heart stuttering at the thought of her. There was a time when we were inseparable, two sides of the same coin, always chasing the next adventure, whether it was finding the best taco truck in the city or planning spontaneous road trips to nowhere. But those moments had felt like a distant memory, dulled by time and the ache of misunderstandings.

Finally, as the sun dipped below the horizon, painting the sky in strokes of orange and purple, I felt the tension in my chest ease slightly. I settled back on the couch and sent a casual message, suggesting a coffee date at our favorite café, the one with the outdoor seating and the best chocolate croissants. I hit send, a little flutter of hope igniting within me.

That evening, I lost myself in a Netflix binge, the screen illuminating my face with flickers of light and laughter, but my heart remained tethered to my phone. Each time it buzzed, my heart raced, but it was never her name lighting up the screen. I tried to immerse myself in the plot, but the characters on screen seemed hollow compared to the vibrancy of real-life connections, the electricity of laughter shared over coffee and pastries.

It wasn't until well into the night that my phone finally chimed, a melodic sound that broke through the fog of anticipation. My heart raced as I grabbed it, breathless, my eyes scanning the words.

"Hey! It's been a while. I'd love to catch up. How about tomorrow at the café?"

A rush of relief washed over me, so powerful that I felt almost dizzy. I wanted to leap up and dance around the room, to scream with joy and disbelief. But I contained myself, responding with a casual enthusiasm that masked the whirlpool of emotions inside me.

Tomorrow. The weight of that single word felt like a promise, an unspoken commitment to step back into a world filled with potential.

As I set my phone down, Marigold leaped onto my lap, nudging my hand with her head. I smiled down at her, feeling lighter, like a weight had been lifted. Tomorrow would be our chance to rewrite the script of our friendship, to revisit the moments that had once defined us, and perhaps even to build something new.

The night deepened, but I no longer felt its shadows looming. I curled up on the couch, the anticipation of the next day wrapping around me like a warm blanket. I closed my eyes, dreaming of laughter shared over steaming cups, the taste of chocolate croissants melting in our mouths, and the rekindling of a friendship that had always felt like home.

Morning light filtered through the curtains, casting gentle stripes across my living room floor, illuminating the dust motes that danced in the air like tiny fairies caught in a sunbeam. I stretched lazily on the couch, remnants of sleep still clinging to me, but excitement buzzed just beneath the surface. Today was the day. My heart thrummed with a mix of nerves and anticipation as I prepared for my long-awaited reunion with Amelia.

I dressed carefully, pulling on my favorite soft, oversized sweater, the color of faded lavender, which felt like a hug wrapped around me. I paired it with dark jeans, knowing they would hold up through whatever the day had in store. As I pulled my hair into a messy bun, I caught my reflection in the mirror. My cheeks still bore the flush of last night's joyous anticipation, and a flicker of confidence sparked in my chest. This was the new me, one willing to face her past, to reach out, to mend what had been broken.

I stepped into the kitchen and brewed a fresh pot of coffee, the rich aroma filling the air like a warm welcome. As the liquid bubbled, I glanced at the clock, counting down the minutes until I would see Amelia again. I grabbed a plate and set out a few croissants—just in case she needed something sweet to accompany our long overdue conversation.

As I poured the steaming coffee into my favorite mug, a cheerful blue one decorated with tiny daisies, I allowed myself to imagine the scene at the café. I could picture us sitting at our usual table, sunlight spilling over the patio as we sank into easy laughter, the world around us fading into a blur. Memories of afternoons spent there flooded my mind—those lazy days filled with giggles and whispered secrets, plans for the future, and dreams that seemed to stretch endlessly before us. I hoped the same magic would weave through our reunion today.

Arriving at the café, my pulse quickened as I spotted the familiar brick facade, ivy climbing its walls like a living tapestry. The scent of freshly baked pastries wafted through the air, mingling with the rich notes of coffee and laughter from inside. I pushed the door open, and the soft chime of the bell overhead was like a gentle nudge from fate.

The café was a mosaic of life, the eclectic mix of patrons creating a vibrant tapestry of sounds and smells. I glanced around, my heart doing a little flip when I spotted Amelia sitting at our table. She looked radiant, her hair a cascade of dark curls framing her face, her smile lighting up the room like a lighthouse guiding me back home.

I took a moment to absorb the sight of her—the way her eyes sparkled with mischief and warmth, the laughter that danced on her lips. Despite the years apart, a familiar comfort washed over me, as though no time had passed at all. Gathering my courage, I approached, a shy smile creeping onto my face.

"Hey there," I said, my voice tinged with a nervous tremor.

"Look who it is!" she exclaimed, her arms opening wide as if to draw me in. I stepped forward, enveloped in her embrace, the warmth of her presence dissolving the tension that had clung to me since yesterday. It felt as if the air between us crackled with unspoken words, the heaviness of our past suspended in the moment.

We settled into our seats, and I handed her a croissant, watching as her eyes lit up in appreciation. The taste of nostalgia filled the air as we reminisced about the little moments that had once defined our friendship—the spontaneous road trips, our epic attempts at cooking, and the ridiculous inside jokes that only we could understand. Each laugh seemed to chip away at the barriers we had built, the walls constructed from hurt and misunderstanding.

But as the conversation flowed, I sensed a deeper undercurrent, the weight of things left unsaid lingering between us like a stubborn shadow. I took a sip of my coffee, gathering my thoughts before plunging into the depths of the vulnerability I had been so eager to embrace. "Amelia," I began, my voice steady yet soft. "I want to apologize for everything that happened. I never meant for us to drift apart."

Her expression softened, and she looked down, tracing the rim of her cup with her finger. "I was angry, you know? But I missed you, too," she admitted, her honesty washing over me like rain on parched soil. "I think we both let our fears get in the way."

I nodded, the truth of her words resonating within me. "I let my insecurities blind me, and I didn't reach out when I should have. I've carried that regret for too long."

As we exchanged stories of our lives since that fateful rift, I felt the ice of the past melting away. Amelia shared tales of her travels, her adventures, and the small victories that had painted her world in vibrant colors. I recounted my journey, the ups and downs, and how Jackson had unexpectedly entered my life, encouraging me to rediscover my passions and confront my fears.

"Jackson sounds incredible," Amelia said, her eyes sparkling with curiosity. "You deserve to be happy, you know?"

Her words struck a chord deep within me, resonating in a way that felt affirming. "I really do feel different now, like I'm finally beginning to embrace who I am," I confessed. "I want to share that with you, to rekindle what we had."

With each shared laugh and confession, I felt the fragile threads of our friendship weaving back together, stronger than before. The café buzzed around us, the world outside continuing its dance, but within our little corner, it felt like we were cocooned in a bubble of possibility.

As the sun dipped lower in the sky, casting a golden hue over everything, I reached across the table, placing my hand on hers.

"Let's promise to keep the lines of communication open this time. I don't want to lose you again."

Amelia's gaze softened, and she squeezed my hand, her smile wide and sincere. "Agreed. Life is too short for misunderstandings and silence. We'll figure it out together."

In that moment, as the sun poured warmth into our little corner of the world, I felt hope blossom within me, vibrant and full of life. The fear of the past slowly faded, replaced by the exhilarating thrill of new beginnings. We talked late into the evening, laughter ringing out like music, weaving a tapestry of memories that would carry us forward.

Eventually, as the café began to close, we reluctantly stepped out into the cool evening air, a comforting breeze brushing against our cheeks. The world felt alive with potential, a stark contrast to the uncertainty I had felt just days ago. I glanced at Amelia, and she caught my eye, a knowing smile spreading across her face. In that moment, we both understood: this was the start of something beautiful, a renewed connection built on trust, understanding, and the shared promise of friendship that would endure through whatever life tossed our way.

We walked down the street, side by side, laughter bubbling up between us, and for the first time in what felt like forever, I felt anchored—grounded in the knowledge that no matter where the journey led, we would face it together. And just like that, the past transformed from a weight I had carried into a tapestry of lessons learned, a reminder that healing often comes wrapped in the simple act of reaching out, opening your heart, and daring to embrace vulnerability.

Chapter 8: A Message Received

The sun dipped below the horizon, casting long shadows across the bustling streets of New Orleans, where jazz music spilled from the open doors of bars like an intoxicating elixir. As I navigated the cobblestone paths, the air felt heavy with humidity and the aroma of gumbo wafted through the night, mingling with the sweet scent of magnolias blooming under the dim streetlights. Each step took me deeper into the heart of a city alive with stories, echoing with laughter, and laced with whispers of longing. My heart thumped loudly in my chest, echoing the rhythm of the city, while my fingers tingled against the cool surface of my phone, its screen glowing like a beacon of hope.

Amelia's response had arrived like a thunderclap amidst a sultry afternoon, sparking a wild mix of emotions I hadn't felt in a long time. She was hesitant, yet there was an openness in her words, a crack in the door I'd thought was permanently shut. The anticipation of seeing her again churned in my stomach, both exhilarating and terrifying. Memories of our friendship flooded back, the laughter we shared, the secrets we confided, and the warmth of her presence that used to feel like home. But with each heartbeat came a reminder of the fracture, the sharp edges of unspoken words and unresolved hurt that had come between us like an insurmountable wall.

As evening descended, I found myself in front of Café du Monde, the iconic beignet shop where powdered sugar floated like confetti in the air, celebrating the simple joys of life. The bustling crowd ebbed and flowed around me, laughter mingling with the soft strains of a nearby street musician's guitar, creating a symphony of sound that felt both comforting and surreal. Jackson stood beside me, his relaxed demeanor a stark contrast to the turmoil swirling within me. He had become my unexpected anchor, a steadfast presence in the chaos of my thoughts.

"You'll be fine," he said, his voice smooth as the dark roast coffee steaming in my cup. "Just take it one moment at a time." His eyes, a shade of warm amber, held a sincerity that eased the weight pressing down on my chest. I appreciated his willingness to step into my world, especially considering how little we had known each other until recently. Yet, he seemed to see me more clearly than most, recognizing the storm beneath my calm exterior.

I took a deep breath, inhaling the rich aroma of chicory-laced coffee and the faint hint of spices wafting from the food stalls nearby. The vibrant life of the city buzzed around me, its energy a tangible force that pushed against my resolve. "You ever think about how this city feels like it's breathing?" I mused aloud, trying to distract myself from the apprehension swelling within.

"Every day," he replied, a small smile playing at the corners of his lips. "It has its own heartbeat, doesn't it? You can feel it in the music, the food, even in the air."

Our conversation flowed effortlessly, a distraction I desperately needed. I wanted to absorb this moment, to lock it away in a hidden corner of my memory, to hold on to the laughter we shared amid the clamor of tourists and locals. But soon, the lightness of our exchange gave way to a heaviness that settled over me, pulling my thoughts back to Amelia. I wondered what her expression would be when I finally faced her. Would she be angry? Hurt? Or perhaps, just perhaps, she would be relieved to see me again.

As the clock ticked closer to our meeting time, the streetlights flickered to life, casting a warm glow over the vibrant landscape, turning the ordinary into a magical tableau. I could already envision Amelia's face, the way her brow would furrow when she was deep in thought, the soft curl of her hair framing her delicate features. Would she remember the last time we met? The silence that had stretched between us like a chasm? The regret hanging in the air like the scent of the beignets we'd shared, both sweet and bittersweet?

Jackson nudged me lightly, pulling me from my spiraling thoughts. "Ready?" he asked, his voice a gentle nudge against my anxiety.

I nodded, trying to muster a smile. "I guess I have to be." Together, we stepped onto the narrow path that led to the café, the ambiance shifting from the carefree laughter to an expectant hush. The patio tables, adorned with flickering candles, illuminated the faces of those seated, their expressions a mixture of delight and indifference, unaware of the internal battle raging within me.

As I approached our meeting spot, I caught a glimpse of Amelia through the throng of patrons. She sat at a small table in the corner, her fingers nervously tracing the rim of her coffee cup, her eyes scanning the crowd. In that moment, the world faded away, the sounds of laughter and jazz melding into a distant murmur. All I could see was her, the girl who had once been my best friend, and now felt like a stranger wrapped in layers of unresolved tension.

Jackson's presence at my side became a tether to reality, his supportive energy guiding me forward. I could feel my heart pounding in my ears, a rapid drumroll marking the moments leading up to this reunion. What would I say? How could I express the myriad emotions swirling within me, the remorse for lost time, the longing for the friendship we once had?

With a deep breath that filled my lungs with the essence of the city, I crossed the threshold into her world once more, ready to face whatever came next.

Her gaze met mine, a mixture of surprise and something deeper flickering in her eyes—perhaps wariness, perhaps vulnerability. In that fleeting moment, I felt the weight of the last several months settle heavily between us, a palpable tension coiling tighter with each second. Amelia had once been the one person who could read my thoughts like an open book, and now, it felt like we were two characters fumbling through a new script, desperately trying to recall the lines we had forgotten.

"Hey," I said, forcing a casualness into my voice that felt like a thin veneer over the nervous tremor beneath. I took a seat across from her, the small wooden table feeling like a barricade in this conversation, a fragile barrier that separated my hope from her uncertainty.

"Hey," she replied, her voice barely above a whisper. The syllables hung in the air, heavy with unspoken questions. She looked different—her hair was tied up in a messy bun, with a few rebellious strands escaping to frame her face, but it was the subtle darkness beneath her eyes that caught my attention. I wondered if it was the weight of our history pressing down on her, too.

The ambiance of the café buzzed around us, a comforting blend of laughter and the clinking of cutlery. The waitress weaved through the crowd, balancing trays of beignets and steaming coffees, their aromas mingling with the warm, sugary scent that clung to the air. I wanted to reach out, to bridge the distance between us, but fear held me back, like a puppet with tangled strings.

"I got your message," she finally said, her voice tinged with caution.

I nodded, feeling a rush of gratitude for her willingness to meet. "I know things have been... weird. I've missed you, Amelia." The words slipped out before I could censor them, raw and earnest. The truth, laid bare between us, sparked a flicker of hope, and I could see the tiniest crack appear in her guarded demeanor.

"I've missed you too," she admitted, glancing down at her coffee cup as if searching for the right words hidden in the dark brew. "It's just... a lot has changed."

The admission hung between us like a charged wire, crackling with the potential to either ignite a flame or send us both spiraling back into darkness. I took a moment, letting the silence stretch, giving her space to find her footing in this precarious dance we were attempting. The last thing I wanted was to rush her or push her back into a corner.

"What happened to us?" I asked softly, my voice barely rising above the chatter of the café. "One moment we were inseparable, and the next..." I trailed off, my heart squeezing painfully at the thought of our shared laughter turned to shared silence.

Amelia's eyes flickered with emotions I couldn't decipher, a mix of regret and resolve playing across her features. "I think we both just got lost in our own lives," she said finally, her words tentative but sincere. "And I didn't know how to reach out when things got tough."

"I didn't either," I confessed, the weight of my own vulnerability pouring out in a rush. "I should have fought harder for us."

We sat in the fragile space of honesty, and I watched as the walls around her seemed to shift slightly, revealing glimpses of the girl I once knew—the one who could laugh freely and talk for hours about everything and nothing. There was a softness in her expression now, a flicker of warmth that suggested the embers of our friendship were still smoldering beneath the ash.

"Do you remember that time we got lost on Bourbon Street?" I asked, the memory a buoy in the turbulent sea of our conversation. "We ended up at that sketchy bar where the band played 'Sweet Home Alabama' on repeat for what felt like an eternity."

A ghost of a smile crossed her lips, the tension in the air lifting just a little. "How could I forget? I thought we'd never find our way back." Her laughter was a balm, soothing the edges of my anxious heart.

"Right? And I was convinced the saxophonist was going to kidnap us," I chuckled, buoyed by the shared recollection. "But instead, we ended up dancing like fools in the middle of the street."

Her eyes sparkled for a moment, the light of nostalgia casting away the shadows of uncertainty. "We made quite a scene."

"Yes, we did," I replied, the warmth of that shared memory drawing us closer, even as the weight of our unresolved issues still loomed over us. "I think that's what I've missed the most—just being able to be silly with you, to not worry about everything else."

"Me too," she said, the admission grounding us both. The hum of the café faded as we locked eyes, an unspoken agreement passing between us. This was our moment to reclaim what we had lost, to mend the fractures of our friendship.

A sudden thought struck me, and I leaned in, lowering my voice conspiratorially. "So, what if we made a pact?" I asked, the idea blooming in my mind like the flowers lining the streets. "Let's make it a point to get lost in this city together again. No matter how busy life gets, we'll find time for each other. What do you say?"

Her eyes widened slightly, surprise mingling with a spark of excitement. "You mean it? You'd really want to do that?"

"Absolutely. We can start small—coffee dates, maybe some live music. Whatever it takes to pull us back together."

A smile blossomed on her face, genuine and bright, illuminating the corners of her expression that had been shrouded in doubt. "I'd like that. I really would."

As we settled into our conversation, I felt the weight of the past start to lift, the barriers that had kept us apart slowly crumbling away. The café around us continued to pulse with life, but it was as if a cocoon had formed around us, sheltering our words and laughter, sealing our promise to rediscover the friendship that had once been a lifeline.

We talked for what felt like hours, the ease of our banter returning like an old friend. Each shared laugh, each wistful memory felt like a thread weaving us back together, reinforcing the bond that had frayed but not broken. In the heart of New Orleans, amid the aroma of beignets and the rhythm of life, we began to reclaim our story, one moment at a time, ready to write a new chapter together.

The conversation flowed effortlessly between us, a dance of words that rekindled the warmth of our shared history. With each laugh, I felt the intricate threads of our friendship reweaving, the past stretching behind us like the winding streets of the French Quarter, each corner holding a story, each alleyway a memory. I caught Amelia's gaze more frequently now, searching for the flicker of old familiarity that still resided in her deep-set eyes, like glimmers of sunlight breaking through a canopy of clouds.

"Remember the Halloween we dressed up as pirates?" I asked, my voice laced with nostalgia. The laughter bubbled up again, bright and effervescent. "You insisted on wearing that ridiculous hat that was twice your size, and we ended up getting lost trying to find that haunted house on Chartres Street."

"I was convinced it was a good idea at the time!" she chuckled, her laughter infectious, brightening her features as she leaned forward, resting her chin on her hands, her posture transforming from reserved to engaged. "And I still stand by my decision to commandeer that ship on the corner. It was a great treasure, despite the dubious quality of the candy."

We both laughed, the sound harmonizing with the lively tunes filtering through the café, the strains of a nearby jazz band adding a rhythm to our reunion. In that moment, the weight of our past disagreements lifted, replaced by the lightness of shared laughter and the joy of rekindled connection. As the night deepened, the café dimmed its lights, casting a soft golden glow that wrapped around us like a warm blanket.

"What if we made a plan?" I suggested, emboldened by the playful energy between us. "Let's explore the city like we used to—get lost in the nooks and crannies of New Orleans, seek out the hidden gems, and maybe even eat our way through the best beignets in town."

Her eyes sparkled with excitement. "That sounds perfect! We can start at the place with the lavender syrup in their lemonade—it was just as good as the beignets!" The enthusiasm in her voice was contagious, a tangible spark reigniting the old flame of our friendship.

The idea of adventure filled me with anticipation, and I felt a rush of warmth surge through me as we began plotting our culinary conquests. It felt as though we were both shaking off the rust of our past, eager to rediscover the joys we had shared. Each suggestion led us further into a cascade of ideas, planning spontaneous outings that would reconnect us to the very heart of our beloved city. The energy shifted; we were no longer just two friends trying to navigate the rubble of old misunderstandings but rather explorers venturing back into the realm of possibility.

The waitress returned with a tray of freshly made beignets dusted with powdered sugar, their golden-brown exteriors a promise of sweetness within. As the warm pastries landed on our table, the sugar dusting fluttered like snowflakes in the soft light, transforming the moment into something sacred and celebratory. I could hardly contain my excitement as I took my first bite, the warm dough melting on my tongue, sending waves of nostalgia crashing over me.

"Best beignets in town," I declared with a mouthful, savoring the delightful blend of fluffy texture and sweetness. Amelia mirrored my enthusiasm, her eyes sparkling as she indulged in the pastries, laughter bubbling between bites.

The warmth of the beignets and the sweetness of our memories merged into a delightful concoction, lulling me into a sense of contentment I had thought lost. But the evening was not just about the food; it was about mending the rift that had kept us apart. We spoke candidly about our struggles, the challenges we faced individually, and the heavy burdens we had carried without each other's support. Each confession was like peeling back a layer, revealing the raw, unpolished parts of ourselves that had been buried under pride and fear.

"I thought I was doing okay," Amelia admitted, her voice dipping slightly as she hesitated, "but without you, everything just felt... hollow." There was a vulnerability in her words that struck a chord deep within me. "I've missed having someone who understands me completely. I've been so focused on trying to keep my life together that I forgot how much I needed you."

The sincerity in her voice was like a balm, soothing the scars of our past. "I felt the same way," I replied, my heart swelling with the knowledge that we were no longer drifting apart but rather embarking on a journey to rediscover each other. "I thought if I kept busy enough, I could forget about the void left behind. But every time I did something fun, I'd just think about how much better it would be if you were there."

The bond we were rebuilding was fragile yet exhilarating, each shared memory stitching the fabric of our friendship back together. I watched as Amelia's expressions shifted—her brows knitted in concentration, the softening of her features as she engaged with my stories. It was in those moments that I realized just how much I had longed for this connection, this simple act of being present with someone who truly understood me.

As the night deepened, we made a pact, a promise that this was only the beginning. We would navigate the winding streets of New Orleans together, reforge our bond with laughter and adventures, and bask in the warmth of a friendship that had once felt as steady as the Mississippi River.

Jackson, who had remained quietly supportive, occasionally chimed in with his own stories, intertwining his experiences with ours. His presence felt less like a distraction and more like a reassuring reminder that life had a way of surprising us, bringing the right people together at the right time. The unassuming camaraderie between the three of us was a tapestry woven with laughter, shared experiences, and the threads of unspoken understanding.

As the café began to close, we lingered over our last bites of beignets, reluctant to let the magic of the evening dissipate. The lingering aroma of coffee and fried dough wrapped around us, a warm embrace that felt like home. With each shared glance, each smile that broke the silence, I could sense the shifts in our relationship, the rekindling of a friendship that had felt lost but was now eager to thrive once more.

Outside, the streets of New Orleans pulsed with life, the night vibrant and inviting. We stepped into the cool air, the gentle breeze a reminder that life was waiting, ready for us to embrace it together. The lights of the French Quarter twinkled like stars, beckoning us into the night.

"Ready for our next adventure?" I asked, a playful grin breaking across my face as I turned to Amelia and Jackson, both looking equally exhilarated.

"Always," Amelia replied, her eyes bright with excitement.

"Let's make sure it's a memorable one," Jackson added, his smile wide, reflecting the contagious energy of the moment.

And just like that, hand in hand, we ventured into the vibrant tapestry of New Orleans, the rhythm of our laughter mingling with the echoes of jazz in the air, weaving our stories into the very fabric of the city we loved. In that instant, it felt as though the world had opened up before us, a landscape of endless possibilities waiting to be explored. Together, we would navigate it all—each twist and turn, each sweet and savory bite, all of it steeped in the warmth of friendship, ready to embrace whatever lay ahead.

Chapter 9: The Reunion

The coffee shop, nestled between a vintage bookstore and a quirky thrift shop, was an oasis of warmth on that crisp autumn afternoon. Sunlight poured through the wide windows, casting playful shadows across the hardwood floors, dancing with the flickering light from the brass lamps hanging above. The intoxicating scent of freshly ground coffee beans mingled with the sweet notes of cinnamon and baked pastries, wrapping around me like a comforting embrace. I could hear the low hum of conversations and the occasional hiss of the espresso machine, all underscoring the symphony of this bustling refuge from the world outside.

As I stepped inside, the jingle of the bell above the door pulled Amelia's attention from the small table where she sat, tucked into a cozy corner. She was alone, her fingers nervously tracing the rim of her cup, a nervous habit I recognized from our younger days. Time had altered our appearances—my hair now bore the weight of subtle waves, and the faintest hint of laugh lines etched my cheeks. But there was something undeniably familiar in her posture, the way she tilted her head slightly as she glanced up, as if expecting a ghost from the past. Her once-vibrant locks were now muted by the gentle hues of maturity, but her eyes—those brilliant pools of emerald—still shimmered with a spark that set my heart racing.

"Amelia," I breathed, as I approached her table, my heart thundering in my chest. The mere sight of her sent a wave of nostalgia crashing over me, dragging me back to the sun-drenched afternoons we spent wandering the local parks, sharing secrets and dreams as easily as we breathed.

"Hey," she replied, her voice a mixture of surprise and something deeper—perhaps vulnerability. We exchanged tentative smiles, each of us searching for the remnants of the bond that once felt unbreakable. "It's been a while."

"Too long," I said, sliding into the chair across from her, my palms clammy on the tabletop. The space between us felt both inviting and intimidating, as if the air shimmered with unspoken words. The coffee shop bustled around us, yet it felt like we were encased in our own bubble, cocooned in the shared history that both warmed and weighed heavily on our hearts.

As our barista approached, a cheerful smile painted across her face, I ordered a caramel latte, the sweet richness reminiscent of our late-night study sessions, where we fuelled our caffeine-driven escapades with sugary snacks and laughter that echoed through the empty hallways of our shared apartment. I glanced at Amelia, her fingers still dancing on her cup, and wondered what she was thinking.

"Do you remember that time we tried to bake cookies?" she asked, a soft smile curling her lips.

"Please, don't remind me. We nearly set the kitchen on fire!" I chuckled, the sound tinged with a hint of regret. "I still can't believe we thought substituting baking soda for baking powder was a genius move."

"Oh, it was more than just genius," she replied, her laughter mingling with mine, lighting a flicker of warmth within me. "It was a disaster of epic proportions."

The memories cascaded, each recollection layering over the last, building a complex tapestry of our past. We reminisced about the reckless adventures of our youth—late-night drives with the windows down, music blaring, and secrets shared under the glow of the stars. Yet, as the laughter subsided, an uncomfortable silence settled between us, thick and charged.

I took a deep breath, gathering my thoughts, my heart pounding like a drum in my ears. "I've missed this—us," I confessed, my voice barely above a whisper. "But it feels like we've drifted so far apart. I don't want that anymore. I regret everything that came between us."

Amelia's gaze flickered to the window, where golden leaves swirled in the breeze, caught in a dance of change. "It wasn't just you," she murmured, her tone laden with unspoken truths. "I thought I was okay, but I was lost. I've been trying to figure out who I am without you, and it's been... harder than I imagined."

Her vulnerability struck a chord within me, the weight of her admission heavy yet liberating. "What happened?" I asked gently, leaning in, craving the details.

"It's complicated," she said, her fingers curling around her cup as if seeking warmth. "After we lost touch, everything spiraled. I thought distancing myself would make it easier, but I just ended up isolating myself. I didn't know how to reach out. I didn't know how to admit I needed you."

The floodgates opened, revealing a rawness I had long buried. It felt like a weight was being lifted, like sunlight breaking through a dense fog. We both had wounds that needed tending, scars left by misunderstandings and silence.

As the barista returned with our drinks, steaming cups filled with swirling foam art, I realized how simple yet profound this moment was. The warmth seeped into my hands, a reminder of the connection we shared—a bond resilient enough to endure the trials of time.

"Do you think we can mend this?" I asked, the vulnerability in my voice palpable. "I don't want to lose you again."

Amelia met my gaze, her eyes brimming with a mixture of hope and fear. "I want that, too. I really do. But it's going to take time. We have to be honest with each other."

I nodded, feeling the truth settle between us like a promise. As we delved deeper into our stories—our struggles, our dreams, our regrets—a sense of healing began to unfold, wrapping around us like the rich aroma of coffee enveloping the shop.

The air thickened with an almost electric energy, buzzing between us as we shared our confessions, each revelation another step into the uncharted territory of our evolving relationship. I couldn't help but marvel at how easily the laughter had returned, as if it had merely been lying dormant, waiting for the right moment to burst forth. The aroma of cinnamon swirled around us, an intoxicating blend that brought with it a nostalgia I thought I had lost.

Amelia wrapped her fingers around her cup, her brow furrowing in thought. "I used to think I was strong enough to handle everything alone. But I was just scared, afraid of being vulnerable." Her words hung in the air like a delicate thread, fragile yet binding. "When you left, I thought it would be easier to shut everyone out, to pretend like I didn't care. But it only made everything worse."

The honesty in her voice touched something deep within me. I knew all too well the perils of isolation—the way it could twist and distort reality until you questioned everything you once believed about yourself. I recalled nights spent staring at the ceiling, heart heavy with regrets, wishing I had reached out.

"I didn't want to come off as weak," I admitted, my voice barely a whisper. "I thought I could just move on without you, but it felt like trying to breathe under water." The imagery danced between us, a vivid testament to our shared experiences. "Every time I saw something that reminded me of us—our favorite songs, the places we used to haunt—it felt like a dagger. I kept thinking I should be over it by now, that I should've moved on."

A soft smile broke through her contemplative expression. "It's strange, isn't it? How the world keeps spinning while you're stuck in your own head? I think we both convinced ourselves that moving on meant pretending the past didn't exist. But it's still there, isn't it? Like an echo."

"Exactly," I replied, relief flooding through me as I realized she understood. "I felt like I was living in a ghost town, haunted by memories that refused to fade. I missed the laughter, the way we could finish each other's sentences, how we never ran out of things to say."

"Those late-night talks about everything and nothing?" Amelia's eyes sparkled with the hint of mischief that had drawn me to her in the first place. "The way we debated the most ridiculous things, like whether pineapple belongs on pizza? I can't believe we wasted so much time on that."

"Or the time we tried to make sushi and ended up with a kitchen disaster that looked like a scene from a horror movie?" We shared a laugh, the kind that wove its way through the heart and stitched up old wounds with threads of humor and shared understanding.

As the conversation flowed, we ventured deeper into our respective struggles, navigating the labyrinth of heartache that had kept us apart. I spoke of the late nights spent wondering if she ever thought of me, how the silence between us had morphed from comfortable to agonizing. She listened intently, her eyes never leaving mine, absorbing my words like a sponge.

"I've been working in a place that felt suffocating," she finally confessed, her gaze drifting momentarily to the window, where passersby hurried along, blissfully unaware of our pivotal moment. "I thought I was doing the right thing by climbing the corporate ladder, but I lost myself along the way. I was chasing something that wasn't really me."

"Isn't it funny how we sometimes think we're supposed to follow a certain path?" I mused, a wave of sympathy crashing over me as I recognized the shadows of my own life reflected in her story. "But the truth is, the path isn't always clear. We often stumble in the dark, trying to find our way back to what truly matters."

With a deep breath, she leaned forward, her voice lowering to a conspiratorial whisper. "I almost didn't come today. I thought about canceling a million times. What if it was awkward? What if I made a fool of myself?"

"But you came," I pointed out gently, feeling a swell of admiration for her courage. "That's what matters. We took this step together, and I think it's important. It's not about perfection; it's about showing up, being willing to face the messiness of life."

"I'm learning that," she said softly, her eyes glistening as she locked onto mine. "Learning to embrace the chaos instead of running from it. I want to find a way back to the person I was before everything changed, and I want you to be a part of that journey."

The sincerity in her voice struck a chord, vibrating through the very essence of my being. I felt my heart swell with hope—a fragile, tentative hope that maybe we could rebuild what had been lost, piece by piece. "I want that too. More than you know."

We spent the next hour navigating through our dreams and fears, unearthing hopes we hadn't dared to voice for far too long. I learned about her passion for photography, the way she found solace behind the lens, capturing fleeting moments of beauty that often went unnoticed. "There's something magical about freezing time," she said, her enthusiasm palpable. "It's like holding onto a memory, preserving it forever."

"And what about you?" she asked, a spark igniting in her eyes. "What are you dreaming about these days?"

"I've been thinking about starting a podcast," I revealed, surprised at my own boldness. "Something where I can share my thoughts, interview interesting people, and really connect with others. I've always wanted to create a space for conversation."

"That sounds amazing!" she exclaimed, her face lighting up with genuine excitement. "You've always had a way with words. I can see you making a difference out there."

In that moment, we forged an invisible thread of encouragement, a silent promise to support each other as we navigated the winding roads ahead. As the sun dipped lower in the sky, painting the room in hues of gold and amber, I felt the weight of the past begin to lift. Each shared dream, each flicker of vulnerability, was a brick removed from the wall that had kept us apart for far too long.

The barista cleared our empty cups, and as I looked around, the coffee shop felt like a sanctuary. It was as if the universe had conspired to bring us back together, wrapping us in the warmth of camaraderie, nostalgia, and the undeniable magic of a second chance. Together, we were beginning to weave a new narrative, one where forgiveness and healing held a prominent place, leading us toward the light of understanding and connection we both craved.

As the afternoon light waned, the coffee shop morphed into a haven of intimacy, the air thick with the aroma of rich espresso and sweet pastries that lingered like cherished memories. Amelia's laughter, rich and melodic, filled the space, and each note danced around me, wrapping me in a cocoon of nostalgia. We spoke of our dreams, our fears, and the paths we had wandered, as if navigating an intricate maze that twisted through the landscape of our lives.

"What about your photography?" I asked, leaning closer, genuinely intrigued. "Have you had the chance to pursue it since we last spoke?"

A flicker of passion ignited in her eyes, and I could almost see the images flashing in her mind, moments waiting to be captured. "I have! I've been working on a series that focuses on the fleeting beauty of everyday life," she replied, her voice swelling with enthusiasm. "I try to capture those tiny, often overlooked moments—like a child chasing butterflies in a park, or the way the light hits a fallen leaf just right."

As she spoke, I envisioned the images she described: golden sunlight filtering through leaves, illuminating the vibrant colors of autumn. I could see the joy in her eyes, the way she came alive at the thought of her craft. "I'd love to see them sometime," I said, my heart swelling with admiration. "You always had such a unique perspective on the world."

"Maybe I'll do a little exhibition," she mused, her expression a blend of hope and uncertainty. "I've been hesitant, afraid of putting my work out there. But I think it's time to stop hiding."

"Definitely! You deserve to showcase your talent. The world needs to see what you can create." My encouragement hung in the air, mingling with the rich, steamy aroma of coffee. The desire to support her felt as natural as breathing.

We continued to delve deeper into our respective journeys, sharing snippets of our lives that had unfolded in the years apart. The more we spoke, the more I felt as if we were peeling away layers of skin, revealing the raw, tender parts beneath. Each word was a gentle caress, healing old wounds and binding us closer together.

"I took a trip to the Grand Canyon last summer," I shared, recalling the endless horizon, the way the sun kissed the rock formations with shades of orange and pink. "It was breathtaking. Standing at the edge, I realized how small we are in the grand scheme of things, how our problems often feel monumental but are, in reality, just fleeting moments in time."

Her eyes widened, captivated by the imagery. "That sounds incredible! Did you take pictures?"

"Of course! I have a whole album dedicated to the trip." I pulled out my phone, scrolling through images of breathtaking vistas and vibrant sunsets. The beauty of the canyon echoed the transformation we were both striving for—a reminder that even the most rugged landscapes can hold profound beauty.

Amelia leaned in, her finger lightly brushing against the screen as she admired the photos. "Wow, you have an amazing eye. It looks like a postcard."

"Thanks! It was one of those moments where I felt like I was discovering a new part of myself. It made me realize that there's so much beauty waiting to be explored if we just step outside of our comfort zones."

Her gaze softened, a knowing smile creeping across her lips. "Maybe we can explore together again? I miss our adventures."

The warmth spreading through me was indescribable, igniting a spark of hope that maybe we could reclaim what we had lost. "I'd love that. Just think about the places we could go—road trips, hiking, all the coffee shops we could visit."

With each word, the distance that had kept us apart began to evaporate, replaced by the golden threads of a renewed connection. There was something sacred about this moment, a realization that we were not merely old friends but kindred spirits striving to rediscover each other in a world that had constantly shifted around us.

As we sat there, time seemed to stretch, the world outside fading into a blur of movement and sound. I could hear the distant laughter of a couple at a nearby table, the clinking of cups, and the soft melodies playing in the background. It felt surreal, almost dreamlike, as if we were suspended in this warm bubble of familiarity and promise.

"Do you remember the time we got lost on that hike?" I asked, the memory bubbling to the surface, pulling me back to that sun-soaked day filled with laughter and a hint of recklessness.

Her eyes sparkled with mischief. "Oh, how could I forget? We ended up wandering for hours, and all we had was a half-empty water bottle and a granola bar. I thought we were going to die out there!"

"I think I still have the granola bar wrapper stuffed somewhere in my bag as a reminder," I chuckled, unable to suppress the grin spreading across my face. "It was the best adventure, though. We ended up finding that hidden waterfall, remember?"

"Of course! That was the best reward after all that wandering. It was so refreshing, and we felt like we'd stumbled onto some magical secret."

As we reminisced, laughter flowed easily between us, the tension that had previously lingered dissipating like fog in the morning sun. I realized that we had weathered storms and faced challenges, but here we were, willing to embrace the uncertainty and take a leap of faith.

With a newfound determination, I reached for her hand, instinctively intertwining our fingers—a gesture that felt both natural and grounding. "Let's make a pact," I proposed, my voice steady. "No more hiding from each other. Let's keep this connection alive, no matter what life throws at us."

She squeezed my hand, her eyes reflecting a mix of gratitude and exhilaration. "I want that too. Let's not let anything come between us again. We deserve to share our journeys, to lift each other up."

The world outside the coffee shop continued to bustle, but within our small bubble, time seemed to freeze. In that moment, we weren't just reclaiming a friendship; we were breathing life into a new chapter—one filled with authenticity, support, and an unwavering belief in each other's dreams.

As the sun dipped lower on the horizon, casting a warm golden glow through the windows, I felt a sense of peace wash over me. Whatever challenges lay ahead, I knew that with Amelia by my side, I was ready to embrace them. Together, we would navigate the winding roads of life, armed with the lessons of our past and a shared commitment to a future bursting with possibility.

Chapter 10: Stirring the Pot

The scent of rosemary and garlic drifted from the open kitchen, curling around me like a comforting embrace as I stepped into Heritage Hearth. The rustic bistro, with its warm wooden beams and glowing Edison bulbs, felt like an old friend. Familiar laughter resonated from the corner table, where a family of four shared a moment that echoed the essence of togetherness. Each plate that passed by carried not just food, but stories waiting to be savored, and I knew tonight would be no exception.

I had invited Amelia here not only to share a meal but to reconnect—two sisters separated by time, distance, and misunderstanding. As I waited for her to arrive, I nestled into a plush corner booth, allowing the faint jazz music to wash over me. The sounds of clinking glasses and sizzling pans formed a symphony of warmth. My fingers danced over the table's surface, tracing the intricate carvings that whispered tales of laughter and love from families who had gathered here before us.

The door swung open, and a rush of cold air heralded Amelia's entrance. She paused, framed by the threshold, her breath forming soft clouds in the crisp evening air. The moment our eyes met, a current sparked between us, grounding and electric, like the first lightning bolt of summer. She looked different—older, yes, but also more vibrant, with an aura of determination that illuminated her features. Her dark hair fell in soft waves, framing her face with a carefree elegance that hinted at the woman she had become while we were apart.

"Sorry I'm late," she said, slipping into the booth opposite mine. Her smile, a mixture of excitement and nervousness, tugged at my heart. "The traffic was a nightmare."

I waved her off. "You're here now, and that's what matters." I leaned forward, my excitement bubbling over. "You have to try the chef's special tonight. It's a savory tart, filled with caramelized onions and goat cheese. I can't get enough of it!"

Amelia laughed softly, a sound that felt like music to my ears. "You always did have a knack for persuading me to try new things."

As we perused the menu, I couldn't help but notice the subtle way her fingers brushed against the paper, a delicate touch that mirrored the careful way we were both approaching this moment. With every word exchanged, it felt as if we were unwrapping a gift, slowly revealing layers of our lives that had been hidden away. I watched as she read through the options, her brow furrowing in concentration, a familiar expression from our childhood days spent poring over cookbooks and planning elaborate meals that we would never make.

"I'll take your recommendation," she finally said, her eyes sparkling with a mixture of nostalgia and hope. "And maybe a glass of red wine? I think I deserve it after that drive."

"Absolutely," I replied, signaling to our waiter, a cheerful soul whose name I'd never caught but whose presence felt like sunshine in a storm. As he scuttled away, I leaned in closer to Amelia, eager to hear more about her journey—the path that had led her back to me.

"What have you been up to?" I asked, genuinely curious. "I can't believe it's been three years since we last saw each other."

She sighed, a wistful smile lingering on her lips. "Oh, you know, life. It has its way of throwing curveballs. I moved to Seattle for a job that turned out to be less than what I expected. Then, I took a leap and started my own catering business. It's been challenging, but also... liberating."

My heart swelled with pride. The Amelia I remembered was a fighter, always seeking adventure even when the world felt daunting. "That sounds amazing! I always knew you had a talent for cooking. I still remember that disastrous Thanksgiving when you tried to roast the turkey by yourself."

She chuckled, her laughter ringing like a sweet bell. "How could I forget? The fire department still teases me about that year."

Our food arrived, artfully arranged and bursting with color. The first bite of the tart transported me to a sunlit meadow, each flavor exploding like confetti in my mouth. I watched as Amelia savored her meal, her eyes closing momentarily in bliss. It was a small moment, yet it felt monumental—like the foundation of something beautiful being rebuilt between us.

With each course, our conversation flowed more freely. We peeled back the layers of misunderstanding that had coated our relationship, uncovering raw truths wrapped in moments of vulnerability. She spoke of her struggles, her dreams of owning a quaint bistro someday, where families could gather to create memories just like we were doing now.

"What about you?" she asked, her gaze penetrating but warm. "How's life treating you?"

I hesitated, the weight of my own choices hanging in the air. "It's been... different. I left my old job, and now I'm working as a food writer, exploring culinary cultures across America. It's a journey I never expected to take, but I'm embracing it."

Her smile broadened, and I could see the flicker of pride in her eyes. "That sounds incredible! I always knew you'd find your way in the world of food. It's in your bones."

As the night unfolded, the world outside faded into obscurity, the only sound that mattered being our shared laughter and the clinking of silverware against porcelain. The restaurant felt like a sanctuary, a place where time lost its grip, and for the first time in years, I felt the chains of regret and sorrow begin to loosen.

Each shared memory wove us closer, stitching together the fabric of our lives once torn by distance and silence. I could see the glimmer of hope reflected in her eyes, an echo of the sisterly bond we had once cherished. This was more than just a meal; it was a reclamation of our relationship, a promise to forge ahead into the unknown together, no longer afraid to stir the pot and explore the flavors of life side by side.

The evening unfolded like a well-written recipe, each element balancing flavor and texture, just as our conversation balanced vulnerability and joy. As the last course of our meal arrived—a decadent chocolate torte topped with a dollop of house-made whipped cream—an unexpected sweetness filled the air. I watched as Amelia took her first bite, her eyes widening in delight, the corners of her mouth lifting into a smile that radiated warmth.

"Wow, this is incredible," she exclaimed, savoring the richness as if it were a long-lost friend. "You always did have an eye for the extraordinary, even in the simplest things."

"Just like you, sis," I replied, unable to resist the urge to reach across the table and squeeze her hand. "Remember when we used to sneak cookies from the oven and eat them while they were still gooey? That was extraordinary too."

The memory hung between us, a shared moment of childhood innocence. It felt effortless to slip back into those days when our lives were uncomplicated, our biggest worries revolving around the cookie jar. But tonight, as we indulged in rich flavors and heartfelt memories, I could see the echoes of the past resonating in our laughter.

"Life has a funny way of steering us back to where we belong," Amelia mused, gazing thoughtfully at the flickering candlelight that danced between us. "Sometimes I wonder how we let so much time slip by without reconnecting."

"It's like we were too caught up in our own lives," I replied, my voice tinged with regret. "But here we are, and I don't want to let anything come between us again."

The warmth in her eyes brightened, and I could see the flicker of hope igniting a fire that had long been dormant. We shared stories of our journeys—her tales of frantic catering gigs and moments of culinary triumph, my adventures in the world of food writing, discovering hidden gems across the country. Each story was a brushstroke on the canvas of our renewed bond, coloring our lives with shared experiences.

The restaurant buzzed around us, the sounds of clattering dishes and bubbling conversations creating a lively backdrop. I watched as the waitstaff flitted from table to table, their laughter mingling with the aroma of freshly baked bread that wafted from the kitchen. It was a comforting chaos that made the bistro feel alive, just like the connection I felt with my sister.

As the evening waned, the once-vibrant dining room softened into a cozy embrace, shadows stretching lazily across the walls. The candlelight flickered, casting delicate patterns that danced on the tablecloth, reminding me of how fragile our lives can be. I couldn't shake the feeling that this moment was pivotal—one that would anchor us amidst the unpredictable tides of life.

Amelia leaned in, her expression turning serious. "I've missed you, you know. It's like I lost a part of myself when we drifted apart."

The sincerity in her words pierced through the casual air, and I felt a lump rise in my throat. "I missed you too. More than I can say. It was hard not having you around to share those little moments—like the taste of a perfect meal or the comfort of a late-night chat."

"I've often thought about how we used to experiment in the kitchen," she said, her voice tinged with nostalgia. "Trying to replicate recipes we found online, our faces smeared with flour and our hearts full of laughter."

"Exactly! We were such a mess, but it was so much fun. Maybe we should start cooking together again, you know, rekindle that part of our relationship?"

Her eyes lit up at the suggestion, and I could see the spark of excitement igniting the air between us. "That sounds like a plan. I'd love to create something together, even if it ends in chaos. It's what we do best."

The idea of reclaiming our shared passion for food felt like a lifeline, a thread weaving through the fabric of our relationship. It was an invitation to embark on a new culinary adventure, one that would allow us to explore not just recipes but the depths of our connection.

As the final remnants of our dessert vanished, I felt a sense of warmth wash over me, a comforting blanket that soothed the frayed edges of my heart. The waiter returned with the bill, a knowing smile on his face, as if he could sense the magic in the air. I glanced at Amelia, our eyes locking in silent agreement.

"Let's split it," she said, reaching for her wallet.

"Absolutely not. This is my treat. I want to celebrate us," I insisted, not allowing her to argue.

She laughed, the sound bright and infectious. "You always were stubborn."

We left the bistro, stepping into the cool night air, where the city glimmered under a canopy of stars. The streets were alive with the sounds of laughter and music spilling from nearby bars, an intoxicating blend of energy and possibility. I could feel the pulse of life around me, reminding me of the vibrant world we had yet to explore together.

As we walked side by side, the distance that had once stretched between us shrank with every step. The city lights illuminated Amelia's features, casting a warm glow that mirrored the joy blooming within me. We wandered down familiar streets, reminiscing about our childhood adventures—riding bikes through the park, chasing fireflies on warm summer nights, and sharing secrets that felt monumental at the time.

"What if we started our own cooking blog?" I suggested, half-joking, yet secretly hoping to spark a new idea. "You could showcase your catering, and I could write about the experiences. It could be our thing!"

Amelia's eyes widened, excitement bubbling in her voice. "That's actually a brilliant idea! We could share our culinary experiments, the good and the bad. It would be like a digital diary of our journey together."

I could see the wheels turning in her mind, each thought spinning into a web of possibilities that shimmered in the air around us. The prospect of creating something together was intoxicating, a testament to our renewed bond and shared passions.

The night wore on, the conversations flowing freely as we meandered through the vibrant streets, the air thick with laughter and unspoken promises. I knew that whatever challenges lay ahead, we had already begun to stir the pot of our relationship, blending the ingredients of our past with the flavors of our future.

As we stood at the corner of our childhood street, I glanced up at the sky, where the moon hung like a sentinel, casting a silvery light upon us. I felt an overwhelming sense of gratitude for this moment, for the warmth of Amelia's presence beside me, and for the promise of new beginnings that awaited us. We were two sisters, bound by love and laughter, ready to create a feast of memories that would last a lifetime.

The warmth of the evening lingered as we strolled down the bustling streets, the vibrant energy of the city wrapping around us like a cherished blanket. Neon lights flickered overhead, casting playful shadows that danced along the pavement. Every storefront and alley held memories—some joyful, others bittersweet—but tonight felt like a fresh canvas, ready to be painted with new experiences.

Amelia's laughter rang out, a melody that sliced through the ambient noise of the city, drawing smiles from passersby who couldn't help but share in our joy. "You know," she said, her eyes sparkling like the lights above, "I always admired your ability to find magic in the mundane. It's something I've tried to replicate in my catering, but I never quite got it right."

"Magic, huh? Maybe that's my secret ingredient," I teased, bumping her shoulder playfully. "But seriously, it's all about perspective. You've always had that creative spark. Remember the time we tried to recreate Mom's lasagna? It was a disaster, but we laughed until we cried."

Her eyes turned soft with nostalgia. "And you insisted on adding too much garlic, thinking it would impress her. We were such little chefs, armed with nothing but enthusiasm and a pantry full of chaos."

"Enthusiasm can go a long way in the kitchen," I mused, watching as a couple walked past, their arms entwined, sharing a slice of cheesecake like it was a hidden treasure. "That's what I love about cooking; it's a journey of trial and error, experimentation, and a sprinkle of audacity."

"Speaking of audacity," Amelia chimed in, a teasing glint in her eyes, "what do you say we challenge ourselves? Let's pick a recipe neither of us has tried and see who can make it better."

The idea sparkled in the air, igniting a rush of adrenaline in my veins. "You're on! But prepare yourself—I won't go easy on you."

As we plotted our culinary duel, we wandered into a cozy bookstore nestled between two lively cafés. The shop, small and intimate, was lined with wooden shelves overflowing with books of all genres. The warm scent of aged paper and polished wood wrapped around us, creating a sanctuary from the chaotic world outside.

"Look at this," I said, pointing to a cookbook prominently displayed near the entrance. "The title claims it can transform anyone into a gourmet chef. Perhaps we should give it a read before we choose our recipe."

Amelia grabbed the book and flipped through its pages, her eyes sparkling with mischief. "If only it came with a guarantee, right? 'Transform your skills in five easy steps!'" She laughed, and her joy was infectious.

The book was filled with vivid photographs of mouthwatering dishes, from delicate soufflés to elaborate charcuterie boards that looked like edible art. "What do you think?" I asked, leaning in to inspect a page featuring a richly colored paella. "A bit ambitious?"

"Why not? If we're going to do this, we might as well go big," she replied, her voice brimming with excitement. "Let's make it a theme night! We can even invite some friends over."

"Count me in," I said, feeling the thrill of the challenge course through me. "Paella night it is! But we'll have to make it truly special—maybe some sangria and tapas to accompany it."

As we exchanged ideas, our enthusiasm spiraled, building upon itself like a carefully crafted soufflé. We envisioned our friends gathered around the table, laughter ringing out like the clinking of glasses, the warmth of shared experiences filling the room. The mere thought wrapped around me, igniting a longing for connection that had been absent for far too long.

With the cookbook in hand, we strolled back into the cool night, our plans taking shape with each step. I felt a sense of giddiness, the anticipation of rekindling not just our bond but the joy that came from shared culinary adventures. We walked past the neighborhood park, where the moon cast a silver glow on the sprawling trees, their leaves whispering secrets to the gentle breeze.

"Let's make this a regular thing," Amelia suggested, her voice thoughtful as we paused to gaze at the stars twinkling overhead. "Cooking together, trying new recipes, and just... being sisters again. Life is too short to let it slip away."

"I couldn't agree more," I replied, my heart swelling with gratitude. "I want to be part of your journey, just like you're a part of mine. No more drifting apart. We're in this together."

Her smile lit up the night, a beacon of promise and hope. "Together," she echoed, and I could feel the weight of our past beginning to lift.

In the days that followed, our plans blossomed. We spent afternoons in the kitchen, aprons donned like badges of honor, each cooking session a new chapter in our sisterhood. Chopping vegetables became a dance, the rhythm of our laughter filling the air as we fumbled through the steps of paella-making, tossing in saffron like pixies casting spells over our pot.

Our friends joined us for the themed dinner, the table transformed into a mosaic of colors and flavors. The paella, a vibrant dish speckled with fresh seafood and vegetables, was a masterpiece born from our chaotic creativity.

As we gathered around the table, the atmosphere crackled with energy, our friends' faces glowing in the candlelight. Stories were shared, laughter flowed freely, and for a few beautiful hours, we created an oasis of connection in a world often filled with distractions.

Amelia and I took turns sharing the backstory of our dishes, our voices intertwining like the rich flavors we had prepared. "This dish is a homage to our family," I said, my heart swelling as I glanced at her. "It reminds us of those messy kitchen experiments from our childhood."

"And it's a promise," Amelia added, her eyes sparkling as she looked around the table, "that we're rebuilding something beautiful here, one meal at a time."

In that moment, surrounded by the warmth of friendship and the aroma of our culinary creation, I felt a sense of belonging I hadn't realized I'd been missing. Our laughter, mingled with the clinking of glasses and the symphony of voices, painted a vibrant picture of what could be—a testament to our commitment to rediscovering each other.

The night wore on, and as the last remnants of paella were devoured and the final sip of sangria consumed, I knew this was only the beginning. The bond we had reignited, forged in laughter and seasoned with love, promised to carry us through the storms of life.

With each recipe we tried, each dish we shared, and every moment we spent together, we stirred the pot of our relationship, creating a rich and flavorful tapestry woven from our past and present. And as I glanced at Amelia, her laughter echoing in the air, I realized we were no longer just sisters; we were partners in this beautiful, messy, and delicious journey called life.

Chapter 11: A Taste of Commitment

The aroma of simmering spices enveloped me like a warm embrace as I stepped into the bustling heart of the food festival. Sunlight spilled across the cobblestone streets of our little town, casting playful shadows that danced between stalls adorned with colorful canopies. I could hear the lively chatter of families, the sizzling sounds of pans heating up, and the laughter of children running from one stall to the next, clutching oversized cotton candy like treasured trophies. Jackson's enthusiasm was contagious, his eyes sparkling with anticipation, and it was hard not to feel swept away in the tide of excitement surrounding us.

Jackson stood beside me, radiating a calm confidence that anchored my swirling nerves. His passion for food was palpable, a warmth that wrapped around me like the golden glow of the setting sun. We had forged a bond over shared meals and long talks that often wandered from the mundane to the profound. His easy laughter filled the spaces between us, and as he introduced me to local chefs, each with a story to tell, I felt a sense of belonging blossom within me. This festival was more than a culinary showcase; it was a celebration of community, connection, and the heartfelt narratives we often served on a plate.

I strolled through the festival, my senses alive with vibrant colors and rich scents. Stalls overflowed with plump tomatoes, their skins shimmering under the sunlight, as if kissed by the sun's own fingertips. Hearty loaves of bread were piled high, their golden crusts crackling with promises of warmth and comfort. I could hardly contain my excitement as I approached a stand that boasted artisanal cheeses. Each wedge was a masterpiece, labeled with the name of the farm, a story distilled into every bite.

Jackson leaned closer, his voice low and teasing, "What do you think? Should we dare to sample the 'Triple Cream Dream' or the

'Smoky Mountain Blue'?" I met his playful gaze with a smile, reveling in the teasing challenge. "Let's go for the 'Triple Cream Dream.' It sounds like a risk worth taking," I replied, my heart racing with a mix of eagerness and trepidation. As I savored the cheese, its richness melted on my tongue, an explosion of flavors igniting my taste buds and prompting an involuntary moan of delight. Jackson watched me with a grin, the light of shared joy illuminating his features.

With each bite, I felt my confidence swell. This was more than just tasting food; it was an immersion into a world where flavors could narrate stories, evoking memories of sun-drenched summers spent at my grandmother's house, where the kitchen was always a whirlwind of laughter, spices, and love. The festival felt like a tribute to those moments, a celebration of the simple yet profound connections that food could foster.

The day unfurled like a vibrant tapestry, woven with the threads of our experiences. We visited a local farm-to-table stand, where fresh herbs perfumed the air, and Jackson demonstrated his knife skills, slicing through fragrant basil with an elegance that turned the mundane into an art form. "You see," he explained, "cooking is about honoring the ingredients. Each herb, each vegetable has its own personality." I watched, mesmerized, as he transformed the simple ingredients into a fragrant pesto. My fingers itched to learn, to create alongside him, to dive deeper into this world that had once felt foreign and intimidating.

As the sun began to dip, casting a warm orange glow across the festival, we found ourselves in a quiet corner, a serene oasis amidst the bustling chaos. It was here that Jackson turned to me, his expression softening, a hint of seriousness threading through the playful atmosphere. "You know, I've always believed that cooking is a form of commitment," he said, his gaze searching mine. "It's about more than just flavors; it's about investing in the moment, in the people you're sharing it with." His words resonated deeply within me, striking a chord I hadn't fully recognized until that moment.

I thought about my own journey, how I had often tiptoed around commitment, not just in relationships but also in my own aspirations. My food reviews had been safe, a way to hide behind my keyboard, rather than fully engaging with the culinary world around me. But with Jackson, I felt a shift, a flicker of determination igniting in my chest. Perhaps it was time to step beyond the safe confines of my comfort zone and truly immerse myself in the world I adored.

As twilight descended, the festival transformed. Strings of fairy lights twinkled above, casting a magical glow over the stalls. The sounds of laughter and music intertwined, creating a symphony of joy that wrapped around us. I took a deep breath, inhaling the mingled scents of grilled meats and caramelized onions, the air thick with possibility. Jackson's hand brushed against mine, a gentle reminder of his presence, grounding me as I contemplated the next step in my journey.

"I want to dive deeper," I confessed, my voice barely above a whisper, yet resolute. "I want to commit to this—exploring food, connecting with people, and sharing these experiences." A smile spread across Jackson's face, illuminating his features with pride and encouragement. "That's the spirit," he replied, his voice steady and warm. "Together, we can create something beautiful."

In that moment, beneath the canopy of stars and fairy lights, I felt a shift within me. It wasn't just about the food; it was about weaving my narrative into the vibrant tapestry of this culinary community. I was ready to embrace the messy, flavorful journey ahead—a journey steeped in commitment, exploration, and a taste for the extraordinary.

As the night unfolded, we wandered deeper into the festival, our laughter mingling with the fragrant steam rising from the food stalls. My senses were alive, heightened by the vibrant atmosphere and the prospect of newfound adventures. Jackson led the way, his enthusiasm infectious as he introduced me to the array of culinary wonders that beckoned from each corner. The sound of a steel drum band floated through the air, lending a lively rhythm that seemed to pulse in time with my own heartbeat. I could feel the energy of the crowd enveloping us, the spirit of camaraderie palpable in the excited exchanges between strangers sharing a passion for food.

"Let's try that!" Jackson exclaimed, pointing toward a stall where a chef was flamboyantly tossing vegetables in a sizzling wok. The colors of the produce burst vibrantly against the blackened steel, and the smell of garlic and ginger danced tantalizingly in the air. As we approached, I felt a flutter of anticipation in my stomach, a little reminder of the childlike wonder that still lingered within me.

"Have you ever had Thai basil?" the chef asked, his hands a blur of motion as he worked. He flashed a bright smile, the kind that made you feel welcome immediately. "It's like regular basil but with a hint of anise—perfect for stir-fries!" I nodded eagerly, eager to experience something new, the vibrant greens and reds swirling in the pan like a kaleidoscope of flavors.

After sampling the dish, I was taken aback by the burst of flavors—a perfect marriage of sweet, spicy, and aromatic notes that lingered on my palate long after the last bite. I turned to Jackson, who was watching me with a knowing smile, as if he had anticipated my reaction. "Told you it was worth it," he said, his voice filled with a mixture of pride and amusement. There was something undeniably enchanting about sharing these moments with him, where each bite became a bridge between our worlds.

We continued our exploration, weaving through the throngs of festival-goers who danced around us like leaves caught in a gentle breeze. Each step drew me further away from the reservations I had clung to, the walls I had built around my heart slowly crumbling under the weight of the laughter and warmth that surrounded us.

Jackson's presence was a guiding light, illuminating the path ahead. He was not just a friend; he was a catalyst, urging me to take the plunge into the rich tapestry of life that had long felt out of reach.

Soon we arrived at a booth where a baker was proudly displaying her pastries, their golden crusts glistening under the fairy lights strung overhead. The sight of them pulled at something deep within me—an old memory of baking with my mother in our sunlit kitchen, flour dusting the countertops like fresh snow. I could almost hear her laughter echoing as we rolled out dough, creating shapes of hearts and stars.

"Let's get one of those," I suggested, pointing to a flaky croissant, its buttery layers whispering promises of decadence. Jackson chuckled, raising an eyebrow as if to say he knew what I was thinking. "You're on a pastry adventure now?" he teased. I smiled, my heart swelling with a sense of belonging that I had craved for so long.

As I bit into the croissant, the flaky layers crumbled beautifully, and the rich, buttery flavor enveloped my senses. I closed my eyes for a moment, savoring the moment. It was more than just a pastry; it was a sweet reminder of home, of connection, and of love. "This is incredible," I breathed, looking up at Jackson, who was watching me with a glint of understanding in his eyes.

We meandered further, sharing stories and tasting more delights, each morsel igniting a spark of joy within me. Jackson spoke passionately about his dream of opening his own restaurant one day, and I found myself captivated by his vision. He described a place filled with laughter and warmth, where families could gather over shared meals and create their own stories. "I want to capture the essence of connection," he said, and I couldn't help but feel that this dream was not just about food, but about creating a haven for the kind of love and community I longed for.

As the festival began to wind down, the sky deepened into a twilight hue, painting everything in soft shades of purple and blue. The stalls were illuminated with twinkling lights, creating a magical ambiance that wrapped around us like a cozy blanket. Jackson turned to me, his expression turning serious amidst the joyous atmosphere. "You know, food is more than just nourishment," he said, his voice low and earnest. "It's about memories, connections, and the stories we share with those we love."

I felt a rush of warmth at his words, a deep understanding blossoming within me. My journey had always been about more than just reviews and critiques; it was about the stories behind the meals, the connections forged over shared plates. And here, in this moment, I felt a powerful resolve to embrace that truth, to commit myself not just to the flavors but to the experiences and relationships that came with them.

Jackson reached for my hand, the warmth of his touch sending a pleasant shiver through me. "Let's make a promise," he suggested, his gaze steady and sincere. "Let's explore this world together—commit to tasting, learning, and growing. We can create something beautiful." My heart soared at the prospect, the thought of diving deeper into this culinary adventure alongside him.

With a nod, I took a breath, feeling the weight of that promise settle around us like a shared secret. "I'm in," I replied, the words spilling out with unexpected conviction. It was a commitment not just to food, but to living fully, exploring the rich tapestry of life, love, and flavors that awaited us.

The night wore on, laughter and music swirling around us, but in that moment, time stood still. With Jackson by my side, I felt as though I could finally step into the vibrant, flavorful life I had always dreamed of, where every taste was a new chapter, every shared meal a step toward connection. We would dive into the unknown together, and for the first time, I felt ready to embrace it all.

The festival's energy lingered in the air like the scent of fresh herbs, vibrant and intoxicating. Jackson and I wandered through the last few stalls, our laughter mingling with the sounds of sizzling pans and clinking glasses. I was surprised at how effortless it felt to be with him, like slipping into a well-worn pair of shoes that fit just right. As we strolled past a stand selling handcrafted pasta, a wave of nostalgia washed over me. It reminded me of my childhood, sitting cross-legged on the kitchen floor while my grandmother kneaded dough, her hands dusted with flour, every crease on her face telling stories of love, loss, and life lessons learned at the countertop.

"Let's grab some of that," I suggested, pointing to a colorful display of ravioli bursting with ricotta and spinach, its surface a kaleidoscope of flavors waiting to be discovered. Jackson nodded, and we approached the vendor, an older woman with kind eyes and a warm smile. "Ah, you have a good eye! This batch is made fresh today," she said, her voice rich with a comforting accent. The ravioli glistened under the soft light, their edges pinched neatly as if to keep their secrets safe inside.

As the vendor prepared our order, I found myself drawn into conversation with her, sharing snippets of my own memories around pasta-making with my grandmother. She listened intently, her eyes sparkling with recognition. "Food carries our stories, dear. It binds us, keeps us close to our roots," she said, her voice wrapping around me like a hug. I glanced at Jackson, whose expression reflected the same warmth I felt. In that moment, the connection between us deepened further, weaving us into the tapestry of the festival, the shared stories and laughter creating invisible threads that pulled us closer together.

Once we had our prize, we found a cozy nook by a tree draped in fairy lights, its branches swaying gently in the evening breeze. The world around us glowed with the amber light of dusk, the sky painted in shades of orange and purple, and I felt as if I were in a dream—a beautiful, delicious dream where everything seemed possible. Jackson opened the container, revealing the delicate pasta nestled among sprigs of fresh basil and a light drizzle of olive oil.

"Ready?" he asked, his eyes twinkling with mischief. "Let's do this properly." With that, he plucked a piece of ravioli, raised it like an offering, and brought it to my lips. The taste was a revelation—delicate yet bursting with flavor, the creamy ricotta mingling perfectly with the freshness of the spinach. I closed my eyes, savoring the moment, and when I opened them, Jackson was watching me, his expression one of sheer delight.

"See?" he said, a playful challenge in his voice. "You're starting to live the experience, not just taste it. That's what it's all about." I smiled back, feeling a rush of warmth flood my cheeks. With every bite, I was shedding layers of hesitation, embracing this newfound sense of adventure. The flavors danced across my tongue, but it was the company—the connection with Jackson—that made the experience truly unforgettable.

As the festival wound down, the air filled with the scent of caramelized sugar and roasted nuts. I noticed a stand selling handmade gelato, and my curiosity piqued. "We can't leave without dessert," I insisted, my excitement bubbling over. Jackson laughed, a sound that sent a flutter of joy through me, and we made our way to the booth, where an array of vibrant flavors beckoned.

The gelato was a work of art, each color more alluring than the last. I chose a rich pistachio, while Jackson opted for a bold dark chocolate. As we savored our gelato, the cool sweetness contrasting with the warmth of the night, I felt an overwhelming sense of gratitude. I had come to this festival as a tentative food critic, but I was leaving as something much more—a participant in a vibrant community, bound by the love of food and the connections it fostered.

"Let's take a walk," Jackson suggested, gesturing towards a nearby park. The path was lined with trees, their leaves rustling softly, creating a symphony of whispers as the wind danced through. We strolled side by side, the world feeling almost suspended in time, each step further reinforcing the bond we had formed.

"Tell me about your favorite food memory," Jackson prompted, his tone light yet sincere. I paused, allowing my thoughts to drift back to my grandmother's kitchen—the warmth, the chaos of preparing family meals, the laughter that spilled over like the bubbling pots on the stove. "I think of Sundays," I began, my voice steady. "We would gather around the table, everyone pitching in. My grandmother would tell stories while we cooked, sharing wisdom between stirring sauces and rolling dough. Those meals felt sacred, a time when everyone came together, leaving the world outside."

Jackson listened intently, his expression softening as I spoke. "That's beautiful," he said, a hint of admiration in his voice. "You're carrying on her legacy by sharing those stories."

I smiled, a warmth blooming within me. "It's more than just food; it's about connection, about sharing who we are through what we cook."

As we continued walking, I could feel the weight of my past loosening its grip on me. With each shared memory, I was inviting Jackson into the intimate spaces of my life, allowing him to see the threads that had woven together to form the person I was becoming. The vulnerability felt liberating, like shedding an old skin, and I reveled in the sense of freedom that accompanied it.

Our stroll brought us to a small pond, the water shimmering under the glow of the moonlight. I caught Jackson looking at me, his gaze steady and contemplative. "I think we all have stories to tell, but it's brave to share them," he said quietly. "You're not just tasting food; you're tasting life. And I want to be there for every flavor."

His words hung in the air, enveloping me in a cocoon of warmth and understanding. I could feel the flutter of something beautiful beginning to unfurl within me—hope, connection, a commitment to embrace this journey alongside him. I realized that my exploration of the culinary world was intertwined with the exploration of my own heart.

With a gentle breeze ruffling my hair, I turned to face him fully, feeling the gravity of the moment. "I want that too," I confessed, my voice steady. "I want to dive into this world and let it shape me, to create experiences and memories. I want to build something meaningful, and I want you by my side."

In that moment, beneath the stars and surrounded by the echoes of laughter, the promise of what lay ahead felt palpable. We stood there, two souls intertwined in a culinary adventure, ready to embrace the flavors, the connections, and the memories that awaited us. Together, we would discover the richness of life, one bite at a time.

Chapter 12: Spices of Doubt

The day unfolded like a vibrant tapestry, each thread woven with the promise of possibility. As I navigated the bustling streets of Portland, the festival blossomed around me—a riot of colors and aromas that beckoned like a siren's call. The sun painted the sky in shades of azure, and the gentle breeze carried the scents of grilled vegetables mingling with the sweet, sticky allure of caramel. My heart danced with the rhythm of laughter and chatter, a symphony of joy in which I longed to partake.

Vendors called out cheerfully, each one eager to share their culinary creations, their faces alive with enthusiasm. A cheerful woman with a riot of red curls enthusiastically promoted her spicy chili oil, her voice bubbling over with excitement. Nearby, a man with an impressive beard was tossing pizza dough in the air, its thinness stretching impossibly under the afternoon sun. I could almost hear it whispering promises of crispy crusts and cheesy goodness. It was a world brimming with flavor, one that danced at the edge of my senses, teasing me with the joy of discovery.

Yet, beneath this culinary carnival, my own doubts simmered. The festival was my moment to share my words, a platform to convey my love for food and the stories it held. I had poured my soul into my writing, crafting pieces that explored the delicate relationship between sustenance and memory. But now, standing in the midst of seasoned chefs and culinary artists, a whisper of uncertainty curled around my heart. Would anyone care about the tales I told? Would my passion translate through the pages, or would it be lost in the din?

Jackson was my anchor in this whirlwind, his steady presence like a lighthouse guiding me through the fog. With his hand resting gently on the small of my back, I felt a flicker of warmth amidst my swirling doubts. He had always had a way of calming the storm inside me, as if he could siphon away the anxiety that so often clung to my thoughts. I turned to him, seeking solace in his familiar smile, and he nodded reassuringly, his confidence in me sparking a flicker of hope.

"Let's taste everything," he suggested, his eyes glinting with mischief as he led me towards a booth filled with vibrant jars of pickled vegetables. The owner, a wiry man with a passion for fermentation, explained his process with such fervor that I could almost taste the tang of the brine on my tongue. We sampled pickled carrots that crunched beneath our teeth, their sweetness exploding against the sharpness of vinegar—a perfect metaphor for life's contrasts, I mused.

As we wandered from booth to booth, indulging in everything from artisanal cheeses to buttery pastries, the doubt that had wrapped around my heart began to unravel. The festival was not just a backdrop for my writing; it was a celebration of flavors, of stories that bloomed with every bite. Each vendor was a storyteller, their dishes filled with narratives that transcended time and space. I felt my pulse quicken, the words I had been mulling over beginning to take shape once more.

The sun dipped lower in the sky, casting a golden hue across the bustling market, and I found myself drawn to a booth draped in fragrant herbs. The aroma of fresh basil and mint wafted towards me, teasing my senses with their vibrant green vitality. A woman stood behind the table, her hands expertly crafting small bouquets of herbs. She caught my eye and smiled, an invitation that felt personal.

"Want to create a little something special?" she asked, her voice smooth like the olive oil that glistened in the jars lining her table.

I stepped closer, intrigued. "What do you have in mind?"

"Let's make a herb-infused olive oil. It's simple, but the flavor can elevate any dish," she replied, her enthusiasm infectious. I watched as she demonstrated, the way her fingers danced over the fresh ingredients with an ease that made it seem magical.

As we mixed fragrant rosemary with peppery arugula, I couldn't help but draw parallels to my own craft. Each ingredient was like a sentence, essential for the overall flavor, contributing to a narrative that resonated with the palate. I scribbled notes in my mind, visualizing the pieces I wanted to weave together, the stories I yearned to tell. The fear that had lingered in the shadows started to retreat, replaced by an exhilarating surge of creativity.

With each taste and every story shared, I felt the weight of my insecurities begin to lighten. Jackson's laughter rang out as he tasted a surprisingly spicy chocolate from a booth that promised indulgence. I turned to find him grinning, a smudge of melted chocolate on his cheek, and in that moment, my heart swelled. This festival was a feast not just for the senses, but for the soul—a reminder that food was a universal language, capable of bridging divides and forging connections.

As the sun set behind the horizon, painting the sky in a wash of pink and orange, I felt a newfound clarity settle within me. My fears were still present, lurking like shadows, but they no longer held dominion over my thoughts. I was here, amidst this vibrant tapestry of flavors and stories, ready to share my own.

The festival buzzed with energy, but within that chaos, I found a sense of calm—a belief that my words could resonate, that my passion for food could be a beacon for others. Jackson caught my gaze, and in his eyes, I saw a reflection of my own determination. Together, we ventured deeper into the festival, ready to embrace whatever awaited us, hearts open to the flavors of life and the stories yet to be told.

As we continued our meandering journey through the festival, the kaleidoscope of colors and sounds only grew more intoxicating. Each vendor stood as a storyteller, presenting their creations with pride and fervor. A couple of booths over, a young chef was plating miniature tacos with the precision of an artist, each one a masterpiece drizzled with vibrant sauces that glistened under the sun. The mere sight of those tiny bites sparked an idea in me, nudging at the corners of my mind like a playful child begging for attention. What stories lay nestled within those layers of flavor?

Jackson nudged me gently, pulling me back into the present moment. "You should try one," he said, his voice low and teasing, as if he could sense the creative spark igniting within me. "You know, for research purposes." He grinned, and my heart swelled. It was moments like these that reminded me how easy it was to be myself around him.

I leaned over the counter, peering at the fresh ingredients, each vibrant color a testament to the chef's dedication. "One please!" I called out, and the chef responded with a smile, expertly handing me a tiny taco cradled in a handmade corn shell. It felt warm in my hands, the aroma wafting up to greet me like an old friend. I took a tentative bite, and the explosion of flavors danced on my tongue—a medley of smoky chipotle, crisp cabbage, and a hint of citrus that brightened the whole experience.

"Tell me that wasn't magical," Jackson said, watching me with amusement as I savored every morsel. I nodded enthusiastically, a wide grin stretching across my face. "See? You're already collecting flavors for your writing."

With each taste, my doubts began to fade, replaced by a burgeoning sense of inspiration. The stories intertwined in each dish began to crystallize, weaving together a narrative that was vibrant and full of life. I envisioned words flowing like the silky sauces that adorned the plates, dancing across pages, revealing the hidden histories behind each culinary creation.

As we wandered deeper into the festival, we stumbled upon a booth decorated with vibrant banners that announced a cooking demonstration. A charismatic chef with a flair for performance was whipping up a seemingly simple tomato sauce. Yet, as I listened to her speak, it was clear that there was nothing simple about it. She spoke of the tomatoes, grown under the warm sun, bursting with sweetness, and how the right blend of spices could elevate a dish from mundane to extraordinary.

Her passion resonated with me, echoing the very essence of what I wanted to convey in my writing. The way she moved—graceful yet energetic—reminded me that food was more than just sustenance; it was a bridge between cultures, a narrative that told stories of struggle and celebration. Jackson squeezed my hand as the chef invited audience members to join her, and before I knew it, we were caught up in the infectious enthusiasm of the crowd.

"Come on, let's make some sauce!" he urged, his eyes sparkling with mischief. With little hesitation, we hopped into the throng, eagerly grabbing fresh basil and garlic cloves from a nearby table. I felt a thrill run through me, like a current of electricity as we chopped and stirred, my insecurities melting away like butter in a hot pan.

The chef guided us through each step, her laughter bubbling over like the pot simmering on the stove. We added crushed red pepper and a drizzle of olive oil, and as the aroma enveloped us, I felt an overwhelming sense of camaraderie with everyone around me. It was as if we were all participants in a grand story, weaving together our own flavors into one harmonious dish.

As the sauce bubbled, I could see Jackson across the table, his focus unwavering as he diced onions with an impressive precision. The sunlight caught the flecks of green in his eyes, and I felt a swell of affection. He was more than a partner in this culinary escapade; he was a confidant, a person who helped me embrace the messiness of creation—both in food and in life.

When the sauce was finally ready, the chef invited us to taste our creation. I leaned forward, the anticipation hanging in the air like the scent of fresh basil. I dipped a piece of crusty bread into the simmering pot, and as the sauce touched my tongue, a warmth spread through me—a realization that I was part of something bigger, a community that celebrated flavors and stories.

The evening deepened, and the festival began to transform. Strings of fairy lights twinkled above us, illuminating faces filled with delight and satisfaction. The crowd swelled, voices rising in a joyous hum that blended seamlessly with the tantalizing scents wafting through the air. Jackson and I wandered toward a stage where a local band strummed gentle melodies, their sound blending effortlessly with the laughter and chatter of festival-goers.

With each passing moment, my earlier doubts began to evaporate like morning fog under the sun. The food, the people, the stories—it was all interconnected, like the threads of a beautifully woven tapestry. My mind began to race with ideas, the words I had once feared now pouring forth with vigor. I imagined the essays, the recipes, the narratives I could share with the world, my heart brimming with excitement.

As we settled onto a grassy patch to enjoy the live music, I leaned against Jackson, feeling his warmth radiate against me. The rhythmic strumming of the guitar mingled with the soft murmurs of the crowd, creating an atmosphere that felt safe and inviting. With a sigh of contentment, I pulled out my notebook, its pages crisp and blank, ready to be filled with thoughts that were now swirling with clarity.

Jackson watched me, a knowing smile on his face as if he could sense the transformation occurring within me. "You're going to do great things, you know," he murmured, his voice barely above a whisper, yet it resonated within me like a gentle promise.

With newfound determination, I opened the notebook and began to write, the words flowing effortlessly. The festival became my muse, each moment a new inspiration—a celebration of life, love, and the undeniable power of food to connect us all. In that vibrant atmosphere, under the glow of fairy lights and surrounded by laughter, I found not only my voice but also a deep-seated belief that my stories were worthy of being told, flavors ready to be savored.

As the evening unfolded, the festival transformed into a vibrant tapestry of shimmering lights and lively conversations. It was a sensory feast, each booth a microcosm of creativity and passion. The stage glowed with the golden hues of the setting sun, illuminating the performers whose melodies wrapped around us like a warm embrace. I felt a sense of camaraderie with the people surrounding me, their laughter intermingling with the notes of the band as if we were all part of a grand symphony celebrating life.

Jackson leaned in closer, his warmth a steady anchor amidst the whirl of sensations. "What are you writing about?" he asked, his voice low, a conspiratorial whisper that made me grin. I had fallen into a rhythm, the words tumbling onto the page like fresh ingredients spilling from an overflowing basket.

"About how food creates memories," I replied, my enthusiasm bubbling over. "Every bite tells a story, doesn't it? Like that taco we had earlier—each layer of flavor is a connection to someone, somewhere." I glanced around, taking in the diverse crowd, the eclectic mix of cultures and cuisines. "It's all these little pieces coming together to create something beautiful."

Jackson nodded, his eyes sparkling with curiosity. "So you're capturing the festival's spirit, then?" he mused, and I could see he understood my vision. The festival was more than just a collection of booths; it was a living narrative, each vendor a character contributing to a shared tale.

We moved through the throng, stopping to sample a dazzling array of dishes—a rich, smoky brisket drizzled with a tangy barbecue sauce, a delicate panna cotta topped with tart berries that danced on the tongue like an enchanting memory. I watched Jackson's reactions closely, his face lighting up with each new flavor. The joy on his face made me feel like a maestro conducting a symphony, orchestrating moments that were both fleeting and precious.

At one booth, a grandmotherly figure served up steaming bowls of pho, her hands deftly ladling broth over noodles with the precision of an artist at work. The aroma enveloped us like a comforting hug, and we stepped closer, entranced. "This is my grandmother's recipe," she shared, her voice soft but filled with pride. "Passed down through generations. It warms the heart as much as it warms the belly."

I felt a spark ignite within me as she spoke, a profound realization that the stories embedded in food were often steeped in love, history, and tradition. I jotted down her words, the weight of her experience resonating deeply with my own journey of self-discovery. As I listened, the fabric of my narrative began to weave together, threads of nostalgia and flavor blending into a rich tapestry of emotion.

With every passing hour, the festival evolved. More people arrived, and the atmosphere thickened with excitement. I spotted a couple dancing under the twinkling lights, their movements carefree and joyous. The energy around us surged, an electric pulse that vibrated through the crowd. Jackson pulled me into the rhythm, and for a moment, we swayed together, swept up in the moment.

"Let's get some ice cream," he said, his eyes alight with mischief. "They have a lavender flavor that's supposed to be divine."

We made our way to the ice cream stand, the cool, creamy concoctions glistening in the light like treasures waiting to be discovered. I watched as the vendor scooped the lavender ice cream into a cone, its pale purple hue reminiscent of twilight skies. I took a tentative lick, the floral notes bursting forth, transporting me to fields of blooming lavender swaying in the summer breeze.

"Doesn't it remind you of summer picnics?" I mused, the taste triggering memories of sun-drenched afternoons spent with friends, laughter echoing through the air as we shared stories and secrets.

"Definitely," Jackson agreed, his gaze thoughtful as he savored his own scoop. "Food has a way of anchoring us in those moments, doesn't it? Like a time capsule."

I couldn't help but smile at his insight. It was as if he could read the thoughts swirling in my mind, unraveling the threads of doubt that still lingered there. Together, we ventured back to the heart of the festival, surrounded by the buzz of voices and the allure of tantalizing flavors.

As night fell, the festival took on an enchanting quality. Lights strung from trees twinkled like stars, and the music shifted to softer, more intimate melodies. I spotted a gathering near the fountain, people sharing their own stories, laughter punctuating the air. Inspired, I suggested we join them, eager to dive deeper into the community spirit that enveloped the festival.

In the circle, a woman shared a story about her grandmother's secret apple pie recipe, her voice imbued with nostalgia. The way she described the scent of cinnamon and nutmeg evoked images of warm kitchens and family gatherings, and I found myself enraptured. As each person took their turn, the atmosphere thickened with connection, an unspoken bond forged through shared experiences and flavors.

The moon hung high above us, a silver sentinel casting its glow on the gathering below. With each story shared, I could feel my own narrative taking shape, words colliding with experiences to create a tapestry of flavors that transcended mere taste. I could envision my writing weaving through these moments, illuminating the bonds that food had crafted among people, how it turned strangers into friends, and memories into legacies.

As the night wore on, I felt my heart swell with gratitude. The festival had become a crucible for my creativity, a space where my doubts melted away like ice cream on a hot summer's day. Jackson's laughter, the warmth of shared stories, the richness of each flavor—all of it coalesced into a tapestry of inspiration that ignited my passion for writing.

"Thank you for being here," I whispered to Jackson, the words tumbling out like the last drop of lavender ice cream. "I don't think I could've done this without you."

He turned, a knowing smile illuminating his face. "You had it in you all along," he replied, his voice soft yet steady. "You just needed to embrace it."

As I nestled into his side, the world around us pulsing with life and joy, I realized that my fears had been merely spices of doubt, easily dispelled by the warmth of connection and creativity. Together, we had created our own story—a narrative rich with flavors, laughter, and the kind of magic that only food festivals can conjure. And as the night deepened, I knew this was just the beginning of my journey, one filled with the promise of untold stories waiting to be savored.

Chapter 13: Unfolding Layers

The festival buzzed with life, a kaleidoscope of sights and sounds weaving together in a vibrant tapestry that wrapped around me like a familiar embrace. Stalls adorned with colorful banners swayed gently in the warm breeze, each one vying for attention, their rich aromas creating an intoxicating perfume that wafted through the air. I moved through the throngs of people, the laughter of children mixing with the rhythmic beats of a nearby band, a symphony of joy that reverberated through the autumn sun.

My eyes darted from one booth to another, each vendor showcasing their passion like precious jewels under the shimmering sunlight. The local artisans flaunted their crafts: handwoven baskets, intricate pottery, and paintings that captured the very essence of our town's spirit. Yet, it was the culinary booth that drew me in, its allure irresistible. A sign hanging above the stall proclaimed "Mia's Culinary Adventure," and below it, an explosion of color greeted me as platters overflowed with dishes that seemed almost too beautiful to eat.

Mia was a whirlwind of energy, her hands a blur as she plated delicate portions of vibrant vegetables and succulent meats, each dish a small masterpiece. I could see the fire in her eyes, a spark of passion that ignited as she worked. She maneuvered through her little corner of the festival with the grace of a dancer, her laughter ringing out like music, infectious and genuine. The way she spoke about her creations made my heart race; her descriptions were laced with dreams and aspirations, each dish carrying a piece of her soul.

As I approached, the fragrant aroma of rosemary and thyme enveloped me, a warm invitation that felt like home. I could almost taste the carefully balanced flavors, an orchestra of freshness that hinted at culinary greatness. "Welcome!" she exclaimed, her eyes glimmering with enthusiasm as she spotted me. "You look like someone who appreciates good food. Can I interest you in a tasting?"

Encouraged by Jackson, who stood beside me with an eager grin, I nodded, unable to suppress the excitement bubbling within. As Mia presented her dishes, I felt as if I were peeling back the layers of her artistry, each bite revealing the stories woven into her food. The first dish was a roasted beet salad, the vibrant colors of the beets bleeding into the creamy goat cheese, garnished with candied walnuts and drizzled with a balsamic reduction that danced on my palate. Each forkful was a testament to her skill, the flavors harmonizing in a way that felt almost like a revelation.

Mia beamed at my reaction, her pride palpable. "It's all about the ingredients," she said, her hands gesturing animatedly. "I source everything locally—each farmer shares a piece of their story, and I try to honor that with my food." Her voice was laced with a conviction that resonated deeply within me, her passion igniting a spark of inspiration I hadn't realized I was missing.

The festival faded around us as I sank deeper into this moment, wrapped in the warmth of her hospitality. She shared tales of her journey, from culinary school to the challenges of opening her own restaurant. I could feel the weight of her determination, the sacrifices made along the way, and it struck a chord within me. In that instant, I recognized the parallel between our paths; both of us navigating uncharted territories, fueled by our dreams yet often overshadowed by self-doubt.

As we continued to taste her creations—a silky butternut squash soup with a hint of spice, and an exquisite herb-crusted salmon—the sense of camaraderie deepened. Jackson, ever the supportive friend, chimed in with playful banter, drawing laughter from Mia as she playfully swatted at him. Their easy rapport brought a smile to my face, the kind of connection that felt like a warm blanket on a chilly evening. The laughter was infectious, breaking down barriers, and for the first time in a long while, I felt buoyed by the sense of belonging that seemed to radiate from Mia's booth.

In the midst of our culinary adventure, she leaned closer, her voice dropping to a conspiratorial whisper. "I'd love to invite you both to an exclusive tasting dinner at my restaurant. It's an opportunity to experience my food in a way that transcends the festival atmosphere. What do you think?" Her eyes sparkled with hope, and I felt a rush of excitement. The prospect of diving deeper into her world was tantalizing, a chance to peel back even more layers of her culinary story.

Jackson nudged me playfully, and I could tell he was already on board. "You should totally do it! I mean, how often do you get to experience a chef's vision firsthand? Plus, it's a food critic's dream, right?" His enthusiasm was infectious, and I found myself nodding, already envisioning the culinary treasures that awaited me at her restaurant.

As I agreed, a thrill coursed through me, a sensation that mirrored the excitement of a first date or the promise of an adventure yet to unfold. Our paths intertwined at that moment, a knot forming between our dreams and ambitions, each of us reaching for something greater. Mia's journey was a reflection of my own, a testament to resilience and the pursuit of passion, a narrative I longed to capture in my writing.

The sun dipped lower in the sky, casting golden hues over the festival as we exchanged contact information, sealing our pact with promises of future culinary explorations. As I stepped away from her booth, the world felt different—brighter, more vibrant. My heart was full, a bubbling cauldron of inspiration, and for the first time in what felt like ages, I felt alive, ready to embrace the unfolding layers of my own journey alongside Mia's.

The dinner at Mia's restaurant was a night I had eagerly anticipated, my heart fluttering with the promise of flavors yet to be uncovered. As we approached the establishment, the exterior glowed softly under the canopy of stars, warm light spilling from the windows and illuminating the brick façade like a scene from a vintage postcard. A small, hand-painted sign read "Mia's Kitchen," an intimate invitation that resonated with a sense of home and comfort. The buzz of the festival faded into the background, replaced by the tantalizing aroma wafting through the air, rich and inviting, like a siren's song drawing me closer.

Inside, the atmosphere was electric yet cozy, the walls adorned with rustic wood and vibrant artwork showcasing Mia's journey—a visual feast that echoed the culinary delights we were about to experience. Each table was meticulously set, the flickering candlelight casting playful shadows that danced on the walls, enhancing the ambiance of culinary intimacy. I felt like I had stepped into a secret world, one where food was not just sustenance but an art form capable of telling stories and forging connections.

Mia greeted us with open arms, her excitement bubbling over as she led us to a charming table near the kitchen. "I'm so glad you could make it!" she exclaimed, her eyes twinkling with a mixture of joy and nerves. "Tonight is special, and I want you to feel every moment." Her enthusiasm was contagious, and as we settled in, I couldn't help but feel enveloped by the warmth of her spirit.

The evening began with a playful amuse-bouche—a tiny, delicate tart filled with whipped feta and drizzled with a honey balsamic reduction that danced on my taste buds. Each bite was a burst of flavor, a tiny explosion that sent ripples of delight through my senses. Mia flitted around the dining room, her presence as vibrant as her dishes, checking in on guests and soaking in their reactions. I watched her with admiration, captivated by the way she poured herself into her craft, every movement a testament to her passion.

Between courses, Jackson and I shared stories, laughter bubbling up like the champagne that sparkled in our flutes. It was a celebration of camaraderie, and I felt the invisible threads of friendship strengthening as the night unfolded. Mia returned to our table, beaming with pride as she presented the next course: a perfectly seared duck breast atop a bed of creamy polenta, accompanied by roasted seasonal vegetables that glistened under a glossy glaze.

"This dish is inspired by my grandmother's recipes," she explained, her voice filled with nostalgia. "She taught me that cooking is an expression of love, and I wanted to create something that honors her." As I took my first bite, I was transported to a sunlit kitchen where laughter and the clatter of pots and pans filled the air. The duck was tender and succulent, the polenta rich and comforting, each flavor dancing together like an intricate ballet. I savored every morsel, feeling the warmth of Mia's heritage weave its way into my heart.

With each course, Mia revealed more of herself, her stories blending seamlessly with the flavors on our plates. A dish of handmade pasta—its silky texture glistening with a fresh herb-infused sauce—was accompanied by tales of her time in Italy, where she had studied under a renowned chef. I could see the pride in her eyes as she spoke, the memories cascading forth like a beautiful stream, each moment shaping her culinary philosophy.

Jackson chimed in with playful banter, teasing Mia about her ability to charm everyone with her cooking, but I could see he was just as entranced as I was. The atmosphere hummed with laughter and heartfelt conversations, the dining room a sanctuary of joy that felt entirely too fleeting. The connection we forged with Mia through food and laughter deepened my appreciation for her artistry, and I could see that she wasn't just feeding our bodies but also our souls.

As the evening wore on, the final course arrived: a decadent chocolate torte, rich and velvety, paired with a scoop of homemade lavender ice cream. The flavors melded in my mouth, an exquisite balance of sweetness and floral notes that lingered long after the last bite. I leaned back in my chair, my heart full, and caught Mia's gaze as she watched our reactions with bated breath.

"Did I mention I'm a food critic?" I said with a teasing smile, my voice playful yet sincere. "Consider this my official review." Mia's laughter rang out, bright and infectious, a melody that encapsulated the spirit of the night. "I think you just might have to come back for another round!" she replied, her face aglow with satisfaction.

We lingered at the table long after the plates were cleared, the warmth of friendship enveloping us like a comforting blanket. Mia shared her dreams of expanding her culinary horizons, exploring new flavors, and eventually opening a larger restaurant where she could share her vision with even more people. Each word was infused with hope and determination, a reflection of the journey that lay ahead for her.

As I listened, I felt a kinship with her dreams, a shared understanding of the struggles and triumphs that come with pursuing a passion. The night deepened, and the sounds of the bustling restaurant faded into a soft hum, the world outside forgotten for just a while longer. We spoke about our journeys, the challenges we faced, and the triumphs that fueled our resolve. In that moment, I recognized that our paths were not only intertwined but also intertwined with those we hoped to inspire.

Eventually, as the last flickering candle cast its glow, we stood to leave, the warmth of the evening lingering in our hearts. Mia enveloped us in a heartfelt embrace, her gratitude palpable. "Thank you for believing in me and for experiencing my journey," she said, her voice a soft melody against the backdrop of a busy kitchen. As we stepped out into the cool night air, I felt a sense of fulfillment wash over me, as if the evening had given me a glimpse of what could be—a beautiful tapestry of flavors, dreams, and connections that transcended the ordinary.

Under the starry sky, I exchanged glances with Jackson, both of us caught up in the magic of the night. It was more than just a dinner; it was the beginning of a friendship built on shared dreams and culinary passions. The promise of more adventures lingered in the air, a sweet anticipation that felt like the first note of a song yet to be composed, a harmony waiting to unfold.

In the days following our enchanting dinner at Mia's restaurant, my heart danced with the memories of culinary delights and laughter. The city, usually so chaotic and indifferent, now felt infused with new life, as if it were holding its breath, waiting for something magical to unfold. As the evening sun dipped below the skyline, painting the world in hues of gold and amber, I found myself wandering the streets with an air of anticipation. The festival lingered in my mind like a fragrant spice, a reminder of the unexpected connections forged amid vibrant chaos.

I decided to visit Mia's restaurant again, eager to delve deeper into her world. Upon arriving, I was greeted by the enticing aroma of fresh herbs and roasted garlic, welcoming me as though I were an old friend. The restaurant buzzed with activity, diners chatting animatedly over their meals, while the clattering of plates formed a rhythmic backdrop, echoing the pulse of life within its walls. Mia spotted me immediately, her face lighting up like a beacon amidst the lively atmosphere.

"Welcome back!" she exclaimed, a sparkle in her eye that made me feel instantly at home. She quickly led me to a table near the window, where the soft glow of candlelight danced across the polished wood, casting warm shadows that seemed to whisper secrets. "Tonight, I'm going to share something special with you," she said, her voice bubbling with enthusiasm. "I'm testing a new menu, and I'd love your feedback."

As the first dish arrived, a vibrant heirloom tomato tart, I was entranced by its beauty. The tomatoes glistened like jewels atop a flaky crust, drizzled with basil oil that glimmered like liquid emerald. Each bite burst with freshness, a taste of summer captured in a single moment, evoking memories of sun-soaked afternoons spent at farmers' markets. Mia's artistry shone through each element, the layers of flavor unfolding like a story told through food.

"This is incredible!" I said, savoring the last morsel, the flavors lingering on my tongue. "You have a gift, Mia."

"Thank you! I just want to create something that brings joy to people," she replied, her expression earnest. As we spoke, her passion for culinary artistry illuminated her face, her words a vivid tapestry of dreams interwoven with memories of her grandmother's kitchen, where love was the secret ingredient in every dish.

With each course, our conversation flowed effortlessly, a river of ideas and aspirations. She revealed her desire to host community cooking classes, a vision that ignited a fire within me. "I want to inspire others, to show them that cooking can be both an art and a source of healing," she said, her eyes alight with possibility.

Listening to her dreams felt like watching a flower bloom, each petal revealing a new facet of her character. I could see the challenges she faced, the doubts that occasionally flickered across her face, yet there was an undeniable strength in her vulnerability. I found myself rooting for her, not only as a chef but as a woman carving her path in a world that often seemed daunting.

Mia's restaurant was not merely a place for culinary experimentation; it had become a sanctuary, a space where dreams mingled with the aroma of freshly baked bread and simmering sauces. I shared my own struggles and triumphs as a food critic, my journey through a world often defined by harsh reviews and fleeting moments of recognition. She listened intently, her understanding deepening with each word I spoke.

That evening, as the sun dipped below the horizon, casting long shadows across the restaurant, I felt a connection that transcended our shared love of food. Mia's laughter rang through the air like music, a melody that harmonized with the clinks of glasses and soft murmurs of conversation. We became coconspirators, our dreams intertwining like vines climbing toward the sun, each encouraging the other to reach new heights.

In the weeks that followed, our friendship blossomed. I returned to Mia's restaurant regularly, each visit unveiling another layer of her culinary genius. She began to introduce me to the stories behind her dishes—the local farmers she sourced ingredients from, the artisan cheese makers she collaborated with, and the small-batch producers who poured their hearts into their crafts. Each story enriched my understanding of her artistry, painting a fuller picture of a chef deeply rooted in her community.

One rainy evening, I found myself at the bar, watching Mia prepare a new dish while droplets tapped rhythmically against the window. The ambiance was intimate, the restaurant lit by flickering candles that seemed to cast a warm glow against the soft rain outside. Mia's focus was mesmerizing, her movements fluid and confident as she sautéed vegetables with a deftness that spoke volumes about her experience.

As I observed her, I couldn't help but feel a surge of inspiration. I asked her if she would be willing to collaborate on a project—one that would blend our passions for food and storytelling. "What if we created a series of articles highlighting the local food scene, featuring stories about the chefs and the artisans behind the food?" I proposed, my heart racing with excitement at the thought.

Her eyes widened in surprise, and then she broke into a brilliant smile. "I love that idea! We could really showcase the heart of this community." The idea of combining our talents ignited something deep within me, a spark of creativity that felt as if it had been waiting for this very moment to burst into flame.

We spent the next few weeks researching, interviewing local chefs, and discovering hidden culinary gems tucked away in corners of the city. Each story was a celebration of passion, resilience, and the extraordinary journey of those who dared to dream. The more we wrote, the more our friendship deepened, a symbiotic bond flourishing in the soil of shared experiences and mutual respect.

One sunny afternoon, we found ourselves at a bustling farmer's market, the air rich with the scent of fresh produce and the sound of laughter. As we wandered through the colorful stalls, a vendor offered us samples of his heirloom tomatoes, their vibrant colors making my mouth water. Mia, with a gleam in her eye, began to dream aloud about a tomato-based dish she envisioned. "Imagine a roasted tomato risotto, creamy and decadent, with a sprinkle of fresh basil and a hint of lemon!" Her enthusiasm was infectious, and I could see the culinary masterpiece taking shape in her mind.

As we continued our exploration, it became clear that this partnership was more than just a professional endeavor; it was a celebration of everything that brought us joy. Together, we were crafting a narrative that not only showcased Mia's culinary journey but also illuminated the heartbeat of our community. Each article was a tapestry woven with threads of friendship, resilience, and the love of food.

With each passing day, I realized that Mia was not just a talented chef; she was a catalyst for change in our culinary landscape. Her unwavering dedication to her craft inspired me to dig deeper into my own journey as a critic, to seek out the stories behind the dishes, and to champion the voices of those who often went unheard.

The fusion of our passions created a ripple effect that reached far beyond the walls of the restaurant. As our articles gained traction, Mia's reputation flourished, and I found a renewed sense of purpose in my own work. Together, we were transforming not just our lives but the lives of those around us, encouraging others to savor the beauty in food and the stories it held.

Our friendship, forged in the heat of the kitchen and tempered by shared dreams, became a beacon of hope and inspiration. In that bustling city, amid the chaos of life, we had found our rhythm—a dance of flavors, stories, and aspirations that promised to unfold in ways we had yet to imagine.

Chapter 14: The Ingredients of Change

The aroma wafted through the air, rich and intoxicating, as I stepped into Mia's restaurant. It was an enchanting evening, a tapestry of warmth and laughter woven with the soft glow of hanging Edison bulbs that seemed to dance in rhythm with the gentle hum of conversations swirling around me. The walls, adorned with local art and vibrant photographs of past culinary creations, whispered stories of those who had come before me, each picture a testament to the love and labor poured into this haven. I could feel it all—the buzz of anticipation and the flicker of hope that lingered, tantalizing my senses like the first taste of a well-aged wine.

Seated at a rustic table crafted from reclaimed wood, I ran my fingers over its surface, tracing the grooves and imperfections that told tales of past gatherings, laughter, and perhaps even tears. Mia flitted around the dining room like a seasoned conductor, her laughter infectious, her energy palpable. She greeted each patron as if they were family, weaving in and out of conversations, her passion for culinary artistry evident in the way she discussed her dishes. It was evident that this place was not just a restaurant; it was a sanctuary where flavors intertwined and souls connected.

Amelia and Jackson sat across from me, their eyes sparkling with curiosity and enthusiasm, a pair of comrades in this culinary adventure. Amelia, with her wild curls and infectious smile, had a knack for drawing people out, and tonight was no different. She leaned in, her voice a conspiratorial whisper, teasing the two of us about our shared obsession with food. I chuckled, the tension of the past weeks melting away with each laugh. Jackson, on the other hand, was the quiet observer, his demeanor calm and thoughtful. He caught my eye with a knowing grin, and in that moment, it felt as though we were cocooned in a world crafted just for us, shielded from the uncertainties that awaited beyond the restaurant's doors.

As the first course arrived—a delicate tartare of tuna, beautifully plated and glistening under the soft lighting—my senses ignited. I took a moment to savor the colors: the vibrant red of the fish against the creamy avocado, the pop of cilantro brightening the dish. Each bite was a symphony of flavors, a melody of sweet, salty, and umami notes harmonizing on my palate. I could feel the artistry behind it, each ingredient thoughtfully selected, each flavor meant to evoke a memory or ignite a feeling. It was a culinary love letter from Mia, each plate a reflection of her journey, her struggles, and her triumphs.

Mia soon joined us, sliding into the seat next to me, her apron still dusted with flour from the kitchen. "So, what do you think?" she asked, her eyes sparkling with anticipation, as if she were waiting for the verdict on her latest masterpiece. The energy in the air was palpable, charged with the excitement of new connections.

I shared my thoughts, words tumbling out in a rush, buoyed by the heady mix of delicious food and warm camaraderie. "It's incredible," I said, my enthusiasm bubbling over. "The balance is perfect. I've never tasted anything quite like it." My heart swelled as I spoke, the truth of my words a testament to the powerful impact of her culinary craft. It felt good to connect in this way, to share not just my opinion but to weave my narrative into hers, becoming a part of this intricate tapestry.

As the night unfolded, so too did the conversations. We shared stories—laughs over mishaps in the kitchen, heartfelt confessions about dreams unfulfilled, and hopes yet to be realized. Each story served as a thread, weaving us closer together, bridging gaps we didn't even know existed. It was exhilarating to let my guard down, to share the struggles that had burdened me for so long. In that moment, I realized I was not alone. Each person at the table had faced their own battles, and we were united in our pursuit of something greater than ourselves.

Mia recounted her journey of opening the restaurant, the countless hours spent perfecting her recipes, and the sacrifices she had made along the way. I hung on her every word, captivated not only by her talent but also by her determination and resilience. It was clear that this restaurant was a labor of love, a space where she could express herself and share her passion with others. I admired her courage, the way she transformed adversity into opportunity, and it ignited a spark within me.

Jackson chimed in, sharing his own story about his recent culinary venture, a food truck that had become a passion project. The joy in his voice as he spoke of the challenges and rewards made me realize that each of us was chasing our dreams in our own way. We were bound by a shared belief in the transformative power of food—a belief that nourished not just our bodies but our souls.

With each course that followed, the connections deepened. The next dish, a luscious risotto infused with saffron, melted on my tongue, the creaminess enveloping me like a warm embrace. Each spoonful was a reminder that food was more than sustenance; it was an experience, a catalyst for change. I felt the weight of my own inhibitions lifting, replaced by a sense of possibility as I ventured into uncharted territory.

As the evening wore on, I couldn't shake the feeling that this gathering was a turning point—a moment of clarity where I realized that I was not merely a spectator in my own life but an active participant. The laughter, the shared stories, and the vibrant flavors ignited something within me, a desire to create, to connect, and to embrace change. Here, in the heart of Mia's restaurant, I felt alive, grounded, and ready to embark on a new journey, buoyed by the bonds formed over shared plates and laughter.

The evening wore on, each passing moment transforming the restaurant into a sanctuary where time itself seemed to pause, allowing us to bask in the warmth of shared experiences. As the last morsels of the risotto disappeared from my plate, I found myself in a state of bliss, both satisfied and invigorated. The energy at the table was electric, a vibrant hum of voices weaving stories that danced like the shadows cast by the flickering candles.

Mia returned to us, a glimmer of mischief in her eyes as she unveiled the evening's surprise: a rich chocolate torte, decadent and adorned with fresh berries that glistened like jewels. It seemed to echo the spirit of the night—bold, luscious, and unapologetically indulgent. I felt a playful thrill rush through me as I watched her serve the dessert, each slice revealing a silky interior that promised a burst of flavor. As she plated it, I wondered if this was what life tasted like when you took risks—sweet and bitter, vibrant yet comforting.

"I hope you've saved room for this," she teased, a knowing smile playing on her lips. "Life is too short not to indulge a little, don't you think?"

Amelia's laughter rang out, warm and infectious, as she declared, "If I had known we'd be having dessert like this, I would have skipped the salad!" Her words hung in the air, a reminder of the moments we often sacrifice in pursuit of restraint, and yet, here we were, surrendering to the allure of culinary delights.

With the first forkful of the torte melting on my tongue, I felt a wave of contentment wash over me. The richness enveloped me like a comforting hug, while the tartness of the berries provided a perfect contrast, a playful dance of flavors. In that moment, surrounded by laughter and vibrant chatter, I recognized that this was what it meant to be truly present—to revel in the beauty of connection, to embrace the fleeting moments of joy that life so generously offered.

As we savored the last bites of our dessert, a lull fell over the table, replaced by the soft sounds of clinking glasses and the distant hum of a jazz band playing in the background. It was as if the universe conspired to create this harmonious atmosphere, wrapping us in its embrace, urging us to reflect on the night's experiences. I glanced around, absorbing the sights and sounds, the joy radiating from our little corner of the world.

"What's next for you?" Jackson asked, breaking the silence with a thoughtful gaze. His voice was gentle, yet there was an underlying sincerity that pulled me in. "Have you thought about what you want to do after this?"

I hesitated, feeling the weight of his question sink in. The truth was, I had been so focused on surviving the chaos of my life that I hadn't allowed myself the luxury of dreaming. The thought of what came next felt both exhilarating and terrifying, a canvas waiting for the brushstrokes of my ambition and uncertainty. "Honestly," I began, my voice barely above a whisper, "I'm still trying to figure that out. But tonight... tonight has shown me that there's something beautiful about embracing the unknown."

Mia leaned in closer, her expression serious yet encouraging. "Sometimes it takes a leap of faith to discover your true path," she said, her words imbued with the wisdom of someone who had fought through her own storms. "Life is like a recipe; you might need to tweak it until you find the right balance. Don't be afraid to experiment."

Her words settled over me like a comforting blanket, inviting me to shed the fears that had tethered me for so long. There was something liberating about the idea of experimentation—of allowing myself the freedom to try new things, to embrace the unexpected flavors life had to offer. I felt an unfamiliar warmth rise within me, a flicker of hope igniting against the backdrop of my uncertainty.

With newfound resolve, I shared my aspirations with them, weaving a narrative of my dreams into the fabric of our evening. I spoke of wanting to write again, to capture the essence of what I had learned through my experiences—both the bitter and the sweet. As I described my desire to create a project that intertwined my passion for food with the stories of those who shared their lives around the table, I could see their excitement mirror my own.

"That sounds incredible!" Amelia exclaimed, her eyes shining with enthusiasm. "You should do it! Your words have the power to bring people together, just like Mia's cooking."

Jackson nodded in agreement, his gaze steady and encouraging. "And who knows? Maybe you'll inspire someone else to take their leap of faith too."

Their belief in me washed over me like a gentle tide, eroding the self-doubt that had clung to me for far too long. In that moment, I realized how profoundly our connections can shape our destinies. I had walked into this restaurant feeling lost, a solitary soul adrift in a sea of uncertainty, but now I felt anchored, buoyed by the love and encouragement surrounding me.

As we rose from the table, our laughter echoing through the restaurant, I took a moment to appreciate the ambiance—the lively chatter, the clinking of glasses, the aroma of spices lingering in the air. It was a tapestry of life, woven together by the choices we made, the moments we shared, and the connections we nurtured. With each step toward the exit, I felt lighter, as if I were shedding the weight of my past, leaving behind the remnants of doubt and fear.

Mia caught my eye one last time, her smile radiant and knowing. "Remember, every dish tells a story," she said softly. "Yours is just beginning."

As I stepped outside, the cool night air wrapped around me like a promise, the stars twinkling overhead like tiny diamonds scattered across a vast velvet canvas. I took a deep breath, inhaling the crispness of the evening, the scent of possibility lingering in the air. There was a beauty in the unknown, a thrill in the journey ahead, and as I walked away from Mia's restaurant, I felt ready to embrace it all. Life was a banquet, and I was determined to savor every bite.

The evening air enveloped me as I stepped outside, the remnants of laughter and warmth still clinging to my skin like the sweet perfume of an evening well spent. The city hummed softly around me, a chorus of distant car horns, the rustling of leaves, and the chatter of pedestrians weaving through the night. With every step away from Mia's restaurant, I felt my heart beating in time with the rhythm of the vibrant life surrounding me. It was as if I had shed a heavy coat of self-doubt, revealing the bright colors of hope and ambition beneath.

I wandered down the cobblestone streets, illuminated by the soft glow of streetlamps casting long shadows, their light painting the night in hues of golden warmth. Each corner I turned revealed a different slice of city life—couples entwined in conversation, artists sketching the world around them, and laughter spilling from nearby bars like bubbles from a shaken bottle of champagne. The city was alive, an untamed beast that thrived on creativity and connection, and in that moment, I felt an overwhelming desire to be a part of it.

My feet led me toward the local park, where a grand oak tree stood sentinel at its center, its gnarled branches reaching toward the heavens as if in supplication. I found a bench nestled beneath its sprawling canopy and settled down, breathing deeply, letting the scents of the evening wash over me. The air was tinged with the crispness of autumn, a reminder that change was inevitable, and much like the leaves that danced to the ground, I too was ready to embrace the shifts in my own life.

As I sat there, my mind wandered back to the evening's conversations. Each moment with Mia, Amelia, and Jackson felt etched in my memory like the most exquisite dish, the flavors still lingering on my tongue. I could almost taste the excitement in Amelia's voice as she shared her dreams of starting a non-profit, helping those less fortunate discover their own culinary talents. Jackson's quiet determination to bring authentic street food to a wider audience resonated with me, igniting a flicker of inspiration. Their ambitions reminded me that passion is often birthed from the deepest struggles, and together we could cultivate something extraordinary.

Just then, I pulled out my phone, the screen illuminating my face in the darkness. I opened my notes app, fingers poised, ready to capture the whirlwind of ideas that surged through me. Writing had always been my refuge, a space where I could untangle my thoughts and transform chaos into clarity. Tonight, it felt imperative to lay the foundation of my new project, a collection of stories that celebrated the flavors and narratives that connect us all. I envisioned not just recipes, but tales woven around the meals that had defined moments in our lives—the laughter of shared meals, the quiet of late-night snacks, the celebration of holidays and the comfort of home-cooked dinners.

As my thoughts flowed onto the digital page, the words came alive with each tap of my finger. I began sketching out the stories I wanted to tell, the voices I wanted to honor. I could see Mia's fiery spirit in the bold spices of her dishes, feel Amelia's kindness radiating through her charity work, and sense Jackson's ambition permeating his culinary endeavors. My vision expanded, and soon I was lost in a web of connections, each story a thread in the rich tapestry of life's experiences.

The more I wrote, the more I felt the weight of my own journey lifting. I was no longer just a spectator but a participant in a grand narrative, one where my voice mattered. The realization that my experiences could inspire others filled me with a newfound purpose. I imagined the people who would read my words, their lives touched by the stories of resilience, passion, and change that I would share.

Time slipped by unnoticed, the soft rustle of leaves mingling with the distant sound of laughter from the park's pathways. Suddenly, I heard footsteps approaching, accompanied by the familiar lilting laughter of Amelia. She appeared, a vision in a cozy sweater and jeans, her eyes sparkling like stars. "I figured I'd find you here," she said, plopping down beside me, her breath visible in the cool air. "I could feel your energy from a mile away. What's going on in that beautiful mind of yours?"

I grinned, closing my phone and turning to her. "Just jotting down some ideas for that project I mentioned at dinner. It's all still very much in its infancy, but I feel like it's bubbling to the surface. It's exhilarating and terrifying all at once."

Amelia leaned closer, her interest piqued. "Tell me everything! I want to hear your vision. We can bounce ideas around like two chefs tossing salad greens."

With enthusiasm bubbling between us, I shared my dreams of weaving together the stories of culinary artists who, like Mia, used food as a means of connection and expression. I painted a picture of recipes not just as instructions but as vessels for stories, each bite a memory. Her excitement grew with every word, her laughter infectious as she encouraged me to pursue this new direction with vigor.

"We need to take this further!" she declared, her eyes alight with determination. "We could collaborate! Maybe a series of pop-up dinners featuring the stories behind the recipes you collect. Imagine—people coming together to savor the dishes while listening to the tales that inspired them!"

Her words danced in the air, igniting a spark within me. A pop-up dinner series was a brilliant idea, a way to bring my project to life while connecting our community in the most delicious way possible. I could envision long tables set under the stars, the laughter and conversation flowing as freely as the wine. The possibility of combining culinary artistry with storytelling felt like the perfect union, the ideal way to bridge my passion for writing with my love for food.

The notion unfolded before me like a blossoming flower, each petal revealing a new facet of what could be. I could see Mia's exuberance as she prepared dishes inspired by her journey, Amelia's passion shining through as she organized the events, and Jackson could provide the street food flair that would keep our offerings diverse and vibrant. The three of us, together, could create something truly special, an immersive experience that would celebrate the power of food and connection.

As we brainstormed under the watchful gaze of the ancient oak tree, the night unfolded like a well-crafted meal, layer upon layer revealing depth and richness. The stars twinkled above us, each one a beacon of possibility, echoing the dreams we dared to whisper into the stillness of the night. My heart swelled with gratitude for this serendipitous encounter, for the friendships blossoming in the shared light of our aspirations.

The hours slipped away, the cool air wrapping around us like a comforting shawl. With each idea we exchanged, each laughter that erupted, the world felt a little brighter, a little more alive. In that moment, surrounded by the flickering shadows and the promise of change, I knew that this was just the beginning. Together, we would create a narrative that celebrated the beauty of connection, one meal at a time. The ingredients of change were all around us, waiting to be combined, and I felt ready to stir the pot.

Chapter 15: Crumbling Facades

The aroma of roasted garlic wafted through the air, wrapping around me like a warm embrace as I entered Mia's restaurant, a charming nook nestled between a dilapidated bookshop and an antique store overflowing with forgotten treasures. The light filtering through the front window played a gentle game of shadows and illumination across the rustic wooden tables, creating an inviting dance that beckoned both familiar faces and curious newcomers. Every time I walked through those doors, it felt as if I were stepping into a story, one layered with the laughter of patrons and the clinking of glasses, all harmonizing with the soft melodies drifting from an unseen speaker tucked away in the corner.

Mia, with her bright smile and an apron dusted with flour, seemed to thrive in this world she'd created—a world where the chaos of life faded, if only for a moment, beneath the heady scent of her garlic bread and the gentle sizzle of her famous chicken piccata. As I settled into my favorite corner table, the one closest to the window, I couldn't help but admire the small touches that made the space uniquely hers: the mismatched chairs, each one a different color and style, stood proudly alongside tables adorned with simple vases filled with wildflowers, as if plucked straight from a sunlit meadow.

I pulled out my notebook, its pages slightly crinkled and ink-stained, and began to write. Each word felt like a brushstroke on a canvas, a way to capture not just the essence of the food, but the very heart of what Mia had built. I focused on the way the pasta twirled effortlessly on the fork, the light glimmering off the perfectly sautéed capers, and how each bite was a conversation, a connection between those who crafted it and those who savored it. The more I wrote, the more I felt the weight of my own aspirations settle uneasily in my chest. I knew that my words were more than just a review; they were a testament to my journey, my growth, and the conflict that tugged at my heart whenever I thought of Jackson.

Jackson had this way of finding light in shadows, drawing me out of my own turmoil with just a glance, a casual smile that sent butterflies fluttering through my stomach. Yet, as our connection deepened, so did my fears. The laughter we shared felt like a fragile glass ornament, beautiful yet precarious, as if a single breath could shatter it. I found myself torn between the intoxicating thrill of being with him and the nagging worry that my career ambitions would overshadow our moments together. Was I really ready to plunge into the depths of a relationship while simultaneously trying to keep my own dreams afloat?

A soft laugh from Mia snapped me back to the present, and I looked up to find her watching me with an affectionate grin. "You look deep in thought," she remarked, wiping her hands on her apron. "What are you writing? Another review, or are you plotting world domination?" Her eyes twinkled with mischief, and I couldn't help but smile back.

"Just trying to capture the magic of your food," I replied, warmth blooming in my chest as I gestured around the restaurant. "This place deserves to be celebrated." I paused, realizing how true those words felt. Mia had carved out a sanctuary for those seeking comfort, a place that offered more than just a meal; it provided a sense of belonging.

Mia beamed, pride radiating from her. "Thank you! That means the world to me. I pour my heart into every dish, hoping it resonates with people." She stepped closer, her voice dropping to a conspiratorial whisper. "And maybe one day, I'll expand the menu to include a signature cocktail." Her excitement was infectious, and I felt my heart lift at the prospect.

But the joy was short-lived, a fleeting mirage, as I recalled my conversations with Jackson. He thrived in the world of corporate hustle, where ambition was currency, and dreams were often sacrificed on the altar of success. I admired his drive; it sparked a flame of inspiration within me, but it also ignited a fear of inadequacy. What if he outpaced me? What if our paths diverged as he climbed higher while I remained rooted in the quest to nurture my budding career as a food critic?

As I continued to write, my mind wandered to that night at the rooftop bar overlooking the city, the skyline a jagged silhouette against a canvas of stars. Jackson had leaned closer, the warmth of his breath a tantalizing whisper as he shared his dreams of launching his own startup. I had listened, hanging onto every word, envisioning a life filled with excitement and challenges, yet the closer I got to him, the more I feared that my own aspirations might feel small in the glow of his brilliance.

I shook my head, forcing myself to concentrate on the words flowing from my pen. The clatter of silverware, the soft murmur of conversation, and the gentle laughter that filled the air began to merge into a symphony, drawing me back into the present. My feelings for Jackson were genuine, yet the unease gnawed at me like an insistent pest. I longed to merge my worlds—the culinary passion I nurtured and the romantic pull of Jackson—into a seamless tapestry of joy.

Mia placed a plate of her signature dish in front of me, a culinary masterpiece that shimmered under the soft light. "Try this. It'll help clear your mind," she said, her eyes sparkling with the knowledge that food held a power beyond mere sustenance. As I took a bite, the flavors burst on my tongue—tangy, rich, and surprisingly complex. It felt like an invitation, urging me to savor each moment, to embrace the duality of my desires rather than view them as conflicting forces.

With each forkful, I began to weave a narrative in my mind, one that didn't shy away from the messy intricacies of love and ambition but embraced them wholeheartedly. The colors of my life swirled together, and I could almost hear the notes of a new story forming, one where I could rise alongside Jackson, hand in hand, while still nurturing my own passions. The unease began to dissipate like steam rising from a hot dish, leaving behind a sense of clarity and determination. I wanted to believe that my happiness was not a zero-sum game; it could be a banquet shared.

I glanced up at Mia, who had returned to the kitchen, her silhouette framed against the light, and smiled. This journey, both culinary and personal, was just beginning. I felt a new resolve take root in my heart, one that would guide me through the uncertainty of my relationship with Jackson while nurturing my ambition. If Mia could create a space filled with love, laughter, and delicious food, then perhaps I could carve out my own place in this vast, beautiful world.

The lingering taste of Mia's pasta still danced on my palate as I stepped out into the brisk evening air, the vibrant city pulsing with energy around me. Neon signs flickered like constellations, illuminating the streets with a kaleidoscope of colors. The night felt electric, charged with a sense of possibility. I took a deep breath, inhaling the mingled scents of street food and blooming urban gardens, letting it fill my lungs, hoping it might also fill the gaps in my heart.

Each step along the cobbled streets felt like a small rebellion against the doubts that had begun to creep into my mind. The world around me thrummed with life, laughter spilling from the open doorways of bars and cafes, where friends gathered, drinks in hand, sharing stories and dreams. I caught snippets of conversation, laughter twirling around me, and for a moment, I let the worries slip away, letting the rhythm of the city draw me into its embrace.

As I wandered, my thoughts kept drifting back to Jackson. He was an enigma wrapped in warmth, a blend of charisma and intensity that captivated me. The way his laughter echoed in my ears, rich and infectious, would often replay in my mind like a favorite song. Yet, with every laugh, a shadow would pass, a reminder of the uncertainty that accompanied our growing relationship. Was I ready to dive deeper into the unknown waters of love while balancing my aspirations? The thought gnawed at me.

Turning a corner, I spotted a familiar art gallery tucked between two towering buildings, its windows glowing with the brilliance of local artists' work. I felt an undeniable pull, as if the colorful canvases called out to me, promising an escape from my swirling thoughts. Pushing through the door, I was welcomed by the scent of fresh paint and the faint whisper of classical music. Each piece on display was a story waiting to be told, an emotion captured in vibrant colors and bold strokes. I ambled through the gallery, allowing the art to wash over me, transporting me to places untouched by the chaos of my mind.

In one corner, a painting of a stormy sea caught my eye—dark waves crashing against a rocky shore, vibrant splashes of white foam breaking through the depths. It resonated with the tumult within me. I could almost hear the roar of the ocean, feel the spray on my face, and in that moment, I understood that perhaps my feelings for Jackson were akin to that sea: wild and unpredictable yet beautiful in their own right. I took a moment, standing there, absorbing the power of that piece, wishing I could bottle it and carry it with me for those moments of self-doubt that threatened to drown me.

As I continued to wander, I felt the warm buzz of my phone in my pocket. I fished it out, heart fluttering at the thought of it being Jackson. But it was just a text from Mia, her excitement spilling through the screen as she shared her thoughts on the review I had written. "You made me cry happy tears! Thank you! Can't wait to celebrate at the launch party!"

Her words enveloped me, soothing the inner turmoil just enough to remind me of the joy my work could bring to others. I typed a quick response, letting her know how much I appreciated her enthusiasm, and slipped my phone back into my pocket. But the momentary respite from my thoughts was fleeting, and as I stepped back onto the street, I felt the familiar weight of uncertainty settle over me once more.

With a resolve I didn't fully feel, I decided to call Jackson. The sound of his voice always made the chaos inside me quiet down, if only for a little while. I dialed, holding my breath as it rang. When he answered, his voice rolled over me like a soothing balm. "Hey! I was just thinking about you," he said, his tone bright and inviting, pulling me closer.

"Hey, you. Just wandering the art gallery," I replied, leaning against a lamppost, watching passersby go about their lives. "What about you?"

"Just wrapped up a meeting," he said, and I could almost picture him, leaning back in his chair, his dark hair falling over his forehead as he ran a hand through it. "I'm free for dinner if you want to celebrate your amazing review."

His invitation sent a rush of warmth through me. "That sounds perfect. I just finished up at Mia's, and I'd love to talk to you."

As we made plans to meet at a cozy little taco place we both loved, I felt my spirits lift. The evening would be an opportunity to share not just our stories, but perhaps the insecurities that lingered like shadows, clouding the bright moments. As I walked toward the restaurant, the city thrumming with life around me, I clung to that hope, a delicate thread woven into the fabric of my desires.

The taco place, with its vibrant murals and the sound of sizzling meat wafting from the kitchen, felt like home. I arrived before Jackson, claiming a table adorned with a colorful woven tablecloth that felt alive beneath my fingertips. The waitress, a woman with a bright smile and even brighter hair, came by to take my order, and I settled on a classic—barbacoa with extra cilantro.

Moments later, Jackson strode in, his presence instantly illuminating the room. He spotted me and waved, his smile wide and genuine, igniting butterflies in my stomach. I couldn't help but admire how effortlessly he commanded attention, yet his focus was solely on me as he approached. "You look beautiful," he said, leaning down to plant a gentle kiss on my cheek, a gesture so sweet that it sent warmth radiating through me.

"Thanks! You clean up pretty well yourself," I teased, taking in his casual yet polished look—a fitted shirt that complemented his frame, jeans that hugged just right. We settled into conversation easily, the light banter flowing as naturally as the music that played in the background.

As we enjoyed our tacos, I felt the atmosphere shift, the playful chatter evolving into something more profound. "So, how's the review for Mia's doing?" he asked, leaning in, his eyes searching mine.

I could feel the corners of my mouth lift as I recounted the joy Mia expressed upon reading it. "She was thrilled, almost moved to tears. It felt good to see her so happy," I replied, my heart swelling with pride. "This place means everything to her."

"That's awesome," he said, his expression softening. "It's nice to see you so passionate about your work. It makes me want to share my dreams too."

The earnestness in his voice stirred something within me, nudging the shadows back just a little. "What are your dreams, Jackson?"

He hesitated, a flicker of vulnerability crossing his face. "I want to create something meaningful—something that makes a difference. I think about starting my own company, one that not only succeeds but also helps others."

His words resonated, igniting a warmth within me that mirrored the fiery salsa we had piled onto our tacos. "You'll do it," I said, my conviction unwavering. "You have this drive that's contagious. It's inspiring."

As we continued to share our ambitions, I felt the walls I had built around my heart begin to crumble, piece by piece. The uncertainty that had shadowed my thoughts began to fade, replaced by a dawning realization that I could pursue my own aspirations while still nurturing this blossoming connection with him.

The evening flowed on, laughter and shared stories intertwining, weaving a tapestry of trust and understanding. We spoke of the future, dreams tumbling from our lips like confetti, and with each word, I felt a surge of hope. Perhaps balancing love and ambition wasn't an impossibility but rather a journey worth taking together.

When the time came to leave, I couldn't shake the feeling that I was stepping into a new chapter—not just in my career but in my relationship with Jackson. As we walked side by side under the soft glow of streetlights, our fingers brushed occasionally, sending sparks through the night. I realized that the path ahead might still be fraught with uncertainty, but as long as we continued to communicate openly and support one another, it could also be filled with adventure and joy.

I took a deep breath, feeling lighter than I had in days. Maybe the facade of my doubts was crumbling, revealing a vibrant world of possibilities, one I was excited to explore, not alone but with Jackson by my side.

The days passed in a vibrant blur, the city morphing into a familiar companion as I continued to explore its many layers. Each morning, I found myself drawn to Mia's restaurant, now an essential part of my routine. It was more than just a job; it was a sanctuary. The aroma of fresh pastries filled the air, mingling with the robust scent of freshly brewed coffee, inviting patrons to linger a little longer. I took to sitting at my usual table, where the sunlight filtered through the window like golden syrup, casting a warm glow on my notebook as I penned reviews, capturing the intricate tapestry of flavors that Mia crafted with such love.

Yet, even within this comforting bubble, the complexities of my feelings for Jackson swirled around me, an ever-present undercurrent. We spent more time together, and with each encounter, the connection between us deepened, weaving a rich narrative of laughter and shared dreams. But beneath the surface of those happy moments, a tension brewed, fed by my own insecurities. I often wondered if I was enough for him, if my ambitions could coexist with his. The thought gnawed at me, a persistent whisper that threatened to unravel the fragile bond we had woven.

One evening, after an impromptu cooking session at my apartment—where flour flew like confetti and our laughter bounced off the walls—Jackson leaned back, a satisfied grin plastered across his face. He had a way of making even the simplest moments feel like an adventure. "You know," he began, a glint of mischief in his eye, "I could get used to this."

"What? Cooking together or making a mess?" I shot back, wiping a smear of flour from my cheek. His laughter bubbled forth, filling the space with a warmth that felt like home.

"Both," he replied, leaning in closer, his voice lowering conspiratorially. "But honestly, it's more about you. I love seeing you light up when you talk about your work. It's infectious."

His words stirred something deep within me, igniting a spark of hope. In that moment, I realized that perhaps I was too focused on the idea of balancing our aspirations rather than simply embracing what we had built together. Jackson's admiration for my passion made the doubts seem smaller, more manageable, like stray leaves caught in the wind.

As the sun dipped below the horizon, painting the sky in strokes of orange and purple, I decided to be vulnerable. "You know, sometimes I worry that I'm not enough," I confessed, my voice barely above a whisper. "That my dreams will hold you back or that I'll never catch up to where you want to be."

He looked at me, his expression softening, the flickering candlelight casting shadows on his strong features. "That's the thing, though. I don't want you to catch up. I want us to grow together, at our own pace. We can be each other's cheerleaders, not competitors."

Those words washed over me, dissolving the lingering unease that had been like a stone in my gut. With each passing moment, I felt the weight of my doubts lift, replaced by a renewed sense of purpose. I could forge my own path while supporting his ambitions—and maybe, just maybe, he would want to walk alongside me.

The next few weeks unfolded like a beautifully crafted narrative, each moment layering into the next. Jackson and I explored new corners of the city, from hidden speakeasies serving craft cocktails to street fairs bursting with local artisans. Every outing felt like a chapter in our story, filled with new experiences and laughter that echoed against the backdrop of city lights.

One Saturday, we ventured to the farmers' market, the vibrant stalls alive with colors and aromas. Fresh herbs and ripe tomatoes beckoned, and I felt my culinary instincts come alive as we meandered through the crowds. I could see Jackson's eyes light up at the sight of artisanal cheeses and handmade pastas, and it was contagious. Together, we concocted a plan for dinner that evening, pooling our finds like eager children playing a game of discovery.

As we returned to my apartment, the sun filtering through the windows, casting a warm glow over everything, I couldn't help but feel a sense of belonging swell within me. We chopped, sautéed, and seasoned our way to a feast, the rhythm of our movements synchronizing effortlessly. It was in these moments—amidst the clattering of pans and the sizzling of garlic—that I truly felt at home, both with my cooking and with Jackson by my side.

That night, as we sat down to enjoy our creation—a beautifully rustic pasta with heirloom tomatoes and a sprinkle of fresh basil—I marveled at how our lives had intertwined. Jackson raised his glass of red wine, a playful glint in his eyes. "To new beginnings," he toasted, his voice warm and inviting.

"To new beginnings," I echoed, clinking my glass against his, my heart swelling with gratitude. The food was rich and comforting, but it was the shared experience that filled me with warmth.

As the evening progressed, the conversation flowed naturally, punctuated by laughter and the occasional playful debate over our favorite pasta shapes. Jackson spoke about his aspirations with such passion, and I found myself captivated not just by his words but by the light in his eyes. In return, I shared my own dreams—how I envisioned my career evolving, the stories I longed to tell, and the impact I wanted to make in the culinary world.

In that intimate space, surrounded by the remnants of our dinner, I realized that I had not just opened my heart to Jackson but also to myself. I was deserving of this happiness, this love, and this beautiful complexity of life we were building together. I could chase my dreams without sacrificing the magic we shared.

Yet, as I settled into this realization, a new challenge emerged. Mia's restaurant was preparing for a big event—a culinary showcase that would highlight local chefs and their unique takes on traditional dishes. When she asked me to write a feature for the event, I felt both exhilarated and terrified. This was a chance to elevate my career but also a potential source of stress, as the spotlight would be on me to deliver something extraordinary.

Sitting across from Jackson one evening, I could feel the butterflies in my stomach dance at the thought of the upcoming showcase. "Mia wants me to write a feature for the culinary showcase," I shared, trying to gauge his reaction. "It's a big deal, and I'm excited but also...what if I mess it up?"

Jackson's expression shifted to one of unwavering support. "You won't mess it up. You've been pouring your heart into your writing. Trust yourself. You've got this."

His confidence in me was a balm to my nerves, and as we talked through my ideas for the piece, I felt a renewed sense of clarity. Perhaps this was the moment I needed to embrace my passion fully, to step out from behind the shadows of doubt and into the light of my ambitions.

The days leading up to the showcase became a whirlwind of creativity and inspiration. I spent hours at Mia's restaurant, tasting dishes, chatting with local chefs, and capturing their stories. Each interaction fueled my passion, reminding me why I loved food and the people who created it. The narrative began to take shape, a vibrant tapestry woven from the threads of flavors, cultures, and the heartfelt connections formed in the kitchen.

The night of the showcase arrived, and as I entered the bustling restaurant, the air crackled with excitement. Local patrons mingled, sipping cocktails and sampling exquisite dishes crafted by talented chefs. The atmosphere was electric, and I could feel the anticipation hanging in the air. I spotted Mia, radiant and bustling around, her energy infectious.

I took a deep breath, my heart racing as I approached her. "This is amazing, Mia. Thank you for trusting me with this opportunity."

She beamed, her eyes sparkling with pride. "You've worked so hard for this. I can't wait for everyone to read your piece."

As the night unfolded, I felt a sense of belonging envelop me. I mingled with guests, soaking in the energy and sharing snippets of my feature. When I finally sat down at a table with Jackson, his warm gaze anchored me, the reassurance I needed.

"Are you ready?" he asked, his voice low but full of encouragement.

I nodded, feeling a mixture of excitement and nerves bubbling within me. "Ready as I'll ever be."

The showcase blossomed into a night of shared stories, laughter, and a palpable sense of community. The chefs showcased their artistry, and I found myself marveling at the beauty of it all—the flavors, the passion, and the connections we forged over food.

When it came time to share my feature, I stood before the audience, a sea of eager faces illuminated by soft candlelight. As I spoke, my words flowed with newfound confidence, each sentence imbued with the love and dedication that had gone into crafting the stories of the chefs. I felt the warmth of Jackson's gaze in the crowd, grounding me as I poured my heart into every word.

And in that moment, amidst the applause and cheers, I understood that my journey was just beginning. The balance I sought between love and ambition didn't have to be a tightrope walk but rather a dance—a beautiful, intricate dance where each step brought me closer to both my dreams and the incredible man who believed in me. With each moment, I felt the walls of uncertainty dissolve, revealing a vibrant world of possibilities, one where I could thrive as both a writer and a partner.

The night concluded in a flurry of joy and celebration, surrounded by laughter and love, and I knew then that I would embrace whatever came next. Whether it was the next culinary challenge or the unfolding story of my life with Jackson, I was ready. Together, we would navigate this unpredictable journey,

Chapter 16: A Season of Growth

The sun hung low in the sky, casting a warm golden hue over the local market as I walked alongside Amelia, the aroma of fresh herbs mingling with the sweet scent of ripe peaches. The air buzzed with a gentle excitement, punctuated by the laughter of children darting between stalls and the cheerful chatter of vendors beckoning passersby to sample their wares. I felt a sense of purpose radiating through me, buoyed by the bond we were deepening through these shared moments.

We wandered from stall to stall, our fingers brushing against the cool, smooth surfaces of tomatoes, their vibrant reds and greens a testament to the summer sun. A local farmer waved us over, his weathered hands cradling a basket overflowing with heirloom varieties. "Try these, ladies," he urged, the corners of his eyes crinkling with warmth. We indulged in the experience, the sweet tang bursting in our mouths, an explosion of flavor that was so much more than food—it was a connection to the land, to the community that cultivated it.

Amelia, with her infectious enthusiasm, spotted a cluster of herbs, their scents dancing in the air. "Look at these! We could use them for our community dinner!" Her eyes sparkled with possibilities, each suggestion more vibrant than the last. We had decided, with an eagerness that felt almost reckless, to host a gathering that would not only celebrate food but the very essence of what it meant to belong. It would be a tapestry of flavors, stitched together with the threads of our local culture.

As we continued exploring, we stumbled upon a family-owned farm stand that felt as if it had emerged from the pages of a storybook. The wooden cart was laden with baskets overflowing with vibrant produce—crimson strawberries, emerald zucchinis, and clusters of sun-kissed grapes that glistened like jewels in the fading light. The couple running the stand, the Rodriguez family, exuded a warmth that enveloped us. Their laughter was like music, harmonizing with the whispers of the wind that rustled the leaves overhead.

"Welcome, welcome! Come taste the best of what our farm has to offer!" Mr. Rodriguez exclaimed, his eyes twinkling as he gestured to a tray of plump strawberries. The aroma was intoxicating, and as I bit into one, the juice cascaded down my chin, each sweet drop a reminder of summers spent running barefoot through fields, carefree and wild.

We lingered, our conversations flowing like the stream behind their farm, rich with stories of generations past. They shared their secrets to organic farming, each word a lesson wrapped in laughter. I felt a spark ignite within me, an exhilarating blend of admiration and inspiration. With every tip they offered, a vision began to form—one where our community dinner would be a tribute not only to the food but also to the hands that grew it.

"Why don't you ladies come help us harvest next week? We could use an extra pair of hands," Mrs. Rodriguez suggested, her voice soft yet inviting. "You'll learn so much about what goes into the food you eat."

Amelia's face lit up, and without hesitation, I nodded in agreement. "Absolutely! We'd love that." The thought of getting my hands dirty, connecting with the earth in a way that felt both ancient and new, thrilled me. It would be a journey, a celebration of the roots—both literal and metaphorical—of our community.

In the days that followed, we immersed ourselves in preparations for the dinner, each task a thread weaving us closer together. The scent of fresh basil mingled with garlic in my kitchen as Amelia and I chopped, sautéed, and laughed. The rhythmic clattering of knives against the wooden cutting board became our soundtrack, and the kitchen morphed into a sanctuary filled with creativity and chaos. I watched her, my sister, flour dusting her nose as she danced around the countertop, her laughter infectious as she recounted the most ridiculous moments from our childhood.

As we crafted our menu, the inspiration from the Rodriguez family infused every dish with a story. Our community dinner would showcase the bounty of local farms—an homage to the hardworking souls who poured their hearts into the earth. With each recipe, we created a narrative, a bridge that connected us to our neighbors, a reminder of the shared experiences that bind us.

The night of the dinner arrived, cloaked in a sky bursting with stars. Strings of fairy lights twinkled above the long table we'd set up in my backyard, adorned with wildflowers that danced gently in the evening breeze. The air was thick with the scent of grilled vegetables and the savory richness of marinades that had soaked into the meats, transforming them into culinary masterpieces.

Neighbors trickled in, each face brightening as they spotted the table laden with food that sang of summer and unity. Laughter floated through the air, intertwining with the music from a nearby radio, creating a melody that wrapped around us like a warm blanket. Conversations blossomed, voices rising and falling in a symphony of connection.

As I surveyed the scene, a sense of fulfillment washed over me. Here, under the vast expanse of the night sky, we had created a space where community thrived, where people shared not just food but stories, dreams, and laughter. The healing power of food was palpable, stitching together our diverse lives, reminding us that we were all a part of something larger.

Amelia caught my eye from across the table, her expression a mixture of pride and joy, and in that moment, I knew that we were not just cooking a meal; we were sowing seeds of friendship and love that would blossom long after the last plate was cleared away.

The clink of glasses and the hum of chatter enveloped us as the evening unfolded, a tapestry woven from the laughter and warmth of neighbors gathering around a long, rustic table. The amber glow of the fairy lights overhead cast a gentle light on the spread before us, each dish a testament to the effort and love that had gone into its creation. The sun had dipped below the horizon, and the night was alive with the sounds of cicadas serenading our little gathering, the air thick with the mingled aromas of grilled vegetables, fresh herbs, and smoky spices.

I watched as Amelia moved gracefully among our guests, her laughter like music, effortlessly drawing people into conversation. It was hard to believe that just weeks ago, we had been lost in our individual worlds, now transformed into partners in this beautiful endeavor. The sight of her animated expressions, bright eyes sparkling with joy, brought a swell of pride. She had become the heartbeat of our gathering, her enthusiasm infectious, stirring something deep within everyone who joined us.

"Try the ratatouille!" she exclaimed to Mrs. Thompson, our neighbor from two houses down, who was known for her sharp wit and equally sharp critiques of potlucks. With a gracious smile, she scooped a generous helping onto her plate, her brow raising in delightful surprise with each forkful. It was a small victory, yet it felt monumental—like winning the neighborhood's culinary Olympics.

I stepped back to soak it all in, finding solace in the rhythm of the evening, where each laugh and shared story stitched us closer. The children scampered about, their delighted shrieks punctuating the conversations of the adults as they darted between the tables. I recalled how Amelia and I used to be just like them, full of wild dreams and mischief, always searching for adventure in our backyard.

As the night deepened, I found myself drawn into a conversation with Mr. Rodriguez, his stories about the challenges of organic farming mingling with tales of resilience that spoke to something profound in my own journey. "You have to be patient with the earth, much like you have to be with people," he mused, a smile breaking across his face. "You nurture them, and over time, they flourish." His words resonated with me, echoing the very essence of what we were trying to cultivate—not just food, but a community, a space where everyone felt valued and heard.

"Food is just the beginning, you know," I said, my fingers absentmindedly tracing the rim of my glass. "It's about building connections, about creating a home within this community."

His eyes glimmered with understanding, and he nodded, "Exactly! When you grow something, you invest a part of yourself in it. You can taste that love when it's served at the table."

The warmth in his voice and the knowledge in his gaze ignited a desire within me to delve deeper into this community spirit. I envisioned a future where gatherings like this weren't just occasional events, but a cornerstone of our lives—a celebration of who we were as a collective.

As the night wore on, I felt an insatiable urge to preserve these moments, so I slipped away to grab my camera, a trusted companion throughout our culinary adventures. The camera felt heavy in my hands, but as I raised it to capture the joyous faces around me, I felt lighter, a sense of purpose igniting in my chest. Each click of the shutter was a promise—a promise to remember these faces, these connections, and the stories woven between us.

When I returned to the table, I found Amelia deep in conversation with the local baker, her eyes sparkling as she discussed the intricacies of sourdough starters. I couldn't help but chuckle at the sight of my sister, who once thought baking was merely an excuse to lick the bowl. Now, she was contemplating the science behind fermentation as if it were a long-lost art, reclaiming it piece by piece.

As I wandered through the crowd, I felt a sense of pride swell within me, each interaction a reminder of how far we had come.

The neighbors I once only waved to now shared stories of their lives—tales of love, loss, and laughter that intertwined with my own. There was Mrs. Thompson, recounting her adventures in her garden, and the Simmons' children racing to show me the fireflies they had caught, their tiny hands clutching glowing jars, sparkling like our dreams in the twilight.

As the first hints of the evening breeze brushed against my skin, I felt the weight of the day settle into my bones—a beautiful exhaustion that spoke of fulfillment. I found a moment of solitude beneath the old oak tree that had witnessed countless family gatherings and whispered secrets over the years. The stars twinkled above like diamonds scattered across velvet, a perfect backdrop to the tapestry we had woven below.

"Hey, you!" Amelia's voice pierced the tranquility, pulling me from my reverie. "Come join us! We're about to toast!" She beckoned with excitement, and I followed her back, my heart racing with anticipation. The clinking of glasses reverberated through the air as we raised our drinks high, the light from the candles flickering in a synchronized dance.

"To community!" Amelia announced, her voice ringing with exuberance. "To family! And to the delicious journey we're on together!"

"To community!" we echoed, a chorus of voices united in celebration, the sound harmonizing with the soft rustle of leaves and the distant hum of crickets.

As laughter erupted, I realized that this night was more than just a gathering; it was a celebration of all the moments that led us here. It was a testament to resilience, connection, and love—the very essence of life that could be savored as richly as the meal before us. I glanced around at the faces illuminated by the candlelight, each one a thread in the tapestry of our lives. In that moment, I understood that the journey we embarked on, rooted in shared meals and stories, would blossom into something profound—a legacy of connection that would echo long after the final bites were taken and the last toast was made.

The flicker of candles illuminated the faces around the table, casting playful shadows that danced with the gentle sway of the evening breeze. As I settled back into the warm embrace of the night, I felt an overwhelming sense of gratitude wrap around me like a soft quilt. Conversations ebbed and flowed like the tide, each wave bringing new laughter and shared stories that intertwined like the roots of the ancient oak tree sheltering our gathering. The scent of grilled vegetables still hung in the air, mingling with the heady sweetness of dessert—an indulgent cherry cobbler that Amelia had insisted we try, her eyes alight with determination to prove that our dinner would end on a high note.

The cobbler, nestled in a buttery, flaky crust, was the epitome of summer, each bite bursting with the flavor of sun-ripened cherries. As I watched the plate disappear under a chorus of enthusiastic forks, I felt a swell of pride. Amelia and I had taken our culinary collaboration to heart, pouring ourselves into every detail. But it was this moment—the joy of sharing food with our neighbors—that made our efforts truly worthwhile.

"Next time, let's include some of Mrs. Thompson's famous blueberry muffins," Amelia suggested, her eyes glinting with mischief as she glanced toward our neighbor, who was busy engaging in a light-hearted debate with Mr. Rodriguez about the best way to grow tomatoes. "Those would make the perfect breakfast for our guests."

I nodded, my mind racing with possibilities. "And what if we incorporated a little competition? A bake-off might spice things up! We could have everyone bring their signature dish and vote on the best one."

Amelia grinned, the idea clearly igniting her imagination. "Yes! We could even have a prize—something like a basket of goodies from the market. It would encourage everyone to participate."

As the laughter settled into a comfortable hum, I took a moment to absorb the warmth enveloping us. This gathering was not just a single night of joy; it was the seed of a tradition that could blossom into something lasting. I envisioned monthly gatherings, each one a celebration of our community's diversity and creativity, where everyone could contribute and share their unique stories through food. It was an idea that sent ripples of excitement through me.

With the evening winding down, the stars above us twinkled like a blanket of diamonds, a reminder of the infinite possibilities that lay ahead. The guests began to gather their belongings, but the atmosphere was anything but hurried. Conversations lingered, fueled by the shared experience of the evening. I spotted Mrs. Thompson leaning in to discuss gardening tips with Amelia, her vibrant laughter ringing through the night air like a bell, and I realized how much these interactions meant to everyone present.

Once the last of our guests had departed, the remnants of our feast began to take on a new life as we cleaned up together, the flickering candles casting a cozy glow over the remnants of our efforts. "What a success!" Amelia exclaimed, her cheeks flushed with exhilaration as she piled the leftover dishes into the sink.

"Truly! I don't think I've ever seen the neighbors so animated," I replied, unable to stifle my own laughter. "You should have seen Mr. Rodriguez; he practically leaped out of his seat to grab a second helping of the ratatouille!"

As we rinsed the plates and shared stories about our favorite moments from the night, I felt a shift in our bond—a deeper understanding forged through this experience. We were no longer just sisters; we were partners in creativity and community building, united by a shared passion for nurturing connections through food.

In the days that followed, our conversations brimmed with ideas about future gatherings. We planned themes, created menus, and even considered inviting local musicians to enhance the atmosphere with live music. The excitement flowed between us like a current, invigorating and inspiring.

One afternoon, as we sipped iced tea on the porch, I leaned back in my chair, gazing at the sun dipping low in the sky, casting a warm orange glow over the horizon. "What if we started a little farmers' market in the community park?" I suggested, the idea bubbling up from my heart. "We could partner with local farmers, artisans, and bakers to showcase their goods. It could be a way to bring everyone together regularly, not just for dinners."

Amelia's eyes widened, and her smile grew broader. "That would be incredible! We could host workshops on cooking with local ingredients, gardening tips, and even how to preserve foods. It would celebrate not just the food but the people behind it, the stories of resilience and love."

We spent the next few weeks laying the groundwork, fueled by our shared enthusiasm. We reached out to farmers, bakers, and artists, sharing our vision of creating a space where community members could gather, connect, and celebrate the beauty of local produce. The response was overwhelmingly positive, each person eager to contribute to this blossoming dream.

As the day of our first market approached, the buzz of anticipation crackled in the air. Banners adorned the park, flapping lightly in the gentle breeze, while booths began to take shape, each displaying a unique array of goods. The vibrant colors of fruits and vegetables mingled with the earthy tones of handmade crafts, creating a kaleidoscope of life and energy.

On the morning of the market, I arrived early to help set up, my heart racing with excitement. The sun cast a warm glow over the park, illuminating the smiling faces of vendors setting up their stalls. Children ran about, collecting colorful balloons and giggling in delight as they flitted between booths.

When Amelia joined me, her infectious energy seemed to infuse the air with a sense of magic. "Look at this!" she exclaimed, holding up a bouquet of wildflowers. "We need to find a way to incorporate these into our community dinners!"

As the market opened, the sound of laughter and chatter mingled with the gentle strumming of a local musician's guitar, filling the air with a lively tune. I felt my heart swell as neighbors poured in, drawn by the colorful sights and tantalizing smells. It was a celebration of everything we had envisioned—a vibrant tapestry of community spirit woven through food, music, and connection.

As I moved through the crowd, greeting friends and neighbors, I caught sight of Mr. Rodriguez showcasing his produce with the same pride he had exuded during our dinner. Each basket was a testament to his hard work, and his smile radiated warmth and love. I knew, in that moment, that this was what it meant to build a community—to lift each other up, to celebrate our stories, and to nourish not just our bodies but our souls.

Amelia joined me, her eyes sparkling with joy as she observed the hustle and bustle. "We did it!" she exclaimed, her voice nearly lost in the din of laughter. "Look at all of this!"

I nodded, overwhelmed by a sense of accomplishment and belonging. As the sun dipped lower, painting the sky in hues of pink and gold, I realized that we had created something beautiful—a tapestry of connections that would thrive long after the last customer had left, rooted deeply in the love of food and the celebration of community. This was just the beginning, a vibrant season of growth that promised even more blooms in the days to come.

Chapter 17: Whispers of Conflict

The moment the phone rang, slicing through the quiet hum of my kitchen, I felt a tight knot form in my stomach. It was the kind of call that came with its own dramatic soundtrack, the ominous notes hovering just beneath the surface. I wiped my hands on my apron, glancing out the window where the late afternoon sun bathed the streets of downtown Charleston in a warm, golden glow. The historic buildings, their faded pastels reflecting a bygone era of grandeur, felt almost like guardians watching over the bustling activity below. I loved this city; its charm intertwined with the vibrant culinary scene made it a canvas for creativity. Yet, as I answered, I braced myself for the tidal wave of responsibility that was about to crash over me.

"Evelyn, we need you to cover the opening of The Fiery Fork," my boss's voice crackled through the line, his urgency palpable. "It's been controversial—lots of negative press. But that's precisely why we want you on it."

The Fiery Fork. The name alone conjured images of scorching pans and sizzling meat, but I knew the reality was far more unsettling. The owner, a brash chef with a reputation for both culinary genius and public antics, had ruffled feathers long before he even opened his doors. Headlines painted him as a culinary dictator, cutting ties with anyone who dared to critique him. I could already hear the click of cameras, the buzz of whispered gossip, and the sharp scent of impending conflict.

I stood there, paralyzed between my sense of duty and my instinct to preserve the integrity of my writing. The thought of amplifying the negativity swirled around in my mind like a pot of boiling sauce, threatening to spill over. I felt the familiar stirrings of resistance; I wanted to shine a light on the local talent, the chefs who created magic in their kitchens without the need for headlines or controversies. Yet, there was something undeniably compelling about tackling the darker side of the culinary world, an arena I had tiptoed around but never fully embraced.

"Are you there?" my boss's voice pulled me back to the moment.

"Yes, I'm here." I hesitated, grappling with my thoughts. It was as if I were teetering on the edge of a cliff, the wind rushing past me, daring me to leap. "I'll do it."

I could almost hear Jackson's soft laughter in the back of my mind. He'd been a steady presence through my ups and downs, a voice of reason who could draw out my thoughts with mere words. I imagined him leaning back against the worn leather of his favorite chair, a glass of bourbon resting in his hand, his brown eyes sparkling with mischief and wisdom. When I mentioned my assignment, he raised an eyebrow, feigning disapproval, but I knew he relished the conflict, the very element that made life interesting.

"It's an opportunity, Evie. You've always wanted to give a voice to the overlooked." His tone was light, but the underlying seriousness made me reconsider. Maybe this was more than just a chance to expose a flawed chef; it was an avenue to explore the complexities of the culinary world and its often-ignored underbelly. "Highlight the good with the bad. Find the truth amidst the chaos."

As the sun dipped lower in the sky, casting a pinkish hue over the cobblestones, I decided to take his advice to heart. I needed to ground myself in the reality of the restaurant scene, so I slipped on my shoes and headed into the heart of the city, where life pulsated like the rhythm of a well-played jazz tune. Each step I took led me deeper into a world of culinary delights. I could hear laughter mingling with the sizzle of pans, the clinking of glasses filled with sweet tea and bourbon, the sound of families gathering around tables to share stories, celebrate life, and savor the food that brought them together.

Walking past bustling restaurants, I inhaled the mingling aromas of garlic, herbs, and spices, feeling a sense of connection to the cooks who poured their hearts into every dish. I turned down a side street lined with quaint cafés, their colorful awnings fluttering like the flags of tiny nations, and paused outside my favorite bakery. The scent of freshly baked bread wafted through the air, wrapping around me like a comforting embrace.

As I stepped inside, the bell jingled, and a wave of warmth enveloped me. Rows of pastries lined the glass display, glistening with sugar and butter, whispering promises of sweet indulgence. I ordered a slice of lemon tart, the tangy zest a welcome burst against my tongue, a reminder that amidst the chaos of culinary life, there were still simple joys to be savored.

With my slice in hand, I wandered back toward the waterfront, where the sunlight danced off the rippling waves, casting diamonds onto the surface. The water shimmered like an invitation to explore, to dive beneath the surface and uncover the hidden gems of the city. I leaned against the rail, taking a moment to let the cool breeze soothe my swirling thoughts.

In that moment, I realized that this assignment could be my chance to embody the very spirit of Charleston—the blend of the vibrant and the flawed. Just as the city wore its history with pride, I could take the shadows surrounding The Fiery Fork and weave them into a narrative that not only exposed the truth but celebrated the resilience of those who dared to dream in a world that often felt overshadowed by controversy.

As the sun dipped below the horizon, painting the sky in hues of orange and purple, I took a deep breath. This was no longer just an assignment; it was a journey into the heart of what it meant to be a storyteller in a city that thrived on passion and conflict. My pen was poised to capture the essence of the culinary world, a narrative that would reveal not just the flaws of a chef but the resilience of a community fighting to uphold its rich legacy. And for the first time, I felt a spark of excitement replace my hesitation.

The clamor of a city bustling with anticipation echoed in my mind as I prepared to delve into the uncharted waters of The Fiery Fork. My heart raced at the thought of confronting a figure as polarizing as its owner, a chef whose reputation for flamboyant displays of authority made him the toast of controversy. I could already picture the anxious chatter of food bloggers and critics, their pens poised, eyes sparkling with the thrill of the hunt. This was not merely an opening night; it was a stage set for conflict, a play where every forkful held the weight of a thousand opinions.

In the days leading up to the grand opening, I found myself spiraling into a vortex of research. I immersed myself in articles, interviews, and social media posts, each piece painting a stark portrait of a chef who thrived on chaos. He was a man who commanded attention like a conductor leading an orchestra, his baton swinging wildly as he orchestrated both praise and scorn. I could almost hear the cacophony in my head, the high-pitched notes of admiration and the deep bass tones of dissent weaving together into a symphony of culinary discord.

As I walked the sun-dappled streets of Charleston, my thoughts shifted from the allure of The Fiery Fork to the heartbeat of the city itself. Each step brought me past vendors selling hand-painted ceramics and fragrant flowers, the vibrant colors competing for my attention. I meandered through the historic district, where the sweet scent of magnolias hung heavy in the air, and the whispers of the past danced between the centuries-old oak trees. I cherished this city, with its quirky charm and rich tapestry of stories woven into every brick and cobblestone.

In the heart of this southern gem, I found solace in the familiar surroundings of my favorite café. As I entered, the rich aroma of freshly brewed coffee wrapped around me like a comforting blanket. The barista, a sprightly woman with a shock of purple hair and a laugh that could fill the room, greeted me with a smile that felt like a warm hug. I ordered my usual—a latte with a sprinkle of cinnamon—and settled into my corner seat, where sunlight poured through the window, illuminating the pages of my notepad like a spotlight on my thoughts.

With each sip, my mind churned with ideas. This assignment could be a dance with danger, a balancing act where I could spotlight the culinary brilliance while revealing the prickly truths lurking beneath the surface. I envisioned how I would weave narratives of the staff—the sous chefs, the line cooks—whose hard work and dedication often went unnoticed in the clamor surrounding their volatile leader. Each person was a thread in the intricate fabric of the restaurant, and I wanted to capture their stories, their passion, the sweat that went into every dish, and the heart that fueled it.

Over the next few days, the city buzzed with excitement as the opening drew near. The Fiery Fork transformed into a spectacle, its entrance draped in crimson fabric that flapped in the wind like a flag of bold defiance. Posters announcing its grand opening plastered the streets, showcasing mouthwatering dishes that promised culinary delights. I found myself standing outside the restaurant, my notebook clutched tightly in my hands, watching as curious diners flocked to the doors, eager to witness the unfolding drama.

As the sun dipped low in the sky, casting long shadows across the pavement, I stepped inside, my heart racing. The interior was a dazzling array of vibrant colors and eclectic decor, an explosion of creativity that echoed the chef's chaotic spirit. Each table was adorned with mismatched china and whimsical centerpieces, creating a sense of intimate revelry amidst the energetic atmosphere. The kitchen, visible through a glass wall, hummed with the intensity of a live performance, where every chop, sauté, and flambé was executed with precision and flair.

I took a deep breath, letting the cacophony of clinking glasses and animated conversations wash over me. The air was thick with the scent of spices and seared meats, enticing yet tumultuous. I watched as waitstaff zipped between tables, their movements fluid and practiced, carrying plates piled high with colorful dishes that seemed to tell stories of their own. The atmosphere crackled with anticipation, and I felt like an intruder in a world teetering on the edge of a precipice.

Then, there he was—the chef himself, a whirlwind of energy and bravado, his hair a wild mane and his voice a booming command. As he moved through the dining room, he wore a confidence that demanded attention, his presence both magnetic and intimidating. I couldn't help but marvel at the way he commanded the room, a lion among lambs, as he stopped to chat with guests, his gestures grand and expressive.

But as I observed, I noticed the subtle tension beneath the surface. A server flinched slightly at his raised voice, a line cook cast a wary glance his way, their faces betraying the fear that lingered behind their smiles. My heart ached for them, the unseen warriors behind the scenes, battling against the storm of their leader's tempestuous personality. I realized this was the heart of the story—navigating the precarious balance between admiration and fear, between culinary artistry and emotional toll.

My gaze swept over the diners, their expressions a mix of delight and apprehension, as they savored the flavors presented before them. I could almost hear their inner dialogues: Was it worth it to indulge in this culinary adventure, knowing the darkness that loomed in the kitchen? Would they leave the experience with satisfied palates or haunted memories? I felt the weight of these questions pressing upon me, an unyielding reminder of the responsibility I bore.

As the night wore on, I found a moment to slip into a quieter corner, where the hum of conversations faded to a gentle murmur. I pulled out my notebook, my thoughts racing as I began to scribble down observations, piecing together a narrative that would resonate with readers beyond the clinking of forks and the buzz of excitement. I envisioned a story that illuminated the complexity of the restaurant world, where passion clashed with ambition and creativity danced on the knife's edge of chaos.

With each word, I poured my heart into the page, committed to capturing not just the glamour but the grit, the struggles of those who labored in the shadows. I was determined to honor the resilient spirit of this community, a symphony of voices waiting to be heard. It was no longer just about the chef's tempestuous reign; it was about every soul who entered The Fiery Fork seeking not just a meal, but a connection to the very essence of Charleston—a celebration of life's flavors, both bitter and sweet.

The air in The Fiery Fork crackled with an electric energy, each table brimming with anticipation and the lingering aroma of roasted garlic and charred meats. I could feel the pulse of excitement vibrating through the room, a collective heartbeat that mirrored my own rising anxiety. The clash of plates and spirited conversation created a backdrop that was both intoxicating and intimidating, as I made my way through the throng of guests, all eager to witness the spectacle unfolding before them.

I positioned myself near the open kitchen, the glass walls serving as a transparent barrier between the chaos of culinary creation and the diners' eager eyes. Through the panes, I observed a team of chefs working with a fervor that resembled a finely-tuned machine, each member aware of their role in this delicious ballet. A sous chef, his brow furrowed in concentration, expertly tossed ingredients into a sizzling pan, while another chef, his tattoos snaking up his arms like ivy, plated dishes with an artist's precision, adding final touches of herbs and drizzles of vibrant sauces.

But as I watched this well-rehearsed performance, my gaze was inevitably drawn back to the chef himself, the magnetic force of the establishment. He was a whirlwind of energy, moving with a frenetic grace that captivated and terrified all at once. His voice rose above the clamor, a sharp command that cut through the warmth of the room, dictating not just the pace of the kitchen but the very mood of the diners. I noted how the waitstaff flinched slightly at his tone, exchanging glances that spoke volumes—an unspoken agreement borne from shared experience, the kind forged in the fires of a demanding kitchen.

A woman at a nearby table leaned in, her eyes sparkling with a mix of fear and fascination, whispering to her companion, "Do you think he's as talented as they say, or is it just the hype?" I could see the flicker of intrigue dancing in her gaze, an invitation to be drawn into the drama that was The Fiery Fork. I chuckled to myself, realizing that this was not merely a restaurant opening; it was a performance piece, a daring exploration of culinary art intertwined with human emotion.

As the evening progressed, I navigated the ebb and flow of the dining room, pen poised over my notepad. I sought out the stories behind the scenes, the quiet whispers of the kitchen that were drowned out by the clamor of exuberance. I approached the sous chef during a brief lull, his apron stained with evidence of a long night's work.

"What's it like working for him?" I asked, leaning in closer, trying to capture the nuance in his expression.

His eyes darted around, ensuring no one was listening, before he replied in a low voice, "It's a rollercoaster. One moment, you're his favorite, the next, you're on the chopping block." His laugh was edged with exhaustion, yet there was pride behind it. "But we make magic here. It's just... you have to be ready for anything."

The tension in his voice resonated with me, a reflection of the turbulent atmosphere I had sensed from the start. This was a family forged in heat and pressure, where loyalty was both a shield and a burden. I scribbled down his words, aware that these insights would shape the narrative I was crafting, a balance of light and dark that embodied the spirit of this place.

As the night wore on, the chaos crescendoed into a peak of culinary prowess, each dish a testament to the skill and creativity of the kitchen brigade. I found myself captivated by a particularly daring dish—a flambéed duck breast that left trails of smoky flavor wafting through the air. Diners oohed and aahed, their reactions a thrilling reminder of the art of gastronomy. I imagined how this moment could be woven into my story, a fleeting glimpse of beauty amid the clashing dynamics of a kitchen.

But the tension was palpable, a thin thread pulled tight, ready to snap at any moment. I spotted the chef making his rounds, his booming laughter echoing through the room, but the moment he encountered a table that didn't immediately rise to his praise, the air shifted. The warmth of the evening turned cool, like the sudden gust of wind that precedes a storm. I watched, transfixed, as he leaned down, his expression darkening, and I could almost feel the collective breath of the room hitch in response.

"What's wrong?" he demanded, eyes narrowing as if he were inspecting a poorly plated dish. The guests at the table visibly shrank, their earlier excitement deflating like a punctured balloon. It was a stark reminder that not all interactions in this culinary playground were joyous celebrations; some were battles fought in the trenches of ego and artistry.

In that moment, I felt a jolt of determination surge within me. This wasn't just an assignment to write about food; it was an opportunity to delve deep into the human experience that surrounded it. The highs, the lows, the triumphs, and the defeats—all of it mattered. I wanted to amplify the voices of those who toiled behind the scenes, the ones who didn't bask in the limelight but made the spotlight possible. I knew then that my narrative needed to reflect not just the chef's bravado but the symphony of stories that played out in the kitchen.

As I jotted down my observations, my pen moving furiously across the page, I could feel the night shifting. The electric atmosphere hummed with possibilities, the tension crackling like the sizzling pans in the kitchen. It was in that moment, surrounded by the intoxicating blend of aromas and sounds, that I realized this was more than just a restaurant; it was a living, breathing organism, with its own rhythm and heartbeat.

I spent the last hours of the evening weaving my way through the chaos, gathering fragments of conversation, snippets of laughter, and glimpses of sorrow, determined to capture the essence of The Fiery Fork in all its multifaceted glory. I spoke with line cooks who shared their dreams of owning their own restaurants one day, their eyes alight with hope. I listened to servers recount stories of diners who had transformed a simple meal into a cherished memory. Each voice added a layer to my understanding, a thread in the intricate tapestry that was this establishment.

As the evening drew to a close and the last diners departed, I stepped outside into the cool Charleston night. The air felt electric, filled with the promise of new beginnings and untold stories waiting to be uncovered. My heart swelled with a sense of purpose, knowing I held the power to bring these voices to light.

I could see the glowing sign of The Fiery Fork reflecting in the moonlight, and as I walked away, I understood that my journey had just begun. The chef, the kitchen, and the people who filled it were more than just subjects of an article; they were part of a living narrative, a beautiful mess of creativity and conflict that demanded to be explored.

With my notepad full and my mind racing with ideas, I embraced the thrill of what lay ahead. This was my chance to illuminate the shadows and celebrate the resilience of those who dared to dream amidst the fiery chaos of the culinary world. I had been given a front-row seat to a tumultuous production, and I was ready to share the story, to uncover the layers that made The Fiery Fork not just a restaurant, but a beacon of passion, perseverance, and the unwavering spirit of those who dared to create something beautiful from the flames.

Chapter 18: Chopping Off Old Habits

The scent of truffle oil lingered in the air, mingling with the sweetness of vanilla-infused champagne, creating a heady concoction that wrapped around me like a warm embrace. My heels clicked against the polished wood floor, a sound drowned out by the laughter and clamor of socialites reveling in the glow of freshly lit chandeliers. Each light was a star suspended in a midnight sky, illuminating the myriad faces that graced the grand opening of a restaurant that promised to be the talk of the town.

With every step, I felt the anticipation swelling within me, an almost electric thrill. Yet, beneath that pulse of excitement lay a tight knot of anxiety coiling in my stomach. I caught glimpses of perfectly curated outfits, the sparkle of jewelry flashing like fireflies against the backdrop of emerald green walls. Influencers, their phones poised like weapons, flitted about, documenting every dish as if it were a piece of art meant to be dissected and critiqued. I was part of this world—a world I had once longed for but had since grown wary of. My heart raced as I surveyed the scene, the vibrant chaos a stark contrast to the quiet corners of my life I often retreated to.

Jackson's familiar figure stood out like a lighthouse on a stormy night. His navy suit hugged him just right, a perfect balance between professional and approachable. His smile broke through the throng like sunshine piercing through a fog, and for a moment, I felt the tension melt away. I made my way toward him, weaving through the crowd, feeling the weight of my responsibilities. Jackson leaned in, his voice a soft murmur against the clamor. "You ready for this?"

I managed a nod, though the unease lingered like an unwelcome guest. "I think so. Just... let's hope the food lives up to the hype."

He chuckled, a rich sound that wrapped around me like a favorite blanket. "With all the critics here, it's bound to be scrutinized." His confidence reassured me, and for a fleeting moment, I allowed myself to imagine that the evening would go off without a hitch. But as we mingled, sipping our cocktails and sampling dishes that looked too beautiful to eat, I sensed an undercurrent of tension—a dissonance that couldn't quite be ignored.

The owner, a charismatic figure who seemed to thrive under the spotlight, paraded around, his bravado as thick as the layers of icing on the extravagant cake displayed on a pedestal. Yet, the more I observed, the more I could see the flickers of desperation behind his smile. It reminded me of a performer who had mastered the art of illusion but was terrified of stepping off the stage.

As the evening wore on, I found myself in a cozy corner of the venue, a quiet oasis amidst the whirlwind. I perched on a barstool, watching the vibrant life of the restaurant unfold before me. The servers flitted from table to table, their trays laden with delicate plates adorned with splashes of color—a kaleidoscope of culinary creativity. I took a sip of my drink, the bubbles bursting like tiny fireworks on my tongue, but I couldn't shake the weight of expectation that hung heavily in the air. The critics, with their discerning palettes and sharper pens, were on the prowl, ready to carve their opinions into the evening's fabric.

I recalled my own past—those moments of doubt when I felt like an imposter, waiting for someone to unmask me. My journey had been a patchwork of experiences, each thread woven with both triumph and failure. As I prepared to write my review later, I realized I had to confront the uncomfortable truths that often lay hidden beneath the surface, just as I had learned to confront my own insecurities. I had a duty to honor the culinary artistry I was witnessing while remaining true to my own voice.

A commotion drew my attention. The owner, with his booming laugh, had gathered a group of influencers, sharing exaggerated tales of the restaurant's inspirations and secret recipes. I could see it—the carefully crafted narrative, a web spun to ensnare the attention of those hungry for a story. I smiled politely, but inside, I felt a pang of empathy for the talented chefs laboring in the kitchen, whose passion was cloaked under a shroud of pretense.

In that moment, I decided I would be a voice of honesty in this glamorous world. My fingers itched to write, to capture the vibrancy of the night but also to shed light on the shadows. Each dish deserved its own spotlight, not just as an artistic endeavor but as a testament to the hard work and dedication of those behind the scenes. I wanted to peel back the layers, exposing the artistry while acknowledging the darker hues of ambition and desperation.

Jackson's voice broke through my reverie. "You look lost in thought."

"Just... reflecting." I smiled, pushing my worries aside for the moment. "You know how it is, trying to make sense of it all."

He nodded, his expression understanding. "You'll do great. Just remember to be honest—your voice is what sets you apart."

As the evening progressed, I realized this was more than just an opening; it was a reminder of the battles we all faced, the masks we wore in public, and the authenticity we fought to uphold in our personal lives. It was about the courage to confront our own truths and the acceptance of our imperfections.

With renewed determination, I stepped back into the fray, ready to capture the essence of the evening while also confronting my own old habits—the ones that held me back from fully embracing who I was becoming. Each clink of glass, every burst of laughter, became a part of my narrative, weaving together the chaotic beauty of the night into something raw and genuine.

As I meandered back into the heart of the venue, the pulse of the evening swelled around me like a living thing. My senses heightened, I could hear the harmonious blend of laughter, clinking glasses, and the soft notes of a jazz ensemble playing in the corner. Each sound intertwined, creating a vibrant symphony that seemed to encapsulate the very essence of the restaurant's ambition. The air buzzed with expectation, as if everyone present was a part of a larger narrative that thrummed beneath the surface, a tale waiting to be told.

I glanced at the artfully arranged dishes making their way to the tables, their vibrant colors practically glowing under the delicate light. A nearby couple gasped in delight as their plates arrived, the aroma wafting toward me, tempting and tantalizing. I had to remind myself that each meal represented a slice of someone's passion, countless hours of work distilled into a single moment of culinary brilliance. The chefs were the unsung heroes, yet their artistry could easily be overshadowed by the sparkling distractions of the night.

Jackson found me again, weaving through the crowd with ease, a calm oasis amid the storm of personalities. "You still deep in thought?" he asked, a teasing grin playing at the corners of his mouth.

"Always," I replied with a smirk, feeling a flicker of warmth at his presence. "Just contemplating the fate of each plate."

"Careful, or you might just become the food critic this place needs," he joked, nudging my arm lightly. "Or at least the one who doesn't sugarcoat the truth."

His comment struck a chord, igniting a familiar fire within me. The truth was a fickle friend—both liberating and daunting. It had taken me far too long to accept that my voice, my perspective, was valuable. In a world draped in facades, honesty felt like a rare gem, precious and powerful.

As the evening unfolded, I caught snippets of conversation that floated through the air like confetti. Tales of ambition and aspiration were woven together with whispers of doubt and vulnerability, threading the fabric of the night into something more tangible. I watched as the owner flitted from group to group, his enthusiasm almost manic, as he eagerly shared the story of the restaurant's conception, the inspirations that had ignited his dreams. It was a story punctuated by passion, yet I couldn't shake the feeling that beneath it all lay a current of desperation.

Jackson leaned closer, breaking my reverie. "You know, sometimes people need to hear the unvarnished truth," he said, his tone suddenly serious. "Even when it's hard."

"I know," I replied, feeling the weight of his words settle deep within me. "It's just... how do I balance that without crushing their dreams?"

"Maybe it's about finding a way to inspire change instead of casting shadows. You're not here to be cruel; you're here to help."

I nodded slowly, absorbing his wisdom. His faith in me felt like a gentle push toward clarity, as if he was unveiling a part of me that had long been buried under layers of doubt and hesitation. The night continued its dance around us, but I felt anchored in that moment, a new resolve beginning to blossom within me.

Just then, a server approached with a dish that demanded attention. The vibrant colors of roasted heirloom tomatoes and creamy burrata practically leaped off the plate, drizzled with a balsamic reduction that glistened like liquid night. As the server recited the ingredients, I could hardly contain my enthusiasm. "This looks incredible!" I exclaimed, reaching for a fork, feeling a surge of joy at the prospect of tasting something so beautifully crafted.

As I savored the first bite, the flavors exploded in a harmonious dance on my palate. The creaminess of the cheese blended with the sweet-tart tomatoes, a symphony that made my heart flutter. I could feel the chefs' artistry in every morsel, the love and labor poured into the creation. "This is what it's all about," I said, turning to Jackson, my eyes sparkling with delight. "It's the connection—the way food brings us together."

He smiled, mirroring my excitement. "Exactly. It's not just about the flavors; it's the experience, the stories behind every dish."

With each passing moment, I became more attuned to the stories unfolding around me—the anxious glances exchanged between chefs, the knowing nods between critics, and the subtle signals of patrons lost in the experience. There was a rhythm to the evening that felt almost poetic, a tapestry of human emotion stitched together with threads of ambition, fear, and connection.

As I navigated through the mingling crowd, I overheard snippets of conversations—some lighthearted, some laced with tension. I caught a glimpse of a young couple discussing their culinary journey, their eyes shining with hope and excitement, while nearby, a seasoned critic was engaged in a serious dialogue about the industry's future. Each voice contributed to the rich tapestry of the night, a reminder that everyone here was seeking something—a moment of joy, an escape, a connection.

The atmosphere shifted slightly as the owner took to a small makeshift stage, his voice ringing out above the chatter. "Thank you all for being here tonight! We're not just opening a restaurant; we're inviting you into our family, our story!" His words were met with applause, but I could sense a vulnerability beneath his bravado. There was a fragile line between confidence and desperation, and I felt an overwhelming urge to support him, to encourage the artistry that lay within.

As the evening approached its zenith, I knew I had to prepare for the task ahead—my review would be a testament to the culinary journey I'd experienced. It was a chance to honor the artistry while reflecting the truth of what lay beneath. I could do this, not just for the sake of the restaurant but for the countless others like it struggling to find their place in a world that often prioritized glitter over substance.

With a determined spirit, I returned to my corner, pulling out my notebook, the pages whispering promises of creativity and honesty. The hum of conversation and laughter surrounded me, a comforting backdrop to my thoughts. I was ready to embrace the messy, beautiful truth of it all, to celebrate the artistry while challenging the shadows lurking in the corners.

As the night carried on, I felt more grounded, the energy of the venue fueling my resolve. I was here to carve out a space for honesty, to champion the connection that food could foster and to remind everyone that sometimes, it's the imperfections that make a story worth telling.

In the dim light of my secluded corner, I pulled my notebook closer, the pages blank yet brimming with potential. The chatter around me was a symphony, a cacophony of laughter and clinking glasses blending into a harmonious backdrop. I could hear the excitement of diners expressing their delight, punctuated by the occasional gasp of surprise as a server revealed yet another masterpiece from the kitchen. The smell of slow-roasted garlic mingled with the sweetness of caramelized onions, wrapping around me like a warm hug, inviting me deeper into the culinary experience that was unfolding.

I took a moment to breathe, letting the atmosphere seep into my bones. The restaurant had taken a gamble on opulence—bold red accents, ornate chandeliers dripping with crystals, and lush velvet banquettes that seemed to whisper secrets of romantic dinners past. Yet, as beautiful as the space was, the decor felt like a mask, a shiny facade that sparkled in the light yet hid the vulnerability beneath. The owner's laughter echoed through the venue, but his eyes flickered with the kind of anxiety that only those on the brink of success—or failure—truly understood.

With Jackson nearby, I felt a certain buoyancy, his calm presence reminding me that I wasn't alone in this tumultuous sea of expectations. He stood beside me, an anchor amidst the shifting tides of ambition and doubt. I glanced at him, a smile tugging at my lips, grateful for his companionship. "Do you think he can sustain this?" I asked, nodding subtly toward the owner, who was currently spinning a tale about his grandmother's secret recipes as if they were the elixir of life.

Jackson shrugged, his brow furrowed slightly. "It depends. Passion is vital, but so is consistency. This isn't just a passion project; it's a business."

"True," I agreed, the reality settling over me like a shroud. "But passion can only carry you so far." I reflected on my own journey, the twists and turns that had led me to this moment. My path had been dotted with uncertainty, and I had learned that the most successful ventures were those that balanced fervor with a realistic understanding of the grind.

As the evening progressed, the air around us thickened with a mix of excitement and apprehension. A prominent food critic I recognized from social media stepped into my line of sight, her gaze sharp and discerning. She navigated through the crowd with the kind of confidence that could silence a room, her reputation preceding her like a herald of judgment. I couldn't help but feel a thrill of recognition as she paused to taste a dish. Her reactions, always so meticulously curated for the camera, were raw and genuine in person. I felt my heart race as I considered the weight of her words, the potential for them to either uplift or devastate the dreams of those working tirelessly behind the scenes.

In a moment of spontaneity, I slid my notebook open, scribbling down my thoughts. "The food is art. It's both a reflection of the soul and a mirror to the heart of the restaurant," I wrote, words flowing freely as inspiration ignited within me. Each bite I had savored felt like a conversation with the chefs, an unspoken dialogue about their hopes and aspirations. This place was more than just a restaurant; it was a dream stitched together with sweat and passion, each dish a testimony to the hard work that had gone into crafting this moment.

With the confidence of a newfound purpose, I ventured back into the heart of the venue. The crowd parted as I made my way through, and I felt a surge of adrenaline, as if I were stepping onto a stage. I approached the kitchen, a warm glow emanating from within, where chefs danced like orchestrated chaos, each movement a testament to their expertise. The sizzling of pans and the fragrant smoke rising into the air felt intoxicating. I could sense the camaraderie, the shared drive that bound them together in this moment of creation.

"Can I ask a few questions?" I ventured, my voice steady despite the whirlpool of nerves beneath the surface. The head chef turned, his brow glistening with sweat but his eyes sparkling with pride.

"Of course," he said, wiping his hands on his apron, a sense of relief washing over his features. "What would you like to know?"

I took a moment, gathering my thoughts, before asking about his philosophy on food, the stories behind the dishes, and the ingredients that inspired him. Each answer revealed layers of passion and dedication, unveiling a narrative that transcended the evening. It was in those conversations that I found the heart of the restaurant—the beauty, the struggles, and the aspirations that intertwined in the creation of each dish.

As I absorbed their stories, I felt a new wave of determination wash over me. My review wouldn't just recount the flavors; it would illuminate the journey, the lives woven into the fabric of the restaurant. I wanted to honor their struggles while remaining grounded in honesty, a delicate balance that could inspire growth rather than extinguish dreams.

Returning to my corner, I penned my thoughts with fervor. "In every plate, there lies a story—a blend of nostalgia and ambition, a tapestry woven with threads of hope. To dine here is to partake in a legacy, to embrace not just the food but the dreams that brought it to life." The words flowed freely, an unfiltered stream of consciousness that felt raw and true.

As the evening reached its climax, I noticed the owner standing alone at the edge of the room, his mask slipping. He watched the crowd with a mix of pride and trepidation, the reality of what lay ahead beginning to sink in. I approached him, my heart racing as I extended my hand, the weight of our shared ambition hanging in the air.

"Your vision is beautiful," I said, meeting his gaze with sincerity. "But remember, it's okay to show the struggle behind the art. That's where the real connection lies."

He looked at me, surprise flickering in his eyes. "Thank you. It's easy to get lost in the performance, to feel like I have to put on a show."

"Authenticity speaks louder than perfection," I replied, my voice steady and warm. "Trust that your journey will resonate."

As the clock ticked toward midnight, the energy in the venue shifted, and I realized that the evening was not just about food and critique but about connection. We were all part of a larger narrative, each voice adding its own unique hue to the night. The room pulsed with life, and in that moment, I felt an overwhelming sense of gratitude—for the food, the stories, and the people who dared to dream.

When I finally returned to my quiet corner, I sat down to finish my review, the words pouring out like a cathartic release. With each sentence, I felt more liberated, shedding the burdens of expectation and embracing the beauty of vulnerability. As I concluded my thoughts, I realized I was not just writing for an audience; I was documenting the raw reality of creation, a celebration of art in its most authentic form.

The night had become a symphony, a celebration of culinary passion that would linger long after the last plate was cleared. As I took a deep breath, letting the evening settle within me, I knew that the words I would share would honor not just the food but the heart and soul that had crafted it. It was my chance to carve a place for truth in a world that often masked itself in glitter and bravado, a chance to inspire and to remind everyone that behind every dream lies a story worth telling.

Chapter 19: A Recipe for Redemption

The sun began to dip below the horizon, casting long shadows across the sidewalk of Main Street, where the aroma of freshly baked bread mingled with the rich scent of roasted coffee. This was a part of town where stories lingered in the air, thick as the humidity that rolled in with the afternoon. I settled onto a weathered bench, the kind that had been painted a dozen different shades over the years, each layer peeling away to reveal the bare wood beneath. With the scent of cinnamon wafting from the nearby bakery, I felt the day's warmth seep into my bones, urging me to remember not just the sweetness but the bitterness as well.

The bustling café across the street beckoned, its glass doors wide open, inviting passersby to escape the sun's embrace. Inside, laughter danced alongside the clinking of cups, each sound a reminder that life continued to swirl around me, even when I felt rooted to this very spot. As I watched, a little girl with tangled curls ran in, her tiny hands cradling a cupcake as if it were the most precious thing in the world. The sight made me smile, but it also stirred the memories of my own childhood—one filled with both joyous moments and painful lessons.

It was here, in this small town, that I had found my footing, albeit wobbly at times. The vibrant mix of storefronts and the relentless beat of daily life had become my refuge, but the reality of my existence felt more like a tightrope walk. For every successful review I crafted, there loomed a nagging fear that my words could shatter someone's dreams. The struggle between loyalty and honesty weighed heavily on me. I had seen the blood, sweat, and tears that the staff poured into the restaurant just a block away, and my pen hovered over the keyboard, torn between admiration and the stark truth.

A familiar figure caught my eye—a tall man with tousled hair and an apron that seemed too large for his lean frame, flinging open the restaurant's door. Jackson. His face bore the marks of long hours, but his smile radiated warmth like the sun breaking through a cloudy sky. He stepped out for a moment, drawing a deep breath as if savoring the world outside before plunging back into the heat of the kitchen. It was no secret that the restaurant was struggling. The numbers didn't lie, but it was the stories behind those numbers that compelled me. Jackson had always welcomed me with open arms, inviting me into his world with a sincerity that made me feel valued. He wasn't just a chef; he was a storyteller who stirred the pot of his life, crafting experiences and flavors that lingered long after the meal was over.

I recalled my first visit to his restaurant, an unexpected detour that turned into a life-changing experience. The moment I stepped inside, the atmosphere enveloped me like a cozy blanket. Strings of warm lights hung low, creating an intimate ambiance that was punctuated by the laughter of patrons gathered around mismatched tables. Each table told a story, a history of shared meals and heartfelt conversations. The walls were adorned with local art—colorful, evocative pieces that spoke of the community's spirit.

Jackson had approached me then, wiping his hands on his apron and extending a welcoming hand. "Welcome! What can I make you today?" he had asked, his eyes twinkling with genuine enthusiasm. I had felt an immediate connection, a sense that this was not just a meal but an experience crafted with love and intention. I had never tasted food like his—each bite was a revelation, a layered masterpiece that reflected the heart of the man who made it. He had shared stories of his childhood, of family gatherings centered around a table filled with the rich, spicy aroma of his mother's recipes. I had been captivated, not just by the food but by the man behind it.

But the glow of those initial moments faded like the last rays of sunlight. The reality of the restaurant industry crept in, bringing with it a relentless tide of challenges. It was easy to critique the culinary world from a distance, to pen words that could lift someone up or tear them down, but standing on that precipice of honesty felt like balancing on a razor's edge.

With Jackson's unwavering spirit guiding me, I felt compelled to dig deeper. The review would reflect more than just a critique of food; it would be a window into the souls of those who made this place what it was. Each staff member had their own story, their struggles echoing in the clatter of dishes and the sizzling of pans. I envisioned the waitress who worked double shifts, her laughter hiding the exhaustion etched beneath her eyes. The dishwasher, a quiet soul whose hands moved deftly but whose heart yearned to be heard.

As the sun dipped lower, the shadows lengthened, and the café began to empty, leaving behind the remnants of conversations shared and memories made. I could hear the soft rustle of leaves in the trees above, a gentle reminder that change was always looming. Inspired, I opened my laptop, the screen illuminating my determined expression as I began to type. My fingers flew across the keys, weaving a tapestry of resilience, vulnerability, and hope.

The words spilled forth, each sentence a thread binding the past to the present. I wrote of Jackson, the beating heart of the restaurant, whose dreams were woven into every dish served. I painted a picture of his kitchen—a chaotic symphony of ingredients, where magic happened amid the chaos. Each chop, sauté, and simmer told a story of dedication, a relentless pursuit of excellence that deserved recognition.

With each keystroke, I felt a weight lifting, the call for compassion echoing in my heart. I knew that my words would carry with them the power to connect, to remind readers that behind every meal served was a story waiting to be told—a recipe for redemption crafted from the ingredients of love, sacrifice, and unyielding passion.

The hum of the café faded into the background as my focus sharpened on the screen before me. With each word I crafted, I felt as though I were painting a vibrant mural of lives lived and dreams pursued within the confines of that bustling restaurant. The air around me shimmered with the echoes of laughter, the clatter of dishes, and the heartfelt conversations that had taken place over countless meals. I could almost see the steam rising from Jackson's creations, curling into the air like whispered secrets shared among friends.

The kitchen was more than just a place of preparation; it was a crucible where flavors mingled, and friendships blossomed amidst the chaos of service. I envisioned the team huddled together, exchanging knowing glances and easy banter as they navigated the intricacies of dinner service. Each member of that crew brought something unique to the table, and their stories were as rich and layered as the dishes they served. I wanted to capture that essence, the intricate ballet of camaraderie that was often overlooked in the relentless pursuit of perfection.

As I continued to write, I felt the weight of my own experiences infusing the narrative. I recalled the moments of doubt that had crept in during my early days as a food writer, the voices in my head questioning my authority and expertise. I had once been an outsider, just a girl who loved food and the stories behind it, but the more I immersed myself in this world, the more I understood the passion that fueled it. I was not just a spectator; I was part of a tapestry woven with the threads of culinary art and human connection.

The restaurant's walls, adorned with photographs of jubilant patrons celebrating milestones, whispered tales of triumph and heartache. It was a sanctuary for those seeking comfort in a bowl of hearty soup or the satisfaction of a well-crafted burger. I imagined the couples who had dined there, sharing their hopes and dreams over candlelit dinners, the laughter of children echoing through the air as they savored the joys of childhood. It was here that people came to find solace, to celebrate life's fleeting moments, and to forge memories that would linger long after the plates were cleared.

In the midst of this reflection, I could not ignore the challenges that threatened to overshadow the beauty. I felt the harsh realities of the industry creeping into my prose, urging me to confront the darkness alongside the light. I thought of the late nights, the exhaustion etched into Jackson's features as he labored tirelessly to create the perfect dish, only to face an empty dining room. The grind was relentless, an uphill battle fought against the tide of changing tastes and economic uncertainties.

Jackson was not merely a chef; he was a visionary, a dreamer navigating a world that often prioritized profit over passion. I admired his tenacity, his refusal to compromise on quality despite the pressure to cut corners. His mission was to create a haven for those who craved authenticity, and I felt a kinship with his desire to share the richness of his culture through food. My fingers danced over the keys, capturing the essence of his journey—a journey fraught with obstacles yet illuminated by the glimmers of hope that emerged in the most unexpected moments.

As I wrapped up the narrative, a surge of excitement coursed through me. I envisioned the reaction of the readers, how they would connect with Jackson's story and the stories of those who worked alongside him. I felt a sense of responsibility to honor their dedication, to shed light on the sacrifices made behind the scenes. This review would not only celebrate the culinary experience but also invite readers to reflect on the human element that breathed life into the restaurant.

With a deep breath, I clicked the "publish" button, my heart racing as if I had just bared my soul to the world. A cocktail of nerves and exhilaration swirled within me as I prepared for the inevitable fallout. I knew there would be reactions—both positive and critical—but I also understood the importance of vulnerability. By embracing honesty, I hoped to foster a dialogue around the complexities of the restaurant industry, encouraging empathy and understanding in a world often clouded by superficial judgments.

My phone buzzed in my pocket, a soft vibration that felt like a gentle nudge from the universe. I pulled it out to find a message from Jackson. "I saw your post. Thank you for sharing our story." His words sent a rush of warmth through me, a validation that transcended the digital realm. I could picture him reading my words, his brow furrowing in concentration before breaking into that signature smile of his.

The sun dipped lower in the sky, casting a warm golden glow across the street. The world around me felt alive, vibrant with possibilities. I rose from the bench, inspired by the thought that my words could spark change, that they might resonate with others who had been silenced by their struggles. I crossed the street, the café's familiar sounds beckoning me closer, urging me to step into that warm embrace once more.

As I pushed open the door, the laughter and chatter enveloped me, washing over me like a comforting tide. I scanned the room, spotting Jackson behind the counter, where he was deftly assembling dishes with the precision of an artist at work. His passion was evident, each movement deliberate and filled with intention. I felt a surge of admiration, recognizing that this was not just about food; it was about connection, community, and the unwavering spirit of those who dared to dream.

"Hey there, food critic," he called out, his eyes twinkling with mischief. "Ready for another round of culinary adventures?"

I laughed, the sound bubbling up from somewhere deep inside me, a spontaneous release of the weight I had been carrying. "Always. Just promise not to hold back this time."

He grinned, that charming smile lighting up his face as he gestured for me to join him at the counter. "I wouldn't dream of it. Let's create something unforgettable."

As I slid into a seat, the kitchen bustling around us, I realized that my journey with Jackson and the restaurant was only just beginning. The scent of spices danced through the air, blending with the warmth of camaraderie, and I knew that together, we would craft stories that transcended the plate. Here, amidst the laughter and the love for good food, I felt truly alive—ready to embrace whatever came next.

The moment I settled into the bustling café, the vibrant pulse of life enveloped me once again. The air was rich with the heady fragrance of freshly brewed coffee and the tantalizing allure of pastries cooling on the counter. A little bell tinkled above the door each time a new customer entered, a joyful announcement that life was still unfolding in its unpredictable manner. I caught snippets of conversation that flitted through the air like butterflies—people sharing their days, their triumphs, their heartaches. It was the kind of atmosphere that reminded you of the world's inherent beauty, even amidst the chaos.

Jackson leaned over the counter, his brow slightly furrowed as he meticulously plated a dish. "You know, I've been thinking about our next special. Something that pays homage to the heart of this community," he mused, his eyes sparkling with ideas. "What do you think about a fusion of flavors that tells a story? We could infuse our dishes with memories."

I watched him as he spoke, a whirlwind of passion and creativity, each word imbued with the essence of his dreams. The way he moved—confident yet grounded—was a dance of devotion, and I felt drawn into his orbit. "How about incorporating local ingredients? The farmer's market has some incredible heirloom tomatoes right now," I suggested, my excitement bubbling over. "We could showcase their vibrant colors and flavors."

"Perfect," he replied, nodding enthusiastically. "Let's do a twist on caprese, but with a touch of spice. Maybe a basil pesto that has a kick to it. We could call it 'Summer's Embrace' or something poetic like that."

I laughed, the sound reverberating in the warm atmosphere. "You're a true romantic at heart, aren't you?"

He winked at me, the kind of playful exchange that felt effortless and familiar. "What can I say? Food is love, and I want everyone who walks through that door to feel it."

In that moment, I realized how intertwined our lives had become. It wasn't just about the food we created or the stories we shared; it was about the connection that blossomed in this space, a sanctuary for dreamers and doers alike. I felt a spark of inspiration ignite within me, a compulsion to capture not just Jackson's culinary vision but the very essence of our community through words. The restaurant had become a microcosm of life itself—a place where vulnerability met creativity, where the mundane transformed into the extraordinary.

As we brainstormed, the restaurant filled with a new energy. Diners filled the tables, their conversations rising and falling like a symphony. I looked around, taking in the vibrant tapestry of people who graced our space: the elderly couple celebrating their anniversary, the group of friends sharing laughter over a bottle of wine, the young parents navigating the chaos of dinner with toddlers in tow. Each individual brought their own story, their own dreams and desires, knitting a complex fabric that bound us all together.

Our chatter was punctuated by the rhythmic clinking of cutlery, the sizzle of pans, and the occasional burst of laughter from the staff, who moved in a choreographed dance. There was Sophie, the bubbly waitress with an infectious laugh, whose spirit brightened even the rainiest of days. And then there was Amir, the stoic but kind-hearted dishwasher, whose quiet presence commanded respect. Each staff member contributed a vital thread to the restaurant's tapestry, and I was eager to weave their stories into my narrative.

With Jackson's infectious enthusiasm fueling me, I pulled out my notebook, ready to capture this beautiful moment in time. I began scribbling furiously, crafting vignettes of the staff, snippets of their lives that would echo the soul of the restaurant. I noted Sophie's tireless dedication, her knack for remembering regulars' orders and their favorite seats, as if each table held a story waiting to be told. Amir's background intrigued me, a tapestry of his own filled with hardships and triumphs that had brought him to this point.

As I jotted down their stories, the connection between our lives felt deeper than ever. This wasn't just a restaurant; it was a community, a living, breathing entity that embraced all who entered its doors. It thrived on laughter and resilience, a testament to the human spirit and its capacity for love and connection.

The evening wore on, and as the golden hour faded into twilight, the restaurant transformed. The warm glow of the lights bathed the space in an inviting ambiance, the clinking of glasses now punctuated by the rich notes of laughter and the melodic hum of conversations. I paused, looking around at the faces illuminated by the soft light, each one a testament to the power of food to bring people together.

"Let's take a moment," Jackson suggested, glancing at the dining room. "What do you say we step outside for a breath of fresh air? The sunset is spectacular tonight."

We slipped out into the cool evening air, the gentle breeze a welcome respite from the warmth of the kitchen. The sky blazed with hues of orange and pink, casting a magical glow over the quaint town square. I stood beside Jackson, soaking in the beauty, feeling as if the universe had conspired to create this perfect moment.

"This is what it's all about, isn't it?" I said, turning to him. "Creating a space where people can connect, where stories are shared over good food."

He nodded, a contemplative expression crossing his face. "Absolutely. It's not just about filling bellies; it's about nourishing souls. Every meal we serve is an opportunity to spark joy, to connect, to heal."

His words resonated deeply within me, igniting a passion that had long simmered beneath the surface. I realized that my role as a writer extended beyond mere observation; it was about weaving those stories together, creating a narrative that celebrated the beautiful complexity of life. I envisioned the words flowing effortlessly, capturing the essence of this place and its people—the laughter, the tears, the dreams intertwined with the aroma of home-cooked meals.

As we returned inside, I felt invigorated, the weight of my responsibilities replaced by a sense of purpose. I was not just a chronicler of food but a storyteller, a bridge between the restaurant and the world outside. I envisioned my next piece—a love letter to the restaurant and its staff, an homage to the dedication that infused every dish with meaning.

The kitchen buzzed with activity as the dinner rush continued, and I dove back into the rhythm of the evening. Jackson moved with grace, his hands working magic as he crafted plates that were as visually stunning as they were delicious. Each dish told a story, a masterpiece that encapsulated the essence of our shared experiences.

As I looked around, I couldn't help but smile at the sight of Sophie effortlessly balancing a tray of dishes while cracking jokes with a table of delighted diners. Amir was there too, his eyes lighting up with pride as he caught sight of the rave reviews the patrons were giving for the night's special. The restaurant was alive with energy, and I felt honored to be a part of it, to witness the unfolding of dreams and the healing power of food.

With my notebook in hand, I began jotting down snippets of the night—moments of laughter, the joy on diners' faces, the palpable sense of community. Each word I wrote felt like a promise to honor the stories that deserved to be told, weaving a narrative that celebrated the resilience of those who dared to dream.

As the night wore on, I knew that this was more than just a restaurant; it was a testament to the human spirit and its relentless pursuit of connection, joy, and love. Together, Jackson and I were crafting something beautiful, a narrative that would linger long after the last plate was cleared. In this kitchen filled with laughter and love, we were creating not just food, but memories that would be savored long after the last bite.

Chapter 20: The Price of Honesty

The morning light filtered through the thin curtains of my cramped studio apartment, casting a warm, golden hue over the cluttered space. The air was heavy with the lingering scent of last night's hastily brewed coffee, and the silence was almost palpable, broken only by the soft buzz of my phone, a constant reminder that my world was shifting beneath me. As I swung my legs out of bed, the cold wooden floor sent a shiver up my spine, snapping me into reality. The notifications piled up like autumn leaves, vibrant yet ominous, each one a testament to the tumult my words had unleashed.

I pulled my phone closer, heart racing as I thumbed through the messages. My review—a piece I had poured my soul into—had gone live the night before, and while it garnered a chorus of applause from those who valued my authenticity, it also unleashed a torrent of anger from the very man whose establishment I had dared to scrutinize. The restaurant owner, a towering figure known for his culinary prowess, had become a titan of social media outrage. He painted me as a jaded critic, wielding my pen like a weapon, intent on dismantling his empire.

With each scathing comment, my stomach churned, a tempest of dread swirling within me. "You're just jealous!" one user proclaimed, while another accused me of wanting my fifteen minutes of fame at his expense. I could almost hear their laughter, mocking me through the screen, as if the digital world had transformed into a gladiatorial arena where I stood, vulnerable and exposed. I was no stranger to criticism; as a writer, I had weathered my share of storms. But this was different. This felt personal, and the stakes were higher.

Just as despair threatened to swallow me whole, the familiar sound of a knock jolted me from my spiraling thoughts. Jackson, my unwavering friend and confidant, strolled in unannounced, his presence a calming balm against my mounting anxiety. With tousled hair and an easy smile, he carried an air of nonchalance that could soothe even the most turbulent of storms. He tossed a bag of freshly baked croissants onto the cluttered table, the buttery aroma wrapping around me like a warm embrace.

"Good morning, sunshine!" he exclaimed, plopping down on the chair opposite mine. "I brought breakfast. You need fuel for the day." His cheerfulness contrasted sharply with the chaos unfolding in my mind, yet it was precisely what I needed.

"Fuel?" I echoed, my voice a strained whisper. I glanced back at my phone, the notifications still pouring in. "More like kindling for a raging fire."

Jackson leaned forward, resting his chin on his hand, his eyes sparkling with mischief. "What are you worried about? This is the price of honesty, right? You knew it would ruffle some feathers."

I sighed, allowing the weight of his words to settle around me. He was right, of course. Honesty, while liberating, often came at a cost. "I just didn't expect this kind of backlash. I wanted to shine a light on the flaws, to help people make informed choices. Instead, I feel like a pariah."

With a knowing nod, he reached across the table and squeezed my hand, his grip firm yet gentle. "Let them say what they want. You're doing something important. This isn't just about one review; it's about creating conversations, challenging the status quo. Remember why you started writing in the first place."

His words resonated with a truth I often needed reminding of. I wasn't just a critic; I was a storyteller, an advocate for authenticity in a world that often preferred to sweep imperfections under the rug. The thought gave me a small flicker of courage, one I clung to like a life raft amid a sea of uncertainty.

As the two of us munched on the warm, flaky pastries, I let the comfort of Jackson's presence seep into my bones. Each bite melted in my mouth, a reminder that life still held simple joys amidst chaos. Outside, the world continued its dance; cars rushed past, horns honked, and the sun climbed higher, casting a radiant glow over the iconic skyline. The city thrummed with energy, a vibrant heartbeat that both exhilarated and terrified me.

"I think I need to go to the restaurant," I finally said, determination surging through me. "I can't just hide behind my computer and let him bully me into silence. I owe it to my readers—and to myself—to face this head-on."

Jackson raised an eyebrow, the corners of his mouth curling into a playful smirk. "You're not going to challenge him to a duel, are you? Because I'm not sure they'd allow it in the dining room."

I chuckled, feeling the tension in my shoulders ease slightly. "No duels, just a conversation. I want to understand his perspective. Maybe even apologize if I went too far."

"Apologize?" He feigned shock, hand over his heart. "Now, that's a twist I didn't see coming! But seriously, if you feel you've crossed a line, it might be worth it. Just remember, you're not the villain in this story."

I nodded, the weight of his encouragement settling comfortably on my shoulders. "You're right. This isn't about me being right or wrong; it's about finding common ground." The thought invigorated me, the kind of energy that made my heart race with anticipation. The prospect of facing my fears, however daunting, was a step toward reclaiming my narrative.

With my resolve firming, I finished the last bite of my croissant, savoring the buttery richness. As I wiped the crumbs from my fingers, I caught Jackson watching me, his expression a mix of pride and amusement.

"Go get 'em, tiger," he said, his voice imbued with affection.

I smiled back, fueled by a sense of purpose that burned brighter than the criticism swirling around me. I was ready to step into the lion's den and confront the very man whose legacy had come under scrutiny. The vibrant pulse of the city beckoned me, and I answered with a heart full of hope, ready to rewrite the story I had inadvertently sparked.

The streets hummed with life as I made my way to the restaurant, the morning sun casting a golden sheen on the iconic buildings that loomed overhead. Each step felt heavy yet invigorating, the weight of my decision pressing down like a leaden cloak while simultaneously infusing me with a surge of adrenaline. The city, with its symphony of honking horns, distant chatter, and the sizzling promise of street food, thrived around me, oblivious to my inner turmoil. I had become a figure in a painting, vibrant yet vulnerable, my brushstrokes etched with uncertainty.

As I approached the restaurant, a sprawling space draped in dramatic black awnings and adorned with potted plants that drooped slightly, I couldn't shake the feeling of being a fool. This was the establishment I had critiqued, its owner—a titan who had built his empire on the very culinary dreams I had dismantled. I straightened my posture, reminding myself of Jackson's words. It wasn't just about facing him; it was about standing up for my voice, about reclaiming the narrative that had spiraled out of control.

The door swung open with a jingle, the sounds of clinking dishes and spirited conversation enveloping me like a warm embrace. I inhaled deeply, the aroma of spices and freshly baked bread wrapping around me, tugging at the corners of my heart with nostalgia. This was not just a restaurant; it was a world of flavors, laughter, and memories, and here I was, a critic standing on the threshold, prepared to confront the chaos I had stirred.

The hostess, a vibrant woman with bright pink hair and an infectious smile, greeted me with a cheerful nod. "Welcome! Do you have a reservation?"

"Uh, no, just here to see the owner," I managed, my voice steadier than I felt.

She raised an eyebrow, curiosity sparkling in her gaze. "He's a bit busy at the moment, but I can see if he can spare a minute. Are you—"

"Is it about the review?" The voice cut through the ambient noise like a knife, rich and smooth like aged whiskey.

I turned, locking eyes with the restaurant owner himself. He was just as I had imagined—tall, with salt-and-pepper hair slicked back, and a look of authority etched across his chiseled features. There was a charisma about him, a magnetic presence that commanded attention, yet it was laced with an unmistakable hint of hostility, as if I had just walked into his lion's den uninvited.

"I'm here to talk about the review," I said, taking a cautious step forward.

"Right this way," he replied, gesturing for me to follow him to a secluded corner table, the atmosphere thickening with unspoken tension.

As we settled into our seats, I couldn't help but notice the decor—dark wood accents and walls adorned with vibrant artwork depicting bustling street scenes and bountiful harvests. This place had character, much like its owner. A waiter approached, setting down two glasses of water, and I could sense the anticipation simmering in the air, a cocktail of anxiety and determination ready to be stirred.

"I appreciate you coming," he said, his voice low yet tinged with defiance. "I didn't think you'd have the guts to show your face after that hit piece."

My heart raced, and for a moment, I was taken aback by his raw honesty. "I didn't come here to fight," I replied, striving for a calmness I barely felt. "I came to discuss my review and the feedback you had. I think it's important for us to understand each other."

"Understand?" He leaned back, crossing his arms. "You think your words don't have consequences? You turned my restaurant into a spectacle for your audience, and now I'm the villain in this story. You've created a narrative that could ruin everything I've built."

The room felt smaller, the walls closing in as the gravity of his words weighed heavily between us. I could feel the heat rising in my cheeks, a rush of defensiveness surging through me. "That wasn't my intention! I wanted to highlight the experience, to foster improvement. I thought that was the purpose of honest criticism."

He studied me for a moment, his expression softening slightly, revealing cracks in his steely exterior. "Honesty doesn't always mean truth. Your truth doesn't reflect my reality. There's a story behind every plate, every ingredient I choose. I put my heart into this place."

I took a deep breath, my own defenses crumbling. "I understand that now. I didn't fully appreciate the weight of my words until they echoed back at me. I just wanted to encourage a dialogue about quality and innovation. Maybe we both need to listen more."

The restaurant owner uncrossed his arms, the tension dissipating slightly as he leaned forward. "You're young, passionate, and unafraid. I respect that. But let me tell you, the restaurant world is brutal. Every decision I make is scrutinized, and I can't afford to falter. I'm not just running a business; I'm maintaining a legacy."

His vulnerability struck a chord within me, a reminder that we were both human, grappling with our own demons. "I didn't mean to put your legacy at risk," I said softly. "I'd like to work together, to highlight the positive aspects of your restaurant while also being honest about areas that could use improvement. Perhaps we could create a follow-up piece?"

A flicker of surprise crossed his face, quickly replaced by contemplation. "You think the audience would be interested in that? A redemption arc, if you will?"

"Why not?" I smiled, emboldened by the possibility. "It could show the growth and evolution of your establishment. It's a chance for us to reshape the narrative together, to show that criticism can lead to improvement, not just destruction."

He chuckled, a low rumble that softened the tension in the air. "You're either incredibly brave or incredibly foolish, but I'm intrigued."

Our conversation began to flow, the edges of animosity blurring as we shared stories of passion and ambition. I spoke about my journey as a writer, the mistakes I'd made, and the lessons I'd learned. In turn, he opened up about his own trials and tribulations—the sleepless nights and the sacrifices that came with pursuing excellence in a world that often favored mediocrity.

As we parted ways, the weight of the world on my shoulders felt lighter, the initial storm of backlash now a distant memory. The sun cast long shadows on the pavement as I stepped back into the city's embrace, my heart buoyed by the unexpected connection we had forged. This wasn't just about me anymore; it was about the intricate tapestry of stories, perspectives, and growth that we were all part of.

And as I walked away, I couldn't help but smile, the thrill of possibility tingling at my fingertips. There was power in honesty, and now, there was hope in collaboration. The price of honesty was steep, but perhaps, in the end, it was worth every penny.

The soft whisper of the wind greeted me as I stepped outside, brushing past the city's familiar chaos. My heart thumped in rhythm with the pulse of the streets, each footfall resonating like a drumbeat in the vibrant cityscape. The sun had climbed higher, drenching the buildings in warm, golden light that spilled like honey over the concrete, illuminating the path ahead. Each step away from the restaurant felt like shedding layers of doubt, leaving behind the anxiety that had clung to me like a second skin. I was no longer just the critic facing down a titan; I was a participant in a narrative much larger than myself.

As I wandered the streets, my mind replayed the conversation, each word unfolding like a delicate origami flower. The restaurant owner's fierce passion for his craft mirrored my own fervor for writing. In the world of culinary artistry, every dish was a labor of love, a testament to dreams both realized and thwarted. And in the realm of writing, every sentence danced with the hope of connection, the desire to bridge the chasm between thought and emotion. With every encounter, I was learning that our stories intertwined like the tendrils of smoke rising from a street vendor's grill, twisting together to form something beautiful.

The bustle of the city provided a comforting backdrop as I navigated through crowds. I could hear the chatter of families sharing meals at outdoor tables, the clink of glasses, and the laughter of children darting in and out of the throngs of people. It was a melody of life that enveloped me, reminding me that I was part of this vibrant tapestry. I smiled at a couple sharing a tender moment over brunch, their eyes sparkling with affection, and felt a warmth blossom within me. In the chaos of my own doubts, love and connection still flourished in every corner of this urban landscape.

With each passing block, the weight of the morning's turmoil faded, replaced by a newfound clarity. I pulled my phone from my pocket, heart racing not from anxiety, but anticipation. I needed to write, to channel the energy swirling inside me into something tangible, something transformative. There was a story to tell, one that could reshape perceptions and bring the city's heartbeat to life through my words.

I settled at a small café adorned with twinkling fairy lights and rustic wooden tables, a haven amidst the clamor of the streets. The aroma of freshly brewed coffee wafted through the air, wrapping around me like a comforting shawl. I ordered a latte, the barista's hands moving deftly as she crafted intricate patterns in the foam.

As I took my first sip, the warmth spread through me, igniting my creativity.

My fingers danced across the keyboard, words spilling forth like an unrestrained river. I wrote not just about the restaurant, but about the passion behind it, the dreams forged in the heat of the kitchen, and the human connections that fed it. I wove a narrative that highlighted the resilience of those who dared to create, who poured their souls into their work despite the relentless scrutiny of the world. This piece would showcase not only the restaurant's flaws but also the triumphs, an ode to the very essence of what it meant to pursue one's passion against all odds.

Just as I lost myself in my writing, the café door swung open, allowing a rush of fresh air to sweep in, mingling with the rich scents of coffee and pastries. In walked a familiar figure, her blonde hair catching the light like spun gold. It was Sarah, my friend and fellow writer, with an exuberance that lit up the room. She spotted me instantly, her eyes brightening as she made her way over.

"Hey, I thought that was you!" she exclaimed, her voice a melodic burst of energy. "Mind if I join?"

"Not at all!" I beamed, motioning to the empty chair.

As she settled in, she glanced at my laptop, curiosity dancing in her gaze. "What are you working on? You look deep in thought."

"I'm rewriting my piece on that restaurant—trying to focus on the heart of the matter, you know?" I gestured animatedly, my enthusiasm spilling over. "It's not just about the food but the people behind it, their dreams, their struggles."

Sarah nodded, a knowing smile gracing her lips. "That sounds incredible. It's so easy to forget the humanity behind businesses, especially in a city that often feels so cold and uninviting."

Her insight sparked a deeper conversation between us, a whirlpool of ideas and reflections. We shared stories of our own journeys, the struggles we faced in the cutthroat world of writing.

I told her about the backlash, how it had threatened to stifle my voice, and how the restaurant owner's vulnerability had changed my perspective.

"It's like a mirror, isn't it?" she mused, tapping her fingers against her coffee cup. "We all have our battles, and sometimes we just need someone to remind us that we're not alone."

Her words resonated deeply, settling in the crevices of my mind. We discussed the importance of empathy in storytelling, the art of weaving narratives that brought people together rather than tearing them apart. In that small café, surrounded by the bustle of life, I felt a spark of hope igniting within me—a reminder that every story, whether sweet or bitter, held the power to change hearts and minds.

As the sun dipped lower in the sky, casting a warm glow through the café windows, I knew I had to channel this energy into my writing. I opened a blank document and began anew, each keystroke an act of defiance against the negativity that had threatened to silence me. I infused my words with the stories of the restaurant staff, their passion for culinary art, and their dedication to serving the community. I wrote of the flavors that danced on the palate and the atmosphere that wrapped around diners like a comforting embrace.

Time slipped away unnoticed, and when I finally paused to catch my breath, I glanced at Sarah. She was engrossed in her own writing, her brow furrowed in concentration. I admired her dedication, a reminder of the bond we shared as creators navigating the unpredictable waters of our craft.

As we gathered our things, the sun began to set, painting the sky in hues of pink and orange. We stepped outside, the cool evening air refreshing against our skin. The city felt different now, alive and full of promise, the chaos harmonizing into a symphony of life. I turned to Sarah, excitement bubbling within me.

"Let's make a pact," I suggested, my voice filled with conviction. "Let's commit to uplifting each other's stories, to ensuring our words reflect not just our own truths but the collective experience of those around us."

She nodded, a smile brightening her face. "Absolutely. Our voices are powerful, and together, we can make a difference."

With that, we parted ways, the city's heartbeat thrumming in sync with our renewed sense of purpose. As I walked home, I felt the weight of my earlier doubts lifting, replaced by a sense of clarity and determination. The narrative I had begun to weave was not just a reflection of my own journey but a tribute to the tapestry of experiences that bound us all.

That night, I settled into bed with a contented sigh, the warmth of the city still lingering around me. My heart brimmed with stories waiting to be told, a kaleidoscope of voices eager to be heard. And as I closed my eyes, I felt a profound connection to the world outside, an understanding that in the end, honesty—while it may carry a price—could lead to a beauty and resilience that transcended the moment, connecting us all in a shared human experience.

Chapter 21: The Comfort of Family

The café buzzed with the gentle hum of conversation, a soft symphony of laughter and clinking cups blending seamlessly into the fabric of the afternoon. Sunlight filtered through the large bay windows, casting golden beams that danced across the worn wooden tables. I could smell the rich, earthy scent of coffee mingling with the sweet notes of buttery croissants and cinnamon rolls that beckoned from the glass display case. Each pastry seemed to whisper promises of comfort, but I was here for something much more substantial than mere calories; I craved the warmth of connection, the reassurance of a friend who understood me better than I often understood myself.

Amelia sat across from me, her dark curls bouncing slightly as she leaned in, her gaze piercing through the noise, anchoring me in this chaotic swirl of emotions. Her vibrant personality lit up the cozy corner where we often found refuge. Today, however, my heart felt like a storm, and I was desperate for an umbrella. I took a deep breath, allowing the familiar scent of the café to wrap around me like a well-loved blanket. "They just don't get it, do they?" I said, my voice tinged with frustration as I ran my fingers through my hair, the strands slipping through my grasp like the fleeting moments of clarity I desperately sought.

Amelia reached out, her hand warm and steady on mine. "You're doing something important, sis," she replied, her tone unwavering, each word a gentle nudge toward the light I had momentarily lost sight of. "You're shining a light on the truth." Her confidence in me felt like the first rays of dawn breaking through a long, dark night. I could almost hear the clattering of coffee cups fading into the background as her words echoed in my mind, taking root amidst the noise.

I couldn't shake the heaviness that had settled in my chest like an unwelcome guest. The recent backlash felt like a tidal wave, crashing over the carefully constructed sandcastle of my beliefs. Each wave had pulled away grains of confidence, leaving behind a shoreline littered with doubt. I had tried to advocate for something that mattered, to raise voices often drowned out by the cacophony of societal expectations. But instead of understanding, I had faced hostility and skepticism that had left me reeling.

"Sometimes, I wonder if it's worth it," I confessed, my voice dropping to a whisper as I stared into my half-finished cup, the surface swirling like my thoughts. "Am I really making a difference, or am I just another voice lost in the noise?" I could feel the weight of uncertainty pressing down on me, and it threatened to suffocate the flickering flame of passion I had fought so hard to ignite.

"Every voice counts," Amelia insisted, her eyes fierce with conviction. "You're not just speaking for yourself; you're speaking for those who can't. You have this incredible ability to connect with people, to make them feel seen. That's rare, and it's powerful." I watched as her enthusiasm poured out, each word colored with sincerity and warmth. She believed in me, even when I struggled to believe in myself.

As the world around us continued its vibrant dance, I could feel my resolve beginning to stir within, a flicker of fire kindling at the base of my heart. The café's walls, adorned with local art and photos of patrons who had come and gone, felt like a sanctuary, a place where creativity and vulnerability intertwined like the patterns of sunlight filtering through the window. I imagined each frame holding a story, a heartbeat from lives lived fully, and it made me want to share my own story even more.

"Maybe I just need to find a way to channel all this," I murmured, letting the idea roll around my mind like a forgotten song, echoing against the edges of my worries. "To transform this frustration into something beautiful."

Amelia's smile widened, and in that moment, I saw the spark of a plan flicker to life in her eyes. "Why don't we do it together?" she proposed, leaning back in her chair, her enthusiasm contagious. "You have your platform, your words, and I have my art. Let's create something that showcases those stories, that highlights the truth you're so passionate about."

A thrill shot through me at her suggestion, weaving between excitement and uncertainty like the intertwining branches of the trees that lined the nearby park. The possibilities stretched before us like a blank canvas, waiting for our brushes to dance across its surface. "You really think we can make that happen?" I asked, my heart racing with the idea of merging our passions into one harmonious creation.

"Absolutely!" she exclaimed, her eyes sparkling with the promise of adventure. "Imagine it: a collection of stories paired with your insights, combined with my artwork. It would be a celebration of voices and truths, a tapestry of experience. We could call it 'Echoes of Truth.'"

Her words resonated within me, striking chords I had almost forgotten existed. The thought of weaving together narratives, of creating a bridge between my mission and her artistic flair, felt like the exact antidote to the weight I had been carrying. With each detail we brainstormed, the fog of doubt began to lift, replaced by a palpable energy that crackled between us.

As we sat there, two dreamers entwined in a shared vision, I felt the roots of my passion deepen into the ground, anchoring me against the tides of uncertainty. I realized then that in the midst of chaos, there was always a way to find light—sometimes, you just had to create it yourself, armed with nothing but the courage to speak and the support of a true friend.

The sun dipped low, casting a golden hue across the café's wooden floors as I watched Amelia sketching furiously in her notebook. Her brow furrowed in concentration, and I marveled at the way her fingers danced over the page, translating the vibrant energy of our conversation into sweeping lines and intricate patterns. I felt a swell of gratitude for her presence, a warm blanket against the chill of self-doubt that often crept in uninvited.

We had agreed that this collaboration would not only be an expression of our individual talents but a celebration of the human experience—the messy, chaotic, beautiful tapestry that wove us all together. I could already envision how our combined efforts might breathe life into the stories I had been so eager to share. "Amelia," I began, my voice barely above a whisper, as though speaking too loudly might shatter the delicate thread of inspiration that hung in the air, "what if we included real voices in our project? Like, invite people to share their stories too?"

She looked up, her eyes sparkling with enthusiasm, and nodded vigorously. "That's brilliant! We could create a space for people to contribute their truths, their experiences. It could be a community-driven initiative!" The idea of opening the floodgates to others' narratives ignited something within me, a flicker of excitement that had been missing from my own writing lately. Perhaps I had been so focused on the backlash and the challenges that I had forgotten the raw power of connection.

As the idea began to take shape, we brainstormed logistics, our conversation flowing seamlessly like the coffee from the barista's pot. I could see it now—an online platform where stories could be shared anonymously, if desired, a safe haven where vulnerability met strength. We would craft prompts that invited honesty, encouraging people to bare their souls and share the truths they often kept hidden, the truths that had shaped them, just as they had shaped me.

The sun continued its descent, the café's ambiance shifting as evening crept in. Twinkling fairy lights began to glow, casting a warm, ethereal light that wrapped around us like a comforting embrace. I could feel the weight of my worries lifting, replaced by an electrifying sense of purpose. My fingers tingled with the desire to write, to create—a feeling I had not experienced in far too long.

"Let's meet every week to work on this," I suggested, my heart racing at the thought of our impending creative journey. "We can set deadlines, keep each other accountable. It'll be like our own little writer's retreat."

Amelia beamed at me, and I could tell she felt it too—the magic of possibility sparking between us. "Absolutely! And we can organize community meet-ups to share our progress, maybe even host a launch event to celebrate the stories we gather."

The notion of bringing together a group of like-minded individuals, all drawn by a common thread of authenticity, sent a ripple of anticipation through me. In that moment, the chaotic backlash I had faced felt like a distant memory, overshadowed by the vibrant light of our new project. It was clear that this would be a labor of love, and I relished the idea of inviting others to share in that joy.

As we crafted our vision, I couldn't help but picture the types of stories that might emerge from this endeavor. Perhaps there would be a young woman sharing her experience of overcoming societal pressures to conform, or a man recounting his journey of self-discovery after a painful breakup. I imagined a rainbow of narratives, each unique yet united in their quest for understanding and connection.

As the evening deepened, the café buzzed with the chatter of patrons and the hiss of the espresso machine. The air was thick with warmth and camaraderie, each person wrapped in their own world of stories, joys, and sorrows. I felt a kinship with them, with all the souls who had ever wandered into this sanctuary seeking comfort, connection, or simply a good cup of coffee.

"I think we should call for submissions right away," I said, my enthusiasm bubbling over like the frothy milk in my cappuccino. "Let's create a social media page, start building a community before we even launch the project."

Amelia nodded, already scribbling notes in her sketchbook, her creative energy flowing freely. "We'll create a hashtag—something catchy that invites people in. It could be as simple as EchoesOfTruth."

The phrase rolled off her tongue like music, and I felt a shiver of excitement at the thought of seeing it spread across screens, a beacon calling others to share their stories. "Yes! It feels like a rallying cry, a call to arms for authenticity."

With every passing moment, the world outside faded into insignificance, and it was just the two of us, lost in a whirlwind of ideas and aspirations. The light in the café had shifted from golden to a deeper, richer hue, enveloping us in a cocoon of creativity. I could feel my heart swelling with hope, my spirit ignited by the knowledge that together, we were forging something beautiful.

As the evening unfolded, laughter and spirited discussions surrounded us, wrapping us in the energy of a bustling community. My eyes wandered around the room, catching glimpses of other patrons lost in their own conversations, the way their hands animatedly punctuated their words, how their laughter cut through the ambient noise like a knife through butter.

Amelia's voice broke through my reverie. "Let's do a soft launch, maybe just a small gathering of friends and family to get the ball rolling." Her enthusiasm was infectious, and I could see the dream of our project blooming like the first flowers of spring.

"Yes! We can showcase some artwork, maybe even read a few pieces. It'll be an intimate gathering to set the tone for what's to come." I felt my excitement bubbling over, a fizzy drink ready to burst free from its bottle.

As we continued to flesh out the details, I realized that this project was not just a diversion from the chaos that had consumed me; it was my lifeline, my opportunity to turn pain into purpose. The idea of crafting a community based on shared experiences felt like a balm for my weary heart, an antidote to the bitterness that had threatened to take root.

With every word exchanged, every idea nurtured, I felt a new sense of direction solidifying within me. Together, Amelia and I were not just creating a platform; we were igniting a movement—a celebration of truth and vulnerability that could ripple through our lives and the lives of countless others. The chaos that once clouded my vision was beginning to clear, revealing a vibrant path ahead, and I knew I wouldn't have to walk it alone.

The days melted into one another as Amelia and I dove headfirst into our project, the echoes of truth reverberating in every conversation and brainstorm. Each morning, the café became our sanctuary, the rich aroma of coffee infusing our spirits with renewed energy as we mapped out the contours of our vision. The barista, a kind woman with an ever-present smile, learned our usual orders—two steaming cups of coffee and a basket of warm pastries. She became an unofficial member of our creative team, her laughter a backdrop to our passionate discussions about community, stories, and authenticity.

We began to reach out to friends, inviting them to share their experiences, their laughter and their tears woven into the tapestry of life. The response was overwhelming. As each story poured in, the richness of human experience began to take shape before us. I felt like a conductor, orchestrating a symphony of voices that blended into a beautiful cacophony of shared truths. Each narrative added depth to our project, transforming it into something far more significant than I had initially envisioned. There was something electric about knowing we were gathering the unvarnished stories of real people—stories of heartbreak, triumph, love, and resilience.

One afternoon, Amelia and I sat together in a sun-drenched corner of the café, our laptops open but forgotten for the moment. Instead, we engaged in a heart-to-heart discussion about the submissions we'd received. Amelia's sketches lay scattered across the table, doodles of people intertwined in a web of colorful threads representing their stories.

"I never realized how similar our experiences can be," I mused, picking up a drawing of a woman with flowing hair and a gentle smile. "It's astonishing how we all face our battles, yet we think we're alone in the fight."

"That's the beauty of it," Amelia replied, her eyes shining with understanding. "In sharing, we not only validate our own experiences but also give others permission to be vulnerable." She glanced down at her sketches, a mixture of determination and hope flooding her expression. "This is what we need more of in the world. A reminder that we're not isolated islands but part of a vast archipelago of shared humanity."

Her words wrapped around me like a comforting scarf. I realized then that this was no longer just a project; it was a mission, a lifeline for so many seeking solace in a world that often felt indifferent. Each submission came with a backstory—some were triumphant, while others were painful testaments to the struggles people faced daily. Yet, amid the sorrow, there was always an undercurrent of resilience, a refusal to be defined by the hardships.

As we delved deeper into the project, we began to notice a theme emerging—a thread that connected many of the stories. It was the concept of "home." Each contributor defined home differently; for some, it was a physical space filled with familiar scents and laughter, while for others, it was the people who held their hearts, no matter where they found themselves. This realization ignited a spark in me, fueling my desire to explore the idea of home further, both in our project and in my own life.

One crisp evening, as the sun dipped below the horizon, I decided to take a walk to clear my mind. The streets were alive with the sounds of laughter and chatter, the air tinged with the scent of autumn leaves. I wandered down familiar paths, my feet guiding me to the small park where I had spent countless afternoons as a child. The swings creaked softly in the breeze, and the old oak tree stood tall, its branches swaying gently, whispering secrets of the past.

Sitting on a nearby bench, I closed my eyes and let the memories wash over me. I thought about my family—my parents, who had always been the steadying force in my life, and how their love had created a sanctuary in the midst of chaos. It struck me that perhaps I had underestimated the importance of that sense of belonging, the unwavering support that came from the people we call family. They were my anchor, a constant reminder that I was never truly alone in my journey.

Inspired by this reflection, I returned to the café, eager to share my insights with Amelia. We spent hours discussing the connection between home and the stories we were collecting. What if we framed the project around this concept? What if we created a dedicated section that invited contributors to explore their definitions of home, both joyful and painful?

The following weeks were a whirlwind of creativity and collaboration. Our initial idea blossomed into a multi-faceted project, encompassing not only written narratives but also visual art, poetry, and even audio recordings. We invited local artists to showcase their work, transforming the café into a gallery of sorts, adorned with vibrant pieces that echoed the stories we were gathering.

As the launch event approached, excitement surged through the air. I could feel the anticipation building, not only within myself but in the hearts of everyone involved. The café buzzed with activity as we prepared for the evening. Amelia and I spent hours arranging art pieces, curating playlists, and designing a cozy reading nook where contributors could share their stories aloud.

On the night of the event, the café transformed into a haven of warmth and light. Fairy lights twinkled overhead, casting a soft glow on the faces of our guests. The air was filled with the mingling scents of coffee and pastries, but more importantly, it was infused with a palpable sense of community. Friends, family, and strangers alike gathered, their eyes alight with curiosity and the promise of connection.

As the evening unfolded, I took a moment to step back and observe. People moved from one piece of art to another, pausing to read the stories displayed beside them. Laughter bubbled up in pockets, and voices intertwined, creating a melodic background that spoke of understanding and camaraderie. It was as if the walls of the café held a heartbeat, pulsing with the stories shared and the connections forged.

When the time came for contributions to be read, a hush fell over the crowd. I felt my heart racing as I introduced the first storyteller, a woman whose submission had struck a deep chord within me. Her words, raw and honest, filled the room, and I could feel the weight of her experience settling over us like a soft blanket.

As each story unfolded, the audience leaned in closer, captivated by the authenticity and bravery of those sharing their truths. I realized that this was precisely what we had aimed for—a safe space where vulnerability was met with acceptance, where stories could weave invisible threads between us, binding our hearts in understanding.

The evening stretched into the night, a beautiful tapestry of shared laughter, tears, and moments of connection. As I looked around, I saw friendships blooming, laughter echoing, and the beauty of shared humanity radiating throughout the café. In that moment, I felt an overwhelming sense of gratitude—for Amelia, for the contributors, and for the unexpected gift of belonging that had enveloped us all.

As the final story was shared, I felt a sense of fulfillment wash over me. This project had become so much more than I had ever anticipated; it was a celebration of life in all its messy glory, a reminder that we are never truly alone in our struggles, and a testament to the power of community. Together, we had created something beautiful, something that would resonate far beyond the walls of the café, echoing in the hearts of everyone who dared to share their truth.

Chapter 22: Whisking Away Doubts

My apartment buzzed with the kind of warmth that makes you forget the chill outside. The smell of garlic and herbs wafted from the kitchen, swirling through the air like a promise of delightful indulgence. The sun dipped below the horizon, casting long shadows across the walls adorned with mismatched art pieces that told stories of their own. Each frame held moments—pictures of laughter, of love, and of a life filled with an abundance of experiences. My heart raced with anticipation as I arranged the mismatched tableware, each piece a little treasure from thrift stores and garage sales, each carrying its own history, like the stories waiting to unfold tonight.

The guests trickled in, first Mia, her curly hair bouncing with each step, a smile stretching wide across her face. She was my confidante, my partner-in-crime, and the sister I had chosen for myself. She swept into the room, immediately taking in the ambiance with an approving nod. "I love what you've done with the place! It feels...alive," she said, her eyes sparkling with mischief. The way she effortlessly filled a room with her energy was nothing short of magical, a talent I always admired.

We quickly moved into the kitchen, where the chaos of culinary creativity thrived. Jackson arrived next, bringing with him the aroma of freshly baked bread, warm and inviting, like a comforting hug after a long day. He had an innate ability to bring laughter with just a glance, his playful banter instantly lightening the mood. Together, we formed a trio as dynamic as the flavors we intended to showcase. Jackson's quick wit kept us laughing as Mia recounted tales from her recent culinary adventures, each story sprinkled with an assortment of spices and a dash of drama.

As we prepped the food, I felt my worries begin to dissolve, whisked away like flour in a mixing bowl. I had spent far too long second-guessing myself, my worth, my abilities, and this gathering was my remedy—a moment to reclaim my passion and share it with others. The vibrant colors of the vegetables brought life to the counter, each one a vibrant note in our culinary symphony. I sliced through peppers, their sweet fragrance dancing in the air, while Mia chopped herbs with the precision of a seasoned chef.

The kitchen transformed into a haven of camaraderie, laughter echoing off the walls, creating an atmosphere so thick with warmth that it felt like being wrapped in a cozy blanket on a cold winter night. Jackson playfully argued about the merits of using butter over olive oil, his arms animated as he brought the conversation to life. I couldn't help but laugh at their antics, feeling a sense of belonging that filled the space beyond the physical boundaries of the room.

As we transitioned from preparation to presentation, the table took on a personality of its own, each dish contributing to the storytelling of the evening. A vibrant salad adorned with edible flowers, glistening under the soft golden light, took center stage. Next to it, a steaming pot of pasta shimmered invitingly, the rich aroma of tomatoes and basil intertwining and filling the air with a promise of comfort. I carefully placed a bottle of wine on the table, its deep red hue a perfect match for the evening's theme of warmth and connection.

Mia and Jackson stepped back, surveying our work with pride. "We did this," I murmured, my voice thick with emotion. This wasn't just a meal; it was a testament to our friendship, a celebration of the lives we lived in this little corner of the world. It was an invitation to share our journeys through the universal language of food.

As the doorbell rang, a flurry of butterflies danced in my stomach. The first wave of guests arrived, bringing with them the promise of shared laughter and stories waiting to be told. Friends, neighbors, and a couple of local chefs we had invited mingled into the room, their eyes lighting up as they took in the vibrant display before them. I greeted each one with a genuine smile, my heart swelling with gratitude for the community that had come to support our venture.

With every new arrival, the room pulsed with life, a vibrant tapestry woven together by our shared experiences. Conversations blossomed around the table, laughter bubbling up like a lively brook as we shared not just dishes but moments—remembrances of summers spent barbecuing in backyards, of first dates at quaint little bistros, of family gatherings where the food was just as important as the people sharing it.

The clinking of glasses marked the beginning of the evening's festivities, and as we raised our cups to toast, I felt a wave of exhilaration wash over me. This was more than just a gathering; it was a celebration of life, of connection, of our unwavering resolve to embrace the joys and challenges that lay ahead.

As the evening progressed, the stories grew bolder, infused with the spirited essence of our personalities, and the dishes became a reflection of our dreams. The pasta twirled like the hopes we nurtured, while the salad sang the praises of our diversity. In this moment, I realized that the food served was more than nourishment; it was a vessel for love, understanding, and shared laughter—a way to bridge the gaps that sometimes felt insurmountable in our busy lives.

With every bite, we tasted the flavors of not just our town but also the shared dreams that connected us. The gathering had blossomed into something magnificent, transcending the mere act of eating. It was a heartfelt tribute to community, a reminder that we are never alone in our journeys. Together, we laughed, we cried, and we savored the exquisite moments that life graciously offered us, as the night unfolded like the petals of a flower, revealing the beauty that lay within.

The night unfurled like a well-worn story, each moment rich with familiarity and delight. Guests settled in, laughter bouncing off the walls like playful echoes, while I poured the wine—a deep crimson that caught the light, swirling like the very pulse of our gathering. Jackson, ever the charmer, was already regaling a group with tales of his culinary misadventures, embellishing each anecdote with exaggerated gestures and the kind of humor that left everyone gasping for breath. His infectious energy acted like a magnet, pulling people into the narrative, turning my humble apartment into a theatrical stage where every guest had a role to play.

Mia, the calm to Jackson's storm, flitted from group to group, her keen eye for detail ensuring that no glass remained empty and no plate went unfilled. She wore her usual apron—one she had spruced up with an array of colorful patches representing all the places she'd traveled. Each patch told a story, just like the gathering itself, stitching together the lives of those present. I admired her ability to navigate the crowd with grace, her laughter genuine and warm, like the comfort of a favorite blanket on a chilly evening.

As we mingled, I took a moment to step back and observe. The scene was a tapestry woven with vibrant threads: the deep laughter of friends from college, the shared glances of neighbors who had lived alongside each other for years yet never truly connected, and the curious exchanges of local chefs eager to showcase their talent. The dining table, a chaotic yet beautiful medley of dishes, told its own story. There was a fresh caprese salad, the mozzarella so creamy it seemed to melt into the sweet basil, and a rich, savory pot of ratatouille bursting with colors that looked like they had been plucked straight from a sun-drenched garden.

The atmosphere was electric, charged with anticipation and camaraderie. I felt like a conductor, guiding this vibrant orchestra of flavors and personalities, watching as the symphony played out in a delightful crescendo. I caught snippets of conversations floating through the air, each one more fascinating than the last. Stories of culinary dreams, of families passing down recipes, and of forgotten traditions resurfacing like treasures buried in the sands of time filled my heart with joy. It was a celebration not just of food, but of life, of every twist and turn that had led us to this moment.

As the night progressed, I found myself wandering from group to group, pausing to savor the laughter, the connections forming before my eyes. At one table, I overheard a discussion about the best pizza joints in town, each recommendation laced with passionate opinions that ignited a friendly debate. Another corner was alive with tales of culinary school—stories of mishaps and triumphs, dreams deferred and realized, a collective experience that bound them all together. Each conversation felt like a thread being woven into a larger narrative, creating a rich fabric of shared experience.

In a quieter moment, I slipped outside onto my balcony, the cool night air brushing against my skin. The stars twinkled overhead, an ancient canvas painted with stories of their own. I took a deep breath, feeling the weight of the past weeks lift, replaced by an invigorating sense of purpose. The doubts that had clung to me like shadows began to dissipate in the warmth of this gathering. I had created something beautiful, something that reflected not only my passion for food but also my love for the community that had embraced me so fully.

Mia joined me, leaning against the railing with a contented sigh. "You did it, you know," she said, her voice soft yet powerful, breaking the spell of the night's tranquility. "You turned that negative energy into something spectacular."

I smiled, allowing her words to settle within me like a warm embrace. "It feels good, doesn't it? To connect people over food, to share experiences."

She nodded, her gaze drifting toward the twinkling lights of the street below. "It's more than just food. You've brought us all together. That's something really special."

Just then, a burst of laughter erupted from inside, and we both turned to look. The sound washed over me, a reminder of why I had orchestrated this evening. I wanted to create an experience that brought joy, that fostered connections, and reminded us all of the importance of community. It was a mission I had only recently discovered, a path I was eager to explore further.

Mia and I stepped back inside, where the laughter greeted us like an old friend. I was drawn to a conversation unfolding between a local chef and a couple of guests who had just moved to town. The chef was animated, describing his passion for sourcing ingredients locally, the pride evident in his voice. I could feel the energy in the room shift, everyone leaning in, captivated by his enthusiasm.

Feeling inspired, I chimed in, sharing my own experiences with local produce, the joys of visiting farmers' markets, and the incredible stories behind each vendor. The conversation took flight, soaring through ideas and culinary dreams, transforming the gathering into a shared journey of discovery.

As the night wore on, plates were emptied, laughter echoed louder, and connections deepened. Each shared dish had been a vessel, carrying with it not just flavors but stories, memories, and dreams. People exchanged phone numbers and promises to meet again, turning fleeting acquaintances into budding friendships. I reveled in the knowledge that my apartment had transformed into a haven for connection, a sanctuary where worries were forgotten, and the beauty of shared experiences reigned supreme.

The clock ticked away, yet time felt elastic, stretching into a delicious eternity. I watched as friendships blossomed like spring flowers, nourished by laughter and the mutual love for good food. I couldn't help but reflect on how transformative this night had been, how it had whisked away the doubts that had loomed so heavily over me just days before.

And as the last guests prepared to leave, I felt a sense of fulfillment wash over me. This gathering was a beginning, a seed planted in the fertile soil of community, ready to grow into something magnificent. I had turned my doubts into determination, my worries into connections, and with each shared dish and every burst of laughter, I had not only embraced the local food scene but had also carved out a space for myself within it.

The door closed behind the last of my friends, leaving behind an echo of laughter that lingered in the air like the last notes of a beautiful song. I stood in the quiet aftermath, the soft hum of the night enveloping me in a blanket of warmth. In that moment, I realized I was not just part of a community; I was an integral thread in its ever-expanding tapestry.

The remnants of the evening lay strewn across the table, an enchanting collage of half-empty wine bottles, colorful dishes now reduced to tantalizing remnants, and laughter still echoing in the corners of my apartment. The soft clinking of glasses and the distant hum of the city outside felt like the afterglow of a celebratory firework display. I savored the warmth that lingered in my heart, a mix of satisfaction and an eager anticipation for what lay ahead.

As I began clearing the table, Mia and Jackson drifted back into the kitchen, engaged in a lively debate about the best way to tackle the dishwashing. I grinned at their playful bickering, a familiar dance of friendship that felt comforting against the backdrop of my whirlwind evening. Jackson insisted on using the "power soak" technique he swore by, while Mia championed the methodical approach of scrubbing each dish to perfection. I could see both their points, yet my heart was far too full to dwell on such mundane tasks.

"I can't believe how amazing tonight was," I chimed in, wiping down the table with a cloth that still carried the essence of the vibrant meal we had just shared. "It's like we sparked something. I haven't felt this alive in ages."

Mia paused, the dish she was scrubbing momentarily forgotten. "This is just the beginning, you know. People crave connection, especially in a city like this." She tossed her curly hair over her shoulder, eyes glinting with enthusiasm. "We should make this a regular thing—create a community dinner series! Local chefs, themed menus... we could really bring people together!"

Jackson's eyes lit up, his trademark grin emerging. "Imagine the possibilities! We could showcase different cultures, seasonal ingredients, and maybe even host a few cooking challenges! A little friendly competition never hurt anyone."

The more they spoke, the more my heart raced with possibilities. We could create something beautiful, an ongoing celebration of community that transcended the ordinary. I could already envision the vibrant themes we could explore—the warmth of Mediterranean feasts, the spiciness of Caribbean nights, or even the delicate artistry of Japanese cuisine. Each gathering would not just be about the food but about sharing stories, cultures, and the kind of connections that often get lost in the hustle of life.

"Let's not just talk about it," I said, my excitement bubbling over. "Let's plan our first dinner!"

In that moment, the kitchen transformed into a war room of creativity and collaboration. We gathered around the counter, our minds racing as we jotted down ideas, flipping through magazines for inspiration. Jackson insisted on a "Farm-to-Table Fiesta," while Mia had her heart set on a "Gastronomic Journey Through Italy." The options spilled out like an endless buffet of creativity, each one more enticing than the last.

Amid our brainstorming session, the doorbell chimed, slicing through the air. Surprised, I exchanged glances with Mia and Jackson, curiosity piqued. Who could it be? I padded toward the door, a mix of intrigue and excitement thrumming beneath my skin.

Opening it revealed a familiar face: Nora, my neighbor from two floors up. She stood there, breathless and beaming, her arms laden with a wicker basket overflowing with pastries. The scent wafted through the doorway like a gentle embrace, an irresistible invitation to indulge.

"Sorry to drop by so late, but I couldn't resist sharing these," she said, her cheeks flushed from the chill outside. "I just baked a fresh batch of almond croissants and thought you all deserved a treat after such a wonderful evening."

The warmth in her voice struck a chord within me. Nora had always been a bright spot in our building—a single mom with a knack for baking and a heart as generous as the portions she served. Her pastries were legendary in our little community, a symbol of comfort and shared moments.

"Come in! We were just discussing our next dinner," I urged, waving her inside, the scent of pastries mingling delightfully with the remnants of our feast. The atmosphere instantly shifted; Nora's presence added an extra layer of warmth, her enthusiasm contagious as she joined our animated conversation.

The croissants vanished almost as quickly as they had appeared, each flaky layer melting into our appreciative murmurs. As we devoured the delicious pastries, laughter filled the air once more, the conversation weaving around the table, from culinary dreams to everyday anecdotes that painted our lives in vivid strokes.

"Imagine a dinner featuring dessert first!" Jackson exclaimed, his eyes sparkling with mischief. "We could have a 'Reverse Feast' where we start with pastries and end with a savory dish. Who wouldn't want to eat dessert first?"

Nora chuckled, her laughter infectious. "You know, that's not such a bad idea. It's all about breaking the rules, right?"

As the laughter rolled on, I marveled at how our little gathering had blossomed into something greater, something that felt not just exciting but necessary. The connections we were forging felt more like threads weaving a tapestry, intricately linked in the fabric of our shared lives.

The discussions turned deeper, evolving into conversations about our dreams and aspirations. I shared my desire to create a space for local chefs to showcase their talent, a platform where creativity could flourish and connections could deepen. Nora nodded in understanding, her eyes bright with encouragement.

"That's exactly what this city needs," she said, her voice earnest. "We're all looking for places to belong, and food has this magical way of bringing people together."

With every exchanged idea and shared laugh, a community began to form—not just around food but around each other. I could see it so clearly now; this was more than a gathering. It was a seed planted in fertile ground, ready to grow into something magnificent.

As the night deepened and the stars twinkled like diamonds scattered across a velvety sky, we sketched out plans for our first community dinner. Each detail felt like a brushstroke on a canvas, each suggestion a splash of color in our masterpiece of connection.

We settled into a rhythm, a joyful cadence that resonated through the room. The gathering, once a simple celebration of food, had morphed into a powerful movement of community, uniting us in our shared passion and purpose.

With our hearts and minds alight with possibilities, I realized that this was what I had been searching for all along. In the laughter and the shared stories, I found the essence of who I was and who I wanted to be—a connector, a creator, and a passionate advocate for the beauty of community.

As we finalized our plans and shared one last round of croissants, I felt a profound sense of gratitude swell within me. Each person in that room had played a part in illuminating my path, reminding me that together, we could cultivate something beautiful, meaningful, and lasting. And in that moment, I understood that the magic of life often lies not in the grand gestures but in the simplest of connections—the shared meal, the laughter that fills a room, and the stories that bind us all.

Chapter 23: The Dinner Party

The evening unfurled like a vibrant tapestry, each thread colored by the laughter and chatter of friends converging in my modest apartment. As I stood in the kitchen, the aromas danced around me—fresh basil mingled with the tang of ripe tomatoes, while the warmth of freshly baked bread created a comforting cocoon that enveloped the space. The soft glow of the pendant lights above cast a golden hue on everything, creating a sanctuary amidst the clamor of the city outside. I felt as if I were crafting a world entirely my own, each dish a brushstroke on the canvas of the night.

Mia flitted about the kitchen, a whirlwind of energy and enthusiasm, wielding her spatula like a maestro conducting a symphony. Her eyes sparkled with the kind of joy that only comes from doing what you love. "Just a pinch of salt, a dash of lemon zest, and voilà!" she exclaimed, her laughter bubbling up like the simmering sauce on the stove. I couldn't help but grin as I observed her in her element, the way her hands danced around the ingredients, transforming simple components into something extraordinary.

As the sun dipped below the horizon, the amber sky gave way to twilight, painting the windows with a soft indigo light. My friends began to filter in, their voices harmonizing with the sounds of sizzling pans and clinking utensils. Emily, always the jokester, burst through the door with a bottle of wine in one hand and a hilariously large cheese platter in the other. "I figured we could all use a little something to drown our culinary insecurities," she teased, a mischievous glint in her eyes. Her laughter was infectious, and soon we were all caught in its embrace, the weight of our daily struggles momentarily forgotten.

The table, set with mismatched plates and flickering candles, transformed into the heart of our gathering. Each dish emerged from the kitchen like a guest of honor, vibrant and inviting. There was

Mia's signature pasta, its delicate strands coated in a rich marinara, fragrant with garlic and herbs. A fresh Caprese salad lay nestled beside it, the red of the tomatoes and the green of the basil gleaming under the candlelight like jewels waiting to be discovered. I felt a swell of pride, realizing this was more than just a meal; it was a celebration of friendship, creativity, and the comforting rhythm of shared experiences.

As we settled around the table, our laughter mingled with the clinking of glasses. "To friendship!" I proposed, lifting my glass of crisp white wine, the bubbles dancing within it like the fleeting moments we cherished. Everyone echoed the toast, their voices intertwining in a melody of camaraderie that resonated deeply in my heart. We raised our glasses high, a moment suspended in time, encapsulating the essence of what it meant to gather, to share, to belong.

The first bites were met with delighted murmurs. "Mia, you've outdone yourself again!" I heard someone exclaim, and I caught Mia's eyes glimmering with satisfaction. It was as if the world outside had ceased to exist, replaced by the warmth and laughter enveloping us like a soft blanket. Each mouthful was a revelation, flavors exploding in a harmonious dance, igniting memories and sparking stories that flowed as freely as the wine.

"Remember that time we tried to cook together and nearly set the kitchen on fire?" Ryan asked, his laughter echoing through the room. The memory floated to the surface, each of us chiming in, recounting the hilarious details of our culinary misadventure, the charred remains of what was meant to be a simple stir-fry, the fire alarm shrieking like a banshee, and us collapsing into fits of laughter, our dreams of gourmet meals dashed. It was these moments that defined us, moments woven into the fabric of our friendship, rich with humor and love.

As the night wore on, the conversations deepened, each one revealing layers of our lives that had remained hidden in the chaos of our everyday routines. I listened intently as Sarah shared her recent struggles with work, her voice steady but tinged with vulnerability. "I just feel like I'm constantly on a treadmill, running but not getting anywhere," she confessed, her eyes searching for understanding. The room fell silent, each of us nodding in empathy, reminding her of her strength and resilience. It was in these exchanges, in the shared vulnerabilities and triumphs, that our bonds solidified, weaving a tapestry of unwavering support.

The dinner party morphed into a celebration of life itself, a reminder that we were not alone in our struggles. We exchanged dreams and aspirations, each word laced with the threads of hope and possibility. As I watched my friends animatedly discuss their ambitions—traveling to far-off lands, starting their own businesses, or simply finding the courage to be themselves—I felt a surge of gratitude. Here we were, a motley crew of dreamers, daring to navigate our lives together, forging a path filled with joy and laughter.

Later, as the last traces of dinner were cleared away, I pulled out the dessert—a rich chocolate cake, its surface glistening like a dark, velvet night. The first slice was met with gasps of delight, each forkful melting in our mouths, a sweet conclusion to an unforgettable evening. We indulged in the decadence, a fitting end to a night filled with warmth, love, and the sweet realization that life, with all its complexities, was better shared with others.

The laughter continued to echo long into the night, and I marveled at how the simple act of gathering had transformed our disparate lives into a shared narrative. With every story told and every laugh shared, I felt the weight of the world lift, if only for a moment, leaving behind only the warmth of connection and the promise of more nights like this.

With the final crumbs of dessert consumed, the soft murmur of conversation lingered like a lingering note in a beautiful symphony. Plates were cleared, laughter still bubbling in the air, as we settled into the comfortable afterglow of the meal. The table was a canvas of empty glasses and remnants of our feast, each piece a testament to the delightful chaos of our gathering. I leaned back in my chair, taking a moment to appreciate the scene unfolding around me—a vibrant tableau of friends, illuminated by the warm glow of candlelight, animated expressions reflecting the shared joy of the evening.

Mia, ever the entertainer, seized the moment with her signature flair. "Who's up for a little game?" she announced, her eyes sparkling with mischief. Instantly, a chorus of enthusiastic cheers erupted, and I felt a rush of affection for this eclectic group of friends who always seemed to find the fun in any situation. Mia proposed a round of charades, a classic that never failed to elicit giggles and playful banter.

We rearranged ourselves into a circle, and the game commenced with unabashed enthusiasm. I watched as Ryan attempted to mime a particularly challenging movie title, his exaggerated gestures drawing uproarious laughter. "Is it Titanic? No, wait—The Notebook?" Sarah guessed wildly, her brows knitted in concentration. The anticipation hung in the air, thick with the kind of camaraderie that only comes from years of shared memories. The atmosphere pulsed with energy, each round drawing us closer, reminding me of childhood sleepovers filled with laughter and spontaneous silliness.

When my turn arrived, I stood and took a deep breath, summoning my best dramatic flair. I chose a classic—Pride and Prejudice. The reactions were immediate; I had ignited the competitive spirit in the room. As I flailed my arms and struck ridiculous poses, mimicking Mr. Darcy's brooding charm, the laughter crescendoed to a near hysterical level. Emily, ever the witty commentator, shouted, "Don't forget to add the angst, darling!" I collapsed into a fit of giggles, the thrill of the game blurring the lines between our adult lives and the carefree joy of youth.

With each round, we peeled away the layers of pretense, revealing the genuine affection we shared. The laughter became a balm for unspoken worries, a reminder that amid our individual struggles, we were united by the simple joys of friendship. As the game wound down, I caught a glimpse of the clock, the late hour creeping up on us like an uninvited guest. But I felt no urgency to end the evening; the magic lingered, and I wanted to hold onto it a little longer.

The evening transformed as we moved from charades to storytelling, each of us weaving threads of our lives into a rich tapestry. We spoke of our childhood dreams, of the ambitions that had once felt so tangible yet had somehow drifted into the background of adulthood. Sarah shared her dream of becoming a novelist, her eyes bright with passion. "I used to write stories about fantastical worlds where anything was possible," she said, her voice a mix of nostalgia and longing. "I want to reclaim that part of myself, to believe in magic again." Her words resonated deeply within me, echoing the ambitions I had tucked away in the busy corridors of life.

In response, I shared my own dream—one that had morphed over the years but had always simmered beneath the surface. "I want to write," I confessed, my voice steady despite the vulnerability it brought. "To create stories that transport people, just like the ones I read as a kid." The room fell silent, the weight of my admission hanging in the air. I could see the spark of understanding in their eyes, a shared recognition of the importance of pursuing our dreams, no matter how distant they felt.

As the clock ticked on, the conversations ebbed and flowed like the tide, each story a wave that washed over us, leaving behind traces of laughter and reflection. With every tale shared, the bonds between us deepened, fortified by our collective hopes and fears. I felt a profound sense of belonging, the kind that reassures you that even amid life's uncertainties, there exists a sanctuary in friendship.

The evening drew to a close with the soft notes of a playlist I had curated—melodies that danced through the air, inviting us to linger just a little longer. We huddled together on the couch, the remnants of our feast now mere whispers in the background. As we listened, the music wrapped around us like a warm embrace, the gentle notes weaving stories of love, loss, and hope.

I glanced around, my heart swelling at the sight of my friends nestled in their spots, the soft light casting a warm glow on their faces. There was Emily, her head thrown back in laughter, her eyes sparkling with mischief; Ryan, leaning against the armrest, his gaze drifting dreamily towards the ceiling as he contemplated his next adventure; and Mia, who hummed softly along to the tunes, her hands cradling a mug of tea, embodying the calm amidst our joyful chaos.

In that moment, I realized how profoundly grateful I was for this life I had crafted, filled with the love of these incredible people. As we reminisced about our favorite moments of the night, recounting the dishes that had made us swoon and the jokes that had left us gasping for breath, I felt a sense of contentment settle within me. It was a comforting warmth, like curling up in a blanket on a chilly autumn evening, safe and cherished.

Eventually, as the clock signaled the end of the night, we began to gather our things, the reality of the outside world creeping back in. But as I stood in the doorway, watching my friends slip into the cool night, I couldn't shake the feeling that this evening had been a pivotal moment—a reminder of the importance of connection, of laughter, and of pursuing dreams. The air was crisp and fragrant, the stars above twinkling like tiny promises, and I felt a surge of hope blossom within me. We were not just friends; we were a tribe, each of us on our own journey but united in our quest for happiness, fulfillment, and the kind of love that lasts beyond the constraints of time.

As the night unfolded, the laughter and shared stories created a tapestry of connection, weaving our individual lives into a vibrant collective narrative. The atmosphere crackled with energy, each person contributing a thread of their essence. I settled deeper into the couch, surrounded by my friends, our conversations weaving around us like a warm blanket. The music continued to play softly in the background, its gentle melodies providing a serene backdrop to the lively exchanges.

At one point, I glanced at the window, where the city skyline emerged like a mysterious silhouette against the night sky. The twinkling lights mirrored the stars above, a reminder of how our lives intertwined with the greater world outside, a city teeming with its own stories and dreams. For a fleeting moment, I considered the people bustling about below, each lost in their own lives, much like us. Yet here we were, huddled together, creating a sanctuary of shared moments that made the chaos of life feel manageable.

Mia, sensing a lull in the conversation, suggested we share our most embarrassing moments. "Come on, we've all had them!" she prodded, a grin spreading across her face. The challenge hung in the air like an unlit firework, daring us to ignite it with laughter. I took a sip of wine, a smile dancing on my lips as I prepared to divulge my own tale, one that had haunted me for years.

"I was in high school," I began, laughter bubbling up as I recounted the time I accidentally sent a text meant for my best friend to my entire class. "It was an innocent message about my crush, nothing scandalous, but it quickly spiraled into an absolute frenzy. Suddenly, everyone was either offering advice or pretending to be him! The poor guy had no idea what hit him." My friends erupted in laughter, their collective amusement washing over me like a wave, making the embarrassment feel less daunting.

As we shared stories of social faux pas and misadventures, each anecdote was met with roars of laughter and gasps of disbelief. Emily recounted her disastrous attempt at karaoke, her voice soaring embarrassingly off-key, while Ryan talked about the time he wore mismatched shoes to an important presentation. Each story was a reminder that we were all beautifully imperfect, navigating the complexities of life with humor and grace.

The clock ticked away, but the sense of time felt suspended, as if we had created our own little universe where laughter and warmth reigned supreme. The bonds we forged through our shared stories acted as glue, solidifying our friendships even further. In those moments, I felt the comforting weight of belonging; I was not just a participant but an integral part of this colorful tapestry of lives.

As the evening wore on, the discussion turned to aspirations and dreams, and the atmosphere shifted from lighthearted to reflective. We shared our hopes for the future, the whispers of ambition surfacing amidst the laughter. Mia spoke of her desire to open her own restaurant, her voice laced with passion and determination. "I want to create a space where people can come together, not just for food but for connection," she said, her eyes gleaming with excitement.

Inspired by her fervor, I felt the need to share my own ambitions. "I want to write a book," I said, my heart racing slightly. "It's always been a dream of mine, to craft stories that resonate with others." I took a breath, the room silent as my friends leaned in, encouraging me to continue. "I want to explore themes of love and friendship, the beauty of ordinary moments, much like the ones we share."

Their supportive nods buoyed my spirits, filling me with the courage to speak my truth. Each dream shared became a thread that added richness to our tapestry, our aspirations intertwining like vines reaching for the sun. In that moment, I realized that the bonds we formed weren't just about shared laughter; they were about supporting one another in our journeys, lifting each other up as we navigated the uncertain waters of life.

The conversation drifted seamlessly from dreams to inspiration, and soon we were discussing our favorite authors, each name sparking a discussion that ignited the room once more. I marveled at the breadth of knowledge and creativity surrounding me, the shared passion for storytelling illuminating the dimly lit room. It felt as if the energy shifted, the very air charged with excitement as we debated our favorite novels and characters, our voices rising and falling like a symphony.

Eventually, Emily proposed a group project—a collaborative storytelling endeavor where we would each contribute a chapter based on our personal experiences. The idea felt electrifying, an opportunity to merge our dreams into something tangible. I could already envision us gathered around the table again, pouring over each other's words, sharing laughter and inspiration as we crafted a narrative that was uniquely ours.

The energy surged as we began to brainstorm potential themes and settings, each suggestion igniting another spark of creativity. Ryan suggested a backdrop of a quaint café in Paris, where our characters would meet and share their lives, while Mia proposed a bustling New York City street, alive with the sights and sounds of life. The ideas flowed freely, and soon we found ourselves lost in the possibilities, the excitement palpable in the air.

As the night crept toward its inevitable end, I felt a pang of longing to hold onto this moment, to etch it into my memory forever. The laughter, the camaraderie, and the dreams shared around that table had created something magical. Each of us had woven our threads into a collective tapestry that spoke of hope, connection, and the beauty of the human experience.

Eventually, one by one, my friends began to gather their belongings, the light in the room slowly dimming as the outside world beckoned. I stood at the door, feeling a bittersweet mixture of gratitude and reluctance. Each goodbye felt like a gentle tug on my heart, a reminder of the precious connections we had cultivated. As the last of them disappeared into the cool night, I closed the door softly, the echoes of their laughter lingering in the air like a sweet melody.

I stood in the silence of my apartment, feeling the weight of the evening settle comfortably around me. The remnants of dinner still sat on the table, the dishes waiting patiently for cleanup, but I felt no urgency to tackle the mess. Instead, I sank onto the couch, enveloped in a sense of contentment. In that moment, I understood that life was not just about the grand achievements or the monumental milestones but rather the small moments—those shared laughs, the dreams discussed, and the bonds forged in the warmth of friendship.

With a smile creeping across my face, I envisioned our future gatherings, the stories we would continue to create together, and the dreams we would nurture in one another. The world outside my window continued to spin, bustling and chaotic, but inside my heart, I felt an undeniable sense of peace. It was in these connections that I had found my home—a place where dreams took flight, and love blossomed in the most unexpected ways.

Chapter 24: Unexpected Revelations

The kitchen was a mosaic of colors, illuminated by the warm glow of hanging pendant lights. The rich, buttery aroma of freshly baked biscuits mingled with the zest of citrus from the fruit bowl on the counter, a veritable feast for the senses. In this bustling little haven of culinary delights, laughter echoed against the tiles, creating a backdrop of joyous celebration. But as the party swirled outside, the clatter of plates and the distant chatter faded into a muted symphony, leaving only Jackson and me in the embrace of our shared solitude.

Jackson stood by the kitchen island, his lean frame silhouetted against the flickering candlelight. The moment stretched between us, the air thick with an unspoken tension. His usually bright, playful demeanor had dimmed, replaced by an earnest seriousness that made my heart flutter in a way I hadn't anticipated. I leaned against the counter, letting the cool marble ground me as I took in the sudden shift in energy. His emerald eyes, often alight with mischief, were clouded now with an introspection that pulled at my heartstrings.

"I wanted to talk to you about something," he said, his voice dropping to a near whisper, like he was confiding a secret that could alter the course of our evening. The casual banter that had filled the space only moments before faded, leaving behind an intimacy that felt both exhilarating and terrifying.

I nodded, urging him to continue, my palms clammy against the cool surface of the counter. In the silence that followed, I searched his face, desperate to find a clue that would unveil the weight of his thoughts. Jackson was a culinary maestro, a magician with flavors, yet there he stood, wrestling with an unease that mirrored my own. It was a revelation I had not expected, but one that made the air around us feel charged with a strange kinship.

He took a deep breath, the sound almost lost amidst the fading echoes of laughter from the party. "I've been feeling... lost lately," he confessed, his gaze darting toward the window, where the twinkling lights of the backyard party flickered like stars against the deepening twilight. "I look around at my peers, the chefs who are getting accolades and recognition, and I can't help but wonder if I'm just a shadow in their spotlight."

The vulnerability in his words struck a chord deep within me. How often had I stood in a similar shadow, wrestling with my own insecurities, feeling inadequate in a world that seemed to reward the bold and the brilliant? I leaned closer, my heart racing not from fear but from a growing empathy. "I get it," I said softly, surprising myself with the honesty that slipped out. "I often feel like I'm barely keeping my head above water in my own field. It's like we're all swimming in the same ocean, but some of us are drowning while others are surfing the waves."

A flicker of understanding ignited in his eyes, the tension that had built between us beginning to melt away. "It's nice to know I'm not alone in this," he murmured, a hint of relief threading through his voice. There was something intoxicating about sharing our vulnerabilities, a connection that felt as if we were weaving our fears into a tapestry of resilience. The invisible thread that linked us tightened, and I felt a warmth spreading in my chest, the kind that comes from being seen, truly seen.

As he spoke, the world around us faded further into the background. The sounds of clinking glasses and the bursts of laughter felt like distant echoes, like I was tuning into a frequency that only he and I could hear. Jackson's passion for his craft poured forth as he spoke about his struggles and aspirations, his words infused with a longing that resonated with my own dreams. I could see the flicker of ambition in his eyes, a fire that refused to be extinguished even amidst the doubts that plagued him.

"I want to create something that people remember," he said, his voice growing steadier as the conversation deepened. "But sometimes I wonder if I have what it takes. I see so many talented chefs being celebrated for their innovation, and I just feel... ordinary." His brows knit together in a frown, the vulnerability he displayed casting a veil of authenticity over his words.

"Ordinary is just a stepping stone," I replied, my own conviction surprising me. "Sometimes, the best dishes are the ones that come from the heart, not just technique. You have a unique perspective, and that's what sets you apart." My voice trembled with passion, the warmth of encouragement filling the air between us. It felt electric, as if I was sparking a light within him that had dimmed, hidden beneath layers of self-doubt.

A smile broke through the clouds of uncertainty on his face, illuminating his features with a warmth that echoed my own burgeoning confidence. The tension that had hung like a dark cloud between us began to dissipate, replaced by something softer, something that felt like possibility. Leaning in closer, I could see the way the candlelight danced in his eyes, casting shadows that hinted at the depths of his thoughts and the dreams he harbored.

In that moment, as we stood together amidst the fading laughter of the world outside, I felt the connection between us blossom. It was a rare bond forged in the crucible of our insecurities, tempered by the understanding that we were both searching for our place in a world that often felt overwhelming. We leaned into that space, letting our hearts share their fears and aspirations, as the aroma of our culinary dreams hung thick in the air around us, a fragrant promise of what was yet to come.

As the warmth of our shared confessions settled around us, the kitchen transformed into a sanctuary, a pocket of intimacy amidst the vibrant chaos beyond. Jackson's laughter, often contagious and rich, had morphed into a melody that resonated with my own experiences, weaving a delicate tapestry of camaraderie between us. I marveled at how, within the confines of this bustling home, we had carved out a world where we could shed our masks, exposing the vulnerable bits that often lay hidden beneath layers of bravado.

"I sometimes wish I could just cook without thinking about what others expect," he said, his fingers tracing the edge of the counter, as if finding solace in the cool marble. "It's like every dish is a reflection of who I am, and when it doesn't resonate, it feels like I'm failing at being me." His eyes flickered with a vulnerability that caught me off guard. It was a reminder of the shared human experience, the collective weight of expectations that seemed to bind us all.

"Imagine," I began, the words flowing from my heart, "if we allowed ourselves the freedom to create without the shackles of expectation? What if every dish was just a story waiting to be told, a piece of our journey that we shared with others?" My pulse quickened as the idea blossomed between us, igniting a fire that spread warmth through my veins.

Jackson's gaze met mine, the air thickening with the weight of unspoken dreams. "A story, huh? That's a beautiful way to put it." The corner of his mouth lifted, a tentative smile breaking through the clouds of doubt. "Maybe that's what I've been missing—a reason beyond just accolades."

We stood in that kitchen, a realm where creativity could flourish, unencumbered by the burdens of judgment. As the party buzzed with energy outside, our moment felt like a secret pact forged in the warmth of vulnerability. With each word, we began to weave an understanding that transcended our individual struggles, transforming our shared insecurities into a potent source of inspiration.

"Let's start with something simple," I suggested, excitement bubbling beneath the surface. "What if we created a dish that speaks to us, one that embodies our stories?" The thought sent a thrill racing through me, like a current of electricity zipping through the air. It was an invitation to shed the weight of expectations and allow ourselves to be the artists we had longed to be.

Jackson's eyes sparkled with renewed determination, and in that instant, I could see the flicker of a fire igniting within him. "I love that idea! Something that reflects not just the flavors we adore but the experiences that shaped us." His enthusiasm was contagious, wrapping around me like a warm embrace.

We began brainstorming ingredients, each suggestion a brushstroke on the canvas of our culinary masterpiece. I shared memories of my grandmother's kitchen, where the scent of simmering tomatoes and basil wafted through the air, wrapping me in a blanket of nostalgia. "Every summer, we'd pick fresh basil from the garden, and the moment we'd tear the leaves, the aroma would fill the air. It was like magic," I reminisced, the memories dancing vividly in my mind.

Jackson listened intently, a soft smile playing on his lips. "That sounds incredible. I have a similar memory with my mom and her lemon tarts. She'd squeeze the juice herself, and the zest would fill the room. It was so bright and vibrant, a perfect summer treat."

As we exchanged stories, the conversation morphed into a delightful exploration of flavors and textures, a dance of ideas that felt exhilarating. With every anecdote, we not only bonded over our culinary journeys but also discovered the essence of what it meant to create from the heart. It was a revelation that deepened the connection between us, solidifying the uncharted territory of friendship—perhaps something even more—beneath the shared laughter.

The kitchen transformed into a whirlwind of activity as we gathered ingredients, our movements synchronized like a well-rehearsed ballet. I felt the thrill of possibility electrify the air, the vibrant hues of fresh produce beckoning us to play. Jackson tossed aside his earlier reservations, diving into the process with a renewed fervor. His hands moved deftly, chopping onions and garlic with an ease that belied the turmoil he had shared moments before.

"Okay, so we start with a base," he declared, his voice now laced with a playful confidence. "Let's sauté these onions until they're golden and caramelized. That'll be the foundation of our story." The way he spoke transformed the mundane into the extraordinary, elevating each step of our culinary adventure.

We worked in harmony, laughter punctuating the air as we bantered back and forth, exchanging playful jabs about culinary disasters and triumphs alike. Each clink of utensils, each sizzle from the skillet, created a symphony that drowned out the distant party, enveloping us in our own world—a world filled with passion, creativity, and the uncharted territory of budding connection.

As the flavors melded together, I watched Jackson transform before my eyes. The self-doubt that had clouded his features began to lift, replaced by a glow of contentment that radiated from within. He was no longer just the talented chef standing in the shadows; he had become the vibrant artist in his own right, forging a new path fueled by authenticity.

The kitchen was alive with the aroma of simmering sauce, the vibrant colors of fresh basil and ripe tomatoes contrasting beautifully against the gleaming pots and pans. I couldn't help but feel that our culinary creation was more than just a dish; it was a representation of our shared journey, a celebration of the moments that shaped us, and a testament to the power of connection.

As we plated our creation, the vibrant colors swirled together like a sunset on a warm summer evening, and I knew in that moment that this was more than just a meal. It was a culmination of dreams, struggles, and newfound camaraderie, a manifestation of our determination to embrace our unique stories and share them with the world.

The dish gleamed on the plate, a testament to our afternoon of revelations and connection. As I gazed at it, I felt a surge of pride for both of us. We had stepped beyond the confines of self-doubt, crafting not just a meal but a bond—one that promised to grow and deepen as we continued to explore the culinary landscape together. In that kitchen, surrounded by the fading echoes of laughter and the warmth of burgeoning friendship, I realized that sometimes, the most unexpected revelations lead us to the places we truly belong.

With every ingredient that graced our makeshift canvas, the kitchen transformed into a battleground of creativity. It was as if we were both sculptors, molding our fears into tangible flavors that danced with the potential of becoming something remarkable. Jackson's hands moved deftly, embodying a harmony of precision and passion, a waltz that began to erase the shadow of self-doubt that had loomed over him just moments before. The onions caramelized beautifully in the skillet, releasing a fragrance that beckoned memories of cozy gatherings and laughter echoing around the dinner table, a reminder of the warmth that cooking can bring.

As I diced tomatoes, their juicy insides spilling vibrant red onto the cutting board, I glanced up at Jackson. He was lost in thought, his brow furrowed slightly as he contemplated the next step of our culinary creation. "You know," he said suddenly, his voice breaking through the delicious haze surrounding us, "cooking has always felt like a puzzle to me. Each ingredient is a piece, and I'm just trying to find the right fit." He looked at me, a spark igniting in his eyes, as if he had discovered a hidden truth about himself. "But lately, I've been so focused on the end result that I've forgotten to enjoy the process."

A warmth blossomed within me at his admission. It mirrored my own journey, the constant pressure to achieve perfection that often dulled the joy of creation. "It's easy to forget, isn't it? To lose sight of the joy in the act itself while chasing the accolades." I leaned against the counter, letting the coolness seep into my skin, grounding myself amidst the whirl of emotions that flowed through our exchange.

Jackson nodded, his hands pausing as if to absorb the weight of my words. "I want to remember why I started cooking in the first place," he murmured, his voice filled with conviction. "It was never about the awards or recognition. It was about sharing something beautiful with others, making them feel at home." The sincerity in his tone enveloped me like a warm embrace, and I could see the passion reigniting within him, glowing like a flame that refused to be extinguished.

In that moment, I felt a kindred spirit emerge in Jackson—a reflection of my own aspirations. We were both artists, navigating the same tumultuous seas, each seeking to anchor ourselves in authenticity. The air around us vibrated with shared hopes, the possibilities unfolding like a delicate blossom greeting the first rays of spring sunlight.

As the sauce simmered gently on the stove, I began to experiment, adding a pinch of oregano and a dash of red pepper flakes. "Let's take it up a notch," I said playfully, flashing him a conspiratorial smile. "After all, we're not just cooking; we're telling a story." The challenge sparked a glimmer of excitement in his eyes, and we embarked on a culinary adventure, blending our unique perspectives into a singular dish that would speak volumes about who we were.

The kitchen became a dance floor, each ingredient a partner swirling in the symphony of flavors. As we chatted, I could sense Jackson shedding the weight of expectation that had burdened him for so long. The laughter returned, bubbling up effortlessly, filling the space with a warmth that felt like sunshine spilling through a window.

"Okay, let's put it all together," he declared, his voice infused with newfound energy. "Time for the grand reveal!" The thrill of creation surged between us, an exhilarating concoction of hope and friendship that hinted at what could bloom beyond this culinary experiment.

As we plated the dish, I marveled at the vibrant hues and enticing aromas that danced before us. The fresh basil leaves were scattered atop the simmering sauce like emerald confetti, adding a final flourish that tied our creation together. "There! A masterpiece born from our collaboration," I exclaimed, stepping back to admire our handiwork. The colors seemed to leap from the plate, each layer a testament to our shared stories, our struggles, and our triumphs.

Jackson's eyes widened in delight, a mixture of pride and astonishment etched across his face. "I can't believe we made this together," he said, a grin splitting his features. "It's beautiful." In that moment, the connection between us felt tangible, a thread woven from creativity, vulnerability, and the courage to embrace imperfection.

We took a step back, our hearts swelling with a sense of accomplishment as we prepared to share our creation with the world beyond the kitchen door. The noise from the party swirled around us, laughter echoing against the walls, an enticing promise of celebration just outside our culinary cocoon. "Shall we?" I asked, a hint of mischief in my voice as I gestured toward the door.

Jackson nodded, his eyes gleaming with excitement. "Let's show them what we've created!" Together, we emerged from the kitchen, the enticing aroma trailing behind us like a fragrant whisper, as if announcing our arrival to the gathering of friends.

As we stepped into the warm embrace of the party, our creation in hand, the buzz of chatter enveloped us. Friends turned to greet us, their smiles infectious as they caught sight of the vibrant dish we had crafted. "What's this?" one friend exclaimed, eyes wide with curiosity. "Did you two whip this up?"

With a theatrical flourish, Jackson presented our creation. "Behold, a culinary expression of friendship and vulnerability!" he declared, his voice ringing with playful exuberance. Laughter erupted around us, the sound bright and joyful, an affirmation of the journey we had just embarked upon together.

I watched as people gathered, drawn to our dish like moths to a flame, eager to partake in the feast we had prepared. The energy surged, a collective sense of anticipation igniting the room. It was a beautiful moment, a culmination of not only our culinary efforts but the bond we had formed in that sun-drenched kitchen.

As the first bite was taken, I held my breath, watching faces transform as flavors danced across their palates. Jackson stood beside me, his eyes shining with pride as the compliments began to roll in. Each word of praise felt like a gentle reminder of the power we held when we allowed ourselves to create freely, uninhibited by the fear of judgment.

In that vibrant room filled with laughter and camaraderie, I felt a sense of belonging wash over me. This was what it meant to share a piece of oneself, to step into the light and embrace the imperfections that made us human. I glanced at Jackson, our eyes locking in a moment of silent understanding. We had both taken a step forward, shedding the weight of expectation and discovering the joy that lay in vulnerability and collaboration.

As the evening unfolded, the conversation flowed, laughter erupted, and friendships blossomed amid the clinking of glasses and the sharing of stories. The world outside melted away, replaced by the warmth of connection and the beauty of creativity. It was a night to remember, a celebration of not only the dish we had crafted but the unbreakable bonds that had formed in the process.

In the end, it wasn't just about the food. It was about the moments that transcended the plate—the laughter shared, the stories exchanged, and the friendships ignited. As I savored the last bite, I knew that this was only the beginning, an invitation to embrace the unexpected revelations that life had to offer, forever igniting the flame of possibility within us both.

Chapter 25: Crossing Boundaries

The sun dipped low on the horizon, casting a golden hue over the bustling streets of Chicago, a city teeming with life and stories waiting to unfold. The soft hum of evening traffic melded with the distant sound of jazz emanating from a nearby bar, each note a reminder of the vibrancy that pulsed through the veins of this urban landscape. I had always found solace in this cacophony, a rhythmic backdrop to my own chaotic thoughts. As I strolled along the winding path of the riverwalk, the gentle lapping of the water against the docks soothed my frayed nerves, a momentary escape from the storm brewing within.

Jackson had always been a steady presence, an anchor in the tempest of my life. With his tousled hair and easy grin, he navigated the world with an effortless charm that drew people to him like moths to a flame. Our friendship blossomed amidst late-night study sessions in the library and long drives through the city, the glow of streetlights reflecting our laughter like little stars scattered across the asphalt. But beneath the lighthearted banter and shared dreams lay a tension that crackled in the air, palpable yet unspoken.

As we found ourselves seated on a weathered bench overlooking the river, the golden hues of the setting sun danced on the water's surface, shimmering like a thousand tiny diamonds. I could feel the warmth radiating from his body, a magnetism that made my heart flutter with each fleeting glance. The conversation ebbed and flowed, touching on everything from our college aspirations to the trivialities of our day-to-day lives. Yet, each word felt laden with unacknowledged feelings, a weight that hung between us like a thin veil.

The evening air carried with it the scent of grilled street food, mingling with the sweet aroma of nearby blossoming magnolias, reminding me of summer nights spent running barefoot through my childhood neighborhood. My fingers brushed against the rough wood of the bench, a grounding sensation that clashed with the whirlpool of emotions threatening to pull me under. I glanced sideways at Jackson, his blue eyes sparkling with a mischief that set my heart racing, and I wondered if he could sense the change in the atmosphere, too.

Then it happened—his fingers grazed my cheek, a tentative caress that sent a jolt through my body, igniting something dormant deep within. The warmth of his touch contrasted sharply with the cool evening breeze that swept through, sending a shiver down my spine. I felt alive, each nerve ending awakened by the proximity of his body, the intoxicating scent of his cologne enveloping me like a warm embrace. Time slowed as he leaned in, his intentions clear, and for a heartbeat, the world faded into a soft blur.

Just as our lips were about to meet, an avalanche of fear crashed over me, a wave of self-doubt that felt insurmountable. I couldn't do this. The line between friendship and something deeper stretched taut, a boundary I had never dared to cross. "I can't," I whispered, pulling back as if my words were a lifeline, desperate to tether me to reason. Panic surged through my veins, the warmth of his presence replaced by an icy doubt that settled in the pit of my stomach.

Jackson's gaze flickered with confusion, a myriad of emotions playing out on his face like a poorly scripted movie. "Why not?" he asked, his voice low and laced with disappointment, but there was an undertone of understanding that tugged at my heart. The city behind him continued its rhythm, unaware of the seismic shift occurring in our small corner of the world. I took a breath, grounding myself in the reality of the moment, the bustling life around us a stark contrast to the tempest raging inside.

"I don't want to ruin what we have," I admitted, my voice trembling as I searched for the right words. "You mean too much to me, Jackson. What if this changes everything?" The truth hung heavy between us, each word a delicate glass figurine poised on the edge of destruction. I feared that crossing this boundary might shatter not just our friendship but the very essence of who we were.

He remained silent, contemplating my words as the shadows deepened around us. The city lights flickered to life, illuminating our surroundings with a soft glow that felt almost ethereal. I longed for him to understand, to grasp the complexities of my heart. It wasn't just about the fear of rejection or the potential heartbreak; it was the fear of losing the only person who had ever truly seen me.

Finally, Jackson leaned back, a pained expression crossing his features. "I don't want to pressure you. I get it," he replied, his voice barely above a whisper. But the disappointment was palpable, each syllable heavy with unspoken words. I could see the conflict swirling in his eyes, the same confusion I felt reflected back at me. I wanted to reach out, to reassure him that it wasn't about him but about the boundaries I had erected in my own heart, fortified by years of self-protection.

The evening grew darker, the world around us shifting into a new rhythm. I could hear the distant laughter of friends, the clinking of glasses at nearby tables, life moving forward while I sat immobilized by my fears. In that moment, I realized how desperately I wanted to embrace what lay beyond the boundary. I yearned for the thrill of uncertainty, the intoxicating promise of love that could transform everything I knew. But fear held me captive, a steadfast guardian of my heart, whispering lies that kept me from reaching for the very thing I desired.

As the stars began to punctuate the dark canvas of the sky, I felt a pang of regret for not taking that leap of faith. The gentle lapping of the river mirrored my heartbeat, a constant reminder of the choices we make, the roads we take, and the moments we let slip through our fingers like sand. With Jackson beside me, I knew the possibilities were endless, yet my heart remained ensnared in the delicate web of doubt I had spun. The question lingered, unyielding and relentless: could I ever find the courage to embrace the unknown?

The air thickened with unspoken words, each breath a tangible thread weaving an intricate tapestry of emotions that bound us together yet threatened to tear us apart. I could feel Jackson's gaze upon me, his expression a mix of confusion and disappointment, a mirror reflecting the turmoil within my own heart. The world around us buzzed with life, but here, in our secluded corner by the river, time seemed to stand still, caught in the liminal space between what was and what could be.

I focused on the ripples dancing across the water, trying to steady my racing thoughts. Each flicker of light from the city's skyline was like a star in the cosmos, distant yet vivid, beckoning me to dream beyond the constraints of my fears. The gentle rustle of leaves overhead provided a soothing counterpoint to my internal chaos, whispering reminders of change and growth. Yet as I inhaled deeply, trying to find some semblance of calm, the scent of night-blooming jasmine filled the air—a sweet and intoxicating fragrance that made my heart ache for something more.

"I'm sorry," Jackson finally said, breaking the silence that had enveloped us like a heavy fog. His voice, usually buoyant, was now tinged with an unfamiliar sorrow, and it felt like a knife to my chest. I turned to meet his eyes, trying to convey the depth of my feelings without words, a silent plea for understanding. The space between us felt charged, alive with possibilities that danced just out of reach.

"Don't apologize," I replied softly, my voice barely a whisper. "It's just... complicated." I glanced away, fearing the honesty of my own admission. The truth was, I was terrified. Terrified of losing him, of ruining the easy laughter we shared, the unspoken bond that had grown so effortlessly over time. But more than that, I feared the unknown—what lay on the other side of this delicate line we were tiptoeing along.

Jackson sighed, the sound heavy with a mixture of frustration and longing. "I get it," he said, his tone resigned. "But sometimes, complicating things can lead to something amazing. You won't know until you try." The earnestness in his words resonated with me, yet I felt paralyzed by the enormity of the leap he was suggesting. Each heartbeat echoed the internal battle raging within me: stay safe in the comfort of friendship or risk everything for the intoxicating allure of love.

As the first stars began to twinkle in the indigo sky, I felt the warm breeze brush against my skin, a gentle reminder of the life swirling around us. A group of friends nearby erupted into laughter, their joy punctuating the air like fireworks, a stark contrast to the storm within me. I couldn't help but admire how easily they embraced their moments, how the unpredictability of life seemed to be a catalyst for their happiness. I wanted that. I craved the freedom to let go, to dive headfirst into whatever lay beyond our friendship, but the shadows of doubt loomed large.

The sound of the river grew louder as the water rushed over stones, a persistent reminder of the choices we make. With a sudden burst of courage, I turned to Jackson, my heart racing. "What if it doesn't work out? What if we lose each other?" The vulnerability in my voice surprised me, but it felt necessary, a truth I had to share. The vulnerability of love terrified me, like standing on the edge of a cliff, staring down at the abyss below.

He studied me, his brow furrowing as if contemplating the weight of my fears. "What if it does work out?" His question hung in the air, a simple but profound challenge. "What if we become something more, something beautiful? Life's too short to live in 'what ifs.'" His conviction ignited a flicker of hope within me, a tiny flame battling against the gusts of self-doubt.

The moments stretched between us, filled with the raw, unfiltered emotions that defined our connection. I could see the depth of his feelings, a well of sincerity that both comforted and terrified me. He was ready to embrace the unknown, to leap into the exhilarating chaos of love, while I stood on the precipice, terrified of what lay beneath.

In that moment, the world around us faded into insignificance, and it was just the two of us—two souls bound by a friendship that had endured storms and sunshine alike. The realization struck me like a thunderclap: I was in love with him. The truth crashed over me, a wave of clarity washing away the fog of confusion. The laughter and chaos of the world faded into the background as the undeniable truth crystallized in my mind.

Before I could fully process this revelation, Jackson reached for my hand, intertwining our fingers. The warmth of his touch sent a jolt of electricity through my body, igniting a fire I had kept buried for too long. My breath hitched in my throat as he leaned closer, his voice a mere whisper that sent shivers down my spine. "Let's take this step together. We'll figure it out as we go."

His words wrapped around me like a warm blanket, offering both comfort and adventure. I searched his eyes, looking for any sign of doubt, any glimmer of hesitation. But all I found was unwavering resolve, a fierce determination that mirrored my own burgeoning desire. In that moment, I felt the dam of my fears begin to crack, the waters of uncertainty threatening to spill forth.

"What if we make mistakes?" I asked, my voice trembling with the weight of the unknown. The question hung heavily between us, both a plea and a challenge.

"Then we learn from them," he replied, his smile warm and reassuring, like the sun breaking through a cloudy day. "Life isn't about perfection; it's about growth."

A laugh escaped my lips, a sound tinged with disbelief and hope. He was right, of course. Growth rarely came from staying within the confines of safety; it flourished in the fertile soil of risk and vulnerability. As I looked at him, I could see a future unfolding—a path filled with both challenges and triumphs, laughter and tears.

In that moment, the fears that had once bound me felt lighter, like the weight of a heavy coat being shed in the warmth of spring. I squeezed his hand, feeling the pulse of his heartbeat resonate with my own. Together, we could navigate whatever came our way, weathering the storms and basking in the sunshine. The decision had been made, the boundaries blurred, and with that, a new chapter began—a chapter that held the promise of love, adventure, and the beautiful unpredictability of life.

As the stars blinked to life overhead, illuminating the darkness, I felt a rush of excitement mingle with my uncertainty. The night felt alive, full of potential and uncharted territory waiting to be explored. The river flowed steadily beside us, a reminder that life continues to move forward, whether we choose to leap or hold back. And in that moment, as Jackson's gaze held mine, I understood that the leap was worth taking, the journey worth embarking on, together.

The weight of my words lingered in the air, and as I leaned back, the tension between us morphed into a palpable presence, an invisible thread pulling taut. Jackson's expression shifted, the warmth of his gaze flickering like a candle caught in a gust of wind. The soft rustle of leaves danced overhead, echoing the turbulent thoughts that swirled within me, yet the world beyond our little bubble faded into insignificance. The city continued its vibrant dance, but here, we were suspended in a moment that felt both electric and terrifying.

His fingers, still intertwined with mine, felt like a lifeline, tethering me to a reality I yearned to embrace. "What if I told you that I'm not afraid?" he asked, his voice steady, cutting through the chaos of my mind. There was an honesty in his gaze, a fierce determination that radiated warmth and possibility. In that moment, it dawned on me that he was standing on the edge of his own fears, ready to leap into the unknown, while I stood frozen, paralyzed by doubt.

A shiver of apprehension coursed through me as I searched for the right words. I had always prided myself on my ability to articulate my thoughts, to weave together sentences that painted vivid pictures, yet here, words eluded me. "You don't know what you're asking," I finally managed, my voice barely above a whisper. "This could change everything. What if we lose what we have?" The question hung heavy in the air, like a thick fog shrouding the possibilities before us.

He sighed, a mixture of frustration and understanding etched on his features. "What if we don't?" The conviction in his words ignited something within me—a spark of hope mingled with the simmering fear that had taken up residence in my heart. I wanted to believe that we could navigate this terrain together, that our friendship could withstand the tremors of change. But deep down, I was terrified of losing him to the whirlwind of emotions that awaited us.

As I looked out over the river, I couldn't help but think of the currents beneath the surface—hidden forces that shaped its course, much like the undercurrents of our relationship. We had built a sturdy foundation over countless late-night conversations and shared secrets, yet the thought of adding romance into the mix felt like tossing a stone into still water, sending ripples that could either disrupt the tranquility or create something beautiful.

"Let's make a pact," he said suddenly, breaking the silence. "If it gets too overwhelming, if it feels like we're losing our way, we can go back to how it was. No hard feelings." His proposal hung in the air, a lifebuoy tossed into a stormy sea, and I felt the tight knot of anxiety in my chest begin to loosen, if only slightly. "But I need to know if you're willing to take that leap with me."

For a moment, the world around us faded into a soft focus, the distant sounds of the city blending into a muted symphony. I glanced back at him, the warmth of his presence enveloping me like a comforting embrace. The sincerity in his eyes held a promise that was both terrifying and exhilarating. As the sun dipped lower, casting a kaleidoscope of colors across the water, I found myself longing for that connection, that chance to explore the depths of our relationship.

With a deep breath, I nodded slowly, a mixture of fear and excitement coiling in my stomach. "Okay," I whispered, feeling the weight of the decision settle over me. "Let's do it. But if it gets too complicated, we promise to go back." The words felt like a spell woven into the air, binding us to an unspoken agreement. Jackson's face lit up, the spark of joy igniting a warmth that coursed through me, dispelling the lingering shadows of doubt.

The night stretched before us like an uncharted map, the stars twinkling overhead as if to celebrate our newfound resolve. Jackson leaned closer, his gaze steady as he searched my eyes for any hint of hesitation. "I promise I'll be there with you every step of the way." The sincerity in his voice sent a shiver down my spine, igniting a thrill of anticipation within me.

And then, in a moment that felt both surreal and inevitable, our lips met. The kiss was tentative at first, an exploration rather than a declaration, but it ignited a wildfire of emotions that consumed me whole. It felt like coming home, like breathing life into a part of me I didn't even know was dormant. The warmth of his lips against mine sent sparks cascading through my veins, igniting a passion that I had long denied.

As we broke apart, breathless and wide-eyed, the reality of what we had just crossed flooded my senses. Everything felt different, yet the familiarity of Jackson's presence anchored me in a way that was both comforting and exhilarating. I could hear the city humming around us, the world bustling with life, yet in that moment, it was just us—two souls entwined on the precipice of something beautiful and uncertain.

We spent the remainder of the evening basking in the glow of our decision, each shared laugh and lingering touch reinforcing the bond that had been forged between us. The stars overhead seemed to shimmer brighter, twinkling as if in approval of our choice to embrace the unknown. We wandered through the winding streets, each corner revealing a hidden gem—a quaint coffee shop adorned with fairy lights, a street musician strumming a soulful melody, and a gelato stand that promised to satisfy our sweet tooth.

Every moment felt infused with a new vibrancy, and I marveled at how the world around us had transformed. I watched Jackson as he animatedly shared stories from his childhood, his hands moving expressively, each gesture punctuating his words with a passion that made my heart flutter. I felt like I was seeing him for the first time, the layers of our friendship peeling away to reveal the man I had yearned for all along.

As the night wore on, we found ourselves sitting on a bench in a quiet park, the glow of the streetlights casting a warm halo around us. The gentle rustle of leaves above accompanied the soft cadence of Jackson's laughter, a sound that filled me with warmth. "You know," he said, glancing at me with a playful smile, "I've always thought of you as a bit of a daredevil."

I raised an eyebrow, surprised. "Daredevil? Me?" The very idea felt foreign, a far cry from the cautious soul I had always considered myself to be.

"Absolutely," he insisted, his tone teasing. "You took a leap tonight, didn't you? That's pretty daring."

I couldn't help but smile, the compliment warming my cheeks. "I guess I did. But you were the one who made it feel safe." The honesty in my voice surprised me, and I felt a rush of gratitude for his unwavering support.

With a newfound lightness in my heart, I realized that this was only the beginning. The road ahead would undoubtedly be filled with challenges, but as long as we faced them together, I felt invincible. The boundaries I had once feared seemed to dissolve, replaced by a landscape brimming with possibilities.

As the stars twinkled above, I leaned my head against his shoulder, a contented sigh escaping my lips. The world felt expansive, full of potential, and with Jackson by my side, I knew we could weather any storm that came our way. Each moment we shared, every laugh and whispered promise, was a thread weaving our story—a tale of friendship blossoming into something extraordinary.

And in that moment, as we sat together in the gentle embrace of the night, I felt the thrill of the journey ahead coursing through my veins, a sweet melody that echoed the promise of a love that would grow with each passing day. Together, we were embarking on a new adventure, one that held the power to change everything. The stars bore witness to our uncharted course, and I couldn't wait to see where it would lead us next.

Chapter 26: Reflections in the Glass

The moment I stepped into the gallery, I was enveloped by an air of expectancy, the scent of fresh paint mingling with the soft aroma of brewed coffee wafting from a small corner café. The walls were adorned with canvases that vibrated with life, splashes of color dancing before my eyes like echoes of laughter. Each piece told a story, and I felt the pull of those narratives tugging at the fabric of my own.

Amelia was already there, a whirlwind of energy in her oversized cardigan, her enthusiasm radiating like the sun peeking through the gallery windows. "You made it!" she exclaimed, her voice bubbling over with excitement as she gestured towards a series of abstract paintings that seemed to sway in rhythm with the gentle music drifting through the space. "You have to see this one!"

I followed her to a canvas that seemed to swirl with blues and greens, an ocean of emotion captured in a moment. As I stood there, lost in the depths of the artist's vision, I felt the tension of the previous evening seep away. The world around me faded, the weight of Jackson's warm gaze slipping through my fingers like grains of sand. I inhaled deeply, letting the mixture of paint and possibility fill my lungs.

Amelia moved on to the next piece, her animated chatter pulling me back from my reverie. "It's all about interpretation, you know? Like, what do you see when you look at this?" She gestured toward a chaotic explosion of color—reds, yellows, and blacks clashing in an unapologetic display. I studied it, my mind racing to decipher the artist's intent.

"Destruction, perhaps," I mused, "or maybe a raw burst of passion that just can't be contained." My heart fluttered at the thought, a reflection of my own chaotic emotions. Jackson and I were like that painting, bursting at the seams with potential yet tangled in the aftermath of our own decisions.

"Exactly!" Amelia nodded, her enthusiasm infectious. "Art is such a brilliant way to explore those feelings. I sometimes wish I could paint my thoughts onto a canvas instead of keeping them locked up in my head."

I glanced at her, admiring the way her eyes sparkled as she spoke. It was moments like these that reminded me how much I valued our friendship. She had an uncanny ability to help me see the world through a brighter lens. "You know," I said, a playful smile tugging at my lips, "you might just be a hidden Picasso. We should totally sign you up for an art class."

Amelia laughed, a sound like tinkling glass. "Only if you promise to join me! We'll become the dynamic duo of creativity!"

As we wandered through the exhibit, I began to notice the people around us. A couple stood absorbed in conversation, their whispers punctuated by gentle laughter. An older man, his face etched with lines of wisdom, stared at a monochrome piece as if it held the secrets of the universe. Each person added a layer to the atmosphere, contributing to the collective appreciation for the beauty that surrounded us.

But still, my mind circled back to Jackson, his voice echoing in my thoughts, that intoxicating blend of warmth and intensity. I felt a twinge of guilt for letting my heart dance on the edge of something uncertain. It was exhilarating, yet terrifying, and I couldn't help but wonder if we had ventured too far into uncharted territory.

Amelia's voice cut through my introspection. "Hey, let's grab some coffee! I need to recharge before we tackle the next set of masterpieces."

The café nestled in the corner felt like a cozy sanctuary. We settled at a small table, the soft hum of conversation enveloping us. I wrapped my hands around a steaming mug, savoring the warmth as it seeped into my palms. The first sip ignited a spark of joy that chased away the lingering shadows of doubt.

"Okay, spill it," Amelia said, her eyes narrowing with playful intensity. "What's been going on with you and Jackson? You were practically glowing when you walked in."

My heart raced at the thought of sharing my whirlwind of emotions, but the safe space of the café made it easier. "It's complicated," I admitted, my voice dropping to a whisper as if the very air held the secrets of my heart. "Last night was... magical. But I can't shake the feeling that it might lead us down a path we're not ready for."

Amelia leaned in, her expression earnest. "Sometimes, you have to take a leap, you know? Life is messy, but that's what makes it beautiful. You deserve to embrace those moments, no matter where they lead."

Her words struck a chord deep within me. What was I afraid of? Was it the risk of losing our friendship, or the fear of confronting my own feelings? The complexities of life felt like the intricate brushstrokes of the paintings surrounding us—beautiful yet daunting, each decision leading to a different masterpiece.

As we finished our coffee, a small group of artists gathered around a large canvas being unveiled. The crowd hushed, anticipation crackling in the air like electricity. I found myself swept away in the moment, captivated by the unveiling of creativity. In that instant, I felt a rush of clarity wash over me, as if the art, the colors, and the people around me were stitching together the fabric of my own desires.

Perhaps it was time to stop hesitating, to stop worrying about the messy implications of pursuing what my heart so desperately wanted. The world around me was a canvas waiting for my brushstroke, and I was ready to make my mark.

The chatter of the crowd grew louder, a symphony of voices harmonizing in appreciation as the canvas was fully revealed. My breath hitched, caught between the swirl of emotions and the sheer beauty unfolding before my eyes. The artwork was a vivid portrayal of an urban landscape, infused with a kaleidoscope of colors that captured the essence of life itself—the bustling streets, the quiet moments in hidden corners, and the electric pulse of the city. Each brushstroke felt like a heartbeat, and for a moment, the chaos of my thoughts quieted, drawn into the tranquility of the scene.

"Isn't it incredible?" Amelia breathed, her eyes wide with wonder. I nodded, unable to form words as the painting spoke to me in a language that transcended speech. It felt like a mirror, reflecting not just the city but also the complexities of my own heart—a blend of yearning, excitement, and the pang of uncertainty.

As the applause echoed through the gallery, I caught a glimpse of Jackson's face in my mind. His laughter, the way his eyes sparkled when he spoke, the comforting weight of his hand on my shoulder—all of it played like a film reel, stirring a pot of emotions that I thought I had neatly tucked away. The risk of venturing into something deeper with him loomed like a dark cloud, yet the prospect of staying within the confines of safety felt increasingly suffocating.

"Come on, let's find the next one," Amelia said, her voice a gentle nudge out of my reverie. I followed her lead, the anticipation of discovery igniting a spark within me. We meandered through the exhibit, pausing at pieces that pulled us in, letting the stories wash over us like waves. With each new canvas, I felt a renewed sense of possibility. The colors danced in front of me, a reminder that life was not just black and white, but a spectrum of experiences waiting to be explored.

After a few more pieces, we stepped outside into the warmth of the afternoon sun. The golden rays cast a glow on everything they touched, the world transformed into a living painting. I inhaled deeply, the sweet scent of blooming flowers mingling with the faint aroma of street food wafting through the air. My heart raced with an unfamiliar exhilaration, as if the universe was conspiring to open my eyes to the beauty of what lay ahead.

"Let's grab a bite to eat," Amelia suggested, glancing around as if searching for the perfect spot. "There's a food truck nearby that serves the best tacos!" Her enthusiasm was infectious, and I couldn't help but smile at her zest for life.

As we strolled down the bustling street, I reveled in the vibrant atmosphere. Street performers showcased their talents, musicians strumming cheerful tunes, and laughter echoed from groups of friends gathered on the benches. It felt like the world was alive, pulsing with energy, and for the first time that day, I allowed myself to embrace the moment, the weight of my worries lifting with every step.

We found the food truck nestled between two towering buildings, its colorful exterior promising a fiesta of flavors. The air was filled with the tantalizing scent of spices and grilled meat, and I couldn't resist the urge to indulge. As we placed our orders, I watched the cook deftly assemble tacos, each movement fluid and practiced, a work of art in its own right.

With our food in hand, we settled at a small picnic table, the sun dappling through the leaves overhead. I took my first bite, the explosion of flavors a delightful surprise. The spicy salsa mingled with the savory meat and fresh cilantro, a perfect harmony that made my taste buds dance.

"See? I told you they were amazing!" Amelia said, her eyes shining with excitement. I nodded, savoring each mouthful, the food igniting a joy that echoed the colorful artistry we had just experienced.

As we ate, we began to discuss our aspirations, each word weaving a tapestry of dreams and desires. Amelia shared her latest idea for an art project that combined photography with painting, envisioning a series of portraits that captured the essence of everyday life. I found myself captivated by her passion, her words painting pictures in my mind.

"I can see it already," I said, enthusiasm spilling over. "You should definitely pursue that! It sounds incredible."

Her face lit up, and I couldn't help but feel a warmth spread through me, a connection solidifying in the shared space of our dreams. "And what about you?" she asked, her tone shifting to curiosity. "What do you really want?"

The question hung in the air, as potent as the spices still tingling on my tongue. I took a moment, the essence of my own desires swirling like the colors on the canvases. "Honestly? I want to explore my creativity more. I've been so focused on my responsibilities, but I feel like there's this part of me that's been dormant for too long."

Amelia leaned in, her interest piqued. "What's stopping you? This is the perfect time to embrace it. You've got the whole world in front of you."

Her encouragement ignited a flame of determination within me, and as I spoke, my heart raced with possibility. "I think I want to start painting again. It used to be my escape, my way of processing everything. I just... lost sight of it."

A soft smile spread across her face. "Then let's do it together! I'll help you set up a little studio at home. We can make it our creative haven."

The idea warmed me from the inside out, a vision of late-night paint sessions filled with laughter, music, and the clinking of brushes against canvases. "You really think so?" I asked, the doubt creeping in.

"Absolutely! You're so talented, and it's time you embraced that part of yourself again," she said, her conviction unwavering.

As the sun began to dip lower in the sky, casting long shadows that stretched across the pavement, I felt a sense of liberation wash over me. I was ready to step into the unknown, to embrace both the light and dark that life offered. The evening held the promise of adventure, and I was determined to seize it with both hands, ready to paint my own narrative on the canvas of life.

The evening air settled over the city like a warm blanket, the vibrant colors of sunset painting the skyline in shades of orange and pink. As Amelia and I made our way back from the food truck, the laughter of nearby groups and the gentle clink of glasses from outdoor cafés created a soundtrack that thrummed with the heartbeat of the urban landscape. I felt alive, every sense heightened by the promise of new beginnings. The glow of the streetlights illuminated our path, and I found myself caught up in the infectious spirit of the night.

"Let's stop by that rooftop bar," Amelia suggested, her voice brimming with enthusiasm. "The view is spectacular, and they have the best cocktails in town!" The thought of sipping a drink while gazing out over the sprawling cityscape felt like a slice of paradise, a chance to escape the ordinary.

We climbed the narrow staircase leading up to the bar, each step heightening my anticipation. When we reached the top, the view took my breath away. The city sprawled beneath us, a tapestry of twinkling lights and bustling streets, a living organism that thrived on dreams and aspirations. I leaned against the railing, the cool metal grounding me as I soaked in the beauty of it all.

As I turned to face Amelia, she was already ordering at the bar, her animated chatter drawing the bartender into the excitement of our evening. I couldn't help but smile at her infectious energy. She had a way of transforming every moment into an adventure, and tonight was no exception.

"Here you go!" she said, handing me a cocktail that sparkled like the stars above. "This is their signature drink—The Urban Sunset. You're going to love it."

I took a sip, the flavors bursting on my tongue—citrusy with a hint of sweetness, refreshing and intoxicating. I felt the alcohol warm my insides, a gentle nudge toward the courage I needed. The city, the art, the vibrant life around me—it all felt like an invitation to embrace who I was and who I could become.

With a drink in hand, we found a cozy corner overlooking the skyline, where we could chat without raising our voices above the ambient noise. The sun dipped below the horizon, casting a golden glow that made the city seem ethereal, a place where dreams could truly take flight.

"So, what's next for you?" Amelia asked, her gaze steady. "You've had this artistic spark reignited. Are you really going to dive back into painting?"

I took a moment to collect my thoughts, swirling the ice in my glass as if it could help me make sense of everything. "Yes, I think I need to. It feels like a part of me that I lost along the way, and I want to reclaim it."

"Good! You should! There's something magical about creating—about putting your heart onto a canvas. It's like speaking a language that everyone can understand but only a few can articulate," she said, her eyes sparkling with inspiration.

The conversation flowed effortlessly, each topic leading us deeper into our dreams and desires. We shared stories of our childhoods—how I had spent countless afternoons in my grandmother's attic, painting whatever came to mind, losing track of time as the world faded away. Amelia spoke of her own journey, the challenges she faced in pursuing art, and the moments when she felt like giving up.

But then, just as seamlessly, we veered into the realms of our futures—the aspirations we harbored and the paths we longed to tread. It felt liberating, sitting there under the vast sky, imagining what could be. I could almost taste the possibilities, each one sweeter than the last.

"Let's have a painting night this weekend," Amelia suggested, her eyes bright with excitement. "I'll bring supplies, and we'll create masterpieces! Just you and me, no pressure."

The idea sent a flutter of joy through me. "I would love that. It's exactly what I need." The prospect of painting with Amelia, surrounded by laughter and camaraderie, felt like a promise—an assurance that I could rediscover a piece of myself that had been tucked away for far too long.

As the night wore on, I became acutely aware of the rhythm of my heartbeat, a reminder of how alive I felt in that moment. I glanced around at the other patrons—friends clinking glasses, couples whispering sweet nothings, and solitary souls lost in their thoughts. The city pulsed around us, and for the first time in ages, I felt as if I were right where I belonged.

"Do you remember that time we tried to paint that giant mural on your garage?" I laughed, the memory bubbling up like champagne. "We thought we were going to be the next great artists of our generation, and instead, we created a disaster."

Amelia doubled over with laughter. "How could I forget? The paint was everywhere—my hair, your shoes! I think we ended up looking like a couple of abstract art pieces ourselves."

The lightness of our laughter mingled with the cool night air, and I savored this feeling—a sense of connection, of freedom, of not having to hide behind a façade anymore. The walls I had built around my heart began to crumble, piece by piece, until all that remained was a tender hope that something beautiful was waiting just around the corner.

As the night deepened, I felt a familiar tug at my heart. Jackson drifted back into my mind like a whisper in the dark. I could almost feel his presence next to me, a shadow flickering at the edges of my thoughts. The warmth of his smile, the way his laughter danced in the air—it all felt like an unfinished story, a chapter I was eager to explore.

"Are you okay?" Amelia asked, her voice pulling me from my thoughts. I turned to her, surprised to see a flicker of concern in her eyes.

"Yeah, I just... I can't help but think about Jackson," I admitted, the name slipping from my lips like a secret. "Everything feels so different now, and I don't know what to make of it."

Amelia regarded me with understanding. "What do you want? What do you hope for?"

It was a simple question, yet it resonated deeply within me. I thought about Jackson—his warmth, the way he made me feel seen, understood. There was a magnetic pull between us, an undeniable chemistry that beckoned me forward.

"I want to explore it," I said finally, my voice steady with conviction. "I want to see where this goes, to allow myself to feel something real."

"Then you should," she replied, her tone unwavering. "Take that leap, and don't look back. Life is too short to let fear dictate your choices."

As I raised my glass in a toast to new beginnings, a flicker of resolve sparked within me. The night continued to unfold around us, filled with laughter and the promise of uncharted territories. I knew that embracing my creativity would open doors I had long kept shut, and perhaps, just perhaps, exploring my connection with Jackson would lead to something extraordinary.

With the city sprawling beneath us, I felt ready to dive headfirst into the vibrant tapestry of life, ready to paint my own masterpiece on the canvas of existence. Each stroke, each moment, would be a testament to my journey, a reflection of my heart, and an exploration of the beauty that comes from embracing both the chaos and the serenity that life has to offer.

Chapter 27: Art and Heart

The gallery pulsed with a rhythm all its own, an intricate tapestry of color and emotion woven into the very fabric of the evening. It was a haven for souls seeking solace and stimulation, the air rich with the scent of oil paints and fresh canvas, mingling with the faint hint of coffee wafting from a nearby café. I stepped inside, the warm glow of soft lighting wrapping around me like a cherished embrace, and paused to take it all in. The walls seemed to whisper, each painting and sculpture beckoning with an allure that promised an escape into worlds birthed from imagination and fervor.

Local artists had poured their essence into every piece, and it showed. I marveled at a swirling abstract of deep blues and greens, its tempestuous strokes mimicking the ocean's might, while beside it, a delicate watercolor captured the fleeting beauty of cherry blossoms in bloom, each petal seemingly alive, drifting on an invisible breeze. It was an exhibition that didn't just invite admiration; it demanded a connection, a dialogue between the viewer and the vision. My heart thrummed in sync with the cadence of this artistic sanctuary, a place where vulnerability met audacity in a brilliant, chaotic dance.

Amelia materialized at my side, her presence a beacon of light amidst the vibrant chaos. With her tousled chestnut hair cascading over her shoulders and her eyes glimmering with enthusiasm, she was an embodiment of the gallery's spirit. "Look at this one!" she exclaimed, her voice a melody above the hum of conversations. She tugged me toward a striking piece that depicted a phoenix rising from the ashes, its feathers painted in fiery hues of red and gold. "It's like it's alive, isn't it?" Her eyes shone with an admiration that was almost palpable, and I couldn't help but smile.

"It's incredible," I replied, allowing the brilliance of the artwork to wash over me. "It feels like a reminder that we can all rise again, no matter how hard we fall." The words slipped from my lips, heavy with the weight of personal experience, and as I turned to meet Amelia's gaze, I saw her nod in understanding, a mutual acknowledgment of the struggles that shaped us.

We wandered from piece to piece, each painting a portal to a different universe. I relished the way Amelia breathed life into the mundane; her laughter echoed through the gallery like music, each giggle an invitation to relish the moment. There was something magnetic about her, a spark that turned a simple outing into an adventure. I felt it—this electric connection forged between us, woven through shared stories and unspoken dreams.

In one corner, a series of photographs captured the essence of life in the city—gritty alleyways speckled with splashes of graffiti, each image a testament to the beauty of imperfection. "This one," Amelia said, her voice dropping to a conspiratorial whisper as she leaned closer, "reminds me of those late-night escapades we had in college." Her eyes danced with nostalgia, and I couldn't help but join in her laughter, the kind that made the past feel vibrant and alive again.

As we settled onto a weathered bench, our legs brushing together, I took a moment to absorb my surroundings. The sounds of gentle conversation and the soft rustle of patrons moving from one artwork to another created a symphony of community, a tapestry of souls intertwined by the shared appreciation of artistry. In this pocket of the world, amidst the paint and the stories, I found a sense of belonging, an understanding that art could illuminate the darkest corners of our existence.

"Do you remember the first time we visited an art gallery?" I asked, letting the memory unfurl between us. "We thought we were so sophisticated, sipping overpriced wine and pretending to know what we were talking about."

Amelia threw her head back, laughter spilling forth like sunlight through the trees. "Oh my god, yes! We were so out of our depth. But we faked it with such confidence!" She leaned in, her expression shifting to one of sincerity. "I love that we've come so far since then. This... this is where we belong."

Her words lingered in the air, settling around us like a warm blanket. In that moment, it struck me how far we had both traveled—not just in miles, but in the layers of our stories, the heartaches and triumphs that shaped us. The world outside faded into a distant hum, the chaos of life muted by the cocoon of creativity that enveloped us.

A small child wandered nearby, her fingers dancing over the surface of a sculpture. She looked back at her mother, her eyes wide with wonder. It was a sight that made my heart swell; innocence and curiosity woven together, a testament to the transformative power of art. I glanced at Amelia, catching her gaze as she witnessed the same scene. "This is it, isn't it?" I murmured, my voice laced with emotion. "Art gives us hope. It reminds us to dream, to believe in something greater than ourselves."

Amelia nodded, her expression softening as she absorbed my words. "It's a reflection of who we are, of our experiences and aspirations. Art can be our lifeline, a way to express what's too complex for words."

And there it was, a realization shimmering between us, igniting a spark of understanding. The gallery was more than just a collection of artworks; it was a sanctuary where hearts could bare their truths and souls could revel in authenticity. Each stroke of paint and each captured moment was a testament to the human experience, a declaration that we are never alone in our struggles, our joys, or our desire to create.

We lingered on that bench, cocooned in a world of beauty and connection, where the stories of artists resonated with our own. In that vibrant space, I felt an overwhelming urge to dive deeper into my own creativity, to explore the hidden recesses of my heart, where dreams lay waiting to be birthed. As the gallery buzzed around us, the essence of art seeped into my very being, urging me to embrace the possibility of new beginnings.

The soft murmur of conversations swirled around us like a gentle breeze as I watched Amelia, her fingers grazing the edge of a canvas adorned with a riot of colors. I couldn't help but marvel at how effortlessly she navigated this world of art, each piece igniting a spark within her, a glow of enthusiasm that seemed to radiate into the very air we breathed. Her passion was contagious, wrapping around me like a warm embrace, urging me to delve deeper into the stories each piece had to tell.

"Have you ever thought about what you would paint?" she asked, her eyes alight with curiosity, a challenge lacing her words. "If you had to capture your essence on a canvas, what would that look like?"

The question lingered in the air, inviting me to peel back the layers of my thoughts. I imagined swirling colors, the vibrant chaos of my emotions, but it felt too simplistic, too shallow. "Maybe a stormy sea," I mused, my mind drifting to the tumultuous moments that had shaped me. "Something wild and unpredictable, but with flashes of light breaking through."

"Perfect!" Amelia exclaimed, clapping her hands together. "It's beautiful—raw and full of life. That's you!"

Her words painted a picture in my mind, a scene alive with movement and conflict, yet buoyed by hope. The artist within me stirred, awakening a desire to translate the chaos of my experiences into something tangible. Here, in this gallery, I felt the quiet hum of inspiration coursing through my veins.

As we resumed our exploration, a nearby sculpture captured my attention, its form both delicate and imposing. It was a twisting amalgamation of metal and glass, reflecting light in a myriad of ways, creating shadows that danced across the floor. I stepped closer, mesmerized by its complexity. "It's almost like it's breathing," I whispered, entranced by the interplay of elements.

"Exactly!" Amelia chimed in, her voice filled with wonder. "It's like it embodies the essence of struggle and grace all at once. You can see the artist's journey in it."

In that moment, I felt a surge of gratitude for this shared experience. Each piece we encountered became a mirror, reflecting our own journeys, our aspirations, our fears. Art had a way of weaving the threads of our lives into a cohesive narrative, reminding us that we are not alone in our struggles.

We ventured into a dimly lit corner of the gallery where a series of portraits hung, each face a study in emotion. One in particular drew me in—a woman captured mid-laughter, her eyes sparkling with mischief. I couldn't help but smile at the vibrancy she exuded, the joy spilling from the canvas like sunlight on a winter's day. "I want to know her story," I said, leaning in closer, almost expecting her to step from the frame and join us in this whimsical adventure.

"Maybe she's the artist's muse," Amelia suggested, her eyes twinkling. "Or perhaps she represents freedom—living life unapologetically."

I considered that, envisioning a life devoid of inhibition, where every moment was seized with fervor. It was an intoxicating thought, and I longed to embody that spirit. "I want to feel that kind of joy," I admitted, my voice barely above a whisper. "To embrace life with such reckless abandon."

Amelia's expression softened, her gaze steady and reassuring. "You're already on that path. Look around! We're here, sharing this moment, surrounded by beauty. That's a start."

Her words hung in the air, a balm for my restless heart. I turned back to the portrait, allowing myself to be enveloped in its warmth. It felt like an invitation—to dance freely through life, to paint my existence in hues vibrant and bold.

As the evening unfolded, I noticed how the gallery began to empty, patrons drifting away like leaves carried by the wind. Yet we lingered, unwilling to leave this sanctuary. The dimming lights cast a gentle glow, transforming the space into a realm where time felt suspended.

"Let's take a picture," Amelia suggested, her phone already in hand, a playful grin illuminating her face. "We have to capture this moment."

We positioned ourselves in front of a large mural that depicted a sprawling cityscape, its skyline a blend of vibrant colors that mimicked the setting sun. The hues melted into one another, each brushstroke a testament to the city's heartbeat. As we posed, arms thrown around each other, I felt a swell of contentment.

The click of the camera shutter echoed in the stillness, freezing our laughter and joy in time, preserving a fragment of this night—a snapshot of our friendship, vibrant and unyielding.

After the photo, we wandered back toward the entrance, the warmth of our connection radiating as we discussed our favorite pieces, reliving the stories that had touched us. The world outside was cloaked in twilight, the soft glow of street lamps illuminating our path. The air was tinged with the promise of adventure, and as we stepped into the evening, the city unfolded before us like a living canvas.

"Where to next?" Amelia asked, her eyes gleaming with excitement.

"Let's find a place to grab some dessert," I replied, the thought of something sweet invigorating my spirit. "I need to indulge after all this inspiration."

We meandered through the streets, the sounds of laughter and music spilling from open doorways, the city alive with energy. The vibrant nightlife beckoned, each corner revealing a new adventure waiting to unfold.

In that moment, I felt a flicker of hope igniting within me—a recognition that life, much like art, is about embracing the unknown and weaving beauty from chaos. As we approached a cozy café, its warm glow spilling onto the sidewalk, I knew I was ready to explore my own creative journey, to dive into the depths of my experiences and emerge transformed.

This was not just an evening of art; it was a celebration of friendship, a reminder of the power of connection. With each step, I felt the threads of my narrative intertwining with those of the artists who had poured their souls onto the canvas. In the heart of this city, amidst the laughter and the stories, I was discovering my own voice, ready to paint the vibrant tapestry of my life, one brushstroke at a time.

The café we stumbled into was a gem tucked away on a narrow side street, its exterior draped in ivy and the warm glow of twinkling fairy lights beckoning us inside. The aroma of freshly baked pastries enveloped us as we stepped through the door, a sweet invitation that wrapped around our senses like a beloved quilt. Amelia led the way to a cozy corner table, the wood worn smooth from years of countless conversations and quiet moments shared over coffee and dessert.

"Do you smell that?" she exclaimed, her eyes wide with delight. "I think they have chocolate croissants!"

I could feel my mouth watering at the thought, the mere idea of that flaky pastry melting in my mouth made my heart flutter. As we settled into our seats, I glanced around, soaking in the eclectic decor. Vintage posters of jazz legends adorned the walls, their expressive faces gazing down at us as if urging us to share our own stories. Soft jazz music floated through the air, weaving a rich tapestry of sound that mingled with the clinking of cups and the hum of friendly chatter.

We placed our orders, my excitement bubbling over as I envisioned the decadent treats on their way. While we waited, I couldn't resist leaning closer to Amelia, intrigued by the fire of creativity ignited within me that night. "Do you think every artist feels this way?" I pondered aloud. "Like they're part of something bigger, as if their art connects them to the world?"

Amelia nodded, her expression thoughtful. "Absolutely. It's like they're channeling their experiences into something that resonates with others. Art is this beautiful dance between the personal and the universal. Every brushstroke, every note played, carries a piece of their heart."

Her words resonated within me, echoing through the chambers of my mind like a beloved song. The thought of weaving my own narrative into art, of leaving a mark on the world, sent shivers of exhilaration coursing through my veins.

Moments later, our desserts arrived, each one a work of art in its own right. The chocolate croissant was a masterpiece of flaky layers, dusted with powdered sugar like a blanket of fresh snow. I watched as Amelia's eyes sparkled with delight, and I couldn't help but giggle at her childlike enthusiasm.

"Dig in!" she urged, breaking off a piece of her croissant and extending it toward me. The rich, buttery flavor exploded in my mouth, and I closed my eyes in bliss, savoring the moment. "I could live on these," I declared, taking another bite as laughter bubbled up between us, filling the cozy space.

As the conversation flowed, we reminisced about our dreams, the aspirations we had whispered into the night during those college years. We had been filled with ideas that danced like fireflies, flickering and ephemeral, yet undeniably beautiful.

"What if we started a project?" I proposed, the idea sparking like a flame. "Something that combines our love for art and storytelling.

We could explore the city, gather stories, and create something tangible—maybe a book?"

Amelia's eyes widened with excitement, her enthusiasm contagious. "That would be incredible! We could interview local artists, dive into their inspirations and struggles, and showcase their work. It could be a celebration of our community!"

The possibilities unfurled before us like a vivid tapestry, each thread bursting with potential. We began sketching ideas, our conversation filled with dreams and laughter, the café fading into a backdrop of vibrant colors as our imaginations took flight.

After polishing off our desserts, we reluctantly made our way back to the gallery, our hearts still soaring from the excitement of our new venture. The night had wrapped around us like a warm shawl, and as we stepped back into the gallery, I felt as if we were stepping into a living dream, a place where creativity and community intertwined in an exquisite dance.

The space felt different now, infused with a deeper meaning as we wandered through the artworks, each piece taking on new life with our shared vision. I couldn't help but touch the edges of a painted canvas, imagining the artist pouring their soul into each stroke. "It's as if we're entering a realm where anything is possible," I breathed, the thrill of our idea sending shivers down my spine.

"Exactly!" Amelia said, her voice bubbling with excitement. "This is where it all begins. We can draw inspiration from the stories that surround us. We'll create a narrative that intertwines art and heart."

As we meandered through the gallery, we found ourselves in front of the phoenix painting again, its vibrant colors capturing the light and reflecting the dreams we had just shared. "Look at it," I said, feeling the weight of its significance. "It's a symbol of rebirth, of rising from the ashes. Just like us."

Amelia nodded, her gaze fixed on the painting, a flicker of determination igniting in her eyes. "This will be our guiding star," she declared, her voice steady. "A reminder that we can soar, no matter the challenges we face."

Time slipped away unnoticed as we discussed potential names for our project, the gallery enveloping us in a warm cocoon of creativity. Each suggestion sparked laughter, our ideas blossoming into vivid images that danced in the air between us. "How about 'Heartfelt Canvas'? Or 'Brushstrokes of Life'?"

"Both are beautiful!" I replied, feeling the energy pulse between us. "But let's find something that captures the essence of our journey, the stories we want to tell."

The late hour settled softly around us, the sounds of the city outside melding with the low murmur of conversation inside the gallery. As the final patrons trickled out, we remained, lost in our own world of possibilities, the night stretching ahead like an unwritten page waiting to be filled.

Eventually, a gallery attendant approached us with a kind smile, gently reminding us that it was time to close. "Thank you for sharing your enthusiasm with us tonight," she said, her eyes twinkling. "It's always a joy to see such passion for art."

As we stepped back into the cool night air, I felt a sense of profound gratitude washing over me. The stars above twinkled like scattered diamonds, and the city hummed with life, a symphony of possibilities unfolding before us.

"Can you believe it?" I asked, turning to Amelia, my heart racing with excitement. "We're on the cusp of something extraordinary."

"Absolutely," she said, a radiant smile lighting up her face. "We're just getting started."

With our hearts full and our minds alight with inspiration, we walked side by side, the night blossoming around us like a canvas waiting for our brushstrokes. The world stretched infinitely ahead, and as we embarked on this new chapter, I felt an exhilarating sense of purpose igniting within me. Together, we were ready to turn dreams into reality, one story at a time.

Chapter 28: The Chef's Challenge

The aroma of sizzling garlic and fresh herbs wafted through the bustling streets of New Orleans, wrapping around me like a warm embrace. It was a typical morning in the French Quarter, where the sun draped its golden rays over vibrant facades adorned with ironwork balconies and vibrant flora spilling over in colorful abundance. I leaned against the cool, sun-kissed brick of Café du Monde, my gaze drifting over the crowd, each face telling a different story. The clatter of plates and the faint laughter of diners created a symphony of life that vibrated through my very core. As a writer, I was acutely aware of the magic in these moments, how they danced just out of reach, waiting to be captured and woven into words.

The recent exhibit had ignited something within me—an insatiable hunger for creativity. I had embraced the thrill of my newfound role as a conduit between art and culinary exploration. The cooking challenge was more than just a feature for the local magazine; it was a celebration of passion, perseverance, and the transformative power of food. The idea of diving headfirst into a culinary adventure, where I could connect with chefs who shared the same fire in their bellies, exhilarated me.

After securing my assignment, I sent a message to Jackson, a rising star in the culinary world. I had met him during one of my visits to a local cooking class, where his fervor for flavors and unyielding ambition had captivated me. I could still recall the way his hands moved with precision, each chop and stir a graceful dance, the way he infused love and soul into every dish. I never imagined I'd be asking him to compete in a cooking challenge, but his enthusiasm was infectious, and I couldn't resist the urge to involve him in this culinary odyssey.

When I shared my idea with Jackson over coffee at a quaint café on Chartres Street, his eyes sparkled with an energy that matched the vibrant murals that adorned the walls. "A cooking challenge?" he repeated, as if savoring the taste of the words. "You mean to tell me that we could create a dish that reflects everything we love about New Orleans? Count me in!"

His eagerness made my heart swell with pride. Together, we began weaving our plans, creating a tapestry of flavors and textures that would echo the essence of the city. Our brainstorming sessions turned into whirlwind afternoons filled with laughter, sketching out the menu like a painter visualizing their next masterpiece. We envisioned dishes that paid homage to the classic Creole and Cajun flavors, yet bore our unique fingerprints.

One evening, as the sun dipped below the horizon, casting a warm, dusky glow over the city, we settled on an outdoor patio overlooking the Mississippi River. The air was thick with the sweet scent of jasmine, mingling with the sounds of distant jazz drifting from nearby bars. It felt as though the city itself was holding its breath, waiting for the culinary symphony we were about to create. Jackson's passion was palpable; every time he spoke about the challenge, his words poured out like a bubbling pot of gumbo, rich and full of flavor.

We decided to incorporate a touch of whimsy into our creation, using local ingredients to craft a dish that would be both familiar and surprising. "How about a shrimp étouffée with a twist?" he suggested, his brow furrowed in concentration as he jotted down ideas on a napkin, the ink smudged with the remnants of our coffee cups. "We can add a hint of coconut milk and lime to brighten it up. Something that reflects our vibrant spirit but feels like a warm hug."

The thought of melding traditional with innovative sent chills down my spine. It was precisely the kind of culinary expression that captured the heart of New Orleans—bold, unexpected, and unapologetically delicious. I could already imagine the judges' faces as they tasted our dish, the blend of flavors dancing across their palates, perhaps igniting a memory or two of their own.

With each passing day leading up to the event, our excitement simmered like a pot on the stove. Jackson and I embarked on scouting local markets, our senses attuned to the vibrant colors and textures surrounding us. The Farmers Market at the French Market was a treasure trove, brimming with fresh produce, fragrant spices, and the lively chatter of vendors sharing stories as old as the city itself. I marveled at the energy in the air, where each purchase felt like a celebration of life and the love that food brings.

As I gathered ingredients, I often found myself lost in thought, contemplating the stories behind each flavor. Jackson would catch my eye and share a quick quip, pulling me back to the present. His playful nature made our journey feel effortless, and every shared laugh stitched us closer together. It became clear that this culinary adventure was more than just a challenge; it was forging a bond that transcended the kitchen.

The night before the event, we gathered to prep, our small kitchen transformed into a chaotic haven of excitement. The scents of sautéed garlic, caramelized onions, and spices enveloped us, a sensory embrace that set the stage for the culinary battle ahead. As we chopped, stirred, and tasted, I felt an undeniable connection to the ingredients, to Jackson, and to the city that had inspired us.

Underneath the bustling surface of this vibrant world, I found solace in the rhythmic dance of our culinary endeavor. With each simmering pot and sizzling pan, I realized we were not just crafting a dish; we were creating a moment—one that would resonate with anyone fortunate enough to experience it. My heart swelled with anticipation, eager for the taste of victory, the warmth of community, and the unforgettable flavors that would bind us all together.

As the sun dipped lower, casting long shadows over Jackson's tiny kitchen, the atmosphere crackled with anticipation. It was our final night of preparation, and the walls reverberated with laughter and the clinking of pots and pans, the kind of joyous noise that harmonized with the culinary chaos. We had a mission to complete, and every detail mattered. The air was thick with the scent of herbs and spices, a fragrant promise of what was to come. Jackson moved around the kitchen with the kind of grace that made his clumsy charm seem effortless, his hands skillfully orchestrating each task like a conductor leading an orchestra.

I couldn't help but admire how the dim light danced off his features, highlighting the determination etched in his brow. "We need to add a pop of color," he mused, glancing at our neatly arranged ingredients, his mind racing through the possibilities. "What if we garnish with pickled radishes and a sprinkle of microgreens? It'll give the dish that vibrant flair." The thought of those bright pink radishes contrasted against the rich, warm tones of the étouffée filled me with a sense of childlike excitement.

Jackson's enthusiasm was infectious, like the lively rhythms of a second-line parade spilling through the streets. I found myself caught up in his vision, surrendering to the intoxicating blend of creativity and passion. Together, we whipped up a storm, occasionally pausing to taste, to adjust, to sprinkle in a dash of this or a pinch of that. Each iteration of our dish brought us closer to the essence of what we wanted to share—a celebration of flavors that mirrored the heart and soul of New Orleans.

As we chopped and sautéed, we shared stories of our culinary heroes—chefs who had paved the way, whose names floated like whispers of legends on the breeze. Jackson spoke passionately about his grandmother, a fierce woman with a heart as big as her cast iron skillet. "She never used a recipe," he said, his eyes glazing over in nostalgia. "Just a pinch of this, a handful of that. Food was her way of loving us, a language without words."

His stories transported me to another time, a tapestry of family gatherings and the comforting chaos of loved ones gathered around the table. I could almost hear the laughter and the clinking of glasses, taste the love woven into every bite. In that moment, I realized that our dish was not just a competition entry; it was a tribute to all those who had come before us, a homage to the culture and tradition that breathed life into our city.

Hours melted away, and before we knew it, the clock was ticking down to our big day. After a flurry of final touches and careful organization, we stepped back to admire our creation, a fragrant étouffée simmering in the pot, its deep amber color promising warmth and comfort. I could hardly contain my excitement; every texture and flavor danced in my mind, waiting to be shared with the world. "We've done it," I breathed, grinning from ear to ear.

The following morning arrived with a vibrancy that seemed almost electric. I stood at the entrance of the culinary challenge, surrounded by the spirited chatter of participants, each brimming with the same mix of nerves and excitement. The venue was an old warehouse transformed into a chic urban space, its rustic charm enhanced by twinkling string lights and long communal tables adorned with colorful dishes. The scent of freshly baked bread mingled with the distinct tang of spices, enveloping me in an aromatic embrace.

As I wandered through the throng, the buzz of conversation swept over me like a warm tide. Chefs and food enthusiasts mingled, sharing snippets of their culinary journeys, each story adding a brushstroke to the rich tapestry of the day. The competitive spirit crackled in the air, but so did a sense of community, as though we were all part of something bigger—a movement, perhaps, to celebrate the love for food that united us all.

Jackson and I set up our station, a modest table overflowing with our carefully curated ingredients. I glanced around, taking in the array of setups from other competitors. Some displayed extravagant setups with colorful garnishes, while others focused on the simplicity of their ingredients. It was clear that everyone here had poured their heart into their creations, and my heart swelled with pride just being part of it.

Once the challenge officially began, the atmosphere shifted into high gear. The timer started, and it felt as though the world around us faded away, leaving only the clattering of utensils and the sizzling of pans in our immediate universe. Jackson moved with the urgency of a well-trained performer, effortlessly balancing the tasks of cooking and plating while I kept our workspace organized, excitedly scribbling notes for the article I envisioned writing.

"Grab the lime!" he called out, his voice a mix of excitement and urgency. I lunged for the zester, handing it to him with a flourish. The way he poured himself into his craft was mesmerizing; each movement was purposeful, each ingredient treated with respect as though it were a precious secret waiting to be unveiled.

With every stir of the pot, the flavors melded and deepened. As Jackson added the coconut milk, I could see the dish transforming, becoming something extraordinary. It was a dance of creativity and tradition, a seamless blend of familiar comforts and bold new ideas.

When the time finally came to plate our dish, adrenaline surged through me. With a flourish, Jackson ladled the étouffée into a bowl, its glossy surface glistening under the warm light. He artfully arranged the pickled radishes and microgreens atop the mound of rich shrimp and sauce, turning it into a visual feast. "Just like grandma would've wanted," he said with a wink, a note of pride lacing his voice.

As we stepped back to admire our creation, I felt a surge of emotion. This was more than a dish; it was a story, a testament to our shared love for food and the journeys that brought us here. In that moment, I realized we had already won—whether or not the judges agreed, we had crafted a memory that would linger long after the last bite was savored. As the sounds of the bustling kitchen faded into the background, all I could hear was the soft, steady beat of our hearts, a rhythm echoing the pulse of the city we loved.

The moment the judges announced the start of the tasting, a hush descended over the venue, thick with anticipation. I felt the adrenaline coursing through my veins, matching the lively rhythm of the jazz band in the corner, their notes curling around us like smoke. Jackson and I exchanged a knowing glance, an unspoken agreement hanging in the air. This was our moment to shine, to share the passion and creativity we had infused into every bite of our dish.

As the first judge approached our table, a woman with an air of authority and a discerning eye, Jackson's smile widened, an inviting beacon amidst the chaos. She studied our plate, her brows furrowing slightly as she leaned closer, inhaling the intoxicating aroma that wafted from the bowl. It was as if time stood still, the clamor of voices around us fading into the background as we held our breath, suspended in this delicious moment.

"Tell me about this dish," she said, her voice rich and warm, like a cup of café au lait on a chilly morning. Jackson dove in, articulating the story behind the shrimp étouffée—its roots in the heart of New Orleans, the infusion of coconut milk and lime inspired by our desire to blend tradition with innovation. The words flowed effortlessly, his passion spilling over like the sauce in our bowl, vibrant and alive.

With a nod of understanding, she took her first bite, and I watched with bated breath as her eyes closed momentarily, the flavor enveloping her in a brief embrace. When she opened them again, a spark of delight lit her features, and my heart soared. Jackson glanced at me, his grin stretching from ear to ear, and in that moment, the world outside fell away.

The judges moved from one station to another, and I found myself enveloped in the lively conversations that swirled around us.

I listened intently, captivated by the stories shared by other participants—chefs whose journeys were as varied as the spices they employed. Each tale painted a picture of determination, of dreams chased down dark alleyways, illuminated only by the flickering glow of a food truck's neon sign.

One contestant, a petite woman with a fierce determination in her eyes, spoke of her family's history in the restaurant business, how she had learned to cook from her mother, who had fled a war-torn country to build a new life in America. "Food was my mother's way of telling us she loved us," she said, her voice steady yet emotional. "Each recipe was a piece of home, a link to the past."

Her words resonated deep within me, reinforcing the notion that food transcended mere sustenance; it was a language spoken through flavors, a bridge connecting generations and cultures. As I absorbed these stories, I felt a sense of belonging in this eclectic mix of dreams and aspirations, a community united by a common love for culinary expression.

After what felt like an eternity, the judges returned to their table, pens poised over notepads, ready to score each dish. Jackson and I leaned in, stealing furtive glances at the other participants, our collective excitement almost tangible. The atmosphere crackled with a mix of nervous energy and hopeful anticipation, and I couldn't help but marvel at the colorful array of dishes—each plate a vibrant reflection of the chef's personality and journey.

As the final minutes ticked away, we busied ourselves with tidying our space, arranging our garnishes just so, as if that might somehow affect the outcome. Jackson took a moment to breathe, leaning against the table, his expression a blend of nerves and determination. "No matter what happens, this has been incredible," he said, his voice steady despite the whirlwind around us. "I wouldn't want to do this with anyone else."

His sincerity struck a chord within me. We had forged something beautiful together, our creativity intertwined in a way that transcended the competition itself. Just then, the announcement came—a hush fell over the crowd, and all eyes turned toward the judges as they prepared to reveal their decisions.

"Thank you all for your outstanding contributions today," the head judge began, her voice echoing through the space. "The passion and creativity displayed in every dish have made this an unforgettable event. After much deliberation, we are ready to announce the winners."

My heart raced, pounding like a marching band's drum, drowning out all other sounds. Jackson stood beside me, his hand brushing against mine, an unspoken promise of solidarity and shared dreams. As the judges called out names, the air crackled with excitement, the tension palpable, each mention sparking cheers and applause.

And then, in the midst of the chaos, they announced our names. "Jackson and our feature writer, the talented creator behind the food and the stories, have taken the prize!" The applause erupted like fireworks, cascading around us, enveloping us in a wave of joy and disbelief. We exchanged astonished glances, the realization settling in—this was not just a victory; it was a celebration of everything we had poured into our craft.

In the following moments, as we stepped up to accept our award—a gleaming trophy that sparkled under the lights—I could feel the pride swelling in my chest, a tangible reminder of our hard work and dedication. The judges commended us for our innovative twist on a classic dish, their praises washing over us like the warm breeze that danced through the open windows.

As we posed for photos, the vibrant spirit of New Orleans enveloped us, the chatter and laughter around us blending into a lively soundtrack. I glanced at Jackson, who was beaming, the sheer joy radiating from him like the sun breaking through clouds after a rainstorm. We had not only created a dish; we had created a memory, a moment etched in time that would linger long after the flavors faded from our palettes.

Later that evening, as we celebrated with friends and fellow competitors at a local bar, the atmosphere remained electric. The walls echoed with laughter and the clinking of glasses, a joyful cacophony that felt like a warm embrace. As we toasted to our success, Jackson leaned closer, a conspiratorial grin spreading across his face. "We should do this again," he said, eyes twinkling with mischief. "Next time, we'll conquer the world, one dish at a time."

I couldn't help but laugh, a sound that harmonized with the jazz notes floating through the air. "How about we just start with brunch?" I teased, my heart full. There was something undeniably magical about this place, the way it fostered dreams and ignited passions.

The night wore on, and as I savored the camaraderie of this vibrant community, I knew that this was only the beginning. The stories shared that day, the flavors experienced, and the friendships forged would weave themselves into my writing and shape the narratives I would tell.

In the weeks that followed, I found myself crafting articles that celebrated not only the culinary scene but the very essence of New Orleans—the resilience, the creativity, the flavors that intertwined to create a unique tapestry of life. Each piece felt like a love letter to the city, a tribute to the artists who transformed everyday ingredients into unforgettable experiences.

With Jackson by my side, our journey continued, rich with flavor and possibility. I realized that food was not just a medium of expression; it was a bridge connecting us all, a reminder that in every bite, in every shared meal, lay the stories that brought us together.

The heart of New Orleans beat strongly in our work, and I was eager to explore every delicious avenue it had to offer.

Chapter 29: Rising Tensions

The sun dipped low in the sky, casting a warm golden hue across the vibrant streets of Charleston. The air was thick with the smell of salt and sunshine, mingling with the tantalizing scents wafting from the open doors of the local restaurants. I could hear the distant sound of laughter spilling out of the bustling cafes, their patio tables adorned with colorful umbrellas swaying gently in the balmy breeze. This place, steeped in history and charm, was my sanctuary—a town where the past whispered through the brick buildings and the present danced joyfully in the rhythm of life.

But today, something was amiss. As I strolled through the cobblestone streets, I felt a heaviness in the air that was different from the usual humidity. It wrapped around me like a damp cloak, a palpable tension that clung to my skin. The upcoming cooking challenge was looming over the culinary community like a storm cloud, casting shadows on the bright, bustling atmosphere. I couldn't shake the feeling that the competition had stirred up more than just the usual excitement—it had sparked a wave of anxiety that rippled through my friends and fellow chefs.

Mia had always been my rock, the one who lifted my spirits with her infectious laughter and culinary genius. But as the competition approached, I noticed her vibrant spirit fading like the colors of a sunset. Her usually bright eyes were clouded with worry, and the sparkle that once lit up her face seemed buried beneath a weight of self-doubt. I couldn't bear to see her like this. She deserved to shine, to bask in the joy that cooking had once brought her.

I decided to invite her over for a little kitchen therapy. There was something about chopping vegetables and blending flavors that seemed to have a magical way of clearing the mind. My small kitchen, filled with mismatched dishware and shelves bursting with spices, felt like the perfect refuge for our brainstorming session. The familiar scent of basil and garlic filled the air, a comforting embrace that promised creativity and warmth.

As she stepped into my kitchen, Mia looked almost ethereal, a wisp of her former self. The loose strands of hair framing her face caught the soft light, and for a fleeting moment, I caught a glimpse of the spirited chef I knew. But that spark quickly faded as she dropped her bag on the counter, her shoulders slumping in defeat. I offered her a reassuring smile and gestured toward the array of fresh ingredients sprawled across the countertop.

"Let's make something beautiful together," I said, my voice gentle yet filled with encouragement. "What about a vibrant ratatouille? It's colorful, alive, just like you."

Mia hesitated, her eyes flitting over the vegetables, each one a small world of potential. I could see her mind working through the possibilities, but the doubt lingered, creeping into her thoughts like an uninvited guest. I grabbed a zucchini, its skin glistening in the afternoon light, and began slicing it with rhythmic precision. The satisfying crunch of the knife meeting the flesh echoed through the kitchen.

"Remember when we experimented with flavors in that tiny kitchen back in college?" I asked, recalling the chaotic nights filled with laughter and unexpected culinary masterpieces. "We didn't know what we were doing, but we had so much fun creating."

Mia chuckled softly, the sound a flicker of warmth in the chilly air. "Yeah, and half of our dishes were disasters."

"Exactly! But we learned from them," I urged, stirring a pot of olive oil and garlic, letting the aroma wash over us. "Every mistake was just another step toward becoming better cooks. You're not just a chef, Mia. You're an artist. Your dishes tell a story, and I want to help you share that story."

Her eyes softened, and for a moment, the flicker of her confidence returned. We resumed chopping, the rhythmic sounds of knives against cutting boards weaving a comforting symphony. As the colors of our ingredients melded together, so too did our laughter, filling the kitchen with a warmth that melted away the tension.

"Let's brainstorm our signature dish for the competition," I suggested, pouring vibrant tomatoes into the pot, their juices bursting forth like little suns. "What do you want to convey? What do you want people to feel when they taste your food?"

Mia's brow furrowed in thought as she stirred the bubbling pot, the rich colors swirling together. "I want them to feel warmth, like a hug from home. Something that reminds them of their childhood, of family gatherings."

"Yes! That's it!" I exclaimed, my enthusiasm spilling over. "We can incorporate flavors that bring back memories—maybe a twist on your grandmother's classic dish?"

Her eyes sparkled for the first time that day. "You're right! I can add a hint of rosemary for nostalgia, a touch of lemon for brightness. It will be a reflection of my journey—how I've evolved as a chef."

I watched as she began to flourish, her hands moving with newfound purpose, chopping and sautéing with an energy that filled the room. Each ingredient was a building block, each flavor a note in a symphony of taste. As we worked side by side, the tension that had enveloped us began to dissipate, replaced by a sense of camaraderie and excitement.

In that moment, the kitchen became a sanctuary, a place where worries melted away like butter on a hot skillet. With every stir and sprinkle, I could see Mia reclaiming her passion, the heart of her artistry returning. The competition no longer felt like a looming threat; it transformed into a canvas for her creativity, an opportunity to share her love for food and her journey with the world.

As the evening sun bathed our kitchen in a soft glow, I felt an overwhelming sense of gratitude. It wasn't just about the cooking;

it was about the bond we shared, the stories woven into each dish. Together, we were crafting something beautiful, not just for the competition, but for ourselves—a celebration of friendship, resilience, and the joy that comes from pursuing our passions.

The evening air shifted as I and Mia continued our culinary escapade, the sun's last rays spilling across the countertop like melted butter. The kitchen transformed into a sanctuary of sensory delight, where laughter intermingled with the sizzling sounds of garlic and onions, creating an aromatic tapestry that embraced us like an old friend. With each chop and sauté, the atmosphere lightened, the burden of competition fading into the background like the sunset retreating beyond the horizon.

Mia's hands moved with renewed energy, her fingers dancing over the vegetables with a grace that seemed foreign moments before. Each slice of zucchini released a fresh aroma, a promise of what was to come, while she crafted our dish with newfound vigor. The melody of our conversation wove seamlessly into the rhythm of our cooking, punctuated by moments of joyous discovery as she recalled flavors from her past.

"It's strange, isn't it?" Mia mused, her voice threading through the fragrant steam. "How cooking can unlock memories? Like when I made my mother's gumbo for the first time. I can still remember the warmth of the kitchen, the sound of her laughter. Food has this incredible way of taking you back, doesn't it?"

I nodded, feeling a wave of nostalgia wash over me. "Absolutely. Every dish has a story, a thread that connects us to our history. What if we infused that essence into your signature dish? A combination of your grandmother's love and your unique twist?"

The spark in her eyes ignited into a flame as she grasped the concept, her enthusiasm palpable. "Yes! I can incorporate smoked paprika, just like she did, but I'll add a hint of orange zest to brighten it up. It will be a tribute to her while still being distinctly mine."

As she spoke, I noticed how her passion for cooking had blossomed, radiating warmth that filled the room. The atmosphere shifted further, becoming a cocoon where fear had no place, replaced instead by excitement and shared dreams. I turned back to the stovetop, stirring the bubbling sauce that had taken on a life of its own, the vibrant colors swirling together in a celebration of culinary artistry.

With each ingredient that slid into the pot, our conversation deepened, veering toward the heart of what it meant to create, to nurture, and to share. "You know, I've always believed that food is a form of love," I said, my hands deftly mixing in a handful of herbs. "When you cook for someone, you're not just feeding them. You're offering a piece of yourself, a moment of connection that transcends the meal itself."

Mia paused, her gaze focused on the simmering pot as if it held the answers to unspoken questions. "That's beautiful. It's so easy to get lost in the pressure of competitions and expectations that we forget why we started cooking in the first place. It's about more than just winning. It's about passion, about sharing a piece of ourselves with others."

The weight of her words hung in the air, an affirmation that resonated deep within me. As the sauce thickened, I could almost taste the stories waiting to be told, the connections waiting to be forged with every plate we served. The very thought made my heart swell with hope and excitement, and I could feel our shared dream bubbling just beneath the surface, ready to burst forth in a colorful, flavorful explosion.

As we plated the ratatouille, the colors danced before our eyes—deep reds, vibrant yellows, and earthy greens creating a feast for the senses. It looked like a canvas splashed with the brushstrokes of our shared memories and aspirations. With a flourish, I drizzled balsamic reduction over the top, the dark liquid glistening like the final touches of an artist's signature.

"Voilà!" I declared, holding the plate aloft like a trophy. "This is your dish, a reflection of your journey and the love you carry with you."

Mia's face lit up, her earlier trepidation replaced by a radiant smile that seemed to illuminate the kitchen. "Thank you for this. I can't believe how much I needed this moment—this reminder. It's not just about the competition; it's about honoring my roots and sharing my story."

We settled down at my small kitchen table, the weight of the day's worries falling away as we savored our creation. Each bite was an explosion of flavors, a symphony that resonated with every taste bud, transporting us back to moments of laughter and love. I could see Mia, lost in thought as she chewed, a look of bliss washing over her face.

"This is incredible," she finally said, her voice almost reverent. "It's everything I hoped it would be and more."

The night deepened outside, the gentle sounds of the world fading into a lullaby of crickets and distant laughter. We lingered over our meal, the plates emptying as the conversation flowed effortlessly, weaving through memories and aspirations like the vines of the ivy climbing the walls of the old brick buildings outside.

"I was so scared," Mia confessed, her eyes glistening with a mixture of relief and determination. "I didn't want to let anyone down, especially myself. But being here, cooking with you, it's reignited something within me. I'm ready to embrace this competition—not just to win, but to share my passion."

I reached across the table, squeezing her hand gently, a silent affirmation of our friendship and shared journey. "You've got this. You're not just a competitor; you're a storyteller, and your food will speak volumes. Just remember that you're not alone in this."

As the evening wore on, our laughter echoed through the cozy kitchen, melding with the soft light that flickered from the candles we lit. The pressure of the upcoming challenge began to feel like a distant memory, replaced by the warmth of friendship and the joy of creation.

With every shared story and every plate we crafted, we solidified a bond that would carry us through whatever challenges lay ahead. I knew that whatever the outcome of the competition, this night would be etched in our hearts—a reminder of the power of friendship, the joy of cooking, and the importance of staying true to ourselves amidst the chaos of the culinary world.

The night unfurled like a well-loved recipe, layered with warmth and laughter, as we settled into a rhythm that felt both familiar and exhilarating. The remnants of our culinary creation lingered on the table, a canvas splashed with vibrant colors that whispered tales of resilience and joy. Mia and I sat among the remnants of our evening feast, the warm glow of the candles casting flickering shadows that danced across the walls, creating an intimate atmosphere filled with unspoken dreams and shared hopes.

"Do you remember our first cooking class?" Mia asked, her voice filled with nostalgia as she absently toyed with her fork, a glimmer of mischief dancing in her eyes. "You nearly burned down the kitchen trying to flambé that banana dessert!"

I laughed, shaking my head as the memory flooded back, an explosion of scents and chaos erupting in a room filled with eager students. "Hey, I was just trying to add some flair! Besides, who knew that a little rum could turn into such a fiery fiasco?"

Mia chuckled, her laughter rich and melodic, echoing the joy that had reclaimed its place in our lives. "I think the instructor's heart nearly stopped. But you know, that's what I love about cooking—it's unpredictable. Just like life."

A comfortable silence enveloped us, our minds wandering back to those formative days when we were still wide-eyed dreamers, clumsily navigating the intricate dance of culinary arts. It was a time filled with laughter, mishaps, and the thrill of discovery. As I sat there, I felt a deep sense of gratitude, not just for the meal we had created but for the friendship that had been forged through fire and flour.

"Do you think we'll ever outgrow this?" I asked, leaning back in my chair, a playful smile tugging at my lips. "The excitement, the creativity? Will we still be here, cooking and laughing together when we're gray and wrinkly?"

Mia's gaze grew thoughtful, a flicker of seriousness breaking through the jovial atmosphere. "I hope so. I want to always find joy in cooking, to keep discovering new flavors and sharing them with the world. It's more than just food; it's about connection, legacy."

Her words hung in the air like the scent of herbs mingling with a warm summer breeze. The notion of legacy resonated deeply, reminding me that our culinary journeys were more than personal; they were intertwined with the community that surrounded us, a patchwork of influences that shaped who we had become.

With renewed energy, we decided to tackle our next challenge: perfecting Mia's signature dish for the competition. The evening morphed into an impromptu workshop, laughter punctuating the air as we whipped up sauces, experimented with spices, and plated our creations with artistic flair. Mia transformed into a whirlwind of inspiration, her previous doubts melting away under the heat of our combined passion.

As the hours slipped by, I noticed the clock ticking toward midnight. The world outside our kitchen had settled into a hushed stillness, the streets of Charleston now draped in the silver cloak of moonlight. The city had transformed into a quiet sanctuary, echoing the serenity we had found in our cooking haven.

"Let's try one more time," Mia urged, her eyes gleaming with determination. "I want this dish to sing."

We moved as a seamless unit, our hands working in tandem as if choreographed. Each slice and stir resonated with purpose, the urgency of the competition blending seamlessly with the thrill of creation. The rhythm of our movements reflected the bond we shared, a language that spoke without words.

As we finished the final touches on our masterpiece, a ratatouille that sparkled with color and flavor, I felt a swell of pride. It was not just a dish; it was a celebration of our friendship, a testament to our journey, and an embodiment of our dreams.

With everything plated to perfection, we stood back to admire our creation. The vibrant colors harmonized beautifully, a symphony of flavors that promised to tell a story—one of resilience, hope, and unyielding passion. I felt a wave of contentment wash over me, knowing that no matter the outcome of the competition, this moment would remain etched in my heart.

Suddenly, the doorbell rang, breaking the serene atmosphere. I exchanged a curious glance with Mia before heading to the door. Upon opening it, I was greeted by the unmistakable figure of Patrick, a fellow chef from the culinary scene and one of Mia's fiercest competitors. He stood there, his expression an intriguing mix of excitement and apprehension.

"Hey, I hope I'm not interrupting," he said, his voice a warm baritone that matched the charm of the town. "I heard you two were having a little culinary soirée and thought I'd stop by."

Mia's eyes widened, surprise mingling with concern as she glanced at the chaos of our kitchen. "Um, we were just experimenting with some dishes for the competition," she said, her cheeks flushing.

Patrick stepped inside, taking in the culinary chaos with a grin. "I love the aroma wafting through your kitchen. It smells amazing! What are you cooking?"

Before I could respond, Mia piped up, her excitement bubbling over. "We just finished perfecting my signature ratatouille! Would you like to try some?"

The invitation seemed to spark something within Patrick, his enthusiasm bubbling over as he joined us in the kitchen. The atmosphere shifted again, this time welcoming an unexpected energy that crackled like electricity in the air.

As we shared our dish with Patrick, I could see Mia's confidence grow. The fear that had once gripped her was replaced by the joy of sharing her creation with someone who truly appreciated the artistry behind it. The three of us savored each bite, the flavors exploding on our tongues like fireworks, and laughter filled the kitchen, creating a vibrant tapestry of camaraderie.

"Wow, Mia," Patrick exclaimed, his eyes lighting up. "This is incredible! You've really captured the essence of comfort food while elevating it to something extraordinary."

Mia beamed at the compliment, her heart swelling with pride. In that moment, it felt like we were all part of something bigger, a community of chefs bonded by our love for food and the shared experience of creation.

The night unfolded into a delightful whirlwind of flavors and laughter, and as the clock ticked into the early hours of the morning, we remained wrapped in our culinary cocoon, savoring each moment. It became clear that regardless of the outcome in the competition, we had already won something far more valuable—a connection built on passion, support, and the joy of shared experiences.

As we eventually cleaned up the remnants of our late-night cooking adventure, I looked at Mia and Patrick, my heart full. We had created not just a dish, but a memory, one that would nourish our spirits long after the competition was over. In the vibrant heart of Charleston, we had found a blend of flavors, friendship, and the sweet promise of a shared culinary journey that awaited us all.

Milton Keynes UK
Ingram Content Group UK Ltd.
UKHW040257181024
449757UK00001B/89